ENDLESS

A Truth or Lies World Collection VI

ELLA MILES

TRUTH OR LIES WORLD COLLECTION SERIES ORDER

ENZO & KAI'S STORY

Taken (Collection I)
Stolen (Collection II)

ZEKE & SIREN'S STORY

Sinful (Collection III)
Broken (Collection IV)

LANGSTON & LIESEL'S STORY

Vicious (Collection V)
Endless (Collection VI)

CRUEL LIES

PROLOGUE
LIESEL

How is it that everything that dramatically changes my life is written in a letter?

The first time it happened was in a letter from my father. That letter was ripped by Langston, so I only got half of the truth.

But this letter, I ripped myself. I destroyed one half and plan on giving Langston the other.

Why did I destroy half of this letter?

The contents scare the shit out of me.

It changes how I think of myself.

It changes who I am.

If true, it changes everything. I won't let my world change all because it was written in a stupid, threatening letter, but I have no way to verify the contents.

Except...

No.

Time will reveal the truth.

Meanwhile, I'm left to wonder if the world is the one lying to me...

CHAPTER 1

LIESEL

I gave up my son without ever having laid eyes on him. I never held him. Never got to see how many of his features matched my own. Never got to smell his sweet head. Never breastfed him. Never changed his diaper. Never dressed him. Never counted his fingers and toes.

I never did any of the things most new moms get to do. Even moms who give their children up for adoption usually hold their child at least once before giving them away.

Not me.

I had an emergency C-section. I was unconscious when he was born, so I never got to hear his first cry. I never met him. I didn't get to name him or find out what his parents named him.

I thought I'd never meet him. That was the plan. When I gave up my son, I did it for him.

I was young and not ready to be a mother, but if keeping him was best for him, I would have figured it out.

I gave him up because of who his father was—the most dangerous man in the world. I had no idea how he would have reacted if he found out the truth. *Would he have tried to kill my son? Would he have tried to brainwash him and bring him under his thumb like he did Enzo? Would he have had to fight Enzo to become the new Mr. Black, ruler of the most notorious crime organization?*

No—I ensured that my son would never be harmed, would never grow up in this dangerous and cruel world like I did.

So I gave him up, ensured he had the best parents possible, that he was hidden, never to be found.

And then, Mr. Black was killed. I could find my son. Kai did find him. It was safe to know my son. To love him out in the open.

But I knew better. Mr. Black dying changed nothing. We are all too connected to money, crime, and power for our enemies not to come and find us. We are always in danger. Enzo, Kai, Siren, and Zeke think they can protect their children while still living in this world—they're wrong. They will never be safe. I did the responsible thing. I kept my son safe. I gave him up a second time.

I thought that was it—I'd never know my son, not even his name, the color of his eyes.

Giving him up the second time was immensely harder than the first. The world turned to shades of gray after I decided to remain out of his life. Nothing brought me happiness or even a tingling of joy. I didn't smile or laugh, and I knew I never would again.

And then, everything changed.

I realized I made a mistake.

I had to find my son for his own survival.

I searched and searched, but I couldn't find him, not with all the resources in the world.

Then, I met Waylon Brown. It seemed like a coincidence at first, but eventually I realized he had ulterior motives. He knew where my son was; he provided proof. But in return, I had to marry him.

I would have married him that day, gave him everything I owned, and kneeled in promise to be his servant forever if he gave me my son. I still don't know what Waylon's real reason for wanting to marry me was.

Did he just find me attractive and want a good-looking, intelligent woman on his side? Or did he want the treasure he thought I had the key to?

The treasure.

Father, what did you put in motion? Why couldn't you just burn your letter?

Why ruin my life and every generation after because of a rumor of the greatest treasure to exist on earth and only a Dunn able to retrieve it?

"Liesel, did you hear me?" Langston asks as he sits next to me on the beach.

I've been staring off into space, thinking about everything I've lost over the years. Langston is included in that list. And yet somehow, my enemy, my best friend, and now my lover might be the man who can give me my son back.

"I heard you," I say, having no idea what to do with the information.

I have so many questions.

"The others? Do they know?" I ask, referring to Kai, Enzo, Siren, and Zeke. I asked them all for help at various times in my search for my son, but none of them had been able to help me. Were they just keeping Langston's secret?

"No, they think he's my biological son."

I nod and look down at my feet. I still haven't looked at the boy Langston claims is my son since he revealed it to me. I'm not ready to see if he has my eyes or hair coloring. I've seen him before, but not up close, not while I was looking to see if he resembled me.

"What's going on in your head?" Langston asks, trying to pry beneath the shield I've put up.

I shake my head, but then I finally speak. There is no use keeping my thoughts to myself. Not when we've shared so much.

"I just don't understand. I don't understand how you could have my son. I don't understand how Waylon said he knew where my child was if you had my son. I don't know who to believe."

"I don't know why Waylon said he knew where your son was, other than he was trying to manipulate you."

"He had proof."

"What kind of proof?"

I shake my head. "It doesn't matter what his proof was, what's yours?"

I look Langston in the eye, and my heart swells. He looks broken from my doubt, but he's lied too many times. We both have. Of course, I don't believe he has my son. *But then, why would he lie?* I could easily get a DNA test and prove him wrong.

Waylon had DNA proof. That's why I believed him. *Will I believe Langston until I have the same proof?*

"I'll tell you my story and get a DNA test if that will make you feel better, but spend one minute with him and you'll realize he's yours."

My heart catches. *How can he be so certain?*

"I met Phoenix when I was a teenager. We met at one of Enzo's father's bars. I don't remember much about that night, except that I was horny and lonely. She was alone and in need of company."

"I don't need to hear this," I say. I don't want to hear about the night they met, fucked, and then how she eventually became his wife.

He grabs my cheeks in his strong hands, holding me so fervently as he peers into my eyes. "Trust me, you do."

I close my eyes, keeping the tears at bay. He was off fucking whores in bars, while I was dealing with the trauma of carrying my rapist's child.

"I was lonely because you were gone. Sure, it had been years at that point since you and I were friends, but even when we were fighting, I felt close to you. But then you took off for Europe. You left. You were gone. That pain was the first intense pain I ever felt. It left a hole in my heart. A brokenness I didn't know I was capable of feeling."

"You seemed to get over it just fine by running off and marrying the first girl you laid eyes on."

"I never got over you. I'm still not over you."

Dammit, my eyes water so much that I can't hide it. His words aren't the truth. They are empty, meant to manipulate me.

"I got drunk that night. I fucked her in the filthy bathroom. And then I left."

I grab his wrists to pull them off my face, but I can't quite do it. I revel in the feeling of his warm hands on my skin—even if I get burned, I want to feel him. That's my problem when it comes to Langston; I have no self-preservation. He's always going to end up hurting me—that's why I should let him go.

"A year later, I found out I had a child."

"Rose?"

He nods. "I knew I'd be a terrible father. I'd most likely end up dead before my child turned eighteen, so all I initially offered was money. I thought it would be better if I stayed out of her life."

He initially gave up his child for the same reasons I did.

"But then Phoenix reached out for help. I made the mistake of agreeing to meet her and my daughter." His eyes water. "Once I laid eyes on Rose, I knew that I couldn't give her up again. I wasn't strong enough."

His words stab me in the chest. Once I lay eyes on my own child, I won't be able to give him up. I need to make sure it's the right thing before I look at him.

"So, I became part of her life. I wanted to spend as much time with her as I could. But Phoenix wanted more than just a father-figure. She wanted me—something I wasn't willing to give her."

"What changed?"

"Fate."

I frown.

"I brought Rose to a playground. She was playing with a young boy her age. When she ran over to where I was sitting on the bench, she was dragging the young boy behind her. He was smaller than her, even though they were the same age. He had dark hair and was too thin in ratty clothes. It was clear he wasn't taken care of as well as he should have been."

I gasp—my son was hungry. He wore ratty clothes. I tried so hard to ensure he didn't have the same life I did. He was adopted by a wealthy family, or so I thought. *What happened?*

"I wasn't going to do anything other than talk to the foster agency and ensure he was placed with a better family. Maybe pay for his food or clothes—"

"I put him up for adoption with a wealthy family; he shouldn't have been in the foster system."

"His adoptive parents had died the year before."

My eyes bulge. *My poor son. Is he fated to live my same broken life? How can fate be so cruel?*

Langston continues, "I was just going to help him out, since Rose had made a friend, something she didn't do often. I'd been coming around for two years at this point, and she never made any friends. So her caring about this boy was a big deal. But then I saw his eyes."

He stares into my own eyes. "I saw his eyes, and it was like I had found a missing piece of my soul. Eyes who hadn't peered at me in years were now looking back at me. Big, beautiful hazel eyes. Eyes that belonged to my best friend. Eyes I would know anywhere."

My eyes.

My son has my eyes.

The tear that I've been holding back finally falls, rolling gently down my cheek.

"I couldn't leave him. I considered reaching out to you, but then I knew that you had given him up for a reason. The choice was now mine, not yours. I talked to the foster agency. I could adopt him; the only problem was Phoenix."

I wipe my tears. "Why was Phoenix a problem?"

"Rose took an immediate liking to Atlas. I knew I couldn't separate them. And I only had partial custody of Rose at the time. I knew I needed her to agree to take Atlas into her life. To love him like a son. She was hesitant to bring another child into our life. Especially when our life was complicated. I was gone working with Enzo for a long time, while she was left behind with Rose. I would come back as often as I could, but it still meant that she had to do more than her fair share of the child-rearing."

He looks ashamed as he says his next words. His head hangs down, and his cheeks pinken. "I told her I'd do anything to make it happen. Atlas was my son, and I needed him and Rose to have the best life. Phoenix has her flaws, but she's a great mother. My kids needed a mother and a father. They needed love from a supportive family, something that you and I never had growing up. So I asked her what she needed to make this happen."

"And what did she ask of you?" My heart is beating a million miles a minute even though I already know the answer.

"She asked for more of my time. For me to spend more time with her and the children."

I nod, imploring him to say the next words.

"And she asked that I marry her."

My heart flatlines. Phoenix has everything I've ever wanted—a child of her own that she can love, my child, and my killer. She has it all, while I have nothing. I've been dealt all the pain, while she's gotten all of the happiness. It's not fair.

"So, you did?"

He nods. "I married her. She knew what she was getting—a man who would never be faithful, who would never love her, but would protect her and our children with my life. For her, that was enough. To have me be hers for an eternity."

I close my eyes, taking it all in. Langston married Phoenix so that he could protect my child; I can't fault him for that. I can't fault him for protecting my child when I failed. I can't fault him at all, even if it all hurts like a thousand needles attacking my skin all at once.

"Thank you," I say, opening my eyes, more tears plunging down my warm cheek.

He stills, like I just slapped him. "What?"

"Thank you, Langston. For everything."

He cups my face in his hands again, wiping away my liquified pain, searching for the heartbreak that was there before. He won't find it. All he'll find is forgiveness and gratitude.

"I mean it. We've been through a lot you and I. We've failed each other so many times. Hurt each other. It stings that you know my child better than I do. That you got part of his life that I will never get. I'm jealous that you married a woman when I always thought deep down that if you ever did marry someone, it would be me.

"But above it all, I'm thankful. My son needed someone to love him. I thought I was protecting him by hiding him away, but you—you showed him love when I couldn't. You found him, protected him, loved him. You became his father when you had no responsibility to do so. He wasn't your blood. He was the lost child of a woman you hated. You didn't have to intervene. You definitely didn't have to become his father. And yet you did. I can never thank you enough for what you did."

"I hid your child. I took him instead of telling you I had him. And I married your cousin when I could have chosen you. Don't thank me for that."

I grab his hands and lift them to my lips, kissing them. "No, you loved my child and became his father. The rest is just messy detail. I'll never be able to repay you for what you did."

He scrunches his eyebrows and gruffs but doesn't argue. "Do you want to meet your son?"

I hear the children laughing just feet away from me. My heart pulls toward them. I want to meet my son. I want to meet Langston's daughter. More than anything in the world.

But I have to make sure it's for the best to meet them. I don't want to bring more enemies into their life. When I meet them, it has to be because it makes their lives better, not worse.

So I answer the only way I can, "No."

CHAPTER 2

LANGSTON

She said no.

My mouth falls open. Her hands slip through my fingers, and my eyes are blinking rapidly. She's joking, or she just said the word because she's used to telling me no.

"Liesel?"

She stands and starts to walk away from me—away from the kids.

"It's okay to be scared. I'll be there with you." I stand, hoping to lure her back. She lived with a man and agreed to marry him because he said he could help her find her son. Now that I told her exactly where he is, she's running. It doesn't make sense to me.

Maybe she's scared? I'm scared too. I'm scared that I'm going to let my feelings for this woman cloud my judgment and change all my plans.

Liesel stops. She doesn't turn her head, but I can hear her words clear as day.

"I'm not afraid. I would love to meet my son, more than anything in this world, but I won't until I know it's safe for him." Then she jogs away, leaving me standing alone, stunned.

Why is she worried about Atlas' life? What is she hiding?

"Don't touch it! It could hurt you," Atlas yells at Rose.

I turn and start walking over toward the kids, quietly observing so they don't notice I'm there.

Rose is bent down in front of what looks like a jellyfish, a small cast still on her arm.

"But it'll die if we don't get it back to the water," Rose says.

"Then, let it die. It's not worth getting stung," Atlas says, grabbing hold of the hem of her black T-shirt and trying to pull her back. It doesn't stop Rose; she bends down and touches the creature. Just like Atlas warned her, the creature stings her.

"Ouch," she pulls her little hand back.

I shake my head at my daughter. So brave that it will get her killed someday, while Atlas is so cautious that he never really lives.

"Let me help," I say, walking over to them.

Rose pouts.

Atlas grins, his face shining like the sun.

"I can do it," Rose says.

"I know, but there is nothing wrong with asking for help."

I squat down and look at the still jellyfish on the sand in front of us. I scoop my hands underneath its squishy body and then carry it over to the water before flinging it into the ocean, setting it free.

I don't know if it will survive or if it has sustained too much damage, but as I stare out at the ocean, I feel a ping of jealousy. Whatever the outcome, the jellyfish is free, unlike me, who is bound by too many lies to count.

"Why didn't it sting you, daddy?" Rose asks.

I turn back to my daughter and hold out my hands. "It did."

Atlas gasps. "Does it hurt?"

"Not as much as watching either of you get hurt does."

Atlas stares at my hand with concern. He doesn't like other people being hurt. He'd rather take on the pain himself.

"Come here," I say to him, holding my arms out.

He collapses into my side as I kneel down and wrap my arms around him. "When you hug me, you take all the pain away."

"Good, daddy. I don't like it when you're hurt."

I smile and watch as Rose approaches me more cautiously but eventually wraps her arms around me as well.

"Piggyback ride?" Rose asks.

"Climb on, you two."

She climbs on my back while Atlas rolls his eyes at her. I know he'd rather keep his feet on the ground, but he trusts me more than anyone else. So when I lift him up in the air and fling him around, he laughs and it's completely carefree.

I glance down the beach toward where Liesel took off. I have an undeniable urge to run after her, but my kids are more important. I have to keep them safe. Liesel will come around.

I carry the kids on my back toward the house, where Phoenix is sitting on the back deck, watching and waiting for us. She doesn't say anything as I set the kids down.

"I'm starving," Rose says as soon as her feet hit the deck.

I chuckle.

Phoenix shakes her head. "There is some fruit and string cheese in the fridge. Wash up first, and then you can eat it."

Rose runs inside with Atlas fast on her heels.

I can't help but smile watching them. They remind me of Liesel and me when we were their age. They seem to fit together even though they aren't biological brother and sister. They still share some blood, being cousins and all.

I look back at Phoenix, who is staring at me intensely. She's wearing her usual outfit of dark jeans and a black long-sleeved T-shirt, thick makeup, and red hair. She hates the beach and the ocean. She'd rather us live in a large city somewhere, but she stays because of me. This is what I need: to be near the ocean. I spend my entire life either here along the beaches of Miami, on a yacht, or basking in the sun on my private island near the Bahamas.

"Why do you put up with me? Why not divorce my ass and find another man who would actually love you?" I ask. It's brazen of me and reveals more about what happened between Liesel and me than I should be admitting, but I have to know why she stays. Maybe if I can understand her, I'll have an idea of how we can move forward.

It doesn't matter what I want. No matter what becomes of Phoenix and I, I can't marry Liesel. I can't love Liesel. Fucking her is all we get, even though it's not enough for either of us to survive on.

"I'm going to need a glass of wine if we are going to have this conversation." She moves to get up, but I grab her wrist, my body begging her to answer me.

She sighs, seeing the pain in my eyes.

"I'm not a good man, Phoenix. I haven't been loyal."

"I never asked you to be."

"I know, but you deserve a man who is."

Her hand touches my shoulder. "Falling in love means you don't get to choose how. You just fall. I know you'll never love me back, but I'd rather have the love of my life in my life than live with no love at all."

I release her wrist, and she walks into the house. My eyes squeeze shut as the wind picks up, hitting me forcefully in the face, as hard as the reality of my situation.

I'm married to a woman who loves me and deserves to be loved back—something I can never give her. A woman who is a wonderful mother to my children.

Yet my body yearns for a woman who hates me and will never love me. A woman I can never love in return. A woman who is the biological mother of one of my children but gave him up.

My life is a fucking disaster.

One of my own creating. If I had just left Liesel alone, I wouldn't be in this mess. I wouldn't be questioning everything. I would be focused on what's important—being a good father.

I hear a car pull up on the gravel drive, so I walk to the front deck, already knowing who it will be.

Enzo and Beckett are stepping out of the car when I walk up to the driveway. Enzo has a heavy scowl, while Beckett is smirking.

"Find Rowan?" I ask, crossing my arms as I lean against one of the poles on the deck.

"Yes, no thanks to you," Enzo says.

I look around into the back of the SUV; I don't see Rowan.

Beckett laughs. "We took him to Enzo's house to have a doctor look him over."

"You should put a bullet between his eyes, not fix his wounds, after what he did to Liesel and me."

"Oh, relax, dude, you're both made of stronger stuff than that. What you two went through was barely a scratch," Beckett says.

My brows pinch. "So that makes what you did okay? Hiring a man to kidnap and torture us?"

"We didn't hire him. He already works for us," Enzo says.

"Fire him or I quit," I say.

"That's not my decision," Enzo says.

I shake my head. "Then tell Kai to get her ass here. I thought you were my family, my brothers, but I was wrong. You are nothing but lying scum."

"Don't blame Kai, she may be in charge of the Black empire, but she didn't make this decision on her own. This was a group decision," Siren says as she walks from behind the car.

I didn't notice the second car pull up.

Siren—*she's really alive.*

My eyes water, and my heart swells, seeing her alive. I've missed her. She's the only person who truly understands me. Everyone else here I consider family, I'd die saving any one of them, but only Siren would I die twice for.

Until now.

"I already know about your betrayal. You faked your own death to hurt me. How could you?"

"How could you kill Liesel's fiancé? How could you kidnap and threaten to kill her?" Siren walks toward me and puts her hands on both of my cheeks. "You were out of control, Langston. Liesel came up with a plan to get back at you—I just went along with it."

I growl and jerk back, forcing her hands to fall from my face. "You don't get to talk to me, not after what you did. You betrayed me when you faked your injury and possible death. And as if that wasn't enough, you decided to risk our lives to manipulate Liesel and me? You're the devil."

Her face falls. I've never been like this to Siren. I expect her to fight back; instead, she gives me space.

That's when I spot Zeke behind her. He lifts his fist and slams it into my face. I knew it was coming. I deserve it.

"That was for forcing my wife to suck your cock. If you weren't a brother to me, I'd castrate you."

I don't fight back, and I don't tell him that Siren sucked my cock willingly to help me. He's the only person who has earned the right to hurt me. All these other bastards had no right.

Kai finally steps forward. "It was my decision to have Rowan kidnap and torture you. Don't blame any of them, blame me."

"I do. And now you can all get the fuck off my property." I turn to walk inside. "Oh, and Kai? I quit."

LIESEL

Atlas is my son.

All the fleeting glimpses I've gotten of him over the last few weeks fill my head as I walk up and down the beach, tormented by what I should do. His dark-colored locks, his laugh, his height.

Is it safe to meet him?

What about what Waylon said? That my son isn't safe. That if Waylon died, so would my son. Is Nolan going to carry on in Waylon's place? Someone else? Or was it all a threat to get what he wanted from me?

The sun begins to set, and I find myself walking back toward the house. I don't know if I should meet Atlas or not. I don't know if I'll be bringing more danger into his life once again, and I refuse to be selfish where he's concerned. I'm glad I now know for sure he's alive and in a loving family. I need to make sure that Atlas is really my son, though, that Langston isn't lying for some gain. And if Atlas is, in fact, my son, I need to warn Langston. He needs to know so he can protect him if he is in danger.

I run my hand through my hair, already knowing that Atlas is my son—Langston wasn't lying. He took care of him when everyone else failed. I can hate Langston for a lot of things, but I'll never be able to repay him for what he's done.

As I walk in the dark, I hope that the children have gone to bed. I need another day before I face them, but I also need to talk to Langston. I need to figure out what we do next. And it's not like I have any money or resources to leave Miami.

I hear voices as I approach the house and find the whole crew— Enzo, Kai, Beckett, Siren, and Zeke—camped out on the back deck, talking amongst themselves.

I stop, my feet halted in the sand. I don't want to speak to any of them ever again for what they've put me through. They had me kidnapped and tortured. They helped conceal my child from me even if they didn't know. They failed to protect me when I was raped. They failed to be there every night when I searched for my son until I had no choice but to accept Waylon's help.

I want to run and hide—but I'm done hiding.

I climb the steps loudly, until every voice on the deck silences at my approach. When I reach the top, all eyes fall on me.

Siren is sitting on Zeke's lap as he plays possessively with her hair. Both are wearing a dark T-shirt and jeans. Kai sits next to Enzo—both of them holding a glass of wine. Kai is wearing a simple sundress, and Enzo is in jeans. Phoenix sits next to Kai in her usual long-sleeved clothing, even though the heat of summer is still suffocating us. And Beckett sits in a chair alone, like he isn't part of the group at all.

I feel Langston sitting across from all of them, but I don't look at him. I'm just thankful he isn't sitting next to Phoenix.

For a moment, the only sound is the gentle flow of electricity through the Edison lights that hang overhead.

My eyes shoot through the souls of every person here, silently cursing them for the sins each of them has committed against me.

I consider my next move. *Should I walk past them all and go into the house, or sit out here and have it out with them?*

No more running. No more hiding.

I spot a seat next to Langston and take it. For once, I feel like it's us two against all of them—something that I haven't felt in a long time. Langston has always been part of them. He always takes their side. But when I feel his pinky brush against my outstretched hand, he's letting me know he's on my side. Whatever loyalty and guilt he has toward Phoenix, whatever brotherhood he feels toward Enzo and Zeke, whatever soulmate bond he has with Siren—none of it matters right now. We've both been betrayed by all of them.

"So, what happens now? You two go after the treasure together?" Kai asks.

I glare at her, and I feel an agreeing animalistic growl coming from Langston next to me. Both of us are still wearing the oversized flannel we got from the cabin we were hiding in.

"You don't get to know anything about our plans," I spit back.

"As the queen of an empire where hundreds of employees and families rely on me, I make it my duty to know."

Langston jumps in. "It doesn't concern you, not anymore. I quit. My enemies will no longer be concerned with going after you."

That gets me to turn and look at Langston in surprise. He quit. I look for the lie in his eyes, but I don't find it.

His frown lightens slightly when I look at him.

"You don't get to quit. None of us do," Enzo says.

We both snap our heads in his direction. "I quit. I used to be part of this family but was thrown out years ago. I was written out of this family. I was considered the villain. So yes, if Langston wants to quit, he can quit."

No one responds.

And then Kai smirks. "At least our plan worked. You two don't want to kill each other anymore; you want to kill us. I can live with that if it means you'll stop bickering."

Her eyes say she knows that we've done more than just stop bickering. We've fucked each other, and if circumstances were different, we'd keep fucking each other until we no longer want to fuck any person.

But I feel Phoenix's gaze.

I'm the devil. I fucked another woman's husband. I don't care about the reason they got married. I don't care that they have an open marriage. It was still a sin—one that I don't regret. I still hurt the woman who has been selflessly raising my son.

I close my eyes, unable to deal with my own shame. I rub my arms, trying to soothe myself as the cool night breeze rattles through the empty place in my chest where my heart once beat. The only heart I have is for that of my son. And I'm more conflicted about what to do about him than ever.

"Come on, it's late; let's leave the lovebirds alone," Kai says, not mincing her words even though she sits next to Phoenix.

Finally, I let my eyes drift to her. She's not looking at Kai; she's looking at me. If my chest cavity wasn't already empty, Phoenix would be burning a hole straight through it.

Kai stands up and grabs Enzo's hand, dragging him behind her.

"Let me know if you need any resources or men to help you," she says as she starts down the stairs of the deck.

"Finish this," Enzo hisses at Langston. He doesn't like anything risking his family or empire. But Langston doesn't like being bossed around, and it's clear that he's done following orders after what they did to us.

Beckett stands and follows his half-brother. He doesn't speak or give us any of his thoughts, but it's clear his loyalty lies with his blood family.

Siren climbs off Zeke's lap and motions for him to follow her. She gives me a slight smile before turning to Langston. "I'm not sorry. You needed this."

She looks back at Zeke, who is standing still as a statue near Langston. I don't know what he's doing, but it appears Langston does.

"Get it over with you big oaf," Langston says, rolling his eyes.

Zeke's fist flies in Langston's face, knocking him back on the couch he sits on.

Siren shakes her head like her husband is a ridiculous overbearing bastard.

"That was the last freebie I'll give you," Langston growls.

"Good, it will give me more reason to hit you harder next time," Zeke snarls.

I realize now as I look at Langston's face, that both sides of Langston's face are puffy. Even in the dark light, I can see the hint of purple forming just under the skin. This isn't the first time Zeke has hit him today.

It makes me giggle.

Langston shoots me an *I thought you were on my side* glare. That only makes me laugh harder.

Serves you right for getting his wife on her knees to suck your dick, I shoot back.

You're one to talk. Langston looks to Phoenix, and my smile wavers. I've committed the same sin. If I was a better woman, I'd let Phoenix take a swing at me too.

Zeke and Siren leave. And then it's just us and Phoenix.

There's a heaviness in the air between us, threatening to choke me if someone doesn't talk soon. I'm sure Phoenix knows what happened between Langston and me. Either because he told her or she's smart enough to figure it out. I just don't know what she's going to do about it.

I don't know what Langston is going to do about it.

I don't know what I'm going to do about it.

Phoenix yawns and then stands. "I'm going to bed. You coming, Langston?"

"Not yet," he says, meeting her gaze.

Not yet—those words hurt us both. Phoenix because he isn't following after her. And me because his words insinuate that he will eventually.

Her jaw ticks in disapproval, but she doesn't tell him off. I don't understand all the ins and outs of their marriage, but if she's married to Langston, she must know that she can't control him. He's a wild killer, and as much as he says he quit working for Kai—he's loyal to a fault. He'll be back to taking orders in no time.

"She can sleep in the guest bedroom in the basement," Phoenix says, not addressing me even though I'm sitting right next to Langston.

I want to snap back that Langston is hers. Even though I fucked him, there is no way he'll leave her. Not when it's the only way to keep both of his children together. Even if I am one of their biological mothers, it doesn't matter. Even if I meet Atlas, it doesn't mean he's mine. I haven't been in his life in years. I haven't proven worthy of being a mother. I will never prove worthy. She'll always win.

I don't say any of that, though. I just watch silently as she walks inside the beach house.

I don't think about how she has two houses, while I have none. I can no longer afford my apartment in New York now that Langston stole everything from me. And I no longer care about reclaiming what was stolen. I have one mission, one goal—to protect my son.

I suspect Langston's reason for going after the treasure is the same as mine. For once, we are on the same side.

"We should talk," Langston says once the night air settles and the surge of our electricity resumes between us. I try to forget about how good it feels to kiss him, to have him plunging inside me.

We have a lot to talk about, but all my body wants to do is feel the thrill of Langston exploring my body.

"We should," I say, not being the one to start the conversation. If I start talking, I'll end up kissing him, and now that we are once again safe, I refuse to become the mistress.

His hand twitches against the fabric of the couch we are both sitting on. Moments ago we were united against our common enemies—friends who betrayed us. Now I don't know what we are. In the very least, we're sinners who stepped into a fire about to consume us both.

"We should go to Peru. We should find the treasure. Then we can decide what to do—use it or destroy it. We have to stop our enemies from attacking us; there is too much at stake," he says.

He means Atlas and Rose. We can't have people coming to attack us for a treasure that we don't even have. We have to put a stop to it.

"I agree."

"Good, I'll see if Beckett wants to watch the kids. He's surprisingly good at it."

"You trust him after what he did?"

"He's the only one I trust. He didn't plan to have us kidnapped. He just went along with it."

I nod. It's not really my place to question the safety of my child, not when I haven't been in my child's life since he was born.

"And then I will book a flight for the three of us," he continues.

"The three of us?"

Langston swallows hard, like he doesn't want to have to state the obvious, but I'm not going to make this easy on him. "Phoenix has to come."

"Why?"

"Because the letter says only a Dunn who is married can seek the treasure. Last I checked, you aren't married."

"No thanks to you."

His eyebrows pull together, and his body tenses. "Actually, thanks to me. You shouldn't be married to a man who used your lost son to blackmail you."

"Ha, you're one to talk since you married Phoenix for basically the exact same reason."

He growls. "So I guess we are doing this? Let's have it. Yell at me for marrying a woman who has been raising your child as if he were her own son. Do it. Tell me how much of a monster I am for fucking you while married. I'm fucking horrible—I know. But I don't care about what you think of me or even what Phoenix thinks of me—the only people I care about are Rose and Atlas. They are safe and loved—that's all that matters."

Silence.

Tears water my eyes, but I don't speak. I can't be mad at him for marrying Phoenix. Even if he wasn't married, it wouldn't change anything. I still couldn't marry him. He'd never be mine...

Phoenix has to come. Even though she hates me. Even though I hate her. Even though I want to thank her and kiss her for everything she's done for my son. I still hate her, but I also owe her my life.

"Fine, Phoenix comes."

Langston settles back, surprised by how easily he won that fight.

"When do you want to leave?" he asks with a soft, bewildered expression.

"Tomorrow. I want everything done as soon as possible."

"Okay, tomorrow it is then."

Silence stretches again, allowing the sultry tingling to reemerge between us. The spark that we stoked, instead of extinguished, is a full-blown fire between us. We have to find a way to put it out, though.

If we don't, it will spread until we've burned everyone we love in the process.

"You should meet Atlas before we leave," Langston says.

I shake my head. "I can't."

"Why?"

Waylon—that's why. Waylon still has a hold on me, even in death. He owns my soul, and I'm not sure if it's safe to see Atlas.

"I just can't." I look down at my hands, picking at my nails nervously.

I hear Langston move against the scratchy fabric as he slides toward me. From the corner of my eye, I see his hands grab onto mine, gently stopping me from anxiously twisting them around.

"You should meet him. It can be brief, and you shouldn't tell him who you are, but I think you should meet him. Just look at him so you can know he's your son."

"I believe you. There is no reason for you to lie to me." I hesitate a second, then ask my next question. "Do you love Atlas as a son?"

"Yes," he says without hesitation.

That's the only confirmation I needed to hear.

"But you won't meet with him?"

"No."

"Why? If something happens to us, he deserves to have met you. Do it for him if not for yourself."

I look up and pull my hands free, staring at Langton's dark eyes, avoiding his lush lips and sharp jaw I want to run my tongue over.

"No," I say definitively.

Langston shakes his head in frustration. His scowl tells me he thinks less of me for not seeing my son, not giving him the chance to meet his birth mother.

He doesn't know that I'm doing it to protect him. Even though Waylon is gone, someone will continue his plans. I don't know who it is, or if they will, in fact, continue Waylon's plans, but until I know for sure, I can't risk it.

For now, knowing his name, Atlas, and knowing that he's safe in Langston's protection is enough. It's more than enough after Waylon led me to believe that he was with a cruel monster who was abusing him. Langston may be a monster, but I've seen how he loves his kids. Atlas is accepted as his child just as much as Rose. He'll protect both of them with his life.

"I'll show you to your room in the basement," Langston says.

"No, I'd rather sleep here."

"Huntress, get your ass inside, now."

I look at the house. I can't sleep under the same roof as Phoenix, and I can't chance that Atlas might see me. I'll sleep out here under the stars, where the sun will ensure I wake up before anyone in the house does.

"Fine," Langston huffs off while I curl up on the couch.

I close my eyes and am just on the edge of sleep, when I see a shadow walking toward me. I'm too tired to open my eyes, but the shadow means me no harm.

A blanket is draped over me, and then his soft lips whisper near my ear. "I don't know if you are the biggest sinner or saint, but either way, you're mine, huntress. Mine."

CHAPTER 4

LANGSTON

I bang the coffee cup down on the counter and slam the cabinet door shut. I should move more quietly so I don't wake everyone up, but I can't. I didn't sleep at all last night. Instead, I spent the night in my office on my laptop, trying to figure out what Liesel is hiding from me.

I pour myself some coffee, and I stare out at the back deck where Liesel is still sound asleep on the couch.

What do I do with you, huntress? What are you hunting now? You've found your child, now what? Do you really want the treasure, or is that just an illusion?

"Morning, baby. What can I make you for breakfast?" Phoenix asks as she twirls into the kitchen.

I narrow my eyes, trying to figure out why she's so happy.

"I'm fucking exhausted and don't have time for games, so tell me what the hell is going on."

Her smile doesn't falter. She grabs a coffee cup behind my left shoulder and then grabs the pot behind me. She happily pours herself a cup before standing on her tiptoes and kissing me blatantly on the lips.

My eyes cut outside, but Liesel is still asleep. I don't have to ask any more questions to know what game Phoenix is playing at. She's trying to let Liesel know that she has me—that I slept in her house, that she's birthed my child and taken care of Liesel's, that she has a secure place in my life, while Liesel has nothing.

I shake my head at her antics. "Liesel being here changes nothing between us."

She tilts her head with an even brighter smile. "I know."

That's what she wants—nothing to change.

I sigh. What a mess I'm in. Two women who both are worthy of the world and I won't be able to give either of them what they deserve. All I do is take from both of them. With Phoenix, I take advantage of her kindness in caring for my children, but I don't want her body or love for myself. With Liesel, I take her body, her lust, her desire, but I don't want to love her.

"Beckett will be here in an hour to take the kids," I say, not giving Phoenix a say in the matter.

She nods. "And then we'll leave after that?"

"Yes."

"Where to?"

I take a sip of my coffee. Finding the treasure is between Liesel and me. Phoenix is only coming along because the first clue said that a Dunn had to be married to seek the treasure. That doesn't mean I'll share anything with Phoenix that she doesn't absolutely need to know.

"You'll know when we get there," I say.

Her smile drops, and her face turns dark. I think she's going to fight me on it, but there is a more pressing issue that we need to discuss.

"When this is all over, what would it take for you to agree to a divorce?"

She blinks rapidly and steps back out of my personal bubble. She swallows and plasters a smile back on her face quickly, acting like I didn't just wound her.

I hate hurting the mother of my children, but I have to be honest with her. I don't want to divorce her so I can be with Liesel, but I'm not sure our arrangement makes sense anymore. I don't want our kids growing up thinking that we are in love, thinking our relationship is what a marriage is supposed to be. I'll never have Liesel, but I don't want to keep leading Phoenix on, giving her hope that someday I'll fall for her. I'll never fall for anyone.

"More than you're willing to give," Phoenix says.

"Money? I'll give you everything I own. Everything that the kids don't need to survive."

She shakes her head.

I set my cup of coffee down and encroach on her space. She's used to me manhandling her, trying to control the situation. I take her cup from her hand and set it on the counter behind her. Then I take her hands in mine. I need her to hear my words. I need her to understand that she's never going to get what she wants from me.

"I'm not a good man, Dunn." She winces when I call her Dunn. She prefers I use my last name as hers, but that's exactly why I call her Dunn. Even though we're married, she's not really mine. Using her maiden name reminds us both of our relationship.

"I take everything and give nothing back. I kill without a thought to the sanctity of life. And I'll never love you, Dunn. All I'll end up doing is ruining you."

She swallows hard, like she might be having doubts about what she's doing with me. "Then ruin me."

Her lips crash onto mine in a desperate attempt to remind me of how good we are together in bed. She's good because she lets me have my way with her. She lets me have control. But after finally having Liesel, there is nothing that will get my dick hard again except her. Fucking Liesel was everything I thought I could never have, and I won't go back.

I pull away gently, trying not to hurt her, but needing to make it clear that I won't be kissing her, fucking her, touching her again.

My eyes flick to the door, already knowing what I'm going to find.

Liesel.

Her eyes are dark, watery, and filled with pain.

Dammit.

Phoenix smirks.

I run my hand through my hair and step back. *Jesus, I'm going to destroy them both.*

Liesel opens the sliding glass door.

My heart pounds.

Phoenix turns with an angry glare, telling Liesel she's not welcome in her house.

Liesel doesn't look at me as she walks into the house, risking Atlas or Rose coming down and her being forced to meet them. All of her attention is on Phoenix, as if I'm not even in the room.

She walks over to us like she's on a mission, full of determination. Whatever she is feeling, it's intense and filling her entire body.

She stops and finally glances at me, but only to indicate for me to move the fuck out of her way.

I do, but I'm afraid she's going to slap Phoenix, so I stay close. Phoenix may have been playing with Liesel's emotions, but she doesn't deserve to be slapped.

I hold my breath as Liesel faces Phoenix. The two women who have twisted their way into my life deeper than I've ever allowed anyone face off. I should stop it, but maybe if they fight and get it out of their systems, they will be able to work together.

Liesel takes another step closer toward Phoenix, who tries to slink back against the counter. Then Liesel wraps her arms around Phoenix.

"Thank you," she whispers through wet eyes.

Phoenix exhales and wraps her arms around her. "You're welcome."

The two hold each other like they are long lost friends. I was wrong. They won't fight over me or stake a claim. They are better than that. All they care about is their shared love for their children.

It's a beautiful moment—one that doesn't happen too often in my life.

Liesel steps back, letting go of Phoenix. "I'm sorry."

"What for?" Phoenix asks.

I think Liesel is going to say for not being there for her child, for forcing her to have to take care of her child. She doesn't mention Atlas, though. "He's yours. I'm sorry for hurting you. I'm sorry for trying to take him from you. I won't again."

I won't again.

Those words are meant for me as much as they are meant for Phoenix.

Liesel won't kiss me again, touch me again, fuck me again. That's what her words mean.

My heart seizes. I thought it would be my cock or lips that was disappointed with her statement, not my fucking heart. It's like my heart can't take the prospect of not having even a chance of falling for Liesel.

I never had a chance of falling for her. I never would allow myself.

Mine isn't the only heart in the room that's breaking. I just can't tell if it's Phoenix's heart knowing what transpired between Liesel and me, or Liesel's knowing she can never be with me again.

"We need to get the kids somewhere safe and leave as soon as we can," Liesel says like she didn't just make a proclamation that destroyed us all.

"Beckett will be here within the hour," I say.

"We can't wait that long," she says, and then she pulls a letter from her pocket and hands it to me. "It was lying on top of me when I woke up this morning. Someone is here."

I grab the note and read.

YOUR CHILD ISN'T SAFE. I CAN GET TO HIM. I CAN HURT HIM. THERE IS *nowhere you can hide him from me.*

Soon, I'll come for the treasure. Give it to me or I'll take him from you forever.

THE NOTE IS TORN AT THE TOP, AND I REALIZE THIS ISN'T THE FULL letter. I flip it front and back like the second half of the letter is going to suddenly appear to me.

"Where is the other half of the letter, huntress?" I ask, glaring at her.

She shakes her head.

"Dunn, go get the kids packed and ready to go. And bring Liesel a change of clothes."

Phoenix nods and runs off, but not before I see the hint of her smirk. Of course, she'd be happy that I'm about to get into a fight with Liesel.

"Give. Me. The. Other. Half. Of. The. Note."

"No."

"Why the hell not? We are on the same side! We both want to protect the kids. I can't help if I don't know what we are facing."

"I gave you the important part. The rest was for my eyes only. It doesn't matter what it said. What matters is we figure out a way to keep the kids safe!"

She's fuming.

I'm fuming.

And when fire meets fire—an explosion happens.

An explosion won't help.

"What are you hiding, huntress?"

"What are you hiding, killer?"

I step toward her. She steps back, until the counter hits her ass, and there is nowhere for her to go.

"You won't again, huh?" I ask, encroaching on her personal space and taking up all the oxygen around her until I control when she breathes. My body hovers over her until a buzzing shoots between us, increasing her pulse.

She licks her lips.

I run mine over my teeth hungrily.

"I won't—I won't hurt her. Not after what she's done for me."

"What if I told you it didn't hurt her?"

"It does. She loves you."

She's probably right that Phoenix loves me, but it can't be true. Phoenix is too smart to have already fallen for my dumb ass.

"And if she were to stop caring about me? What then?" I breathe over her lips, tempting her to close the gap.

"Then..." she purrs but doesn't answer.

"How do you feel, huntress?" My thumb touches her swollen lip, begging her to give in to me. To want me. To let down her guard so I can figure her out. "What do you want?"

My tongue darts out of my mouth to taste hers.

She closes her eyes as my tongue brushes against her lip. They fly back open a second later.

"No." She puts her hand on my chest and pushes me hard. "You can tease me, tempt me, lust after me, but it's a waste of time. I don't regret what we did. I thought we were going to die in that tower. But things are different now. I won't hurt the mother of my child."

The mother of *her* child. The mother of *my* child.

I take a deep breath and sigh.

"Then I guess I'm the bigger monster between the two of us because I want to sin with you no matter who it hurts."

CHAPTER 5

LIESEL

I'm stronger than I ever imagined. It took every bit of my strength to resist Langston. The wetness of his tongue against my lip, the heat from his breath, the pull of my soul. My body comes alive when I'm with Langston. I've never felt so alive as when he's inside me. And I'll never feel that alive again.

I meant what I said—*never again.*

I will take the memories with me forever, but that's all I'll take.

Langston's words will taunt me, though. They beg me to give in, and I'm sure his latest attempt was only the beginning. I can't be alone with him. I'm strong, but I'm not strong enough to keep saying no. Especially not now that I know how it feels to be with him.

I hear footsteps upstairs—Phoenix getting the kids ready. If I could make him fall in love with her, I would. It would be better for everyone.

All I can focus on now is the threat made against Atlas. My entire life has been about keeping him safe. It's the only thing I've succeeded at, and I'll do everything I can to keep him safe.

Langston is desperate to know what the note said, but it's my burden to bear. It's my fault Atlas is in danger. And Langston knowing will just get him killed.

Monsters come in all shapes and sizes, but they all hide in the dark. Creeping through the shadows, pretending that they have the power to destroy, but that makes them easier to catch. This monster left a clue as to who he is. Now, all that's left to do is to decide if I want to set a trap and catch the monster or give in to his demands.

There's a rough knock on the door.

"Beckett got here early," Langston says, running to the door.

Thank god.

I hear footsteps coming down the stairs, and I creep back. This isn't how I'll meet my son, not like this.

I run out back before the kids make it down the stairs. I exhale sharply as the sun beats down on me, making me sweat. My hands are clammy, and my nerves shot. I need to run to get some energy out and make myself feel better, but I can't.

Instead, I do something that might actually help protect my kids. I call Siren.

"Hello?" Siren answers.

"Hey, it's Liesel. I need your help."

"I'm out of the faking my death business. Besides, I don't think Langston would fall for that one again."

"No, it's nothing like that. The kids..." I find I can't finish before tears fill my eyes.

"Say no more. What do you need us to do?"

"Make people believe that you all are moving precious cargo. Beckett will be the one who has them, but anything to make people believe that you or Kai or someone else might be hiding them, the safer they'll be."

I hate asking. They all have kids that this could be putting at risk as well.

"Done."

I exhale sharply after holding my breath, waiting for her answer.

"We all have kids. We know how terrifying it can be to be worried about your children. Don't worry about what was said or done before. When it comes to our kids, we will always protect them."

"He told you then?"

"That Atlas is your son? Yes. He told us, but I've always suspected."

"Thank you," I say before we hang up.

I hear voices and the opening of a car door. It's safe to go back into the house now and hide until they are gone. Saying goodbye as my son is driven away is not the way I should meet him. I haven't earned the right to meet him, not until I know he's safe from this world forever.

But I can't fight the pull. *Maybe I'm not as strong as I think? Or maybe I just love my son more than I care about Langston?*

I walk up the side of the house, following the sound of the sweet little voices. One is thrilled about the new adventure she's going on. The other concerned and dubious of why the adventure is being sprung on them.

I force my feet to stop when I get to the side of the house, where a row of bushes gives me a spot to hide. I crouch down, blending with the greenery.

And then I look through the branches and leaves.

I see a scrawny fair-haired girl in a pink dinosaur shirt, black shorts, and sparkly shoes. She has a black bandana in her hair, and she's talking Langston's head off about how he has to promise he'll be coming with on the next adventure.

He promises.

I smile. She has him so wrapped around her little finger. He gives her a tight hug, and I see how clearly her hair color matches his. She didn't get her coloring from her mother unless Phoenix's darker hair is dyed that way. She moves to hug Phoenix next while Langston moves to Atlas.

His hair is much darker, and he's more reserved. He doesn't say much. I find myself afraid that Langston is going to behave differently toward him since he's not his biological son, but he kneels down in front of him in the same way he did to Rose.

"Keep Rose out of trouble for me, okay?"

"I promise."

He wraps Atlas in a hug and then whispers something into his ear that makes him smile.

I gasp when I see Atlas' eyes and smile. There is no doubt in my mind that he's my son and that Langston loves him as his own. My only role in my child's life is to ensure that he's safe. I don't get to know him—that will only bring more danger into his life.

Phoenix is his mother.

Langston is his father.

And I, I'm his protector.

CHAPTER 6

LANGSTON

I plant my feet firmly on the ground on my driveway as I watch Beckett drive away with my kids in the backseat. Every instinct in my body tells me to run after them. I'm their protector. I'm supposed to keep them safe. I need to be with them.

My feet don't move, though. The weight of the world is the only thing keeping me from running after Beckett's bulletproof SUV. The only way to protect them is to get the damn treasure and destroy our enemies. If they stay with me, they will be a target.

So I let them go, even though I physically feel pain letting them out of my sight. Even though I trust Beckett. Even though I know the rest of the Black empire—Enzo, Kai, Siren, and Zeke—will protect them. We would all lay down our lives to protect the kids.

I turn around just as the SUV turns a corner and escapes from sight.

Liesel.

She's standing on the side of the house.

I smile—she couldn't help herself. She took a peek at the kids.

I wish she had done more, met them, but that's her decision. The monster inside me isn't satisfied with that, though. I can forgive Liesel for a lot of things, but not when it comes to her child.

She looks back to the house and walks over to where Phoenix and I stand.

"We should go now," Liesel says. She rushes toward the car in the garage.

Phoenix and I exchange glances before we follow her to the car. I sit in the driver's seat, Phoenix next to me, and Liesel behind me. Phoenix tosses Liesel a change of clothes as I start driving us to the airport.

We aren't out of the garage for two seconds when a nearby explosion rocks our car.

Phoenix shrieks.

My heart stops.

Liesel just stares down the road, completely unfazed.

"It's gone," Phoenix says, drawing my attention away from Liesel and back to the house.

Flames dance across the shattered remains. This house is where my kids have grown up. It's where I first brought them home, where we became a family.

I try to push out the dozens of stuffed animals, bikes, and pictures that were just taken from us. We are all safe—that's what matters.

But my blood boils. Liesel isn't surprised at all that the house just exploded. *The letter threatened us, but did she hide details from me? What else is in that damn letter?*

I grip the steering wheel in rage and look back at Liesel through the rearview mirror. I've only been this pissed at her one time before. But this time, I'm not going to let her get away with it.

Phoenix is still sobbing and carrying on next to me. It's just a house, just stuff, but I feel her pain. Something was taken from us today, and whomever it was is going to pay—even if the woman in the back seat had something to do with it.

I reach across and find Phoenix's hand. I lift it to my lips and kiss the back of her hand.

"It's going to be okay, Phoenix. We are all safe. Everything inside is replaceable. And I'm going to make every person who had anything to do with this suffer."

Liesel's eyes meet mine when I say those words, intending her to know that whatever has happened between us doesn't matter. I don't care that we survived hell together. I don't care that she's Atlas' birth mother. If she had anything to do with this, if she hid this from me, then I'll make her pay.

I watch as her eyes drop to where my fingers are intertwined with Phoenix's. She doesn't react, at least not on the outside, but I suspect Liesel is raging with jealousy.

For the next few minutes, the only sounds that fill the car are Phoenix's quiet sobs and hiccups.

"We're being followed," Liesel says carefully.

I glance in the rearview mirror and force myself to look beyond Liesel to the road. A blacked out sedan creeps after us.

I make a last-minute right turn onto a side street, and sure enough, the car turns as well.

"Shit," I say.

"Oh my god! We are going to die. I should have gone with the kids. The kids are going to grow up without parents," Phoenix howls.

I let go of Phoenix's hand and grip the wheel. I don't have time to deal with her hysteria. I have to get the car behind us off our tail.

I make another sharp turn, and Phoenix screams at my sudden speed.

"Slow down!" she shouts.

I don't.

I take my gun out, preparing to shoot the tires of the trailing car behind me.

"Langston! Don't shoot them! I—"

Slap.

Liesel has unbuckled herself, climbed in between us, and slapped Phoenix in the face.

"Stop it. Now isn't the time to freak out. It's not helpful. If you want to be helpful, shut up and do whatever Langston tells you to do. If you do that, your kids will grow up with a loving mother and father. If you don't, then I'm going to throw you out of this car to ensure that your kids at least grow up with a father," Liesel says, getting into Phoenix's face.

I raise an eyebrow, not sure that's the best technique to get Phoenix to stop.

Phoenix sniffles then nods.

Then both women turn toward me.

"At the next intersection, I'm going to spin us. Then, I'll fire some shots out my window that will stop the car from pursuing us. I need you both to duck down. The car is bulletproof, but the windows are the most vulnerable."

Phoenix sucks in her snot and then ducks down, flinging her arms over her head.

"Seatbelt, then duck," I say slowly to Liesel.

Liesel rolls her eyes, then digs under my seat before coming back up with a gun in her hand.

"What are you doing?" I ask.

"Stepping up."

"You could get killed."

"Then I'll die doing something good for Atlas."

My heart swells. Maybe I was wrong about Liesel.

I give Liesel a look of preparation.

She grabs onto the door, and we both lower our windows.

And then I sling us around.

I aim out the window and start firing at the tires. I hit the first before moving to the second and seeing that it has already been blown out by Liesel. Then we both start shooting at the driver.

The men in the car barely get a return shot off before I'm spinning us back around and stepping on the gas.

"Is it over?" Phoenix says from the floor as Liesel and I roll up our windows.

I glance in the rearview mirror; the car behind us has stopped. I look to Liesel, who purses her lips and lets out a slow breath. She's always said she doesn't belong in this world and that she hates firing a gun. She hates the violence, but she fits in better than she will ever admit.

"Yes, the car isn't following us anymore," I reply.

"Good," Phoenix pants next to me. Her hair is disheveled, and her forehead is sweaty. Now I'm regretting bringing her along; that car chase is going to be the least dangerous thing we go through.

The rest of the drive is uneventful as I pull up to the tarmac where one of Kai's private jets is waiting.

"Huntress, go into the jet and tell them we'll be ready to take off in five minutes. I need to talk to Dunn here."

Liesel hesitates as she opens the door, but then she climbs out, still holding onto the gun like most women would a purse, completely at ease with herself. She's turned into a mama bear willing to do whatever it takes to protect her child—fucking finally.

Phoenix carefully watches Liesel climb the steps into the jet.

"We're on the same side," I say.

Phoenix pulls the visor down and starts blotting underneath her eyes, where her mascara has run. She pinches her cheeks and then runs her hand through her hair before she faces me with watering eyes.

"We're not."

"Yes, we are. Liesel cares about Atlas and Rose just as much as we do."

She shakes her head. "She hasn't been around. She gave Atlas up. She—"

"She didn't have a choice. Giving Atlas up was the best thing for him."

"I don't trust her."

"She's Atlas' mother. She knows Rose is my kid. Don't let your jealousy impede your thinking."

She slaps me.

"I'm not jealous of Liesel. You can stick your dick into anyone you want. The only people I care about are Atlas and Rose, and I don't trust your whore. She gave up Atlas, and Rose means nothing to her."

"You're wrong."

"I'm not willing to risk our kids' lives on your hunch, which is based entirely on wanting to fuck the woman."

"What do you want, Phoenix? We need Liesel in order to end this. The kids are safe. So you either trust her enough to finish this together, or you go hang out with the kids until this is over—which will it be?"

She huffs like the decision is going to be the death of her, and then she pops open the door. "I'm coming, but it doesn't mean I trust her yet."

"You don't have to trust her. You have to trust me." I grab onto her hip, pulling her back into the car. "Can you do that? Trust me?"

"I trust you."

I release her, and then we both get out of the car and walk up the stairs to the plane.

I don't spot Liesel initially when I step into the aisle. For a second, my heart skips, thinking that she took off. We need her help to get the treasure, to protect the kids.

I need her.

But then I spot her blonde locks peek up over the last seat in the back of the plane. There are a dozen seats between me and her. Phoenix takes the first seat at the front, purposefully making me choose between her and Liesel.

I sigh and take a seat next to Phoenix. I don't know how to fix the iciness between the two of them, but I'll let Liesel think she's safe for now hiding in the back of the plane. She's not safe—not from me.

This is never going to end.

Atlas will never be safe.

And it's all my fault.

The plane takes off with Phoenix and Langston sitting in the front while I occupy the last seat—the furthest away I can be from them. I quickly change out of my flannel and sweatpants and into new clothes —dark jeans and a tight white T-shirt. At least it's not a long-sleeved shirt like Phoenix usually wears.

I need to think, and Langston distracts me. My body comes alive when he's close, and if he touches me...forget it. There won't be any blood left in my brain to function.

I swore when I gave Atlas up that I was doing it to protect him. Everything I do is to protect him. I won't let anyone distract me.

The words of the letter burn into my head. There is only one way to protect Atlas now, and I'm not sure I'm strong enough to pull it off.

I close my eyes and lean my chair back so I can be well-rested when we get to Peru.

"What aren't you telling me, huntress?" Langston asks, jolting me awake.

My body heats, and my pulse races, even though my eyes remain closed.

"You can't ignore me, huntress. You are trapped on a private jet with me for another two hours. Talk to me, or I'll make you talk."

My eyes fly open, and I stare him down as he stands above me. I'm tired of his threats. His harsh words should tamper down the heat in my body, but the heat only rises. I prefer us being enemies to friends, even if we are enemies on the same side. It reminds me that I can never have Langston; he isn't mine.

"Your threats mean nothing to me."

"I know, but they should." He sinks into the chair next to me.

I think I prefer him towering over me to sitting so close. He leans over, invading my space as his hot breath dances across my skin on my neck.

"Won't Phoenix be missing you?"

"Phoenix is a big girl. She can sit on a plane for a few minutes all by herself."

I glance her way and see a thin black cord hanging down from her ear. She's listening to something, and her eyes are closed.

I sigh. There is no one to save me from Langston. Right now, I'd even take Phoenix's snarky comments—anything to not be left alone with Langston.

Langston turns sideways in his seat. He places one hand on the window behind me and his other hand on my chin.

"What aren't you telling me?" he asks again.

Everything. I'm not telling you everything because it's not your burden to bear. You've done enough. You've protected my son when he wasn't even your own blood. I'm the only one who can save him now.

"I've told you everything." *Everything that you need to know.*

"I don't believe you, Liesel. I know you're lying. You tore the note in half before you gave it to me. You knew the house was going to explode. What aren't you telling me?"

His grip under my chin strengthens as his resolve weakens. His voice is low and grumbly. He's trying to look strong and unbreakable, but there is a hint of the boy I used to know underneath his blonde eyelashes. He wants me to tell him not because he's worried about our safety but because I want to share information with him. Because I trust him. I do trust him more than he'll ever know. If I didn't trust him, I'd take Atlas far away from him. He's the only man I trust with my son.

I just can't let him further into the depths of my dark soul. I know what I have to do, and Langston will hate me for it. I can handle the hate if I didn't know anything else, but I can't handle him hating me after feeling his love.

"I'm not hiding anything from you, killer. I've told you everything you need to know to keep us safe."

"What was on the other half of the note?"

"Just a personal attack against me. Something about calling me a bitch and whore, I didn't think you needed to read it."

His eyes narrow, and his tongue licks his lips. "Liar."

Of course I'm lying, but I refuse to tell him the rest. Not until I know it's the truth myself. Not until I've done what needs to be done.

"So what if I am lying? You're not going to be able to get me to tell you the truth, so drop it."

"Kai and Siren are going to be disappointed their plan failed so quickly. Just like that, you don't trust me anymore."

"I never trusted you."

"I beg to disagree. You seem to trust me plenty with my cock in your mouth and tight cunt. Should I remind you?"

"You wouldn't do that to Phoenix." My chest rises and falls in hushed breaths.

Langston smirks. His eyes turn a wicked shade of black.

My mouth dries, just imagining his lips on mine. It's all I ever crave. If it wasn't for Atlas, my every thought would be consumed with Langston. I'd fuck him right here and not give a damn about hurting Phoenix's feelings. But she's Atlas' mother. She will always be his mother. I can't do that to her.

I shake my head and finally pull myself out of his grasp. I'm still trapped in my seat, boxed in beneath his arm.

"Phoenix needs to face reality." He tilts his head as a lock of his hair falls into his eyes. I want to reach up and swipe it out of his eyes, but I remain motionless.

"What do you mean?"

He huffs. "I asked her for a divorce."

I blink. I must have imagined him. There is no way he wants to divorce Phoenix. She's the mother of his children.

"Don't act like you didn't hear me. I asked Phoenix for a divorce."

"And..." my voice cracks. "What did she say?"

"Phoenix and I are getting a divorce as soon as this is all over."

"Sure, you are. And I'm going to be the next Queen of England."

His eyes roam down my body. "You'd make one hot as fuck queen."

I roll my eyes.

And then his lips graze my cheek.

"What are you doing?"

"Getting you to tell me the truth or fucking you in the back of this jet. The choice is yours."

I swallow, but the lump in my throat barely moves. My palms sweat, and my body tingles. I'm not going to survive his form of torture.

I should just give in and fuck him. Everyone already thinks I'm a bitch who steals other people's men. Phoenix certainly does. I might as well live up to my reputation.

I have a wicked soul that's been hardened by years of pain. I'll do enough horrible things with what remains of my life. I don't have to hurt Phoenix. Not like this.

"I'm not telling you anything, and you aren't fucking me either."

His tongue flicks over my earlobe, causing my lips to part and moan.

"You can pretend you have control over your body all you want, but it's not the truth. The truth is you and I were made for each other. We've resisted for years because we knew that if we ever gave in, we would never stop. Now that we've had each other, there is no stopping the inevitable. You can't stop us from happening. Phoenix can't. None of our enemies can. We are meant to be together, huntress."

"We hate each other, killer. That will never change. Being together hurts too many people."

He kisses down my neck to my clavicle. "I didn't mention anything about love. All I said was we belong together. We belong hating each other. Fighting together. Fucking together. Our lives became more intertwined than either of us ever expected. The second I tore your father's letter out of your hand all those years ago, you and I became an 'us.'"

My eyes are trained on the ceiling as my mouth parts. I breathe heavily through my mouth as his hand pushes up my shirt, his fingers walking up my stomach.

He's right—love may not be in the cards for us, but everything else is fair game.

I'm a horrible, sinful bitch.

"Talk to me, huntress, and this stops." He kisses the corner of my mouth as his hand continues to climb higher on my body until he's cupping my breast.

I suck in a breath as his thumb brushes over my nipple. My eyes dart to Phoenix.

Please, god, let her be blasting her music and not look back here.

"I can't."

He grins against my lips. "Can't or don't want to?"

I gasp, and then his mouth is on mine. I try to close my mouth, but I'm not fast enough. His tongue is in my mouth; his lips hungrily eat mine. My mind is mush as he devours me.

Can't.

Don't want.

Definitely want.

My hand grabs his neck as I deepen the kiss. I denied wanting Langston for so long that every time I kiss him, I think it's a dream. It can't be real. None of this is real.

But then his tongue dances across mine, he lets a throaty growl out, his hand pinches my nipple, and I realize just how real it is. As real as all of the horrible things I've ever experienced.

Langston's hands start moving lower off my breast and down my stomach as he continues to attack my mouth, using his tongue as a weapon.

"Talk to me, huntress, or I'm going to fuck you with my fingers until you scream so loud that Phoenix will hate you forever."

"You wouldn't."

He grins. "Let's see how quiet you can be when I give you an orgasm that shatters every nerve ending in your body."

I gulp.

My eyes drift to Phoenix. *Maybe it's for the best that she hates me?* We don't need to get along. We both just have to play our roles in protecting our children.

No!

Get ahold of yourself. You're better than this.

His hands keep traveling south, and I only have moments to decide. I don't have much strength in telling Langston no, but I'll have none left once his hands reach my pants.

He kisses me again, and I moan, quickly losing my ability to control this situation. I'd rather him be holding a gun; I'd have a better shot at defeating him than with his tongue in my mouth.

I don't know which way Langston would rather me choose either—telling him the truth or letting him fuck me until I lose control. Whatever I choose, he wins.

Forgive me, Phoenix.

We were always doomed to become nemeses. My cousin, who gets to love the boy I grew up with freely. She carried his child, got him to put a ring on her finger and vow eternity to her. I know he says that he wants to get divorced, but when it comes down to it, Langston is an honorable man. He won't divorce Phoenix unless she agrees.

With every tantalizing kiss, I'm becoming more and more of the tragic whore I was always destined to become. I'm the thorn in his side. The darkness that overshadows his children and brings the monsters in the night.

I may be the cheater, but I won't be the monster that brings children anymore suffering. It's just one of the many reasons that Langston and I are not meant to be together. He's wrong—we don't belong together in any way. Our lives have become intertwined because of that damn letter that he stole from me and because fate played a sick game on us by having Langston adopt my child.

Knowing that every kiss we exchange is going to break our hearts that much more when this ends doesn't stop the kisses. It doesn't stop our teeth from clashing, our tongues from wrestling, and our moans from escalating.

Each kiss brings me further away from reality. I forget to be quiet to prevent Phoenix from hearing, and I no longer flail my arms in failed attempts to push him away. Instead, my fingers curl around the neck of his shirt, holding him tight against me so I can invade his mouth with my tongue.

His fingers continue to drag down my flat stomach filled with enormous butterflies that build into a swarm of feelings that I'm never going to be able to decipher.

"I want this," I say as his hands lower.

We both lock eyes. I expect a cocky grin; instead, he gives me a seductive gaze that has my insides melting. His hand finds the top of my jeans and begins to unbutton them. We've stopped kissing, both intensely focused on what his hand is doing.

This is wrong.

So wrong.

But my whole life has been wrong. After this is over, I may regret the pain I've caused, but right now, I just want this man—the only man left in the world that I trust to make me feel good.

"Can you be quiet, huntress?"

I nod as his hand pushes beneath the fabric of my jeans and cups my sex. I moan loudly, before realizing my mistake and biting down on his shoulder to keep from making another sound.

He chuckles. "I'm not going to let you be quiet. I'm going to make you scream until the pilot comes back here thinking he needs to make an emergency landing."

"Your fingers aren't that good."

His scruff rubs against my cheek as his tongue tickles the rim of my ear. "Liar. Everything about me is that good—fingers, tongue, cock. I'm going to make you scream my name with each one."

All of my brain cells burst with his deeply arrogant words. I slant my head as I resume kissing him. I no longer remember why I don't want to make a sound, just that I don't. Kissing him muffles any sounds that escape. He's right; I will moan, groan, and scream every time he touches my clit or pushes himself inside me.

His fingers push aside my panties and spread my lips before dipping inside.

I moan around his bottom lip that I've pulled into my mouth and sucking ferociously, trying to control myself.

"So wet for me already."

His fingers push further inside me, spreading me and making me feel whole. His thumb brushes over my clit.

I bite down with everything I can—using his lip like someone might bite down on a belt in olden days when they are about to lose a limb. Langston is doing the same to me—except instead of losing a limb, I'm losing my soul.

His thumb is merciless as he rubs faster and faster on my clit until water stings my eyes from trying to keep my screams inside. I taste his blood in my mouth, but he doesn't surrender. It seems he's happy to pay the price in blood to make me pay in sin.

I crumple as his fingers thrust in and out, crushing all my walls I've built to keep him out.

His hand slides down my back before he dips me sideways in our row of seats until I'm lying on my back. He settles between my spread legs, his hand still inside me, but our mouths separated. I no longer have his lip to bite down on, nothing to muffle my cries.

He smirks down at me, knowing once again that he's won.

Why did I need to keep quiet again?

With one hand still inside me, his other hand moves to my stomach, pushing my shirt up before running down my center. Then his fingers dip lower, tracing over my C-section scar.

A scar he has avoided touching or commenting on until now.

My scar.

Atlas.

I prop myself up on my elbows abruptly, pushing through the fog that has surrounded my head since he started touching me.

"Stop."

He does, but he doesn't remove his fingers from my slit.

"We can't." I shake my head. "I'm already a cheater, a whore, a bitch. And as bad as my body wants me to become a cheater again, we can't. I won't hurt Phoenix. I won't hurt the mother of my child.

Before, I thought we were going to die. Now, we have a choice. I won't make the same mistake again."

My breathing is erratic, and my hands shake. My entire body is calling me a fool for telling Langston to stop.

"Tell me what you're hiding, or I keep going," Langston says with a devilish smirk.

"You wouldn't."

"Try me."

My breath hitches, and my heart rate skyrockets. *How do I get out of this with my body and sanity intact?*

Tell him the truth—at least what you can of it. Tell him the why.

"You tell me I should trust you. That we are on the same side—both looking for the treasure and a way to protect our kids."

He nods.

"I trust you," I say.

His eyes widen at my admission.

"And now I'm asking you to trust me. I can't tell you any more than I already have. At least not yet. It's not safe."

"Not safe for who?"

"For you! Our kids need a father alive."

He pauses, and I'm not sure what he's going to do—keep torturing me to tell him the truth or let this go.

Slowly, he slides his fingers out of me. He pushes my panties back in place and even zips up my jeans and fastens the button.

Then he lifts his fingers to his lips and sucks my juices off them. I'm so close to coming that I'm afraid just watching this enchanting man suck his fingers is going to make me come, so I look away.

"They also need their mother to stay alive," he says as he holds out his hand to me.

I take it, and he helps me sit back up.

"They already have a mother," I say, my eyes locking on the back of Phoenix's head. She's still looking straight ahead, and I have no idea if she knows what happened between us.

He stands up and looks at me sadly. "Maybe they need two."

CHAPTER 8

LANGSTON

*T*rust her.

That's what Liesel wants—trust.

I sink back into my chair next to Phoenix. She doesn't even glance up from her phone. She can pretend she doesn't know what I went back to Liesel for all she wants, but pretending we are one big happy family isn't going to make our children's lives any better. We have to face the truth.

Liesel said she trusts me. I assume that must be true since she didn't immediately demand her child be removed from my custody. To some extent, she must also trust Phoenix.

But do I trust her?

I want to. I want to trust her desperately. I want to trust that everything I thought I knew about Liesel isn't true—that she didn't do the horrible thing I discovered. I want to believe that the reason she's hiding things from me is truly to protect our kids. I want to trust her.

But I don't.

She's broken my trust so many times, as have I.

I don't know why she's changed her mind and now trusts me. Or maybe that's a lie, like everything else she speaks.

I do know that we have to figure out a way to trust each other if we are going to survive this; I just don't know how.

Phoenix finally looks at me and smiles weakly as she puts the hood of her hoodie up over her head and then leans on my shoulder, her hand resting against my inner thigh. It doesn't bother me how blasé she is with touching me. Phoenix has earned the right to touch me however she wants.

The problem is I don't crave her touch. I crave the spicy blonde in the back who wants to castrate me as much as she wants to fuck me. The woman hates as much as she loves me. The woman who is mine and yet will never actually be mine.

When Liesel told me to stop, I thought I was imagining it. There was no way I could be feeling like I felt touching her, and her have the capacity to tell me to stop. The burning desire bolting through me was buzzing through her body too. I saw it in her hooded eyes, her parted lips, and the way she bit down on my lip.

I tortured her with my body not because I actually thought it would lead her to tell me the truth, but because I needed something to ground myself in her again. I thought she needed the same—an escape from reality together.

But then she asked me to stop.

Does she have more control over her urges than I do? Or is her lust just not as strong as mine is?

I move my head, and a drop of blood splotches Phoenix's cheek. Her thumb swipes across her pale cheek, and then she looks at the red-colored liquid on the tip of her thumb.

I don't know how she's going to react to seeing evidence of my interactions with Liesel. I watch curiously as she waits a beat before placing her thumb into her mouth, sucking the blood off.

Nothing.

A sight like that in the past might get me hard and horny as hell. I'd be pulling her into the nearest bathroom to fuck her senseless. That was who I used to be—a horny bastard content on fucking everyone.

My eyes sear back to where I left my heart—sitting next to Liesel, my huntress.

Phoenix sits up and examines me closer until she finds the source of the blood—my bottom lip. A lip that Liesel bit down on to keep from screaming my name as I fucked her with my fingers—fingers that still smell like her.

Phoenix's eyes glaze over into a frosty shade. I can see the damn icicles hanging from her eyelashes.

I prepare myself for her slap, bite, hit, rage. I deserve it. Even though we have an open marriage, I know that I hurt her. I hate hurting her. She's one of my closest friends, and I'll always owe the world to her. I married her never thinking I'd want another woman as a constant in my life. I was wrong, but so was Phoenix for thinking that she could make me fall in love with her.

The slap never comes. Instead, she leans close to my lips, uncomfortably close, until we are sharing oxygen.

"Dunn," I warn.

"You vowed your body to me forever. I let you fuck other whores, but you will always be mine. We aren't getting a divorce. You don't want that. You're just confused by old feelings. You want me."

I shake my head, careful not to let our lips brush against each other.

"She hurts you." Her thumb brushes over my swollen, bleeding lip. "I heal you."

And then she presses her lips against mine. She might call it a kiss, but for it to be a kiss, I'd have to kiss her back. That doesn't stop her. She licks her tongue over my wound, trying to heal me with her saliva.

I give her one more second to get whatever jealousy she's feeling toward Liesel out of her system. Then, I grab her shoulders and hold her back.

She tilts her head, her brows pulling together.

"Stop," I say, repeating the word that Liesel said to me.

"You're my husband. You don't get to tell me to stop. You're mine."

I shake my head. "I was never yours. We have an agreement on paper to protect the kids; that's all. I care about you deeply, Dunn. And that's why I'm going to spend the rest of the flight in the cockpit."

I stand up before I release her.

"Baby, please," she begs.

"I care about you. I'm sorry for hurting you, but I can't, Dunn—not anymore. I'm sorry."

And then I walk to the cockpit. I don't allow myself to glance back at either of the women. I don't want to see the pain I'm causing both of them.

All I know is I'm a stupid man who thought I'd never care about a woman more than I do Phoenix. I wasn't sure I had a heart. Even Siren thought I'd never fall in love and agreed that marrying Phoenix was for the best.

Then Liesel came back into my life and fucked up all my plans.

I GOT THE SILENT TREATMENT FROM BOTH WOMEN DURING THE entirety of our landing and drive to our hotel. The sky is dark, so we won't be searching for any treasure tonight.

I park the rental car in front of the swankiest hotel I could find. I chose the best not because I need us to rest in luxury, but because expensive hotels have the most cameras to hack into ensuring our safety.

Phoenix continues to give me an icy glare from the passenger seat next to me. Liesel stares out the window, completely lost in thought like we aren't even here at all. If Liesel is upset that Phoenix kissed me, she's not showing it.

I get out of the car, scanning every person on the street, my gun at my back, my fingers tingling to grab it. After the explosion at my house, I don't trust that we aren't being followed.

A couple walks by holding hands, and my mind immediately goes to them being dangerous. A woman is carrying a baby in one hand while holding the hand of a crying toddler with the other—an obvious enemy in my paranoid mind.

Liesel steps out of the car, her eyes scanning just like mine, searching for the devil inside every person who walks by.

Another door slams. Phoenix struts by us and walks through the automatic doors of the hotel, her anger overtaking any fear she has.

Liesel and I exchange a glance wordlessly, and then we walk inside.

"Do you still have a gun?" I ask.

She nods.

"Good girl."

She rolls her eyes. "That's not going to work. You can't seduce me by saying things like 'good girl.'"

"I'd bet everything I own that your panties are wet right now." I wink at her.

Her ears pink, and I know I'm right.

We hit the lobby floor, and our flirting stops. People are milling about everywhere—the reception desk, the lounge, the bar. People walk briskly past us and danger could be anywhere.

"Stay close," I order.

She nods, walking next to me. Phoenix emerges from the bar with a dry martini in her hand as she settles into a walk on my left.

"Don't leave my side again, Dunn."

Both women look at me. I should really stop calling Phoenix, 'Dunn.'

"Why? Miss me already?" Phoenix bats her eyelashes at me as she grips my arm.

"Just do what I say so you don't end up dead."

Phoenix gasps and then grips my arm tighter as I walk up to the reception desk.

"How can I help you, sir?" the man behind the desk asks.

"Can I get a suite with two adjoining rooms?"

I don't have to turn my head to feel the two sets of eyes from each woman burning into my side.

"I want my own room," Liesel says.

"Me too," Phoenix huffs.

"Two adjoining rooms or a suite with two bedrooms and a couch," I say to the gentleman.

"We have a suite with two queen bedrooms and a spacious living room pull out couch."

"Perfect."

I pull out cash to pay. I don't want anything tied to our names revealing our location. The man slides me three room keys.

"Can we talk? I don't think it's a good idea for the three of us to share a suite," Phoenix says, tugging on my arm.

"If we want to all stay alive, it is."

I look over to Liesel, expecting more of a fight from her as well, but her eyes are scanning the crowd.

My eyes follow her gaze. *Does she sense some danger that I'm not seeing?*

Carefully, I position Phoenix behind me as I put my hand on my gun.

"What is it?" I ask Liesel.

She smiles.

I frown.

She starts running excitedly in the direction of the bar.

"Looks like I don't have anything to worry about after all," Phoenix says, stepping next to me again as she sips her martini.

Liesel jumps into the arms of a man in a suit and jealousy rears its head inside me. So much so, that it takes me a second to recognize the man whose arms she flung herself into.

Maxwell.

I thought we had agreed that he was too shifty to be trusted, but she's acting like she just met up with a long lost friend.

I hand Phoenix a room key. "Go to the room and don't leave."

"Why? I want to watch the show."

"Dunn," my voice is serious and commanding, so Phoenix will do as I say. That's one of the traits I can always count on with her. When our lives hang in the balance, all I have to do is give her an order, and she'll follow it. Phoenix rolls her eyes and saunters toward the elevators.

I walk over to Maxwell and Liesel, my hands itching to grab the gun, but I don't since we're in a crowded lobby. That won't stop me from killing this bastard, though.

"Get your hands off her," I growl at Maxwell.

He doesn't budge an inch. His hand remains on the small of her back. His rigid, clean-cut appearance does nothing to make me trust him. That's why he appears the way he does in a suit and tie; he looks like a trusted businessman instead of the scum I know he is.

"Langston, it's so nice to see you again."

"Let her go," I roar through gritted teeth.

He chuckles. "Liesel is the one who called me. I'm not holding her hostage." He waves his hand, showing he has no weapon pressed against her back. "I'm here to help her."

"It's the truth. I called him," Liesel says.

"And why the hell would you do that?" I spit in her face. *How dare she pull a move like this without talking to me first!*

Her eyes implore me to trust her, but we've already established that I don't.

"Waylon wasn't the one in charge at his organization. He was second in line. The man in charge is still after me. He still demands that I give him what he wants. Now that Waylon's dead, he's impatient. He wants this over. Maxwell has met him before. I told him to meet us here so we could talk to him about what he knows," Liesel says, giving me more information that was in that damn letter.

She's lying. Or at least, she's hiding something—*from me or from Maxwell?* That's the question.

"What is this man's name?" I ask Maxwell.

"Corbin."

I square myself, looking at Maxwell. He has a couple of inches on me. At first glance, it would seem he has bigger muscles than me. But he doesn't know I grew up fighting Zeke, the biggest, physically strongest man I know. I know how to fight hulks, and I know how to win.

I want to order Liesel to go to the suite, so I can beat Maxwell's ass into telling me everything he knows before I kill him. But I know that she will never allow that.

Instead, I flag down a waitress.

"Table for three, please."

She smiles at the three of us. "Right this way, please."

We sit at a table near the bar, surrounded by people. The only good thing about sitting at a restaurant this crowded is that Maxwell is less likely to make a move.

We each order a drink, and then I say, "Start talking."

CHAPTER 9

LIESEL

The vein on Langston's forehead is bulging as he glares at Maxwell. I'm surprised Langston hasn't already climbed across the table and strangled him. Right now, all of his anger is focused on Maxwell, but soon his intimidating glare will turn toward me. But he won't do it, not as long as Maxwell, the bigger threat, is sitting at the table.

Langston doesn't know why Maxwell is really here. I'm not even sure why he's here. Call it a hunch. After I got the threatening note, I knew that Waylon was behind it.

I just didn't know if somehow Waylon was alive or if it was someone working for Waylon or this Corbin guy who sent the threat. It was a risk bringing Maxwell here—a huge risk—but my gut says Maxwell might be the only way to get the truth.

I understand why Langston is practically growling and shooting daggers at Maxwell. Langston has no idea if Maxwell is on Waylon's side or ours, and when our kid's lives are at stake, you don't let anyone into our lives that could threaten theirs.

What annoys me is that Langston has yet to show that he trusts me.

After everything we've been through together. After fucking each other. After learning he's raising my son. After all of it, he still doesn't trust that I would never do anything I think could hurt us, any of us—Langston, Phoenix, or our kids.

Maxwell's gaze turns to me, waiting for me to tell him where to start. He's here for me, not Langston.

I open my mouth just as the waitress brings over our drinks on a tray. Our silence stretches as the woman places three scotches in front of us. I give her a tight smile but don't offer a thank you. The air is too intense for any of us to mumble a word that could be seen as a weakness to the others at the table. The waitress senses something is off about the three of us and scurries off as fast as she can.

We return to our staring contest. Langston glares at Maxwell, while Maxwell stares at me. And I am torn between the two men.

"Waylon is dead, correct?" I ask, deciding to start with what I think will be an easy question for Maxwell to answer. In our world, people die and then come back to life. I basically faked Siren's death. It wouldn't be impossible that Waylon did the same.

Except, Langston was the one who killed Waylon, and there would be no reason for him to fake that. Plus, I was the one who discovered Waylon. He was covered in blood and had no pulse. Unless he has an identical twin or he has literal powers to return from the dead, he's dead.

"Waylon is dead," Maxwell says.

Both Langston and I study him closely, looking for any tell that he's lying. When you've been lied to by people as often as Langston and I have, you learn to read people better than most.

"So if Waylon didn't send me that threatening note, who did?" I ask.

Maxwell drinks down his entire glass, like he needs courage for the next part.

"Corbin, his brother."

I narrow my eyes. "Waylon doesn't have a brother. He's an only child."

"He has a brother."

"And how do you know that?" Langston asks, gripping his glass hard so he doesn't punch Maxwell in the face.

"He's the one who hired me," Maxwell answers.

My breathing stops, and for a second, I think I made a mistake bringing Maxwell here. I let him get close to the next clue that could lead us to the treasure.

Langston's leg bounces under the table, and I grab it, trying to get him to calm the fuck down.

He doesn't so much as glance my way. He just shakes my hand off his thigh and keeps bouncing like I'm nothing more than an annoying fly that just landed on his leg.

"Tell me why I shouldn't kill you right now," Langston says in a low, deep voice.

"Without me, you won't be able to find him."

Langston laughs. "I'm sure I can figure it out."

It's then that I realize Langston has his gun trained on Maxwell underneath the table.

Maxwell senses it too, but he doesn't seem concerned. He makes no move to get up, to defend himself. Instead, he looks at me with warm eyes.

"Waylon's brother hired me to keep you safe, Liesel. My job is still to protect you. Whether my loyalty lies with him or you, it doesn't matter. I'm your only shot at staying safe."

"Like hell you are! I'm her only shot at staying safe," Langston says.

Maxwell ignores Langston and keeps looking at me.

"I was sent to blow up the house, killing everyone but Liesel to send a message that he can get to you any place at any time if you don't cooperate. I chose to wait until you were all out."

He shouldn't have said that. Now he's a dead man, and there is nothing I can do to protect him.

I can feel Langston boiling next to me, itching to drag this man into an alley and kill him.

"He has your son, Liesel. He knows where he is. Waylon wasn't lying about that."

I don't react. I don't want Maxwell to be able to read me at all. I don't want him to know that I don't believe him because Langston is the one who has my son. And he's currently safe in hiding with Beckett.

Maxwell smirks, though, thinking he has the key to getting us to do whatever he wants.

"That's not a reason for me to keep you alive. That's a reason for me to kill you," Langston says.

"I know. I didn't realize that a child was involved. If I did, I would have never agreed to work for him. The money was good, and with my criminal record, I couldn't get a job that paid half as well. After I learned they're holding a child hostage to get you to do what they want, I vowed I would do whatever I could to protect you both. Believe me or not, but I'm here to help you, Liesel."

It doesn't matter if I believe him or not. I won't let another man risk my child's life.

"Prove it. Tell me everything about Corbin. Tell me where my son is," I say. My eyes connect with Maxwell's. I plead with him to stop hiding the truth from me.

"His name is Corbin Brown. He's two years older than Waylon. He inherited his father's drug smuggling organization and doubled it in size. While Waylon, being the much more charming and less evil of the two, decided getting law enforcement and government in his pocket was the best way to help the business instead of handling the day to day organization. So he ran for office. They also had a third brother. He was the youngest. He was killed in a shoot-off with a rival organization just before his eighteenth birthday. And a sister, who I don't think involves herself in the illegal stuff."

I bite my lip, and my heart aches for Waylon. He had two brothers. One dead. The other a criminal.

"Both men wanted a way to increase their power and money so they would never have to worry about losing one of their own again. They heard of this legend from your father, Liesel. More money than they earned in the last decade. That kind of money would give them the power to never be threatened again. So they worked together to get you under their control. Waylon courted you, while Corbin took your son. You were the key to getting everything they ever wanted. With Waylon's murder, nothing will stand in the way of Corbin doing whatever it takes in order to get you to give him the treasure. Nothing."

The concern in Maxwell's eyes feels real, too real. He's either a good actor, or he truly is concerned for my son's life. My son, who is perfectly safe. *But if my son is with Beckett, whose child does Corbin mistakenly have?*

"Why are you here telling me all of this? I've been trying to figure out who Waylon works with for months," I say.

"Because I made a mistake working for them, and I want to help fix that."

Langston scoffs, like it's not possible.

"Tell me where Corbin is keeping my son," I say.

Maxwell's eyes water. "I don't know."

"You're a dead man," Langston says.

"No! He's not." I slam my hand down on the table, getting the attention of an older couple nearby who looks at me in disgust for my inappropriate outburst. I don't care, though. My outburst got the attention of the two men.

"I don't trust you, Max, but I haven't sentenced you to death yet either. What did Corbin tell you to do?"

"My assignment is to convince you to trust me, that I'm on your side, and to keep you safe. To help you get the treasure and then convince you to give it to Corbin in exchange for him keeping your child safe." His eyes lighten with the truth.

His words may be true, but are his intentions?

"You're only helpful to me alive if you can help me figure out where my son is. Is that something you can do?"

"Yes, that's all I want. I don't want an innocent child hurt. I would never knowingly work for a man who would do that."

"Killer," I say, rubbing Langston's arm, trying to calm him down. But the second my fingers graze his muscular bicep, I feel the zing of electricity. This time it isn't attraction between us—it's rage flowing freely off his skin.

"We are going to search him, find any bugs, any electronics he could be using to send back to Corbin. Then we are going to tie him up in our suite until we get all the information we can from him. Understood?" I ask Langston.

I'm not sure he heard me, but then Langston nods his head the slightest amount in agreement. I doubt he agrees with my plan. I'm sure he wants to kill Maxwell, but we have to keep him alive. We have no leads on Corbin. And he has a child hostage. I have no doubt that Atlas is my son, but Corbin is holding an innocent child thinking he's mine. We have to do something to save the child and stop him from discovering Atlas. Maxwell is the only lead we have.

Langston digs some cash out of his wallet and throws it on the table.

"After you," he says to Maxwell.

Maxwell and I both stand. Maxwell keeps his eyes on Langston. I turn my head back and forth between the two men, trying to get a read on either of them. They seem to be playing a silent game between themselves I don't understand.

Without a word, we walk out of the bar. Maxwell in front, followed by Langston, and then me trailing them both.

Maxwell walks to the elevator banks and presses the up button, while Langston and I flank his either side. If he plans to run, we'll stop him. I still have the gun I took from Langston's car. I have no problem shooting this man.

The doors open, and we all step into the lift. Langston presses the fifth-floor button, waits for the elevator to rise, then presses the emergency stop button. Langston turns to Maxwell with his arms crossed as he stands in front of the door.

The corner of Maxwell's mouth lifts, and then he starts pulling out his phone, gun, wallet, and watch. He flings each on the floor at Langston's feet.

Maxwell raises his eyebrows. "Satisfied?"

"No, not until you're dead." Langston walks over to Maxwell and starts patting him down, looking for any other electronic device on him. When he's finished, he walks back to his place in front of the doors.

"Does Corbin know where we are?" Langston asks.

Maxwell shakes his head. "I told him I was going to Patagonia and just had a layover for tonight in Peru."

"I don't have anything with me to scan you to see if you have a tracking device in your body, but if you are lying to us and still communicating with Corbin in any way, you'll wish I killed you here on this elevator," Langston growls.

Maxwell nods. "I wouldn't expect anything less."

Suddenly, Maxwell seems smaller. Anyone else might see them as two alphas fighting for power over the situation. In reality, Langston is always the alpha, always in control.

Langston fists his hand and slams it over the emergency stop button. The elevator starts creeping up again until we reach our floor. This time Langston motions for me to step out first, so I do. I walk to our room and insert my key.

As soon as all three of us are in the room, Langston turns on Maxwell and attacks him viciously. A fist flies in Maxwell's face before he can react, followed by a swift kick to his ankles, knocking him on the mahogany-colored carpet.

Langston is on top of him a second later, pulling Maxwell's arms behind his back roughly.

"Get me something to tie him up with," Langston says to me.

Just then, Phoenix exits one of the bedrooms in a robe while carrying a martini glass. Her eyes pop. "I thought I had to come up here because it wasn't safe for me down there. But you all just brought the danger up anyway."

I ignore Phoenix. I need to find something to tie up Maxwell with.

I start opening cabinets, digging through drawers trying to find something to use. I walk over to an end table, yank a phone cord out of the wall, and toss it to Langston.

Langston snatches the cord mid-air and then ties Maxwell's wrist together so tightly I'm afraid that he's going to amputate his wrists. He grabs Maxwell by the collar and forces him to his feet.

I feel concern for Maxwell. He's protected me before, looked out for me, and if he's telling the truth, he doesn't deserve to be treated this way. I called him here for a reason. I just can't figure out what that reason is yet, what my instincts were screaming at me to get Maxwell here for. Then Maxwell winks at me, and my concern vanishes.

Langston marches him through the suite to one of the bedrooms. He slams the door shut until it's just me and Phoenix both standing awkwardly in the living room, staring at each other.

"So I take it he's not on our side?" Phoenix asks.

I shrug. "We don't know."

Phoenix shakes her head. "I don't know what it is about you that makes Langston fall over his feet to do whatever you say."

"He doesn't do that."

She scoffs. "He does. Because if what you are saying is true and that man isn't on our side, then Langston would shoot him dead, not tie him up."

The bedroom door opens, and Langston remerges. He stares me down, shooting daggers my way as he motions for me to come with him. He walks into the other bedroom. I follow.

As soon as I'm inside the room, Langston slams the door behind me before slamming me against the door, his hand at my neck as he squeezes.

"Tell me what the hell is going on right now, or I'm going to fuck it out of you."

I've never been so furious with Liesel in my life, and that's really saying something as I'm always angry with her. She brought the enemy with her. We ran, and she left a trail for the enemy to follow. He blew up my house, threatened my children, and she invited him here for drinks.

My hand grips her neck, while I try to decide between strangling her to death or fucking her. *No, it's not a decision—I want to fuck her to death.*

Liesel's lips part, and her tongue settles between her teeth. Her breath is slow and steady, unlike her raging pulse. She wants me to believe that she's relaxed in my grip, but her heart says otherwise. She's either scared shitless, turned on, or both.

"It was a hunch," she whispers through her parted lips.

"What?"

"A hunch, that's why I told Maxwell where we were. That's why I told him to come here. My gut told me he's the key to bringing Corbin down."

"You're a foolish woman."

She licks her lips. "And you're a wicked man."

I move in close to her until my mouth is hovering over hers, but

I'll deny us both kisses. This isn't about pleasure. This is about getting answers for my brain and wetness for my cock.

I grab her bottom lip, sucking it into my mouth and biting down hard.

She doesn't wince. Her eyes bore into mine, enjoying the pain.

"Tell me why you made the horrible, fucking wrong decision to bring Maxwell here without talking to me first. Or I'm going to fuck you so hard my wife and the entire hotel will know you're mine."

"I don't belong to anyone. I'm a loner. You can't have a wife and have me."

I grin. "Good, because soon I won't have a wife. I'll only have you."

I tug on her bottom lip again until it's swollen and red. "What was on that note?"

"Nothing."

I grab her by the waist, spin her, and slam her back hard against the dresser. My hands snake down the sides of her body, and I watch delicious goosebumps pop up on her smooth skin.

"Why. Is. He. Here?"

"I told you—a hunch. Waylon's brother sent the note, and I've always suspected Maxwell was pretending to be a little incompetent as a bodyguard. I sensed something deeper in Maxwell, something I don't understand. So I lured him here, away from the kids. Now, we can get the information we need from him and then kill him."

"Or we could just kill him."

She shoves me hard in the chest, pushing me off her body.

I think she's going to run away, but she surprises me. She sprints at me until I'm falling back on the bed. Her legs land on either side of my waist as she reaches for her gun and aims it at my heart.

"No, we can't kill him—not yet. Not until he's told us everything."

She grinds her hips over mine, and my cock springs up against the zipper of my jeans, trying to get to her.

She wants to play—dirty and rough. She won't back down and let me control her. She won't let me use sex as a weapon. She's willing to throw it right back at me.

"I won't let you make me feel bad for wanting to fuck you. I'm not a nice woman, never have been. I'm thankful to Phoenix for raising my child. But if I fuck you, I won't be the one cheating—you will be. If that's how you want to repay the woman you owe everything to, then so be it. But I'm not going to let your threats get to me."

My jaw ticks looking at the sexiest woman in the world straddling me with a gun in her hand like she's completely in control. It's adorable that she thinks that. My heart beats faster, though, because maybe she's right. She's more in control of this situation than I am.

"You don't know what you're talking about. Phoenix fucks who she wants, same as me. An open relationship is not cheating."

"Oh, Phoenix is okay with you fucking me?"

"Yes."

She shakes her head with a smug expression. "Now, who's lying?"

I toss her off and roll onto her as I fling the gun out of her hand. She growls, and I pin her hands over her head, my hard body slamming into every part of her softness.

"Maxwell has to die," I say.

"You don't get to make that decision."

"Just like you don't get to make the decision to bring him here without consulting me first."

I come down hard on her lips—getting a taste of her fiery sweetness before sudden pain overtakes me.

I roll off her after she knees me hard in the balls.

She moves to get off the bed, but I grab her shirt. It starts to tear as she reaches for the gun. I throw her back on the bed, ripping her shirt completely off of her.

She gasps when I stare at her bare stomach and kiss her skin above her belly button.

For a moment, she lets me touch her. She strokes my hair as I kiss her tenderly.

We won't be fucking each other tonight, no matter how much we both need it—not with my wife in the next room. Neither of us is that cruel.

I won't be fucking Liesel again until I convince Phoenix to divorce me. Even then, it's a long shot. The only reason she fucked me before is because we thought we were going to die. Now, that time has passed.

Good thing in our world, the threat of death is just around the corner.

I inch up to kiss her breasts, when she slaps me across the cheek.

She grabs my shirt and rips it the same way I did, right down the fucking middle. Her nails dig into my skin next before her teeth bite and nip over my abs.

My eyes roll back in my head with each touch of her mouth against my skin. I shouldn't moan—Phoenix will make me pay for all the sounds I'm making in here, thinking I'm fucking Liesel when I'm not. But dammit, I can't control myself around Liesel.

"Huntress," I warn when her lips lower to just above my pants.

She grins as she continues to kiss down my happy trail.

I grab her chin, lifting her up.

"Don't fight fire with fire," I say.

"Why not?"

"Because I can handle getting burned, but you can't."

"I've been burned before."

"I know—but I can't handle being the one who burns you."

She gasps.

I make my move.

I flip her onto her back and sink my hand back beneath her panties, finding the sweet spot that controls her whimpers, cries, and moans. I rub my finger slowly over her clit, feeling her panties soaking around my fingers.

She's silent at first, and then the first glorious whimper pushes through her luscious lips.

"Please, stop torturing me," she whispers.

I stop.

Her hips buck, begging me to finish her.

My eyes darken. I need answers. I need her to come.

I lean down and kiss her slowly, torturously. It's a real kiss that floods her body with emotions and drenches my hand with her precum.

"Talk to me, huntress. Tell me everything. Trust me with your soul and body." *Trust me with your heart.*

She shakes her head. "Trust me."

My fingers move again over her clit until she can't talk. Her breath is heavy, more gasping than breathing.

A single tear drips down her cheek as I bring her closer to the edge of an orgasm. So close, in fact, that I feel the first ripple before I once again stop.

"I can't," she whispers.

I grit my teeth to keep from slamming my mouth over hers and fucking her senseless.

"But I do know that we can't kill Maxwell, not yet. The child—"

"Isn't yours. Atlas is your child. If you want a DNA test to be sure, we can do that."

"No, I know Atlas is my son. I saw the similarity of our eyes."

"So, Corbin is obviously lying. He doesn't have your child. I have your child. He's safe with Beckett."

"But he has someone's child."

I still, looking at her closely. There have been moments when I'm not even sure she cares about her own child. For her to care about a stranger's child isn't like her.

"You're confusing as hell, huntress."

My fingers dance over her clit again.

Her eyes close as she feels me. She licks her lips and arches her back in ecstasy. One more touch and she'll be screaming my name.

She grabs my wrist, though, stopping me.

"Go back to your wife, killer. You chose her. I'm just a whore you fucked because there was no one else around in the face of death."

I frown. She couldn't be more wrong, but I understand that I caused this mess. I chose Phoenix, and Liesel thinks I still hate her. She doesn't know I've spent my entire life wanting her, dreaming of fucking her.

And now that I've had her, I can't imagine fucking any other woman but her.

CHAPTER 11

LIESEL

Sleep was impossible.

Even though I had my own bedroom and a large queen-sized bed to myself, sleep never came. And neither did I.

After Langston suddenly left, I touched myself. I rubbed furiously while I tried to finish the job Langston started. No amount could bring me to orgasm, though. It's like my body no longer knows how to work without Langston.

I get out of bed as soon as the sun starts rising. My clothes are ripped from Langston, so I walk to the small closet in the room and put on a hotel robe.

My fingers and body wreak of sex. My hair is a mangled mess, but the only way to get to the bathroom to try and tame my hair is to make my way through the common areas. Hopefully, Phoenix and Langston haven't woken up yet. I don't want Phoenix to think I fucked Langston last night. And I don't want Langston to realize I still haven't come.

I open my door carefully, and my eyes peek around the dark room. I don't see anyone.

I creep out, tiptoeing across the room as to not wake anyone.

I make it halfway across the living room before the other bedroom door opens, and Phoenix and Langston stand in the doorway. Phoenix is wearing a robe just like mine. Her hair is bushy on her head, her cheeks warm and pink. Langston stands in nothing but his boxers behind her.

They look like a happy couple.

Phoenix smirks at me.

I know, you won. He's yours. Take him, I don't want him.

It's all a lie. I've never wanted a man more than Langston. But even if Phoenix wasn't in the picture, I could never really have him. I'm the huntress. I have to continue hunting. I've spent my whole life hunting for something that I'm not even sure can be found. And Langston, despite all his faults, is a good man. He doesn't deserve to be dragged down into my despair.

I cut my eyes away from them and dash into the bathroom. I can breathe again as soon as I shut the door. But I know the feeling is only temporary. I relieve myself and am trying to comb through my hair when there's a knock at the door.

"Stop hogging the bathroom. Some of us need to pee, you know," Phoenix says.

Stop being such a pussy, I tell myself before I slap a smile on my face and walk out of the bathroom, past a waiting Phoenix.

"It's all yours," I say.

She steps inside, leaving Langston and me alone.

"Huntress, it's not—"

"You were with your wife last night. I understand. I'm going to make some coffee."

He frowns but doesn't try to explain himself. It's obvious he slept in her room last night instead of the untouched couch. I don't need to know any more details than that.

I refuse to feel jealous as I make the coffee in the small kitchenette area. But the banging I'm making betrays me.

Finally, I finish pouring four cups of coffee.

"Four? Really?" Langston asks.

"Yes, Maxwell gets a cup too."

Langston rolls his eyes.

"Go get him, now."

His lips thin into a single line. For a moment, I think he's going to argue with me, but then he turns and disappears into the bedroom.

He reappears with Maxwell still tied up. He sits him down in one of the living room chairs and then grabs a knife from the kitchen to release his bindings before handing him a cup of coffee.

Maxwell smiles at me as he takes the cup of coffee, knowing this was my doing.

Langston pulls a gun out from the waistband of his boxers.

"If you move, I'll shoot you dead with pleasure," Langston says, casually lifting his cup of coffee to his lips.

"Noted," Maxwell says, drinking his own coffee.

We all sit in the living room in an awkward silence as we drink our coffees. Maxwell in a single chair. Langston and Phoenix are sharing the small loveseat. And me sitting in the other single chair.

"What did I miss?" Maxwell asks, looking between the three of us.

"Nothing. What's the plan?" I look to Langston.

"Oh, now you're going to discuss plans with me? I thought you just made plans on your own," he shoots back.

I sigh. "I have no problem deciding, if you'd rather."

"Will you two stop? The sooner we figure out how to work together, the sooner we can never see each other again," Phoenix says.

"We all go to the sacred ruins, then we get the next clue," I say.

"I already called to have new clothes brought up for us, and a car should arrive in the next twenty minutes," Langston stares back at me.

He didn't argue with me about us all going.

I don't know what to do with that. All I know is that I need to get out of this hotel room before I suffocate in the thoughts of him fucking Phoenix after touching me.

♡

Langston rented a six-passenger van and driver to take us to the ruins. The drive is long, winding, and silent.

None of us speak about what we are going to do when we get there. Langston and I don't share any of the information we know about what we might face. We don't discuss what we are going to do with Maxwell or what Phoenix knows.

Eventually, the driver stops and points down a dirt road. Apparently, this is as far as he goes.

Each of us climb out. I feel for my gun, but don't remove it. Just knowing it's there brings some comfort. I'm nowhere near as skilled with a gun as Langston is, but at least I have a weapon to defend myself.

Maxwell asked for a gun, but we refused him. And Phoenix just scoffed when Langston tried to get her to carry a gun.

We all march down the abandoned dirt road, walking as much apart as we are together. If anyone were to notice us, I'm not sure they would be able to deduce if we are a group or four separate strangers. Fog hangs in the air, masking much of the greenery of the surrounding mountains as we continue through the chilly air.

"How much further do we have to hike?" Phoenix pants as the road climbs up the side of the hill.

Langston points to the top.

She sighs.

"I can give you a piggyback ride if you want?" Maxwell asks her.

We all freeze, not sure what Phoenix or Langston is going to do.

Phoenix grins. "Hell yea."

"Dunn, is that a good idea?" Langston asks.

"I'm exhausted. I wasn't made for climbing. So unless you are offering a ride, I'm taking Max here up on his offer."

Langston rolls his eyes and continues climbing. Phoenix climbs on Maxwell's back. I take up the rear.

"You smell good," I hear Phoenix whisper to Maxwell, who chuckles gruffly.

Langston keeps walking like he didn't hear her.

After an hour or more of hiking, we finally reach the sacred ruins.

"Now what?" Phoenix asks, still clinging to Maxwell's back.

Langston stares back at me, like he thinks I have the next clue.

He's right—I do.

My eyes scan the sight. It's beautiful, eery with haze and clouds hanging low in contrast to the bright green grass and broken remains of stone buildings. There are a few tourists and locals milling about, but nothing compared to the hoards of the more famous ruins like Machu Pichu.

"This way," I say, finding a trail to the right of the ruins and following it. I feel Langston fast at my heels as I head down the trail. I expect him to ask me questions about what comes next, but he doesn't. He just follows closely with Maxwell and Phoenix struggling to catch up.

I stop abruptly when I spot the small cottage nestled in the rolling hills.

I look to Langston. I don't know what to do next. He has the next clue.

He walks forward, taking the lead.

I hear Maxwell's feet stopping behind us, and Phoenix climbs off his back.

Langston motions with his head for me to follow him to the side of the house. I do. Maxwell and Phoenix don't follow us.

Langston approaches the small wooden door on the side of the house. He knocks four times and then waits.

My heart is pumping wildly, waiting for what's going to happen next. A minute goes by and nothing happens.

My heart sinks.

This was all a wild goose chase, wasn't it, father? You sent me here to ruin my life.

The door opens.

My eyes widen, and then an older bald man with a white beard steps to the door. He doesn't speak, just stares at Langston.

"A Dunn is here to collect what's hers," Langston says.

The man's eyes go from Langston to me. His eyes look like he's seen a ghost. His ears perk like he can't believe what he just heard.

"You married?" he looks between the two of us, looking for a ring.

My thumb traces my bare ring finger—a finger that will never have a ring.

I look to Langston. He's not wearing a ring either. Weird—I guess I never noticed or thought about it before.

"No," I say.

"I am," Langston says.

The man pokes his head out of the door as if to ask where his wife is then.

"Dunn," Langston calls.

Phoenix steps forward. Her head is proud and boisterous as she saddles up next to Langston, gripping his bicep like she owns him.

She does.

"Come in," he says, opening the door wider for Langston and Phoenix.

They step inside without glancing back at me.

I move to follow, but the old man steps in front of the door, blocking my way.

"Are you married?" he asks.

I shake my head.

"I'm sorry," he says, closing the door.

I step back, staring at the small house as my hand traces down the door. I need to be inside. I need to know what is going on. I need to help keep Atlas safe.

But I'm not married. And for some stupid reason, my father made that a term in finding the treasure.

I walk back to the front of the house, where Maxwell is still standing. I still don't understand his motivations or why I decided to tell him where we are. I'm also surprised he hasn't tried to pull some crap yet.

I hug myself as I stare at the house, trying to decide my next move.

"We could break in. I'm pretty sure we could take that old man," Maxwell says.

I shake my head. I'm sure we could, but it's not getting in that would be the problem. It's getting him to tell us the next clue.

The only way to get inside is if you're married.

I bite my lip, trying to come up with a different way. My eyes cut to Maxwell, hating my plan.

"Fuck this, let's go," I say.

"Where are we going? I thought—"

"We are going to fix our situation so we can get into the house."

CHAPTER 12

LANGSTON

We step into the small one-room house. There isn't much to see, but a small bed in the corner with some books strewn over it and a rocking chair in the other corner. This man either lives a simple life or doesn't live here full time.

The door whooshes closed behind us, sinking the room into darkness.

Phoenix jumps, leaning further against me as the room turns pitch-black.

I hear the light of a match striking, and then we can see again as the man walks toward us.

"What's your name?" I ask.

He shakes his head.

I frown. If he isn't even going to tell me his name, I have little faith I'm going to learn much about how to find the treasure.

"I need proof that you two are married." He turns to Phoenix. "And I need your blood."

She shrivels back, using my shoulder to shield herself from him—not that I think she should be worried about such a small, frail man.

I pull out my phone, where I have a saved image of our marriage license, and hand it to him.

He nods, taking the phone from me and sliding it into his pocket. Then he produces a knife and stares at Phoenix, waiting.

She looks up at me. "No."

"Phoenix, he's just going to draw a couple of drops of blood. He's not going to cut off your hand."

She huffs but relents, placing her hand out in front of him. He pricks her finger with the tip of the blade.

He nods his thanks and then disappears out the back door.

"What was that about?" Phoenix asks.

"My guess is he's verifying our marriage license and that you are a Dunn."

She frowns and grips my arm tighter.

I want to tell her to relax. She could be outside with Liesel and Maxwell right now, wondering what the hell is happening and being forced to trust me that I'll tell them what I find out.

I'll tell Liesel everything she needs to know, but I know she's not going to trust a word I say.

The man returns less than a minute after he disappeared.

"I'm sorry, but your marriage isn't valid," he says, handing me back my phone.

"What do you mean it isn't valid?"

I take my phone and stare down at the document that I know is legal.

"It isn't valid."

"How? I mean, what part isn't valid? Do we need to legally marry in this country? Is there some type of ceremony we need to do?"

He shakes his head. "I can't tell you any more other than you need to leave until you fix the problem. Return once you are truly married."

He walks to the door and opens it.

"But..." Phoenix stutters, just as confused as I am.

I take Phoenix's hand and drag her out the door. I look back one more time at the man who has an intense glint in his eyes. I don't know what just happened, but I'm going to figure it out.

"Liesel, we have a problem..." I stop talking and let go of Phoenix's hand when I round the house and don't find Liesel or Maxwell.

"Liesel?" I shout louder, hoping they just found a more comfortable place to sit and wait for us, but that's not Liesel's style. She would be pacing impatiently just outside the door or looking for a way to break in.

"Where is she?"

A chill creeps down my spine as a thought crosses my mind—a clue to where she might have gone.

Phoenix steps up to my side and rubs my arms in a comforting manner.

"Do you think Maxwell took her?" she asks.

I examine the scene, looking for any sign of a struggle, any sign that Maxwell could have hurt her, but I know better.

"No."

Phoenix narrows her eyes and pulls her brows together as she stares up at me.

"She went to get married so she can enter," I say.

CHAPTER 13

LIESEL

I found a small white church in the center of the small town. I've talked with the priest, and he's agreed to marry us. Now, I just have to wait for Maxwell to get back with the paperwork.

I sit in the very last pew, staring up at the stained glass window at the end of the small chapel. The light twinkles as it hits the glass and then flickers into my eyes, making me squint. This doesn't seem real—it feels like a dream, or in reality, a nightmare.

I never wanted to get married. Definitely not to a man who might be more devil than angel. A man I can't imagine kissing, let alone fucking.

We just need to get the paperwork done. That's all this is. A contract that we can eventually annul.

But it won't change the fact that for a short time, I'll be married to Maxwell. I'll promise my life and love to him.

I hear the door open behind me. My eyes water, but I quickly blink them away.

I never imagined myself married. Never thought of myself as a wife or mother. Never wanted the big white dress and lasting love. So marrying a man I don't love just so I can find a treasure shouldn't feel like I'm giving anything up.

But why is my throat tightening, my neck sweating, and my hands clamming up? Why does it feel like I'm losing something I never knew I wanted?

"Ready?" Maxwell asks as he towers over me.

I nod.

He holds out his hand to me.

I try to wipe the sweat off on my pants before I put my hand in his and he helps me stand.

He smiles at me, gently.

"Don't worry, you're still the boss. And I already know there won't be any fucking." He winks at me.

"That's not what I'm worried about. I still don't know if I can trust you."

"You can. I didn't realize who I'm working for. You have my complete loyalty."

I shake my head. "It doesn't matter. You're just a pawn I'm using to get inside that house. You're still our prisoner. I will have no problem killing you when I no longer have a need for you."

He grins. "I have no doubt that you will."

We start walking down the aisle as a woman sits behind a piano and starts playing. The sudden music makes me falter in my step, but Maxwell keeps walking me forward until we are at the altar.

The music stops, and then our priest begins speaking.

I know he's speaking, but I can't hear his words over the beating of my own heart. I can't believe I'm this nervous. All we are doing is speaking meaningless words before we sign a piece of paper.

I close my eyes and steel my heart, forcing it to close tighter than a bank vault. When I open my eyes, I feel strong and ready to do this. Ready to marry this man so I can do what I came here for—to get the damn treasure and protect Atlas in the process.

"Do you take Liesel Dunn—"

"Wait!"

I turn my head and see Langston jogging down the center aisle with Phoenix right behind him.

I blink rapidly.

Langston stops right in front of me, huffing profusely like he ran the whole way here. He doesn't glance at Maxwell; he just grabs my hand and jerks me to the side.

"We'll be right back," Langston mutters as he pushes me out of the side door of the church.

We stumble outside—him out of breath, me not able to breathe. Finally, we come to a stop in a small alleyway between the church and the coffee shop next door.

"What happened?" I ask when I'm finally able to breathe and remove my hand from Langston's grasp.

He growls as I pull away, but he doesn't make a move to take my hand back.

"Don't marry him," Langston says.

I fold my arms across my chest and take a step back. "If you came here to tell me what to do with my life, you can forget it. I don't want to be left out in the dark the next time. I'll marry him, and then we'll kill him. What's the big deal?"

He runs his hand through his hair, and he huffs out a long breath trying to figure out his next words. His eyes are zipping around, crazy with anger.

I don't understand why he's acting this way. It's not like—

"Phoenix and I aren't legally married."

"What?" I gasp.

"We aren't legally married."

"But I saw your marriage license. How could that be?"

He paces a foot. "Some sort of mixup at the registry. He knew almost immediately that our marriage wasn't valid. I called while we were running over here to verify. It's true—I'm not married to Phoenix."

I nod, slowly, unsure of reality.

"So you didn't get the next clue?"

He shakes his head, slowly mimicking my movements. "No, he kicked us out before he told us anything."

"Stupid father, thinking I need to be married before I get any real money. Like being married will mean I'm somehow protected."

"I don't know why your father thought any of this was a good idea either, but what are we going to do now?"

"I'm going to walk back into the church and get married to Maxwell. You can marry Phoenix for real or not. But at least one of us needs to be married in order to get the next clue."

I take a step toward the church.

He puts his hand on my waist, stopping me from moving. His breath is hot, fire against my lips. I think he's going to say something that will change both of our lives. Something that speaks a lot more of love than of hate.

Instead, he says nothing.

With a twitch of his hand, he pushes our bodies together. Our hips bump, and our mouths land. My eyes close a second later as I taste a man I want but can never have.

This isn't a proposal. He didn't bring me out here to tell me not to marry Maxwell. He knows I have to. He brought me out here for one last goodbye kiss.

Maxwell's and my marriage might be fake, but once we are married, I'm pretty sure the kissing and torturing Langston will have to stop. At least until we get the treasure, since we need the man in charge of hiding the treasure to think I'm married. And after we find the treasure, there is no hope for us.

The sky must agree that this kiss is defiantly wrong in every way as rain starts pouring down on us. It pelts down on us so hard that I can barely breathe. But I'm thankful for the rain because it hides the tears spilling down my cheeks.

Langston notices anyway and rubs my cheeks with his thumbs even though we are both soaked.

I shiver.

"We should go back inside."

He nods.

I start to brush past him, but he doesn't let go of my waist. He doesn't let me move past him.

"Huntress—"

"Don't—you belong with Phoenix."

"But—"

"I was never yours, killer. Let me go."

He does, and I stumble back into the church, sopping wet. Everyone's eyes are on me as I march back to my place in front of Maxwell.

"Where were we?" I ask with a smile.

CHAPTER 14

LANGSTON

I re-enter the church through its beaten-down wooden door. I'm soaking wet, and with each step I take inside, I leave a puddle of water behind me. I don't feel the water, though. All I feel is the heat between Liesel and me, even though she's standing far away at the altar with Maxwell.

I walk over to Phoenix in the second pew and sit next to her. Liesel doesn't so much as glance my way. She's staring intently at Maxwell like he's the only man she sees. If a stranger walked into the church right now, they might even deduce from the sight of Maxwell and Liesel together that this is a romantic wedding where the two are so desperate to get married that they can't even wait for her to change clothes.

All I see is the most beautiful woman I've ever met standing in front of the devil about to sign her soul away.

"What's happening?" Phoenix whispers next to me, staring with wide eyes as the priest starts talking again.

"They are getting married." I curse under my breath. "And then we will get married again here."

I don't look at Phoenix to judge her reaction. I'm sure she has a smug expression on her face, knowing that not only did I marry her once, but I'm going to marry her again. She thinks she's won, that she has a claim over me that Liesel will never have. And yet, I can't stop looking at Liesel.

She will always be mine, even if she's married to another man. She will always be mine.

"I do," Maxwell says.

My heart feels like it's just been hit with a hammer, exploding from two little words. I can't imagine how it's going to feel when she says them.

This is for the best. I can never forgive her—never love her. Getting married is necessary, for both of us.

I try to close my eyes, so I don't have to watch Liesel pledge her life to another man, but I can't seem to force my eyes closed. They are fixated on the tragic nightmare in front of me.

Silence stretches around the room, and I know the priest has just asked Liesel if she takes Maxwell as her husband. All that is left now is for her to answer. For her to reach into my chest cavity and pull out what's left of my disintegrated heart.

"You know they are going to have to fuck, right?" Phoenix says.

I snap my head toward her. "What?"

"That old man will know if their marriage isn't real. They are going to have to consummate the marriage or he'll know. I don't know how, but he seems to know everything. I don't know if this will work if they don't act like a married couple."

"Fuck," I curse. *She's right. I know she is. They are going to have to fuck, to pretend to be in love. And then they'll have to do god knows what in order to get the next clue.*

I glance to Phoenix. I'm going to have to do the same with Phoenix.

This is truly goodbye. I have to let Liesel go. In order to get the treasure, she has to be committed to being married to Maxwell, and I Phoenix. And after all that, she won't want me.

Finally, my eyes are able to close. I slam them shut, sealing myself from the extraordinary pain that only Liesel can cause me. For decades, I've been chasing her—hating her, yet wanting her, knowing how wrong we are for each other, yet assuming we would end up together no matter how wrong it is. In reality, we were destined to get the briefest of moments together and then be lost to another forever.

I keep my eyes closed as a single painful tear escapes. My tear duct takes its time purging the tear, and then the liquid is even slower to descend over my cheek, stopping at each pore to remind me just how painful this moment is.

I hear Liesel breathe, and I open my eyes, knowing this is the moment she says 'I do.' The moment she marries another man.

"Wait!" Phoenix shouts.

I blink, trying to flush the rest of the tears from my eyes so I can figure out if this is a dream or not.

Phoenix pushes me out of the way as she runs up to the altar. She whispers something to Liesel that I can't hear as she takes her hands in hers.

Liesel gasps in shock at whatever she says.

"Are you sure?" Liesel asks.

"More than anything. I was a selfish bitch before."

The two women hug.

I narrow my eyes, trying to understand what the fuck is happening.

Then, Phoenix rushes back to my side. She takes my hand and pulls me out toward the back of the church.

"Wait, I can't leave—"

"Trust me," Phoenix says, yanking me out the doors.

Maybe she's right. Maybe it's for the best I don't want Liesel stomp all over my heart.

We are once again outside in the pouring rain.

"Marry her," Phoenix says.

"What?" I ask.

"Ask Liesel to marry you. You love her or, at the very least, want her. You don't want me. I've done a lot of selfish things in my life. I've stolen you from her and demanded you be mine for years when I have no right. You two belong together. Only the two of you are going to be able to do the tasks required to get the treasure. This is the only way this will work."

I frown. "What about you?"

"I love you. And if I love you, I have to let you go. All I ever wanted to be was a mother, and you gave me that. So I think it's time I return to the thing I love the most—my children."

My heart thumps so loudly in my chest that it blocks out the roar of the thunder.

"You're wrong," I say.

Phoenix looks up at me, even though the rain is pelting down, stinging her cheeks.

"I don't love Liesel. I love you. I'm just not in love with you, Dunn."

"I know." She gives me a weak smile. "But that doesn't change that she's the one you want to marry, not me."

"I'm sorry."

"Don't be. Loving you was one of the best parts of my life."

"I'll love you forever, Dunn."

And then my lips consume hers. It's a kiss that tells her how much I love her. How much I appreciate her. How fucking incredible she is —the most unselfish person I've ever met.

For me, I hope it's a goodbye kiss, but it's also a moment for her to change her mind. If she says she can't give me up yet, that she wants to stay and marry me, then I will. Not because I'm selfless, but because this woman deserves the best man. I'm not the best—but I can give her my best for as long as she wants.

She pushes my chest hard, breaking the kiss.

Her eyes sear into mine—knowing that was a test to see if she can really give me up. The fire in her eyes tells me she can; she already did.

"Go get the girl you love," she whispers.

"I don't love her."

She shakes her head. "Sure, you don't. You can fight it all you want, Langston, but it doesn't make it not true. Stop lying to yourself."

I nod, but I can't, because the only sin I refuse to commit is loving Liesel. Loving her will destroy us both.

CHAPTER 15

LIESEL

"Wait!" Phoenix shouts.

Jesus, if this wedding gets interrupted one more time, I'm not sure I have the guts to go through with it.

Phoenix rushes up and stands between Maxwell and me.

She takes my hands in hers and then whispers, "He's yours. He always has been. I thought I could make him love me, but I was wrong. I won't step in the middle of the two of you again. Being between the two of you doesn't help me; it just means I'll end up getting burned from the inferno you two are bound to create."

"Are you sure?" Liesel asks.

"More than anything. I was a selfish bitch before."

"Thank you," I whisper as she runs back to Langston, dragging him out of the church.

My eyes water once again.

Dammit, I have to stop crying.

"Are we getting married or not?" Maxwell asks me with an annoyance to his voice.

I smile. "No, we aren't."

"Damn, I was sort of looking forward to the honeymoon." He winks at me.

I roll mine.

"Sit your ass down and don't move, or I'll tie you up."

I really should tie him up. Or lock him up. Or kill him. Something. I don't trust Maxwell.

No, you were just going to marry him.

Maxwell sits in the first pew, looking bored.

I wish I knew whose side he was really on and what the hell to do with him. All I know is there is something inside me, a warning bell of sorts that tells me I can't kill him—yet.

I don't know what to do with myself. I want to go outside and talk to Langston, but I should let Phoenix and him have their time.

So I pace.

Back and forth in the front of the altar.

The priest has walked to his back office, realizing this wedding isn't going to happen. It's just me and Maxwell.

"You need to stop doing that," Maxwell says.

"Why?" I keep pacing.

"You have nothing to worry about. That man loves you and will jump at the chance to marry you."

"He can't love me," I whisper more to myself than to Maxwell. I won't let Langston love me.

The door at the back opens, and Langston appears. The sun forms a halo of light around his body as the rain is now nothing more than a pitter-patter behind him.

"Come," he orders.

I hate when he gives me orders. I'm too nervous to protest or ask questions, though, so I walk to him.

"Where is Phoenix?" I ask, looking behind him.

"I got her a car to take her to the jet. She's headed back to watch over the kids."

"I don't think I could have picked a better mother for the kids than her. She's the most amazing, selfless woman I've ever known. I'll never be able to repay her for everything."

"No, we won't," he agrees.

We stare into each other's eyes as our breathing deepens. I can feel my pulse in my throat—a big, giant heartbeat that wrecks my whole body, taking over every other emotion.

Neither of us speak; we just stare. I'm not sure what to do or what this means.

Are we getting mar—

I can't even finish my own thought in my head, let alone speak it aloud or ask Langston if this means what I think it means.

Langston takes my hand and, without a word, leads me out of the church. Away from the church—that means I was wrong. We aren't getting married.

He moves us quickly, practically running through the streets.

"Where are we going?" I ask.

He doesn't answer. He keeps moving us through town until he stops so suddenly I almost slam into him.

"Wait here," he says, leaving me standing on the side of a road.

He disappears into nearby greenery until I can't see him.

"Langston," I hiss, completely confused by what's happening.

He doesn't answer. He takes his time doing whatever he's doing. Returning a moment later, he wordlessly takes my hand, and then we continue on. The road leads to a hill, but that doesn't stop him. We start climbing up the hillside, both of us still wet from the earlier rain. My feet are going to have blisters from all the walking in wet shoes.

We reach the top of the hill when he stops. I have no idea why, but I turn and look out at the view, and my breath catches. It's stopped raining completely now, a low fog hangs in the air over the town in the Sacred Valley between the mountains, and the sun shines down as if it's shining only on us.

"I hate you," Langston says.

What?

I turn my head toward him, not having a clue what this is all about.

"I hate you, huntress. You've been a thorn in my side since we were kids. You taunted me with your beauty. You tortured me with your smart mouth. You lied to me. Resisted me. Refused to bend to my will. And you hated me in return."

I frown.

He smirks and continues.

"We've both done horrible things—the worst things. Things that can never be forgiven. You're a sadistic princess, and I'm a cruel manwhore. Most of the time I still want to kill you. And yet, we were made for each other."

Only most of the time? I really should ask him why he wants to kill me and why now he only wants to kill me most of the time.

My mouth dries as I gape at him. *What is he doing?*

He bends down on one knee. "I'm not going to say I love you because that would be a lie."

Thank god.

"I'm not going to promise you a lifetime of happiness because that would be a lie."

I bite my lip.

"I'm not going to promise you any of the things a husband should promise his wife, but that isn't going to stop me from asking you to be mine. Huntress, will you marry me?"

He reaches into his pocket and produces a ring. A ring he's made out of twisted together flowers similar to roses, but not quite. It has a green vine, thorns, and red petals.

I look into his eyes—eyes that say he cares about me way more than he should. He said he didn't love me. *Please, don't let him be lying about loving me. Please, let him hate me.*

"I hate you, too," I whisper back.

"Is that a yes?"

"Yes."

He grabs my hand and holds the ring over my ring finger. Then he hesitates as he realizes the thorns are going to cut into my skin as he puts it on.

"Do it," I say, not able to think of a better way to represent our relationship than with this ring. A ring of both thorns and petals—a ring of pain and beauty.

He slides the ring onto my fingers, producing little droplets of blood as it slides in place. Then he stands, takes me in his arms, and we kiss.

It's a kiss I never thought I'd experience—a kiss of a man who wants to marry me. A man I want to marry despite knowing the pain this will cause us both.

I feel the tears welling as his tongue pushes between my lips, but I hold them back. I won't cry in this moment. I won't allow any sadness to warp this memory.

I wrap my arms around his neck and pretend he just proposed to me in the most romantic way. It may not have been sweet, but it was honest, raw, and true. It made me fall for him even more.

Finally, he sets me down, releasing my lips. We smile at each other, before Langston takes my hand, and we start walking back to town. I make him stop at the same spot we did on the way up and grab more flowers to make him a ring too. Finally, we head back into town to go back to the church to get married.

Before we make it to the church, Langston stops at a small shop in the middle of town. He turns me in the direction, and I smile.

"Give me just a minute," I say as he hands me some cash and I step into the small dress shop. When I was marrying Maxwell, I didn't care what I looked like, but now that I'm marrying Langston, I have this urge to get married in a white dress.

Most of the dresses in the small shop are beautiful vibrant patterns of the traditional Andean culture, to the point where I almost give up on finding a white dress. I decide to settle on any dress when I spot white lace fabric at the back of the store. The dress is simple—a low v-neck with thin straps and not much shape. It's perfect.

I pay for the dress and quickly change at the back of the store. I can't do much about my wet hair except scrunch it and hope it dries in beautiful waves instead of a frizz ball. Then I step outside, where Langston is waiting for me in a loose-fitting white long-sleeved shirt and dark jeans.

I drool just looking at him.

"Ready to be my wife?"

I blush, still not sure what being his wife means, but I'm excited to find out.

Together we walk back into the church, where surprisingly, Maxwell is still sitting.

The woman behind the piano starts playing, and the priest is once again at the far end of the aisle. *How did they know?*

We make it to the end when I realize that this won't be legal. "We didn't file for a marriage license."

"Shit," Langston curses, now realizing that we are going to need that.

Maxwell steps up, holding a piece of paper out to us. "Actually, I went back to the registrar when you took off with Langston assuming that you would be needing this and filed for you."

We both stare at him, completely confused why he's helping us.

"I didn't want to have to wait for you two to get your shit together. The sooner you're married, the sooner we can finish what we came here for," Maxwell says.

I suspect he's here to steal the treasure once we have it. But until then, he could be of some use to us.

Langston pockets the piece of paper, and then the priest begins. I get lost in Langston's eyes as the priest speaks, prompting Langston to lean in and whisper in my ear, "If you want to marry me, you have to say 'I do.'"

"I do," I say, biting my lip.

Then Langston holds out his hand, and I place the ring on his finger, drawing a trickle of blood as I push it on.

It all happens so fast that I'm not sure it's real. That is until Langston kisses me like he owns me. And for the first time, he actually does.

CHAPTER 16

LANGSTON

I'm a fucking married man.

I thought I was before—to Phoenix. Turns out something got fucked up with our paperwork. Even though we lived that life, it wasn't true, at least not in the eyes of the law.

This isn't real, either.

And yet, when my mouth crashes down on her soft lips much harder than I've ever kissed her, I know that this is as real as it gets for me.

I dip her back in my arms, claiming her with every part of my body, slipping my tongue between her parted lips. My hand is already running down the front of her white lace dress that I plan on ripping from her body as soon as we don't have any eyes on us. I've spent my entire life sharing her—I'm done. I won't let any other man even get a glimpse of her ever again.

I start to pull away when she groans into my lips—her voice pulling me back to her.

How am I ever going to let her go?

I'm not.

She's mine.

My hand slides up her thigh, hiking her dress up her toned leg until I reach her ass.

"Get a room," a man's voice says.

I stop, realizing I'm taking things too far.

Our eyes open, and we stare at each other as my lips gently pull off hers. She pulls her bottom lip into her mouth as her cheeks pinken. I swear I see stars in her eyes.

Oh, baby, you have no idea what I'm about to do to you.

I pull her back up onto her feet, then take her hand. We need to get out of here now, before I take her into the church bathroom and fuck her in a dirty stall.

I turn, and then I see my biggest problem—Maxwell.

He's sitting in the second pew with a smug look on his face. I don't know why in the hell Liesel thinks we need to keep him alive. She thinks I was controlling before; she's about to find out just how controlling I can be.

"Stand up," I tell Maxwell.

He stands casually, putting his hands in his pockets like he's not worried for his life.

My jaw ticks. I hate that he thinks so little of me. He thinks that Liesel will save him.

I consider my options. I don't want to leave Liesel alone for a second, but I also don't want her to have Maxwell on her conscience.

I pull out some cash and hand it to Liesel. "There is a hotel two blocks over. Get us the most expensive room they have for the night."

She looks at me, wide-eyed. "What about him?"

"I'll take care of him."

She opens her mouth, I assume, to argue with me, to beg for me not to kill him, but she shuts it before rising on her tiptoes and kissing me with plenty of tongue. "Hurry," she whispers before she walks out of the church.

I stand frozen, watching her walk away. I can't stand to see her go, even though we'll only be apart a few minutes. I still ache.

Maxwell frowns.

I grin.

Liesel trusted me. She let me decide what I do with Maxwell. I don't know when that changed, why she decided to trust me now with him, but she did.

"Shit," Maxwell mutters.

I stalk toward him—expecting him to run, to beg, to fight.

He does nothing.

What game is he playing?

I pull my gun out.

He keeps his hands in his pockets, surrendering to his fate.

"You going to kill me here, in the church? Isn't that like a double sin or something?"

"Why do you assume I'm going to kill you?"

"Because you are."

"Move," I say, nodding my gun toward the church's basement door behind the altar.

Maxwell walks with slow and steady steps, not like a man about to die. He walks like he isn't afraid of death.

He's like me—always knowing death will come sooner for him than it will for most people. It's one of the many reasons why my marriage to Liesel isn't real. It won't last, so what's the point?

We descend into the dark basement. This is the moment where I could torture Maxwell, get answers to my questions, ensure my family is safe and free the boy Corbin kidnapped. But Liesel is waiting for me in a hotel room, hopefully naked. My only goal is to secure him so I can spend the night with my wife. Tomorrow, I can deal with this bastard.

Every second I spend with Maxwell is a second I don't get back with Liesel. I may have just married her, but tomorrow is never promised. Tomorrow she could hate me, divorce me, kill me.

I grab pull ties from my pocket while keeping the gun on Maxwell.

"Put your arms behind your back," I say.

Maxwell slowly removes his hands from his pocket and slips them behind his back.

I walk behind him, jerking him backward until his arms are around a pole. I tie his arms with the pull ties, and then I walk to the door.

"I knew you didn't have the balls to go against her," Maxwell snickers.

I fire.

He yelps and then stares at his thigh, where blood oozes out.

"Fucking bastard," he yells at me.

I smirk; there's his reaction. He is human, after all.

"I'll be back in the morning, to see if you survived the night." And then I walk the fuck away, to go find my wife.

CHAPTER 17

LIESEL

I pace back and forth in the hotel suite, still not believing what just happened. I have to stare down at the thorn-covered ring on my finger as the only proof I have that I just married Langston.

I. Married. Langston.

What the hell was I thinking?!

I shouldn't have married him. This will fuck everything up. It will distract us both from the task at hand. It will end up hurting him in the end.

And as much as I used to enjoy hurting Langston, I don't want to put him through the pain I know I'll end up causing.

So I pace—trying to find a way out of this that won't end in destroying Langston even more than I already have. He's my killer. My protector. He has a hard exterior capable of enduring any explosion, but inside he's sweet, kind, and warm.

Inside, he's a beautifully sensitive soul who cares about me more than he will ever say out loud. I pray that I haven't already ruined that soul. A soul that has to survive long enough for our kids to grow up with a father after I'm long gone from their lives.

I hear a keycard enter the door, and my feet stop. I gulp in huge amounts of oxygen as I wait for Langston to open the door.

The door opens like he's pushing the weight of the world away. He steps through and slams all outside forces out until it's just the two of us remaining. Everything else vanishes.

Langston enters alone, which doesn't surprise me. I want to ask what he did with Maxwell. *Did he kill him?*

It doesn't matter. I trust him.

Why?

I shouldn't.

He's a monster.

A killer.

But he's my killer. And now he's my husband. There are plenty of vows we couldn't speak to each other because we wouldn't keep them. But being loyal and trusting to my husband is something I plan on doing for as long as we are married.

My gut told me to keep Maxwell alive, but tonight, I'm trusting Langston's gut. If it told him to kill Maxwell, then so be it. We'll find Corbin and the kid he kidnapped with or without Maxwell.

Langston has a predatory gleam as he looks me up and down. I haven't changed out of my wedding dress, my hair is dried in long waves, and I've been itching to drink something from the minibar to calm my nerves but thought better of it. I want to be completely sober for whatever happens between us tonight.

I throw his look back, pinning him with my stare as I take in his thick muscles that his white linen shirt is clinging to.

The atmosphere changes now that Langston's in it. The air is warm, electric—a brewing storm.

He walks toward me; words have yet to be exchanged.

Tonight isn't about words. For the first time, I can fuck Langston without taking something from another woman. Phoenix gave him up. I still have to make a lot of things right between me and her. I owe her my life, and I plan on repaying, but I don't have to worry about hurting her with every kiss.

Langston grabs the back of my neck, and he pulls me into a wicked kiss. One that involves teeth, tongue, and swollen lips. One that radiates down my entire body setting me aflame. One that cements him in my soul, refusing to let go of this man ever again.

I have to be careful tonight. I have to guard his heart. I have to protect him.

"Why do you still want to kill me?" I ask him as his open mouth comes down hard on mine for another kiss.

They're the first words I've spoken to him since we got married in the church.

He stops his kiss, his lips pausing on my upper lip. He pulls back gently, giving me just enough room to breathe but not enough to not be exchanging oxygen with him. He thumbs the vein in my neck.

"Why do you still hate me?" he asks, answering my question with a question.

Because I can't love you, I can't keep you. All I'm going to do is hurt you. And I hate you for turning me into a killer. I already know my first kill is going to be the slaughter of your heart.

I nip his top lip.

He grabs my ass as I wrap my legs around his waist. His kisses turn soft, graceful like a choreographed dance as he carries me toward the bed.

Warning bells go off inside my head, reminding me that we shouldn't fuck in a bed like normal people. That level of intimacy, now that we are married, can only lead to heartbreak.

I grab his hair and yank hard, pulling his lips off mine.

He growls, not liking that I'm taking control or stopping his possessive kisses.

"Don't fuck me in the bed," I say.

He cocks his head, searching for the truth in my words, in my eyes. And then he grins deviously.

"I can still blow your mind whether I fuck you in a bed or against the window for everyone to see."

I shake my head as he kisses me tenderly. I know what kind of sex he's expecting. The kind that says more than I'm just a good fuck. The kind that has feelings and emotion behind it.

"I'm damaged, killer."

"I am too, huntress."

He tosses me back onto the bed. His body covers mine before I have a chance to escape. His hips press against mine until I feel his bulging erection pulsing against my sex.

He's mine.

I'm his.

But being his is as far as this can go.

I push against his chest, and my hips wiggle beneath his pelvis, only causing his hardness to rub against my clit through my clothes, inciting my brain with euphoria and making it harder for me to focus on getting my words out. But I have to—it's important.

"Don't make love to me," I whisper.

The corner of his lip tilts up as if to laugh. "I never make love, huntress. I fuck—hard. I control and sin with the darkest pleasures. I never make love."

I twist out of his grasp as I knee him in the crotch, springing my escape. I run to the wall, pushing my back against it as Langston groans before standing up and stalking toward me.

"Promise you'll never love me," I beg.

He grabs my wrists and pins them behind my back. He twists me around until my front hits the wall. There's no way I can knee him now.

"I could never love you, huntress. You're a fucking liar. How could I ever love you?"

My eyes cut to his, and I know his words are a lie. I can see it in his amused expression. He can't promise that he won't love me.

"Promise me that a part of you will always hate me," I say, hoping that even if he ends up loving me, the hate will always remain.

He grabs the hem of my dress, his nails clawing up the back of my thigh as he raises it up. They creep around my cotton panties until he dips his fingers inside, pushing between my lips and trying to enter me.

I growl, not ready to let him have control of my body even though he already has control of more than I'm willing to admit, even to myself. My thighs squeeze shut, keeping his fingers locked between my folds.

"Promise," I demand.

His teeth clamp down on my earlobe until I squeal.

"I promise that a part of me will always hate you."

He releases my earlobe; I release his fingers.

Then I kick back against the wall, pushing him off me until I have control of my body once again. I run toward him, barreling my body into his open arms. I grab the hem of his shirt and rip the thin fabric in two right up the middle.

He pants hard, his abs contracting with each breath, taunting me with his fitness.

My nails scrape down his front, feeling every ripple on my way to his pants to rip them off his body.

He catches my wrist in my hands, denying my touch until he has what he wants first. His eyes drop to look at my dress, but he can't rip it until he lets go of my wrists.

He grins, as if he can read my mind.

"You want to play, huntress? Let's play."

With my wrists still in his fists, he dips his head down to the v of my dress. His teeth sink into the fabric, and then he pulls down —hard.

The fabric starts to fray, then rips in half as his teeth continue their assault on my dress. He continues downward until the dress is split in two, and my body is displayed in front of him in nothing but my white thong panties between us.

I yank my arms free before fleeing the bedroom. The bedroom is too personal, too sweet, too romantic. It's the opposite of who we are and what we can be.

Langston doesn't chase me. He walks slowly and deliberately after me, knowing that I want to get caught; I just don't want to fuck in the bedroom.

I glance around the living room, trying to come up with a way to have the upper hand when it comes to Langston. We've fucked before, and it was always incredible, but how long can that last? *How long can I give myself up to him before I lose myself? Before the raging panic returns, as will the nightmares of my past?*

Langston catches the fear in my eyes—so much fear mixed with want. It's a cataclysmic combination.

It only makes him move slower as I scan the room for a plan. I have nothing. All I can do is fight or surrender, and I'm not one to surrender.

Langston removes his shirt, baring all of his glorious muscles to me before he puts his hands in the pockets of his pants and stands still, watching me.

I let my dress fall to the floor before putting my hands on my hips, mirroring his action.

We both breathe slowly; our eyes grazing each other's burning flesh.

"You're mine," Langston says in a deep, controlling voice.

"Then, come and get me."

I bite my bottom lip.

He moves.

I move.

One step.

Two steps.

And then we both attack. Both grapple for control of the other.

I grab his pants, needing them off his body, needing him as vulnerable as I feel.

I yank them down his legs as he grabs me once again in his arms and slams me back until I knock the lamp off the small table behind me.

I shove him hard, until his back crashes against the full-length mirror behind him. The glass shatters, no doubt some slicing into his back.

His eyes twinkle with arousal.

I reach between us, finding his cock beneath his boxers. I want to wrap my lips around him. I want to suck him so well that he'll never want another woman sucking his dick ever again.

He smirks and cups my chin. "You don't have to worry, huntress. I'm yours."

He once again reads my thoughts.

Then he slams me back toward the couch. We end up knocking the TV off the wall as we stomp by.

I keep squeezing his cock. He ravishes my mouth with his.

And then, all at once, he releases me until I fall back on the couch with him standing over me.

"Spread your legs."

I throw them closed, purposefully defying him and loving the thrill it brings me when he seethes and bosses me around.

He steps forward, kicking my ankles apart. "Spread. Your. Legs."

As I do, he steps between them, his hand moving over my thighs, spreading me wider. He kneels in front of me.

My heart is shuddering in my chest, feeling like a deer that's just been caught by a tiger.

Langston licks his lips like he's about to devour a feast. His eyes are a wicked shade of dark brown, swirling with the devious things he wants to do to my body.

And then he leans down, his fingers swiping my panties aside as his tongue licks down my slit.

I bite my lip to keep from screaming his name with one touch, but my hands can't stand to not touch him. I grab on his hair, pushing his head deeper between my folds.

He stops, his head popping up as he grabs my hands and places them on either side of the couch.

"If you touch me, I'll stop, and you don't want me to stop, baby."

I frown. "Why would you stop?"

"You don't get to control this."

I dig my fingers into the couch cushions, trying to give up a little control as Langston once again licks my clit with his tongue.

My eyes roll at the pleasure shooting through my body. My lips part, needing more oxygen. Needing to grab him, but needing Langston to continue more.

He takes his time relentlessly licking over my clit like an endless lollipop. It's torture, when what I really want is him to suck, twirl, and hum to bring my body to orgasm quickly, instead of this slow, torturous slog.

He has me so worked up that I can't control myself, and I grab his hair.

He stops, once again moving my hands to the couch before continuing.

"You decide when you come, huntress. Not me."

"What?" I breathe, confused because he's clearly the one deciding by going so slowly.

He smiles between my folds before his finger plunges into me. "When you trust me, you'll come."

"I trust you."

"You don't."

I frown, realizing I don't trust him because the fear is still there. The fear that a man I care about could possibly not be enough. I could revert to my nightmares having hold of me.

"Let go," he hums against my clit.

I do, exploding on his tongue as my orgasm pours out of my throat, and I call out his name.

I collapse against the couch, my head falling back as I catch my breath.

"My turn," I say, eyeing his crotch.

He stands and exhales, as if blowing out smoke. "I'm going to bed."

"What?" I snap up. He just gave me one hell of an orgasm, but it didn't do anything to quench my thirst for him.

He grins. "You're welcome to join me in bed."

I sigh and lean back, refusing to give in. No matter how much my body wants it, I can't give in.

"What's the problem? We've fucked in a bed before."

His eyes search mine.

"I'm afraid," I whisper.

"Me too, but I already promised not to love you. Isn't that enough?"

"No."

"Whether I fuck you in a bed, or against the wall, on the floor, in an alleyway, a car, the moon, it makes no difference."

"Then why do we have to fuck in a bed tonight?"

"Even though you'll never love me, you need to trust me. Trust that I won't ever let the fear win. The pain you're afraid of will never come as long as you're with me."

Truth—his words are the truth. At least as far as he knows.

I stand up until we are once again face to face.

"Okay."

With that, he takes my hand and leads me into the bedroom. He lays me back on the bed before hovering over me and kissing me so sweetly on my lips that it burns, already bringing on the pain. And he hasn't even fucked me yet.

"I've got you, huntress. I know you better than anyone. I've failed you more than anyone, but I've also protected you more than anyone." He kisses his way down my body, stopping to suck one of my puckered nipples before making his way down my stomach and over my C-section scar. He licks its length, before pulling my panties off my body.

He pushes his boxers off before reaching for a condom and gliding it on. We've fucked without a condom before, but I'm thankful he has one now. I've already failed as a mother; there is no reason to make me one again.

He carefully parts my legs as he settles himself between my legs until I can feel his hardness against the heat of my pussy.

"Trust me," he whispers.

I nod.

And then he sinks inside me in one pulverizing thrust, the kind that has my head spinning with everything I've been missing, suddenly filling me and making me whole. I'm never going to be complete without him again.

"How have I gone so many years without you?" he growls, as always matching my thoughts.

"Miserably," I say.

He chuckles before his eyes return to his normal dark orbs. He lowers his mouth once again to kiss me.

I accept, and then he's rocking into my body. Taking his time. Protecting me from my demons. Caring about me when he shouldn't.

All the time he thrusts, one word hovers between us but is never spoken. Neither of us can deny it's there.

"Killer," I cry out as literal tears fill my eyes. *God, I'm going to cry when I come.* I don't care.

"Huntress," he returns my cry.

And then we fall over the devastating cliff together. One that will ruin us and leave us even more broken than before.

Tears roll down my cheeks as Langston holds me to his body, us both breathing frantically as we hold onto each other with enduring need. Like another force is already at work trying to pull us apart.

"You're mine," he whispers into my hair.

I nod.

His words are the truth.

I hate him.

I hate him. I hate him. I hate him!

Those words are a lie. I don't hate him.

I love him.

But I will never say the words out loud. I'll never allow myself to even think them again. The words are toxic and lead to nothing but pain.

I pull his arms tighter around my body, knowing that we are going to spend the rest of the night fucking—*no, making love.* Although, neither of us will use that word to describe this.

I can love him forever, but Langston can never know. I may be the devil, but the pain my loving him would cause is something I could never inflict on him. So I'll keep lying until our marriage eventually dissolves—that's the only way to not hurt him.

CHAPTER 18

LANGSTON

I leave Liesel snoring in bed. I don't want to leave her, but I should check on Maxwell. And there is no room service in this hotel, so I have to venture out for coffee and breakfast anyway—and new clothes since ours are ripped. I don't care if Maxwell lived or died last night; I just need to ensure that he's still in the basement of the church and didn't escape to go tell Corbin where we are. My need to protect Liesel and my kids trumps my ache to stay in bed with Liesel and watch her wake up in my arms.

The sun hasn't even risen yet as I stomp the couple blocks over to the church in nothing but my jeans. We barely slept last night, and I want to get back to Liesel as soon as I can. Hopefully, she won't wake up until I return.

My mind races with everything that happened last night. Every position we fucked in. Every sound she made each time she came. The way her thoughts spun between fear and something else that I couldn't figure out.

The fear is what fucked me up the most. She's afraid, terrified her demons will return with me like I'm sure they have with every other man she's been with. Afraid of giving up control to me. Afraid I'll fall in love with her and hurt her. That's the one thing she'll never have to worry about—I won't be falling in love with Liesel Dunn.

When I get to the small church, I run down the stairs and find Maxwell right where I left him.

He groans and looks up at me.

"Did you have a good night?" I ask, leaning against the doorframe.

"Better than you did," he says.

I laugh. "So you spent the night fucking the most beautiful woman in the world?"

He shakes his head. "No, but I didn't spend the night fucking a woman I'm going to destroy." He looks at me with a snarl. "I'm going to kill you if you hurt her."

"Liesel isn't yours to worry about. But don't worry your pretty little head about her. I won't be hurting Liesel."

"Says the man who has threatened to kill her multiple times."

I grind my teeth to keep from exploding on this man. He's not worth it. It's true that I've threatened to kill her, but I won't anymore. She probably still deserves it, but I'm not as much of a monster as I used to be.

"I'll be back," I say, turning to go back up the stairs. I take my time in case he decides to beg—beg me to let him go, to give him something for the pain, give him food and water. He doesn't beg. He's tougher than he looks, but that won't save him in the end.

I stop by two local shops. One for clothes, the other for coffee and picarones before I head back to our hotel room. When I get to the bedroom, I find it empty. My heart skips as I see the light on under the bathroom door.

She's still here, I breathe out.

I knock my knuckles against the door. "Liesel, I have coffee and breakfast."

She doesn't answer back right away. There's a rattling sound coming from the bathroom that I can't quite make out.

"Liesel?" I ask again.

"One sec," she says back.

I relax and start laying out the breakfast in the small nook while I wait. A moment later, Liesel appears in a white hotel robe. Her cheeks are flush, her hair wet, and a soft, knowing smile on her lips. All my fears disappear as soon as I see her.

"Coffee?" I say, holding out a cup to her. Her eyes rake down my bare chest.

She takes it, and I pull her into a kiss before I sit her down on my lap instead of letting her sit in the chair opposite me. She doesn't argue.

We wordlessly touch and explore each other while we eat our Peruvian donuts and drink our coffees. There's a level of comfort with each other that shouldn't be there so fast. Even though we've known each other practically our whole lives, it shouldn't be this effortless to just sit with her.

My thumb brushes over the ring I made for her. "I'll get you a real ring soon."

I don't know why I say it. This isn't a real marriage. We don't even love each other. I wouldn't have proposed if it wasn't for the stupid treasure. But it's important to me that she has the ring of her dreams because now that we're married, she's truly mine. I'm not letting her go to any other man—not without a fight.

She frowns and turns to me. "This is a real ring."

Her words have a deeper meaning, almost as if she's saying this is a real marriage.

I nod, but it doesn't change the fact that I will be getting her a real ring soon enough. Before long, the flowers I made this ring out of are going to wilt and die. I need to get a real ring before that happens.

Liesel shudders in my arms.

"You okay?" I ask.

She nods. "Just cold. We should get dressed and go. We have a long day ahead of us." She climbs off my lap before I can answer.

"Okay," I say.

We both quickly get dressed—I in jeans and a T-shirt, her in cutoff shorts and a tank. Then we head back to the small cottage hand in hand to await our fates.

Whatever is inside the small house waiting for us doesn't matter because it brought me Liesel. It made her mine, forever. Whatever awaits us will be worth it.

LIESEL

The door opens to the small shack-like house. The old man with wrinkles around his brown eyes wears a stern expression as he welcomes us in wordlessly.

Langston reaches into his pocket to produce our marriage license. "Do you need this? We just got married yesterday, so I'm not sure if it will show up in the record system yet."

The man shakes his head. "I confirmed with the priest that you two are, in fact, married."

He turns to me. "I do need your blood, dear."

He pulls out a knife, and I automatically stick out my hand, offering this man to take whatever he needs from me. I'll do anything to protect my son.

Langston tenses next to me as the man pricks my finger.

I smile up at Langston, loving how protective he is over me. I didn't use to like it, but it sets my heart aflutter when he does it now that we're married.

"I'll be right back," the man says, carrying the knife with my blood on it away.

Langston hasn't let go of my hand as we stand in the small candlelit room, waiting.

"What happens next?" I ask Langston.

"I don't know. This is as far as Phoenix and I made it."

My stomach rolls when he says her name. I still can't believe how kind she is. Langston deserves a girl like her, not me.

"Don't," Langston says.

"Don't what?"

"Compare yourself to her. She has made plenty of mistakes with her life, just like you have. Don't forget she blackmailed me into marrying her."

"She also adopted the son of her enemy. She's a much better woman than I am."

Langston growls and squeezes my hand, obviously disagreeing with me.

"Have you heard from Beckett or Phoenix yet? Or the kids?"

"No, not hearing from them is a good thing. They will only contact us if there is a problem. It's safer this way."

I nod, knowing he's right. But after learning Atlas is alive and well, I want to know where he is every second of every day.

"Thank you for waiting, Liesel. If you will, please follow me now. Langston, if you will wait here," the man says.

I nod and start following the man out the back door, but Langston's grip on me tightens.

I lift his hand to mine and kiss it. "I'll be right back."

Slowly, his release on me loosens enough for me to pull my fingers out of his grasp. I feel every tingling nerve of anxious energy burst through him, and I want nothing more than to go back to our hotel room and spend the rest of the day getting lost under the covers to soothe him.

Instead, I do the right thing. I let go and follow the old man out of the house. The sun is shining down on us through the trees as we walk down a small winding path to a clearing by a creek.

"Sit," he says, pointing to a small tree stump on the ground.

I sit while he walks over to a makeshift table that has a pot of tea and two cups. He pours each of us a cup and hands one to me before he sits on a log opposite me.

"I'm Diego, I knew your father well. I'm sorry he's gone."

"Nice to meet you, Diego. But you don't need to be sorry for my dead father. He was never around. I didn't know him."

"I'm sorry that your father didn't know how to be a father. You were better off without a father."

I disagree, but I don't say so.

"I bet you're wondering why your father sent you on this crazy quest. If he had so much money, why not just give it to you?"

I nod. "It does seem strange."

"He didn't want it to destroy you like it did him. He wanted to ensure you'd be strong enough to wield the kind of power that goes with the kind of money you would inherit."

"I don't know if I'm strong enough or not; I just want to ensure that my child doesn't grow up constantly facing danger and threats of people trying to steal from him. I just want him to be safe. I couldn't care less about the money."

"I think you have what it takes, Liesel. I can see it. All that's left is to prove it."

"And how do I do that?"

"There are three qualities your father wanted to ensure that you possess. Once you demonstrate them, you'll have all the clues you need to find the hidden treasure."

He sips his tea. I do the same and its warm, grassy tasting contents soothe the ache in my stomach.

"How do I prove these qualities?"

"Each of the locations you are sent to will give you a task. Completing the task on your way to the next location will be one step closer to proving your worthiness. We will be watching for proof, so no need to bring anything physical with you. But your next location is in Egypt."

"Egypt?"

"Yes, your father had friends who like to live where there are fewer people."

Like him.

He shows me the address of the next location, and once I've memorized it, he burns it in the fire crackling between us.

"What is the quality I have to show?"

"Betrayal."

I frown, not liking the sound of this. "Betrayal to who?"

"Your husband."

My heart thumps to a stop. "My father wanted me to get married just so I could betray him?"

He nods. "He wanted you to prove to yourself that even if you loved a man, you don't need him. That his love isn't enough."

I stand up as my blood boils. I'm beyond pissed. I want to go to my father's grave and pull him back to life just so I can kill him all over again. Everything I just went through was for nothing. I married Langston for nothing.

"What exactly do I have to do to betray him?"

"The only way that matters to Langston."

"Which is?"

"Be claimed by another man. Make Langston believe you're no longer his."

"How will you know if I betray him or not?"

"Trust me, we'll know."

"And if I choose not to betray him?"

"Then, you won't get the next clue, and you'll never find the treasure."

And my son will never be safe from greedy hunters.

I look down to the ground, knowing if there is a heaven and hell, my dad is most definitely in hell for what he's putting me through. *You couldn't be a father for the first twenty-plus years of my life, and now that you're dead, you decide to teach me some lessons?*

I look at Diego, defeated. "What do I do now?" *What if I love him?*

"You betray him. You get the treasure. You protect your child. That's what you do."

I squeeze my eyes shut, but the tears fall anyway. I don't know why Langston hates me. I don't know why he wants to kill me. But after I betray him—he's never going to forgive me.

CHAPTER 20

LANGSTON

I've worn down every inch of the dirt floor with my pacing in this one-room house while I wait for Liesel to return. Fear floods my head with horrible images of what could be happening to her.

Is she in pain? Is she suffering, and I'm not helping her? I could never forgive myself if so.

Finally, light streams into the house as the back door opens, and Liesel steps back into the room alone.

I run to her and wrap her possessively into my open arms. She doesn't speak. I assume she's going to act tough and try to pull away; instead, she sinks into my chest, letting me hold her as tight as I want.

I slow my breathing, trying to slow hers. Hers stays quick for several minutes before finally meeting my steady breath. Only then do I speak.

"What happened?" I ask.

"He just told me where the next location is."

My hand is nestled on the back of her neck behind her hair. I tilt her head up to look at me, and rage spreads inside me at what I see—puffy, red eyes.

"What happened?" I try again, this time as softly as I can manage, so I don't scare her with the fire I feel inside.

"We had tea, and he told me where we have to travel to next."

I can see the truth in her eyes—but she's also hiding something from me.

"What did you do to get that information?"

She takes a step out of my arms; she's not going to tell me. I could beat it out of her, threaten her, but it wouldn't work. There is no threat violent enough to get her to tell me—to trust me.

We haven't been married but a day, and she's already keeping things from me. The only thing I can do is earn her trust while keeping the burning disappointment that I'm not enough for her at bay.

Her long eyelashes flicker up at me—telling me to trust her. There's a reason she can't tell me, it's not by choice.

I sigh and run my hand through my hair.

"Let's go get Maxwell and then get out of here."

"You didn't kill him?"

I shake my head. "You didn't want me to, so I didn't."

"Thank you."

I grab her neck and pull her back into my arms, my lips kissing the top of her head. "I'll always do my best to do right by you. I promise."

I link our fingers together, and then I pull her out of this place of darkness that has caused her so much pain in such little time. I may not know what happened, but at least I can be the one to take her away.

I watch her closely, looking for any sign of injury as we walk back into town. I find none. Whatever he did to her was mental.

We walk back into the church. It feels surreal to be standing back in the place where we got married so soon. Then I show her downstairs to where Maxwell is still tied up with a bullet wound in his thigh.

"You really didn't kill him," she says to herself in disbelief at the sight of Maxwell. She lets go of my hand and approaches him.

I'm not sure what she's going to do to him. What I didn't expect to see is her down on her knees next to him, ripping the bottom of her shirt to tie around his leg.

"I'm going to get you some water and pain killers, and you'll feel better soon," she says to him.

I frown, glaring down at him. I want to put a bullet between the bastard's eyes, but apparently, we're bringing him with us.

"Knife," Liesel says, holding her hand out to me in an annoying tone.

I pull out my knife from my boot and hand it to her. She starts working on the pull ties around his wrists.

"Are you annoyed with me?" I ask.

"No," she snaps back.

I roll my eyes. "So that's a yes."

She cuts the tie, and Maxwell falls forward, barely conscious.

"Did you really have to shoot him?"

"Yes, I had to ensure he stayed put and didn't run to Corbin."

"I think the tie was sufficient. You didn't need to shoot him." She slips her arm under his shoulder, while I do the same to his other arm and help him up.

We start walking him up the stairs. "He isn't a good man. He works for our enemy."

"He still didn't deserve to be shot."

She looks at him, and I swear there's a longing in her eyes when she looks at him, but I'm sure I'm just mistaking it for pity. She doesn't want Maxwell; she just doesn't want him dead. At least, not yet.

I call a cab, and then we all pile in and drive to the private airport. I'm on the phone making arrangements for our flight, while Liesel holds Maxwell in her lap, stroking the golden locks of his hair mindlessly.

Our pilot asks me where we are flying to. I snap to Liesel. "Where to?"

I don't expect her to answer, but she does. "Egypt. I'll give him the exact coordinates once we get to the airport."

I tell my pilot and then sit in silence for the rest of the drive, trying to understand what changed with Liesel between last night and right now.

We get to the airport, and I pull Maxwell out, carrying him sideways in my arms so Liesel won't have to touch him. He barely groans as I carry him toward the airplane.

Once inside, I lie him down on one of the couches at the back.

Liesel walks up beside me, carrying a first aid kit. "Do you want to do it or should I?'

I grab the kit out of her hands. I don't want her touching this guy.

I set the kit on the floor as I kneel next to him. I pop it open with a thump and begin searching for the items I'm going to need—gauze, tweezers, alcohol, bandages, stitches.

I go to work on his leg like he's a member of my team—not the enemy he is. I'm so focused on getting the job done quickly and cleanly that I don't notice Liesel holding his hand.

My eyes keep cutting to their joined hands. I want to rip her hands from his and suck every finger clean of the mere touch of him. I don't because I don't want to deepen our fight.

"I'm finished," I say, basically clearing my throat in a grumbled, grumpy way to get Liesel to stop touching Maxwell.

She doesn't immediately let go of his hand. Instead, she digs through the first aid kit until she finds a bottle of pills. Popping the lid off, she pours a couple into her hand and then puts them in Maxwell's mouth.

"These will ease the pain and help you sleep," she says to him before holding up some water to his lips. He sips the water, barely conscious. The pills will knock him out. He won't feel any of the pain within minutes. It's too kind if you ask me.

Maxwell's eyes flutter closed, and only then does she let go of his hand.

"Why are you being so nice to him?" I ask.

She purses her lips, looking at Maxwell like she has a pull to him that even she herself doesn't understand. "I don't know, really. It just feels like the right thing to do."

I hate her answer, but I'm not going to fight with her about it. Maxwell will meet his demise soon enough. I start walking a couple of rows up and take a seat. I don't want to look or think about the bastard.

"What are we going to do about Corbin?" Liesel asks, sitting down next to me.

"I already have Enzo and Zeke looking for him."

She smiles. "You forgave them already?"

I growl.

She smirks and takes my hand in hers. The same hand that was just holding that monster's.

I remove my hand from her grasp and look out the window, annoyed with her already. This is why we would never work out.

"Don't—don't be like that. I don't care about Maxwell. I just think we should keep him alive and taken care of until we figure out how to use him to get to Corbin and save the child he's taken, that's all."

"I say we kill him. Corbin will come after us for revenge if he cares about the bastard at all."

She frowns. "I'd rather not piss Corbin off and risk our lives for nothing."

She's soft on Maxwell. She cares about him. And she's not a killer—that's my job.

"We can't keep him around forever. At some point, we have to take a stand."

"I know, and I think we should after we have the treasure."

I disagree with her, but there is no point arguing right now. All I did was stitch Maxwell up and keep him alive until we get to our next stop, where I'll once again have to tie him up and disable him while we go in search of the treasure. It's actually kinder to just kill him now.

"Look at me," Liesel says.

I take a deep breath and then turn and face her. I'm annoyed with her about how she's handling Maxwell. I'm frustrated that she doesn't trust me enough to tell me what she had to do to earn our next clue. But when I look into her big hazel eyes that hold the weight of the world—all of that vanishes. In her eyes, I see something I've never seen before staring back at me—an emotion that neither of us can describe with words.

She runs her tongue over her teeth as she climbs on top of my lap until she's straddling me in my chair.

"Kiss me," she says with a longing to her voice. She thinks I won't kiss her.

I don't hesitate—I grab the back of her neck and pull her down until her soft lips touch mine. I just had her last night, but that seems like a lifetime away. The bitterness that I felt melts away with a single kiss.

"I needed that," I say when she pulls back.

"I need more."

She reaches between the seats and flicks the lever that dips the seat back. Her eyes ignite with a burning desire as she rips her tank top off her body until two peaks are staring back at me.

My head darts behind me to where Maxwell is hopefully asleep and not looking at my topless wife.

"What are you doing?"

She grins as she undoes the button on my jeans. "Fucking you."

"You can't—Maxwell is three rows behind us. The pilots—"

"Are you my husband?"

"Yes..."

"Then fuck me. I don't care about anyone else on this plane. I need you."

Fuck me.

She doesn't wait for my answer. Her hand slips into my pants, taking complete control.

"Don't." I grip her wrist, stopping her.

"Why?" Her eyes sear, demanding this.

"I'm angry."

"So?"

"Maxwell could wake up and see you."

"He won't."

Her lips come down hard on mine, clinging to me like I'm the only thing in her world. "I need you."

"I'm yours," I concede.

Her next moves are frantic, crazed as she moves quickly to undo my pants. I match her frenzied state, unbuttoning her shorts off just as quickly.

I don't know what happened to her. I don't know what she did, what she gave up to get the next clue. I do know it was painful, though. And I will do anything to take away her pain.

She kicks her shorts off and angles me between her legs, straddling me again.

I move to reach for a condom in my pocket, but she's already sliding down on my cock. I don't give a damn if I get her pregnant. Kids I'm good with. And if she wants to have my babies, I'll give her as many as she wants. What's most important now is giving her all of myself without any barriers.

I thrust up as she slides her hips down over my cock—up and down like she's sprinting, trying to chase an orgasm that will escape her if she doesn't find it quickly. I don't know why she feels the need to rush, but I match her speed, not questioning her.

I tug her nipple into my mouth that's been bouncing at eye level as she grasps onto my hair, giving her more grip to fuck me harder.

"That's it, baby, get it all out. Fuck the pain away."

I grab her hips and lift her up and down, helping her move as quickly as her body demands her. Helping her to chase away her fears.

Harder.

Faster.

Deeper.

I thrust into her. I focus on giving her all the pleasure in the world —thrusting deeper into her cunt, lapping at her swollen nipples, pinching her sensitive clit. I don't even realize I'm on the edge of coming until she's exploding around my cock, and I shoot my cum inside her.

She breathes deeply as I grip her hips. Her head falls forward against my chest, and she inhales and exhales sharply.

I stroke her hair, letting her have a moment to feel and breathe normally again. Her breathing does slow, but her eyes close as she falls asleep against my chest.

I shake my head as I lift her gently in my arms. I find a blanket a couple of rows up and drape it over us. Both of us are half-naked and my cum is sticking to her thighs, but none of that matters as she sleeps in my arms.

"What happened to you, baby?" I whisper into her hair, devastated by whatever it is she went through.

I close my eyes and tug her tighter to my body, kissing her hair. *How does she feel so perfect in my arms?*

"I lov—" I start and then stop myself. I run my hand through my hair, scolding myself for the almost slip.

It was just reflex. I don't love her. The only problem is I don't know if I'm lying to myself or finally admitting the truth.

CHAPTER 21

LIESEL

I wake up as the plane lands; our rough landing jars me awake.

I blink several times, trying to remember where I am and what's happening. Then I breathe in Langston—his musky smell mixed with sweat and sex. I smile and snuggle into his chest.

"You're going to have to wake up and get dressed, baby."

Get dressed?

I take an assessment of my body and realize I'm naked except for the blanket covering me. Langston is naked, too, lying underneath me. And then I remember fucking him—how desperately and furiously I fucked him with everything in my body, unsure if it would be our last.

Betray him.

My heart begins to crumble just thinking about hurting Langston. I'm going to blast both of our hearts into a thousand pieces when I betray him. I've been cruel to Langston before but never when he was mine. I don't know how I'm going to go through with it.

Langston lifts me up so he can search my eyes. He knows that something is up with me. He just thinks it's something I've already done, not something I'm going to do.

If he didn't already hate me, if we didn't have a history of lying to each other, if we loved each other, then maybe we could survive my betrayal, especially once he realizes that I only did it to get the treasure and protect Atlas.

But we don't love each other. We never will. Our marriage will end with my betrayal.

I force myself to smile and kiss Langston gently on the lips before I climb off his lap and find my clothes in a pile. I start putting my jean shorts and tank top back on, peering through the aisle back to a still sleeping Maxwell. His chest rises and falls, so I know he's still alive.

Langston gets dressed beside me as well.

"What's the plan?" I ask.

"It's dark, so we should head to a hotel to sleep for the night. Tomorrow we can go in search of the next clue."

I nod.

He gets up and walks to the back to wake Maxwell. He says something, and Maxwell pops up.

Langston gathers a few things in the back before walking back to me. He has a gun in his hand that he holds out to me. I take it and tuck it into the back of my shorts.

Langston nods his approval.

"Follow me, we have a car waiting."

I stand and follow him through the aisle and out of the plane. As I walk, I hear footsteps behind me.

"Are you feeling better, Max?" I ask, without turning my head.

"Good as new."

I smile.

Langston growls, irritated with me for talking to Maxwell. The easiest way to betray Langston is by fucking Maxwell. Maxwell is good looking enough. He's injured, and Langston already thinks I have a thing for him. It would be easy to make him believe that. I'm just not sure I'm strong enough to do it.

My mind is spinning with how I could pull it off, how I could use Maxwell to hurt Langston as I follow Langston down the stairs. A flood of anxiety rattles through my chest, shaking me with every fucked up thought I have of kissing Maxwell, sucking his cock, letting him touch me—all so I can hurt Langston.

I try to think of all the reactions Langston could have. Him yelling, beating Maxwell until he's dead, or just wordlessly walking out and sending me the divorce papers later. I don't know which is worse.

"Wait," Maxwell says suddenly, before we step into our waiting SUV.

His words barely register in my whirling head.

Langston understands the single word, though. He pulls his gun out and starts firing before anyone fires at us.

I duck down and grab my gun, watching as bullets whizz by my head.

"Huntress!" I hear Langston shout. His voice is far away. I can't hear him. I don't see him.

I shoot in the direction the bullets are flowing from, but I can't make out who's shooting.

And then I see a bullet coming straight for me. I try to flatten myself out—it's all I can do in the fraction of a second I have to react before it hits me.

A body hits me instead—Maxwell.

He groans from the bullet lodging in his wrist as he pushes me out of the way.

Suddenly, the bullets stop.

Maxwell hovers over me, still trying to protect me.

I knew there was a reason to keep him alive. I just don't know why he saved me.

I look around the tarmac, but I don't see Langston.

A man appears, standing less than ten feet away from me in suit pants, a jacket, and an unbuttoned collar without a tie. His hair is slicked back with a few gray strands. He looks so similar to Waylon that I know who he is at once.

"Corbin Brown," I say as I stand.

Maxwell stands, too, cradling his bleeding wrist.

"What do you want?" I demand.

"I thought my letter made my demands clear."

My eyes scan the tarmac until I spot a body lying face-first on the ground.

No!

Corbin laughs, drawing my attention back to him. "Don't worry, your husband isn't dead. Just knocked out."

I don't react. I don't want Corbin to think he can use Langston to control me in any way. He already has a child he can use to do that. He doesn't need Langston.

"If you think I care about him, you haven't studied me very well. I only married him to get the treasure. I was about to marry Maxwell; Langston just ended up being closer."

Corbin's dark eyes glance from me to Langston, trying to decide if I'm lying or not.

"I don't have the treasure yet," I say.

"I know. I'm here to ensure you give it to me when you do."

I see Langston stirring out of the corner of my eye. A man stands over him with a gun pointed at his head.

I have to save him. *How?*

Maxwell is still standing to my left. He protected me from a stray bullet. He seems on our side. And as soon as Langston comes to, he'll try to fight. I have to protect him.

"I may not care about Langston, but you can't kill him. I have to remain married to him to complete the clues to get the treasure," I say, demanding that Corbin not harm Langston.

"I wasn't planning on killing him."

"Then, why are you here? You sent your minion to watch over us while we got the treasure. You kidnapped my child to ensure my cooperation. I'll give you the treasure; I just need more time."

Corbin's eyes run up and down my body, telling me exactly what he wants in addition to the treasure—me. I know exactly what I have to do to earn a little of Corbin's trust while destroying Langston's. Somehow, I have to use this opportunity to get the upper hand on Corbin.

I give him a wicked smile back as I run my tongue over my bottom lip slowly. Then I bite it as I sway my hips and start walking toward him. I rake my eyes over his body, pretending he's the hottest man I know.

When I reach him, he sucks in a breath, not expecting my reaction.

"I loved Waylon. It may have started off as him blackmailing me, but I fell for him. I always fall for the bad guys, the villains. I prefer the darkness to the light. I'm sure I could fall for you too." I pause, digging my nails into his chest. "If you want me, all you have to do is ask." *And tell me where you're keeping an innocent child.*

I wink as I let my nails dig down his chest, and then I strut toward his Bentley sedan behind him. I resist the undeniable urge to look at Langston. To see if he heard my words. To see if I've already broken him. To see if my cruel lies destroyed him.

CHAPTER 22

LANGSTON

Liesel winked at Corbin.

She flirted, used her body to seduce him. She touched him like she already knew him.

What is happening?

My mind buzzes, trying to remember everything that just happened. Every look she gave Corbin. Every unspoken exchange. Every word she muttered.

If you want me, all you have to do is ask.

She said it so flippantly. Like it meant nothing to her. Like she'd fuck him without thinking twice about it.

When she was just fucking me just hours earlier. When she's married to me. When she's *mine*.

I try to rack my brain for answers, but I only find more questions. Corbin didn't even ask to fuck her. He didn't threaten her. He didn't say he would force her. She just willingly offered her body to him. *Why?*

Has she been working with them all along? Did she lie to me? Was she really in love with Waylon? Does she actually want Corbin, not me?

None of her actions make sense.

And then another memory springs into my head like a bulldozer driving into my heart.

Kissing.

I was in the back of the van, barely conscious, but I saw Liesel kissing Corbin.

I open my eyes to darkness and find myself locked in a dungeon. Metal bars surround me, chains bind my wrists to the wall above my head, but the bars and chains are nothing compared to the darkness encapsulating my heart.

I shake my head, trying to shake off the memories that have to be lies.

Liesel cares about me, not Corbin. She wouldn't betray me like that. My memories must be wrong. She's in danger, same as me. She might be locked up in a dungeon nearby. Corbin could be torturing her, forcing himself on her. I have to break free. I have to go find her and save her.

I try to move my arms, but the chains holding my arms to the wall don't budge.

Fuck.

My feet are free, so I dig them into the ground, trying to gather some leverage to yank the chains off the wall. No amount of strength is going to get these chains to move.

I glance around the dark room for something I could use to pick the lock with, but the room is empty. I move my ass against the floor, trying to see if they left my wallet or phone. My pockets are empty. I move my foot around in my boot, but they don't find the knife I usually keep there.

I have nothing to use to break free.

I'm going to fail Liesel again.

I flail one more time, trying to pull the chains off the wall, but I have to force myself to stop no matter how hard it is for me to sit here and do nothing. If I do get an opportunity to get free, I'm going to need all of my strength to fight my way out of here, to protect Liesel.

A door opens, and light floods down into my dark little space.

I squint, hating the light. I prefer the darkness.

The door closes again as heavy footsteps creep down the stairs.

"Maxwell," I practically growl as he stops just outside the metal bars.

"It seems like our circumstances have changed. Now you're the one tied up, while I'm free to do as I please."

"Just shoot me and get it over with."

He chuckles. "Only an unhinged man would shoot a man while he's tied up. Especially when those men are on the same side."

"We aren't on the same side."

"Aren't we?" Maxwell grabs onto the top of the bars, his body slouching relaxedly as he waits for me to remember.

I glance up at one of his hands, wrapped in bandages.

He took a bullet for Liesel. He protected her.

I frown, completely confused about which side anyone is on anymore. But I do know that no matter whose side Maxwell is truly on, I owe him.

I sigh. "I owe you one for protecting her."

He smirks. "You're about to owe me twice."

He reaches for the lock and inserts a key, opening the cage. Then he walks to me and pops open the locks on each of my wrists until the chains fall off.

I rub my wrists as I stare, completely confused by Maxwell.

"What do you want?" I ask, knowing he's only doing this in exchange for something.

"I want you to go get the woman we both love. I want you to take her and get the treasure. I want you to save the kids. And I want you to destroy my brother."

"Brother?"

Maxwell nods. *Corbin is his brother. Waylon was his brother. He's a liar. Why should I trust him now?*

"You love Liesel?"

He nods. "I do. But unlike every other deranged man who has fallen for her, I know she will never be mine. The best I can do is protect her."

I don't correct him that I don't love Liesel. That I can't love her.

"You're here to help us?"

"Yes." He flings a gun at me.

I catch it with wide eyes. A man I've shot before just freed me and willingly gave me a gun. I don't know what his true motives are, but right now, it seems our goals are aligned.

"Where's he keeping Liesel?" I ask.

He frowns. "I'm not sure if Corbin is keeping her or if she's working with him willingly. She seems fascinated by him."

"Where is she?"

Maxwell scratches his head like he's not sure he wants to tell me. "Follow me."

I hold the gun in my hand as we jog up the stairs. Maxwell has his gun out, too, as we reach the top. "If anyone approaches, I'm going to pretend to knock you out. They still think I'm on their side."

I nod.

Then he opens the door, and we're standing in the hallway of a grand house. Without even taking a step out of the hallway, I can tell how big the house is. There are voices, but they are far off. The hallway is long, with dozens of doors.

"This way," Maxwell says, sneaking us down the hallway until we get to the end and it suddenly opens up into a grand room where the voices are coming from.

Liesel is standing in the center of the room with a drink in her hand, while Corbin sits in a chair opposite her with his minions strewn about the room, sitting on various pieces of furniture, all looking up at Liesel like she's the one in charge.

Maxwell crouches down beneath a sofa; I slide over, doing the same as I watch Liesel through a crack between two sofas.

She licks her lips, her eyes darting around to every man in the room like she's taking her pick of the litter. I know Liesel uses sex as a weapon. I've witnessed it plenty of times. I just never thought she'd try it after she was mine.

She's not—it can't be true. Corbin is forcing her into this position.

Liesel struts over to Corbin, her eyes set on him. I know what she's going to do before she does it. I have to stop her.

"No," Maxwell whispers in a hushed command.

"I have to help her."

He shakes his head. "You do and we're all dead."

I know he's right. I count over thirty men in this room—all with guns. Maxwell is basically useless, and I'm good, but I can't take down thirty men while keeping Liesel from getting shot in the process. But I can't just sit here and watch this.

Maxwell looks at me and just shakes his head like he thinks I'm ridiculous. "You're an idiot."

Maybe I am—for falling for a girl who is followed by trouble like a hurricane leaving devastation everywhere. I know I'm about to once again risk my life to save her, but I'll do it gladly.

"What do you want in exchange?" Corbin asks, his eyes raking up and down her body like she's his.

"Nothing," she grins. "I'll fuck you and any other man in this room who wants me for free."

My heart breaks into a million pieces, each sharp edge stabbing at my ribs and organs, killing me from the inside out.

But then Liesel's eyes catch mine. She sees me hiding—looks right at me as she breaks my heart and snickers.

My head falls back, and I glance over at Maxwell, who is just as stunned as I am. I'm not seeing things—Liesel just willingly offered up her body to any man in this room. She doesn't want anything in return.

Liesel Dunn is a liar.

She's never been on my side. She's always been on Waylon's and now Corbin's. She's the villain in my story. I should have killed her when I got the chance.

I couldn't then, and I sure as hell can't now.

Maxwell is right; I am an idiot.

For falling in love with a girl who was never mine. For still wanting to save her when she doesn't want to be saved. For still loving her even when she betrays me.

CHAPTER 23

LIESEL

etray him.

Do it—it's just sex. Something that's been taken from you so many times before. Fuck this man and whoever else he wants me to fuck to get the treasure, to protect my son, to end this war.

It will hurt Langston—but it will also save him. It's better this way. Make him hate me now so he won't get hurt worse later—so that there is no chance he'll fall in love with me.

I don't know what I was thinking, letting Langston propose to me like that. Getting married in a white dress with a handmade ring and vows. I should have just dragged his ass into the church and had a quick wedding like what I was going to do with Maxwell.

Instead, it was romantic and sweet and led to more. But we can never have more.

So I'll end it now.

My father was a cruel fucking man. If he wasn't dead already, I'd kill him myself for making me fall for a man only to hurt him in the worst possible way. Even if Langston figures out why I'm doing this— it's still unforgivable. It will still change everything between us.

I lazily look around at the men in the room. Corbin sits in his chair like it's a throne, while the other men salivate in my direction.

I have no problem fucking men, taking away their power with my pussy. It's when they try to take from me, that's when I have a problem. Sex is a weapon when you wield it correctly, and I'm an expert.

Before the last twenty-four hours, I would have had no problem fucking Corbin, making him believe I'm on his side, getting him to let his guard down in order for me to win. But now...

My eyes cut to the boy I used to love. The boy who is all grown up now and hiding behind the couch, staring at me like he's about to kill me.

I'm going to have to give the best performance of my life to pull this off. I have to betray Langston in order to get the next clue. If I fail, my son will forever be in danger. There will be no reason for Corbin to keep Langston or I alive. I have to succeed.

Before Langston came looking for me, I made a deal with Corbin. I'll do whatever he wants in exchange for getting to see the boy he's keeping hostage, a boy he thinks is my son.

I turn off my emotions as I throw back the rest of my drink—the alcohol burns all feeling in my throat as it sinks down into my stomach.

I'm saving Langston. I'm saving him.

That's the last I allow myself to think of Langston. My eyes focus in on my target—Corbin. He's sitting in a red velvet chair in a full suit. The only thing missing is his tie. He thinks the clothes make them look more powerful. And maybe he is powerful. He has loyal men, wealth, weapons. He thinks he has me.

He can fuck me, but I'll never be his. I already gave my heart away...

I straddle Corbin's lap. I hover over him, careful not to touch any part of him as I raise an eyebrow challenging him.

We doing this here, baby? In front of everyone?

His nostrils flare, taking the bait.

Why do I want to do it here in front of everyone? Because Langston is here. As much as it's going to kill him to watch me do it, I also feel safe and connected to him. I only have the strength to do this if he's here.

I grab his shirt, ripping the expensive buttons on his white Louis

Vuitton shirt as I pop it open. I have to make the first move, and I just made it.

I'm the one in charge, not him.

I repeat that mantra over and over in my head as I roll his jacket and shirt off his arms. Corbin doesn't move to touch me. He thinks of himself as the king, and my job is to serve him. That makes my job easier. I'll be in complete control of everything.

I consider my next move carefully. I don't want to take off my shirt. I want to strip him first, so he knows I have all the power. But giving up part of myself, controlling his eyes with my body is more important. I'm the most confident person in the world and have absolutely no problem fucking him is what I need him to believe.

I need every man in this room to believe.

So I pull my tank top off like it's nothing, like I strip in front of dozens of men every day.

I can hear men clearing their throats. Others groan. Some look away, embarrassed. But most of their eyes are glued to my pointed nipples, inches away from Corbin's pupils.

But I'm not done yet. I stand up with nothing but tiny shorts that barely cover my ass. Turning around, I stick my ass out as I swoop it over Corbin's crotch and undo my button and zipper.

I force myself not to glance at Langston. I don't want the men in the room to know that he's hiding, but I feel his heated stare on me more than any man's in the room. His eyes are trying to demand that I'm his, trying to convince me to come back to him and stop this.

I can't.

Instead, I slide my shorts and underwear down my body.

There is a collective gasp in the room as I stand naked in front of a room full of men.

Corbin still hasn't touched me. He hasn't said anything either.

I turn back around, eyeing Corbin's crotch like I want to eat him for dessert.

He doesn't react. He just stares at me intently, not moving.

I trade his stare. I'll fuck him in his chair, just like I did to Langston on the plane.

"Such a brave woman to come into the lion's den and offer yourself up willingly," Corbin says.

I hold all my tension in my jaw, but I don't react. I don't let out any fear.

I can't help but think my father did this as punishment for all the pain I've caused.

He knew I was a terrible daughter, and I'd make a terrible mother, a terrible friend.

I think about Phoenix. I took the man she loved only to destroy him. I deserve to feel whatever pain Corbin is planning on sending my way.

"Kneel," he says, attempting to take control from me. But one thing I've learned from my time with Langston is that no one can take anything from me without my consent. He can boss me around, and I can follow. He can touch me without my permission, but until I give him something, he has nothing. He can touch my body all he wants; all I care about is my heart, and he won't be coming near that.

"With pleasure," I say, kneeling in front of him.

Corbin's eyes widen as he realizes just how far I'm willing to go.

"You really don't love your husband, do you?"

"I really don't, but I love to fuck." My eyes cut left, then make a slow circle around the men in the room before landing back on Corbin with a grin. "So who is going to give me the pleasure of fucking me first?"

I purposefully spread my knees, giving Corbin a direct view of my pussy.

He stops breathing.

I smirk.

"I want you to suck me and then every other cock in this room. Show us what a dirty slut you are," he says.

In my head, I roll my eyes. Men are such simple creatures; always with the dick sucking like that is somehow demeaning me. They would do anything I say for a simple blowjob.

I inch forward and grab onto Corbin's pants, yanking them down.

His cock springs free, already hard. It's thick and long, a decent looking cock, but my pussy doesn't get a drop wetter. When he fucks me, it's going to be dry and painful.

I lower my head to his cock, but before I touch my lips to his tip, I'm jerked back by my hair.

Langston.

He starts shooting.

Shit.

I thought he understood I didn't want him to save me.

Bullets start flying all around us. Then I see Maxwell. I look at his wrist and remember that he protected me. He's on my side.

End this, I mouth to him.

He jumps over the couch and is by my side in an instant with his gun at my temple.

"Stop or she dies," Maxwell yells.

Langston stops, turning his head to stare at Maxwell. I know he's confused about whose side Maxwell is on, and I'm not going to help him.

"Drop the gun, Langston," Corbin says.

"You won't kill her; you can't kill her," Langston says, looking between Corbin and Maxwell.

"Not yet, we can't. But we can kill her child," Corbin says.

Langston smirks. "No, you can't. Because I have her child."

Corbin laughs. "So sure you have the correct child? And even if you do, you're willing to let an innocent child die? Even if she did love you, she'd never forgive you for letting a child die."

Langston sucks in a breath, and then his eyes fall to Maxwell, who nods, telling Langston to surrender. Langston still doesn't look at me.

Killer, put the gun down before you ruin everything.

Finally, Langston looks at me. For a second, I let a moment of truth fill my eyes.

Trust me.

His eyes glide side to side over mine, and I know he got the simple message, but he's searching for more—the reason I'm doing this.

His gun drops to the floor.

There's silence for a split second, then all of Corbin's men have Langston at gunpoint.

"You can stop pointing that thing at me, now," I say to Maxwell.

He doesn't lower his gun. He looks to Corbin for permission.

"Tell Maxwell to lower the gun or I won't fuck you. And I won't give you the treasure."

Corbin looks at me curiously. "There are almost thirty men in this room, all who work for me. If I want to fuck you, I'll fuck you. If I want the treasure, you'll give it to me. You have no power here. My brother will do as I say."

I shake my head. "You forget—I know who you are, Corbin. You're just like Waylon. You want me to want you willingly. You want me to offer myself up on a platter to you. Force me, and you're no more of a man than any other monster on the street. You don't have any power."

Corbin nods, and Maxwell lowers the gun. Apparently Corbin and Waylon's other brother didn't actually die—it's Maxwell.

A sick idea forms in my head. I want Corbin to trust me. If he does, he won't send his men to follow me when I go and get the treasure. I'll be able to finish the job on my own with Langston.

I could give up the whole ruse and fuck a random man on the street to betray Langston, but that only serves one purpose.

I walk up to Corbin, still completely naked. I wrap my arms around his neck and tug on his bottom lip roughly.

He growls.

And then, I whisper my filthy plan into his head. A cruel plan that is going to end Langston and set him free once and for all.

He'll hate me, forever.

He'll want to kill me and, this time, he might actually do it.

Most importantly, it will ensure I have the strength to finish off my own soul.

CHAPTER 24

LANGSTON

Liesel Dunn is a huntress.

She's always hunting, always searching.

And because of that, she's always been the enemy.

But now she's my wife.

I thought she was my friend. I thought that me taking care of her kid would have meant something to her. That our relationship, if not a real marriage, was at least sacred because I'm raising her son.

But everything I ever think when it comes to Liesel is a lie. *Why should this be any different?*

Who is she lying to, though?

Me? Probably.

Corbin? Definitely.

Herself? Absolutely.

Liesel is hiding huge secrets. She's hiding her very soul. I wish I knew if this wicked woman before me, playing her games, is the real Liesel or the one I had back in my bed a few hours before.

She's playing games with all of us. I don't see fear when I look into her eyes. I see a badass woman completely in control. A woman capable of burning this entire house to the ground, destroying us all.

I made a mistake trying to save her. She's more than capable of saving herself, and I lost my element of surprise. My skin is crawling from the way both Corbin and Liesel are looking at me right now—a failed protector.

Liesel is still standing naked in the center of a room filled with disgusting men. They devour her with their eyes, imagining filthy, vile things they want to do to her.

"We're going to play a little game," Corbin says, glaring at me.

I still have a dozen guns pointed at my head, so I don't move. I won't until I have a better plan, anyway.

"Langston, hold Liesel's arms behind her back," he continues.

Feeling any part of Liesel in my arms right now is going to heal my heart while simultaneously stir a storm that will wreck us. I don't think too hard about why he wants me to hold Liesel's arms behind her back, I just do.

A spark surges from her to me when I touch her first wrist. When I grab the second, I feel grounded again for the first time since I married her. My whole world came crashing down at me all at once at the single touch of her soft skin.

I hold her arms firmly behind her back, pulling her back to my front. No matter what happens here, she's mine.

Corbin grins at my reaction. "Since you already know I can't kill either of you until after you retrieve the treasure, I will have to resort to a different kind of threat for you, Langston. A game Liesel already agreed to play. You will hold her arms back so I can do whatever I want to her body. You will ensure that she obeys my commands. And if you let go, if you try and save her in any way, I will slice through her skin."

Jesus, it was bad enough when I had to watch her throw herself at him while hiding behind the couch. Now I have to hold her while he fucks her.

Maxwell gives me a look to say, "*See, I told you to stay put.*"

I roll my eyes at him and then focus on how I'm going to survive this.

"We can still fight our way out of this," I whisper into Liesel's hair.

"I don't want to. I like sex. I like to fuck handsome, powerful men." Her words sound so strong, so sure.

"I don't believe you," I whisper back, trying to see if she's lying or not.

"That's why I wanted you to play, so you can see first hand how much you can't tame me. I don't care if you are my husband."

Corbin sits back in his chair as he grips his cock in his hand.

"Bring her here," he says.

I quickly scan to find every exit and count every man blocking each one.

"Husband, bring me forward so I can suck Corbin's cock," Liesel says seductively.

She wants him. I can feel her aching need pulsing through her. She doesn't have a good relationship with sex. Sometimes she controls it; other times, it controls her. She never thought she'd get married, and ours is a marriage of circumstance, not reality. I shouldn't fault her for wanting another man's cock—even that of the enemy.

Slowly, I push her forward until we are standing in front of Corbin.

"Lower," Liesel hums before licking her lips.

I can't watch, and yet I can't not watch.

I push her onto her knees, as I stand over her, holding her arms back. At least I can keep her from touching him with her hands. At least I control one tiny part of this.

"I can't reach, hubby."

I growl as I push too hard, and her lips come crashing down on top of Corbin's cock.

This has to be a nightmare. This can't be happening.

I hear her gag on his cock as I pushed too far, but the sound quickly changes to moaning like she can't get enough.

I can't do this. I pull her off his cock, and yank her back.

Corbin's eyes shoot to me in an angry glare.

He snaps his fingers, and all his men descend on us. Arms yank Liesel from me and drag her toward Corbin while I'm held back.

Corbin twirls his knife around, and before I can blink, he slices it across her left breast.

"No!" I yell in complete shock.

She doesn't make a sound. She's strong, good with pain, but that had to hurt.

"Now, are you ready to behave?" Corbin asks me.

"Yes," I say through gritted teeth. I'll do anything to touch her again, to know that she's okay. Her back is currently to me as she stares at Corbin. I have to have her in my arms again.

The men release me, and I run to her, grabbing her cheeks and making her look up at me. All I see is hate.

She hates me.

All I do is hurt her.

I release her cheeks.

"Please resume holding her arms and hair while she sucks my cock," Corbin says.

I gather her hair in a ponytail with one hand, while the other grabs her wrists and holds them back. This is about protecting her, ensuring he doesn't spill any more of her blood.

I hold her head to his cock and watch as she sucks him, moaning with each head bob up and down. Over and over I watch, until my own eyes begin to water from this terrifying scene.

The room is quiet except for the sounds of her saliva and tongue licking over his length.

He grunts, and he's coming down her throat.

It's almost over.

I hear her swallow his cum, and I about lose it again. But I see drops of blood soaking the floor near my feet and I remember the price of me stopping this.

Finally, Liesel pulls her head back.

It's finished.

Corbin leans forward with a smile on his face like she just blew his world.

"You said I'm just like my brother. That I wanted you to come to me willingly, Liesel." He licks his lips. "In some ways, I'm like him, but there is something I enjoy more than a woman willingly submitting to me—revenge."

He snaps his fingers, and two men approach. Each takes one of her legs and lifts her up.

Shit.

I feel her body tense as I still grip her arms, now holding her torso up in the air. I feel a pull of her body to mine.

Corbin stands as the two men pull her legs apart.

I can't do this, but I don't know how to get us out of this. I have to find a way, watching her suck his cock was enough.

I don't know if the tense feeling I'm getting from her is real or if I'm imagining it. I don't know if she's begging me to save her or desperate for him to sink his cock inside her.

As Corbin tugs on her legs, she feels more like mine than his. *She's still mine.*

No matter what pain she puts me through.

No matter the agony.

No matter how many men she chooses over me, my heart is still hers. And hers still beats for me.

I don't know how to get her out of here safely, but I can take away her fear until then.

I find the spot on her neck—a pressure point used to put people to sleep, and I press my thumb against it. It takes a few minutes for it to work, and I don't know if I have that kind of time.

She squirms in my arms but tries to keep a composed face. At least, that's how my mind has morphed this situation.

"Trust me," I whisper.

I'm not sure she hears me. She continues to tense and then relaxes in my grip until she suddenly goes limp, falling into a heavy sleep.

I take a deep breath, finally able to breathe now that I've protected her consciousness from the pain. Now, to protect her body.

I'm going to have her words begging for him, her mouth willingly sucking him, in my head forever. And yet, I still fucking love her. Love is a strange thing I've yet to fully understand, but I do know that by the time we leave here, everyone in this room will know she's mine.

CHAPTER 25

LIESEL

I'm drenched in sweat as my body bounces up and down.

What's happening?

Where am I?

I open my eyes, feeling the weight of my body get tossed around in a leather seat. I'm in the backseat of a car, I realize when I see buildings flicker by out my window. I'm wearing my shorts and tank top again.

My eyes snap to the driver's seat, expecting to see Corbin, Maxwell, or any of their men.

"Langston?" I croak out, my throat dry and scratchy.

He doesn't turn around to look at me, but his shoulders tense, and I know he heard me speak.

I play through everything I remember.

Purposefully seducing Corbin.

Sucking his dick with Langston holding my arms. The connection I felt to Langston in that moment, making it easier for me to surrender myself to the cause.

And then Corbin approaching me, ready to tear me apart.

I remember feeling fear for the first time. But then I felt Langston holding onto me, and it didn't matter who was about to fuck me; all that mattered was my connection to him.

And then blackness.

I have no memory after that.

Did Corbin fuck me?

I look to Langston and around the car. There is no one else here in the car with us. I slowly sit up and look behind us, but I don't see anyone following us either.

Or did Langston burn all those motherfuckers to the ground?

The latter is more likely, but damn, do I feel sore and queasy. It doesn't matter either way. Sex with a man who isn't Langston is meaningless. Other men can do what they want to me, but I only belong to Langston.

"What happened?" I ask tentatively.

Once again, Langston doesn't answer. He doesn't turn around. His eyes don't so much as flicker in my direction. But the vein on the side of his neck bulges, and his grip on the steering wheel tightens as he makes a right turn.

Clearly, I won't be getting any answers from Langston, not that I deserve them. I destroyed a good thing he had going with Phoenix, and then I betrayed our marriage within the first forty-eight hours. I don't even think it's the betraying our marriage part that he's pissed about. The destroying our friendship and not trusting him part—that's what infuriates him.

I purse my lips and breathe out slowly.

I succeeded. I betrayed and hurt him. Now we can get the next clue. We can get one step closer to saving Atlas—that's what I have to focus on.

I assume Langston is driving us to the next location to get the next clue. I told Langston the exact address earlier, so I don't ask where we are going.

I just try to focus on my breathing and soothing the rattle in my belly, but I fail.

"Pull over," I say suddenly.

Langston doesn't listen, and I don't have time to argue with him.

I throw the door open just as the contents of my stomach come up.

"Jesus," Langston curses as he pulls the car to a stop.

I don't pay attention to what he's doing as acid expels from my stomach. I continue until I'm dry heaving. Even when there is nothing left in my stomach, my muscles continue to rid my body of all the shit I've been through.

"Here," Langston says. He's standing outside the car, just outside the spray of vomit on the ground.

I don't have the strength to look up. I barely have the strength to lift my hand to take whatever he is offering me.

A napkin.

I cling to it as I try to wipe my mouth.

Langston grumbles something I can't make out, and then he gently lifts my head up, takes the napkin from my hand and wipes my mouth. Then he lifts a bottle of water to my lips.

"Drink."

I do, but the second the water hits my stomach, I start heaving again.

Langston pulls my hair back as I dry heave this time. When I finish, he once again wipes my mouth but doesn't offer me water.

He looks at me curiously but doesn't speak.

When it looks like I've finally finished, he lifts my feet back into the car, then does my seatbelt before climbing back into the front seat to continue driving us.

My eyes water, not from the lack of food or pain in my stomach, but from the way Langston still took care of me even though he can't stand to talk or look at me.

He truly hates me, and this time, I won't be doing anything to change his mind on the matter.

A tear rolls down my cheek as I hug myself in the back seat. My life is truly cruel—to give me a man I could love and then rip him away from me so quickly.

Langston stops the car on the edge of town, parking it along the side of the round. He steps out and opens the door for me, offering his hand to help me out, but I can't take it. I have to start getting used to not depending on him.

I climb out on my own. Langston doesn't talk to me, look at me.

We walk in silence in the direction of the desert, down a path to a small house that sits on the furthest edge of town.

When we reach the house, Langston knocks, and we wait in silence until a middle-aged woman opens the door. Her hair is dark and long, and she wears a long tan dress. She looks between us and then motions for us to come inside.

It appears that Diego has told her to expect us because she doesn't ask who we are or why we are here.

"Sit," she commands as we enter a living area containing four chairs.

Langston and I both sit as the woman heads into her kitchen and returns with a cup of tea for each of us.

She doesn't speak, and I'm beginning to get used to the silence. After what I've done, no one will ever want to speak to me again. She looks back and forth between us, her eyes judging us.

"My name is Ramla. Please, drink your tea."

We both drink, hesitantly, like the tea is poisoned with a truth serum or worse. I brace myself for getting sick again, but the tea soothes the ache in my belly, and I'm able to keep it down. Not only am I able to keep it down, but the tea rejuvenates me and makes me feel more like myself.

Ramla continues to study us like she's looking for answers in the way we drink our tea.

"You did it," she says to me. It's not a question, it's a statement, but I nod my head in shame anyway, knowing she's referencing my betrayal of Langston.

Langston looks at me for the first time, frowning like he doesn't understand. I'm not going to tell him now; the damage is done. We need to get the clue and move on with our lives.

She looks to Langston. "I need you to come with me."

I frown, afraid of what is going to happen. I had to betray him, *what will he have to do to me?*

Hurt me?

Sell me?

Kill me?

There is no telling what my father's twisted game will require next. If we could bury the treasure forever with my death, then I'd kill myself. But it would only cause everyone to shift their focus to my child, thinking he can still find the money they desire.

Langston stands. He looks at me one last time, and then he follows the woman out of the room. I'm left behind to drink my tea and hope for forgiveness.

CHAPTER 26

LANGSTON

How can I want to wring Liesel's neck at the same time I want to worship at her feet?

Liesel is hiding something from me, and I think I know what it is. I can't think about it too much, though. Right now, I need to focus on the task at hand. Whatever Liesel had to do before she left the house in Peru really tore her up. Something changed in her after that. I need to focus so that I'm prepared for what awaits me.

"Sit," Ramla says, pointing to a chair at her small dining room table.

I sit, and she brings me more tea.

I politely drink the stuff even though I don't like the taste. I have no idea what awaits me. No idea what task I'm going to have to do.

"Tell me everything you are feeling," she says.

I frown. I wasn't expecting that.

"Um…" I rub the back of my head. "I'm feeling confused, tired, angry, sad, frustrated." *Horny*—I don't say the last one.

She nods and gives me an encouraging smile as if I should say more.

But what should I say? I don't know what answer she's looking for or why this turned into a therapy session.

"I'm feeling hopeless, lonely, lost, heartbroken, miserable."

"Liesel hurt you."

I nod; she has no idea how much.

"Do you want to divorce her?" she asks.

"No," I say automatically. I want the opposite of a divorce. I want Liesel to be bound to me forever.

She doesn't react to my answer. I don't know if I gave the correct answer or the wrong one.

"Do you hate her?"

"Yes, but—" I cut myself off; I can't finish that sentence out loud.

She nods as if she understands.

"Do you forgive her?"

I blink at her, realization hitting me like a bus all at once. Liesel didn't do something to get a clue in Peru. She had to do something in order to earn this one. She had to hurt me, be unfaithful to me, break me, and she did.

"Yes." I forgive her. I already did before I even knew why she did it. That's why I was so frustrated with her—as much as I keep trying to hate her, I can't.

Ramla gives me a slow smile, before reaching into her pocket and sliding an envelope toward me on the table.

I put my hand on the envelope and slide it toward me.

"Be careful. There is a lot more darkness and danger coming your way. More tests to prove that your love can endure anything. Don't lose sight of what's important on the way to riches," she says.

"Thank you," I say as I tuck the envelope into my pocket before standing to return to Liesel.

She's still sitting in the same chair where I left her, sipping her tea like it's the only thing keeping her alive, which is probably true. I don't see any signs that she vomited again, so hopefully, she's starting to feel better.

She looks up at me with giant, expressive eyes screaming of her shame and fear.

Oh, my huntress, you have no idea how much I'm still yours. How I'll always be yours.

I reach down, and she flinches.

I deserve that after how I've treated her. She doesn't even realize that all I want to do is hold her hand.

I try again, this time making my intentions more clear as I take her hand.

"Did you get what we need?" she asks, looking behind me for Ramla.

"Yes," I say, and then I lead her out back to the car parked on the side of the street. I put her in the passenger seat next to me before hopping into the driver's seat and driving us away. I don't know where I'm heading, just that I need a safe place where we can talk.

Thankfully, Liesel doesn't talk, and she no longer seems sick—the pink has returned to her cheeks, and her eyes no longer look hollow as I drive.

I don't know how long I've been driving or why I stop, but it feels like the right place. There are no cars around, no people, just what looks to be some Egyptian ruins. Nothing big or grand like some of the more well-known places, but a few stones and an archway.

I climb out of the car and take Liesel's hand once again and lead her into the ruins.

"Sorry, maybe I should have taken you somewhere to get some food," I say, realizing my mistake.

She shakes her head. "I'm not hungry."

I open my mouth to say the words I'm desperate to say—*I love you*. But I snap my mouth shut again, knowing those words will just make everything worse. Instead, I say the next best thing.

"I forgive you, not that there is anything to forgive."

She gasps and blinks rapidly, trying to pull her hand free of mine. "You can't."

"I do. That's why I was so upset, not at you, at myself for wanting you no matter how much you hurt me."

She steps back.

I step into her space, my predatory stare boring into her. "But there was nothing to forgive, was there? You were told to hurt me. That was the only way we would get the next clue."

A tear slips from her eye as she nods. "Yes." She takes a deep breath. "I'm sorry."

I swipe the tear off her cheek. "You have nothing to be sorry for. You were given a task, and you did it. If the roles were reversed, I would have done the same thing."

"But I chose Corbin...I chose the worst thing I could think of to hurt you."

I shake my head. "You made the best out of a bad situation. Corbin trusts you now. He thinks you hate me, that you will do anything he asks just to ruin me."

"But I almost got us killed. I put you through so much pain. I made you watch while he fucked me."

"No!" my voice booms, halting her ramble.

I pull her into my arms, until our bodies are pressed together. "I didn't let Corbin fuck you. I couldn't. Maxwell couldn't either. We fought our way out of there."

"Maxwell helped you?"

"Turns out your instincts were right. I'm pretty sure Maxwell is a good guy."

"Where is he?"

"Hiding, Corbin won't forgive his brother easily. But you don't have to worry about Corbin hurting the child he has; he thinks you are going to betray me to help him. You played your role well."

"Thank you for saving me. It wouldn't have mattered to me if he fucked me—I'm yours either way. But thank you," she says.

I tuck a strand of her hair behind her ear.

"Don't fucking thank me for claiming what's mine."

Then I tilt her head back and kiss her. We are standing in the middle of ancient ruins, in the middle of the desert, with no one around, and it feels like we are on top of the world. This kiss says *I'm sorry*, *you're forgiven*, and *I love you* more than any words ever could.

I don't know how I'm ever going to stop kissing her, but before I have to worry about that, I feel wetness hit my lips. Her tears have rolled down her cheeks and landed on both of our lips.

"What's wrong?" I ask.

"You were supposed to hate me."

I frown, not understanding.

"Promise me you hate me." She shakes me, demanding for me to hate her.

"I hate you," I lie. It's one of the most obvious lies I've ever said. I don't hate her. There is nothing that could make me hate her. *Nothing*.

LIESEL

I'm going to end up hurting Langston worse now. If he can't hate me for what I've done, then he's never going to hate me. In fact, there's a chance he loves me. That would be the thing that ends up killing him.

"Show me how much you hate me," I say.

"I hate you so much."

He grabs my thighs and lifts me up until my legs are around his waist as he kisses my lips again, stealing my breath, my pain, my fear. He consumes everything as his tongue bursts between my lips, commanding everything. My hands grip his head as he carries me toward a stone wall with hieroglyphics on the side.

"I hate you so much that I want to fuck you until your body realizes my cock is the only cock for you."

His eyes sear into mine, and I know he's serious, just not about the hate you part. He's saying one thing, but it's almost as if the way he says *hate* he means *love*.

My ass hits the top of the broken wall as he moves between my legs. I've never wanted or needed him more than I do right now. I need him to heal the chasm between us. I need to know that all the pain we endured and are going to endure is worth it.

His hand slides up my stomach underneath my shirt until he finds the point of a nipple. He squeezes, sending delicious currents through my body, familiar wetness spreading between my legs at the single touch. He knows my body better than I know it myself.

"I hate you more than I hate my father," he says.

I love you more than I hate my father.

I grab his shirt, lifting it off his body and throwing it down onto the sand. He frantically does the same with my tank top. He looks over my naked top half before he leans down and takes one of my nipples in his mouth, biting down hard enough to punish me for letting other men look at my body, touch my body.

"I hate you more than I hated Waylon," I say.

I love you more than I hated Waylon.

He growls at my words and kisses hungrily down my stomach as he undoes my shorts.

My hands find the front of his pants, and I start undoing them. I shove them down hard at the same time he rips my shorts from my body.

"I hate you more than I hate Corbin for touching you," he says.

I love you more than I hate Corbin for touching you.

And then he storms inside me in one long thrust, claiming every inch of my pussy. He doesn't stop to sheath himself with a condom. He doesn't stop to see if I'm ready. He just claims me.

"Killer!" I scream for the whole world to hear. A single word claims him as mine, just like he did me with his thrust.

In our world, getting married isn't enough. Loving someone isn't enough. The only way to keep someone is to do it over and over and over.

He fucks me like an animal. I claw at him like a raven ripping apart its food.

Every thrust inside me is deep, all the way to my cervix. He relentlessly pounds into me, and I want it all.

Every time I fuck Langston, I think it could be the last, and this time is no different. I desperately cling to every moment for as long as I can.

We fuck frantically like we are running out of time to be together.

We are. We could have seconds, minutes, days, weeks, years. Our time together is ending, just as it's finally beginning.

I try to hold off my orgasm, not ready for this time to end, but I can't.

"Langston!" I yell as I come undone. I lose all of my senses as the universe shatters around me.

I don't know if Langston comes or not until I come back down to earth. I smile at his grin and feel his cum dripping down my thigh.

I shiver, and he cradles me in his arms as we sink to the sand, both of us still naked as we lean into each other's arms against the ancient stones.

"I have a question for you," I say.

"Same. You go first." Langston strokes my hair as I lean my head on his shoulder.

"Why did you want to kill me?"

He stiffens. "Atlas was really sick."

"What?" I interrupt him.

He frowns as his thumb strokes my face. "He *was* sick. He isn't anymore."

I exhale.

"His adoptive parents at the time contacted you for help. They didn't have the money or resources to get him help. And if he was going to die, they thought you might want to say goodbye."

I scrunch my nose, completely confused by why he would want to kill me. But I'm also heartbroken that Atlas was so ill.

"They said you refused them. You refused them money. You refused to help with treatment. You refused to see him."

I swallow the pain.

"I hated you for it, hated you for leaving your son to die." He pauses. "But looking at you now, I'm not sure how much I know is true."

I blink back tears. He hated me because he thought I would just let my son die. I regret asking my question now, but I need to know what his question is.

"What was your question?"

His thumb traces the outline of my collarbone. "Well, now, I have two. One is, did you know that Atlas was sick? And two..." I can hear the pain and frustration in his voice. "Are you pregnant now?"

I can understand why he's conflicted if he thinks I would abandon my son; he's not sure he wants me to be pregnant now. And yet, he's not sure any of it is true. If it's not true, he's hated me and wanted me dead this long all for nothing.

I don't need a test to tell me if I'm pregnant or not.

I know how I should answer about whether or not I knew Atlas was sick and in trouble.

One will be the truth. The other will be a lie. Both will hurt him.

CHAPTER 28

LANGSTON

Waiting for her to answers seems like a millennium.

I suspect she might be pregnant, although, I don't know when she would have had time to take a pregnancy test, so it's really not a fair question. But she's been throwing up, and I've fucked her numerous times now without a condom or any other form of protection. It's a real possibility.

It's also a possibility that she just has food poisoning or hasn't eaten in a while and got motion sickness.

Still, she's constantly hiding things from me, and I want to know if I'm about to become a father again.

Liesel looks stunned sitting in my lap, like I just spilled a world of secrets onto her lap. That's why I'm not worried about hating her anymore. I will never hate her again. She didn't know about Atlas—that much I'm certain about.

"If you need me to take you to a pharmacy to get a pregnancy test, I can," I offer.

She shakes her head. "No, I already know."

My heart stops.

I love kids. This is the moment I become a father, again. And this time, I'll get to be there every step of the way.

She looks up at me like she knows she's about to break my heart. "I'm not pregnant."

My heart rattles around in my chest, not believing her words. But before I can call her out for lying, she continues.

"And I knew." She runs her hands through her hair in anguish. "I knew there was no way I could save him. No money in the world would be enough for his treatments. And me being in his life would only cause him to be hunted by my enemies, so I stayed away. I thought the kind thing to do was to let him die."

I stand to my feet, throwing her to the ground. "You were wrong. Atlas could've been saved. He's well now because I did what it took to save him. I found a treatment when there was none. I didn't give up on him."

Tears roll down her cheeks as my fury explodes at her.

How could she be so cruel? So heartless?

I'm steaming. I can't look at her. I march around the grounds, still naked, trying to reconcile everything I know about her.

Liesel is manipulative. She's controlling. And she has one mission in her life. She wouldn't let us give up on a child who wasn't even hers; there is no way she would have given up on Atlas, her own flesh and blood.

Something doesn't add up.

She wants me to hate her.

She's trying to force me into hating her.

It's not going to work, not this time.

I march back toward her, where she's crumpled into a naked, broken ball on the ground. Sand sticks to her skin. She looks hopeless and in pain.

Without a word, I scoop her back into my arms. She tries to fight me, tries to get me to let her go. I don't.

"What are you doing?"

"I'm putting you back in the car, driving you to a hotel room where I'm going to clean you off, fuck some sense into you, and then hate you for the rest of my life!"

Her eyes narrow, looking up at me in complete confusion. She knows every time I've said the word hate, I mean the word love. It's a word I can never speak out loud, but it doesn't stop me from feeling it.

"I hate you, too," she whispers.

Her head falls against my chest, relenting to me. She's given up trying to protect me by getting me to hate her. I know a world of suffering awaits us, a pain like neither of us have ever felt before. But that's not going to stop me from loving her.

I kick up our clothes from the ground with my hand before carrying her back to the car. I pull my shirt down over her body and slip my jeans back on before I start driving us to the nearest hotel room I can find.

The hotel room isn't much, but we just need some place to clean up, fuck, and regroup. We can't stay here; it's not safe.

I carry her inside the room and examine it. It isn't much more than four walls, a bed, a toilet, and a hose hanging from the ceiling that can be used as a shower, but it will do.

I carry her straight to the shower, strip her shirt off, remove my pants, and then turn on the water. It's freezing cold, as I expected, but we are both in too much pain to feel it.

I claim her mouth with mine, once again possessing her.

"Your pain is mine; stop hiding it from me," I say, kissing her under the stream.

"It's not my pain I'm worried about."

"Stop suffering because you're afraid to hurt me. Stop lying and hurting me now to prevent future pain. I want the truth, not the lies."

She shakes her head. "You don't know what you're saying."

"I'm saying I'm yours as much as you are mine. I'm saying I'll hate you forever, and nothing you say can change that."

I kiss down her body, stopping at her stomach that looks swollen to me, but it's probably my imagination. She said she isn't pregnant.

But she lied—*about hurting Atlas or about being pregnant or both?*

Liesel grabs my arms, shaking me fiercely under the water. "Hate me! Hate me for real. I need it to be real." She bites down on my bottom lip, then slaps me. She's flailing desperately for me to truly hate her. She's purposefully trying to be cruel. But I see her clearly for the first time. I may not know all of her secrets, but I know her heart. Everything she's ever done is to protect her son.

She's the opposite of cruel. She is beauty and strength and all good things in the world. I'm the stupid idiot who ever thought differently of her. I just don't know why she's so desperate to add me to the list of people she wants to protect. *Why does she think me loving her is going to hurt me?*

I decide we aren't leaving this room until she gives me an answer.

My phone starts buzzing in my pocket.

Strange.

I don't answer. I need her. I need answers.

It eventually stops buzzing, only to start right back up again.

I groan and grab a nearby towel before picking up my phone. It's an unknown number; a tactic Beckett would use to contact me.

"Hello?" I answer as soon as I see the number.

"I fucked up," Beckett says.

"What happened? Are the kids…?" Safe? Alive? Dead? I can't think any of the words out loud. But the mention of the kids has Liesel scrambling out of the shower, dripping wet with a towel and barreling toward me.

I put the phone on speaker so we can both hear.

"Phoenix took Rose and—" Beckett says.

"Okay? She's her mother. Just call her and tell her to come back to the compound where it's safe," I say.

"No, I mean she kidnapped her," Beckett says.

Liesel and I trade stares. "She's her mother. She can't kidnap her."

"Well, she did. She said she was just taking Rose downstairs to get ice cream. But they are both gone, and she left a note."

"What does the note say?"

"To give her the treasure or else she'll kill Rose," Beckett says.

I glance at Liesel, whose eyes are spinning. Yet again, she knows something she isn't telling me.

"Where is Atlas?" I ask.

"Maxwell took him. I tried to fight him off, but I wasn't strong enough."

"Fuck."

I throw the phone down in frustration, watching it shatter into a billion pieces.

Liesel sinks to the floor.

"They're all working together," Liesel says suddenly.

"What?"

She comes out of her daze and looks up at me. "They are all working together. Corbin, Maxwell, and Phoenix. Corbin played the bad guy, Maxwell our friend, and Phoenix the loving mother."

She stands up suddenly. "Did you ever figure out why you and Phoenix weren't legally married?"

I shake my head.

"I don't think she's my cousin. I don't think she's my blood. I think you weren't married because her last name isn't actually Dunn, it's Brown, same as Waylon. Same as Corbin. Same as Maxwell."

I rack my brain, but her theory makes sense.

"What else?" I ask, knowing she has more.

"The letter I got; it said something crazy. Something I didn't think was possible."

"What?" I beg frantically.

"You were at the hospital the day Atlas was born."

I nod. "I wish I had told you, and I could have held your hand when you went into surgery. I could have held you when you cried, but I was too angry with you. I was always furious with you because you never chose me."

She frowns. "I was pregnant with triplets."

My eyes widen.

"The day I gave birth to Atlas, I thought I lost the other two. That's what the nurses said, but the letter I got from Corbin said differently. He said I had three kids, and he'd have all three soon enough. I thought he was bluffing, but now I'm not so sure. You didn't take my kids and hide them away?"

I shake my head.

"You think all three survived?"

"Yes, and I think they have all three," she says in disbelief.

"Who are the three?"

"Maxwell has Atlas, who we both already know is mine. Corbin has

Declan, according to his letter. Waylon's DNA proof all these years wasn't proof of Atlas, it was proof of Declan, I just didn't know it. And Phoenix has Rose."

"This doesn't make any sense, Rose is Phoenix's and mine," I say.

"Phoenix lied to you, Langston. She said she had your child, when really she had mine and wanted to keep you close to control us both. I think you've known for a long time. I suspected it when I got the letter, but I didn't want to hurt you. I didn't want to take away a biological kid from you because I know how that feels. But Atlas, Declan, and Rose are my kids. Somehow, they all survived."

I collapse on the bed in shock, as I come to so many realizations at once.

Finally, I lift my head and look at Liesel. "And now they have them all."

DANGEROUS LIES

PROLOGUE
LIESEL

I always knew that falling in love was dangerous.

I could fall in love with the wrong person.

A monster.

Criminal.

Devil.

A man who could hurt me.

Rape me.

Ruin me.

That was always my biggest fear—that I would fall in love with a man who would hurt me, a man I couldn't escape. That I would love him even when I shouldn't. That my love for him would kill me.

It turns out, I didn't fall for the devil.

I fell for a good, compassionate man. A man with the biggest heart. A man who loves me as his equal. A man who loves my kids as his own.

I found a man who completes my heart—a man I want to spend the rest of my life with and beyond.

But falling in love with him was still dangerous.

And I don't know if we can survive our love.

CHAPTER 1

LIESEL

Beep, beep, beep.

An annoyingly high-pitched sound infiltrates the fog in my brain. I try to open my eyes, but my eyelids are too heavy. My legs feel numb, and my teeth chatter from the chill surging through my body.

Beep, beep, beep.

The sound continues, trying to pull me back to reality. I don't know what happened, but I do know that I don't want to return to reality. Whatever happened was bad. I may not have much of a heart left, but I have to protect it.

Stay asleep; life will be easier if you just sleep.

"Miss Dunn, can you open your eyes for me?" I hear a sweet voice say.

No!

It's a trap. I won't open my eyes.

I feel a hand running through my hair, brushing it out of my face before it lands on my cheek.

"You should open your eyes now. It's time," her voice is still sweet, yet firmer now.

I shake my head gently back and forth. "I'm scared."

Her hand moves down my body until she's gripping my hand. "I know. I'm going to be right here holding your hand the whole time, though. You won't have to face the truth alone."

The truth—that means something terrible did happen. It wasn't supposed to be this way. I wasn't supposed to be asleep when I gave birth. *What happened?*

"Open your eyes, sweetheart. Then we can talk. You still have time to decide."

Decide?

I've already made my decision. Nothing is going to change that.

"On the count of three," she says.

"One."

"Two."

I open my eyes before she gets to three. I don't like doing what I'm told.

"There you are." She smiles, still gripping my hand. "How are you feeling? Do you need more pain medicine?"

"I just need you to cut the crap and tell me what happened."

Her lips thin, and her smile drops, but she nods.

"You gave birth to a beautiful, healthy boy."

My eyes scan hers, waiting for her to say more. She said boy —singular.

"And the others?"

She shakes her head as a tear rolls down her cheek. "I'm so sorry. We lost them."

We.

There is no we.

She didn't have triplets. I did.

I failed.

I didn't provide a good enough home for them. I didn't eat healthily enough. Exercise enough. Take my vitamins. Reduce my anxiety. I didn't do enough.

I failed.

And now they are gone.

I want to scream, break things, explode into a million pieces.

My grief doesn't allow it. My grief streams down my face in

burning silent tears. Tears that pour down each cheek for each of the children I've lost.

My tears are the only external sign of my pain. Everything else I keep inside. The pain rages through my veins like branding fire until my heart can't pump the agony through any longer. It flees from my body to go with my children. I no longer have a heart. A soul. A purpose.

I'm nothing.

I know the woman is hugging me, trying to comfort me, but I don't feel her arms. I'm numb. I feel nothing anymore. I doubt I will ever feel anything ever again.

"The couple is here to adopt the boy," she says. Those words get through the pain.

She waits; I don't say anything.

"There is still time. You can still keep him. You'd make a great mother."

"No, I'd make a terrible mother." Even if I wouldn't, I won't bring a child into my world. He'd end up dead just like my other two children.

"Do you want to hold him before...?" she trails off.

I shake my head.

"Dear, I really think you'll regret not meeting him before you give him up."

My tears stop, and I push back out of her arms as the pain settles into my body. I might as well get used to it. This is my life now—an all-consuming amount of loss. Everywhere I go, I'll feel it. Nothing will take the pain away. Nothing.

"No! I don't want to hold him. I killed them! It's my fault they are dead. If I hold him, I'll just end up killing him too!"

I notice someone at the door, but then he's gone as soon as I get a glance. A lock of blonde hair is all I see as he walks away from me.

Good riddance.

He's the only one who could ease my pain right now. The only boy who would know the exact words to say. The only boy who could love me. And he can't do that—loving me is dangerous.

Plus, I want to feel all the pain. I don't want him to take it away. Not now, not ever.

. . .

THAT WHOLE STORY WAS A LIE.

The nurse lied to me!

All three of my children survived, not just one. They are all alive. I didn't fail. Langston overhearing that my children died was a lie. All of it.

The pain I've carried with me since that day was a lie.

I have three kids.

None of them are mine.

I didn't fail them that day, but I have now.

Atlas was taken by Maxwell.

Rose was taken by Phoenix.

Declan was taken by Corbin.

Three kids—all taken.

All because I didn't do something sooner. After seeing Atlas myself, I was sure that Corbin and Waylon claiming they had my child was a lie. They had to be bluffing. I knew the second I saw Atlas that he was mine.

Even though I saw the similarities between Rose and me when I saw her, I convinced myself that she was Langston's.

If I hadn't been so afraid, then maybe I could have prevented this. I could have done more to stop it.

I stare at Langston, who is still processing everything. He's basically been frozen in place, his eyes wide, his lips parted, his hair wild since he found out the truth. Rose isn't his child. I have three kids all gone.

I can't imagine how he's processing this.

For a moment, I thought he could have been the one telling me my children died the day they were born. I thought he hated me that much and wanted to punish me.

But despite all the lies we've told each other over the years, he wouldn't tell me that. When he realized Rose wasn't biologically his— it shocked him, hurt him. There is no hiding or faking the kind of pain that comes with losing a child.

If it wasn't Langston who was behind pretending my children died and hiding them from me, then who was it?

It seems important to find out.

But right now, I have more important things to worry about. I need to ensure Langston hasn't gone into shock and figure out a way to protect all three of my kids that are with three separate monsters. I have no idea if Langston is still willing to do this with me or not. Now that he realizes he actually has no biological children, he could just run—file for divorce and live his life. He has no loyalty to me.

In some ways, it might be better if he did. The longer he stays with me, the higher the possibility of him falling in love with me. Other than getting my children back, the next most important thing to me is ensuring he doesn't fall for me.

But what if he already has?

"Langston?" I speak tentatively.

He runs his hand through his hair and immediately snaps back out of his trance.

"Talk to me. What's going through your head?" I ask.

My heart skips waiting for his answer. Somehow this is more important than all the other words he's given me.

"We have three kids we have to get back."

There's that word again—*we*. We have three kids. He speaks about them as if they are his. I guess even though they are all biologically mine, he has a much closer relationship with at least two of them. They call him father. It's clear in his eyes and the words he uses that he won't let that change any time soon.

He grabs my neck and yanks me into his chest until I'm consumed with his smell—pine, sweat, sex—that's him. For a second, I can breathe again. *Would this have happened if, instead of walking away from my hospital room, he walked toward me? Would I have felt like I could breathe again? Like I could face another second of a day? Would I have kept enough of my heart to keep living instead of turning in a shell?*

"I hate you," he says.

I love you.

Fuck. Fuck!

He's not supposed to love me, and I'm not supposed to love him. I don't have a heart left to love him with, *right?*

Something is keeping him from saying the actual words, though, so instead of saying he loves me, he says he hates me. *Maybe he senses the fear in me? Maybe he thinks I'd run if he said he loves me? Maybe he's too stubborn to say the actual words?*

Whatever it is that is preventing him from saying the words I'll hold on to that for as long as I can. It doesn't actually change anything, but it makes me feel like we are safe for a few more minutes.

"I hate you more," I say back.

He smiles, knowing the truth of my words. That's what we do—we lie.

"What are we going to do?" I ask.

"We are going to get our kids back. We are going to get the damn treasure. And we are going to kill anyone who gets in our way."

He speaks his words as if it's already happened, without fear. He's not afraid of failing because it's not a possibility. We are going to get our kids back.

I, on the other hand, am not so sure.

"Hey," he lifts my chin as if sensing that I need comforting. "I'm not going to let anything happen to those kids—all three of them. I love them. They are mine as much as they are yours. I won't let anyone hurt them. We are going to get them back and then never let them out of sight again. Beckett won't be babysitting again; no one will. We'll homeschool them, do whatever it takes to keep them safe. I'm telling you the truth, huntress. Believe every word I'm telling you."

His lips lower, and he seals his promise to me with a kiss. Our lips touch only for a second, but with that kiss, he breathes new life into me.

"What do we do now?" I ask, my head spinning, trying to decide between getting the treasure to pay the ransom to get our kids back and going after them now before getting the treasure.

"Now, we get the crew together. We fight. We get the treasure, and we get our kids."

The crew—he means Enzo, Kai, Zeke, Siren, Beckett.

"Do you trust them after what they did?"

He nods. "I think we've punished them enough. We have three kids to keep safe, being kept in three separate locations. We need their help."

I don't want to trust anyone, not even them. Beckett failed to keep my kids safe. The others betrayed us and manipulated us to try and get us to like each other. But we need help, and they are the closest thing to family that we have.

Langston calls for a car, and then we are headed back to the airport. We are in our private plane in record time. I should ask Langston about the treasure, about what he found out about what we have to do next. But all I can think about is my kids and about what Langston said about Atlas being sick.

I have to choose my words carefully, so he doesn't know that I was lying. I had no idea that Atlas was sick and dying. If I did, of course, I would have done what I could to help him. Langston holding on to that little piece of hate might be the only thing that ends up saving him in the end, but I have to know what happened.

I'm lying against Langston's chest as the plane takeoffs. "Tell me about when Atlas was sick. How did you save him?"

CHAPTER 2

LANGSTON

I don't want to talk to her about Atlas being sick. Up until this point, it was the worst time of my life. I had her child, and he was dying. Terminal, the doctors said. I had to live with the fact that Liesel knew and did nothing.

But did she really know? The fear she feels about him now is real. I can't imagine she wouldn't have felt the same fear then if she had known. She would have tried to save him, just like I did.

Liesel lies to protect those she cares about. *So why is she lying to me?*

Right now isn't the time to get the truth from her.

I can't talk in great detail about Atlas. It will break me. Although, she deserves to hear a sliver of the truth even if she won't give it to me, so I say a single sentence and hope she reads into it.

"I went to the end of the world to find a cure for him."

She sits up, her eyes blinking as she soaks in my words, trying to decipher what I'm not saying. Her eyes light up, and her head tilts. She's smart—it took her less than three seconds to realize what I'm not saying.

"The cure that Siren and Zeke had. That's why you went after it? For Atlas?"

I nod.

I would have done anything for that boy. I'll continue to do anything for him.

"Thank you for everything, killer."

There is so much truth behind her words. But I didn't do it for her—I did it for him.

She takes my hand in hers, and then we think about the kids the rest of the flight. About Atlas and Rose, who were taken from us. About Declan, who neither of us has met. And about how together we will do whatever it takes to save them.

I glance at her stomach, and something stirs inside me. I have five lives to worry about—Atlas, Rose, Declan, Liesel, and the baby in her womb.

LIESEL AND I DROP HANDS AS WE WALK UP THE PORCH TO KAI AND Enzo's house. Sure, we are together. We're married. We are in this fight together. But we don't want anyone in the house to look at us as a couple. We don't want them to think they somehow were in the right to kidnap us and try to form a bond between us. Our bond has nothing to do with them. It has everything to do with us.

Liesel and I have always been a couple, even when we fought it, even when we hated each other, even when we were apart, even when we lost. It's always been us—even when being together means a lifetime of pain. There is no stopping us.

We give each other a knowing look before I open the door without knocking and step into the three-story mansion. We don't have to be holding each other's hand to gain strength from each other. We don't even have to be sharing the same oxygen. The strength we possess is from knowing that no matter how much we fuck up, lie, cheat, or kill, we are unstoppable together.

We don't even have to say we love each other for it to be true. We just always have.

Kai comes fluttering into the hallway. I'm sure her security system notified her of our arrival.

"Living room, now," I say, marching past her with Liesel right behind me.

Kai nods. She's not used to taking orders from other people, but if she wants to help, Liesel and I will be the ones in charge, not her.

We walk into the living room, where I find Enzo, Zeke, and Siren already on the couches. Siren's eyes are puffy, like she's been crying. Zeke rubs her back in slow circles, like that is somehow going to bring my kids back. Enzo sits sternly, completely lost in thought.

Then I spot Beckett walking in from the kitchen. He looks like a wreck. Puffy eyes, pale skin, a slumped curve of his spine as he walks. The pain he feels is immense—good. He had the most important job. I trusted him. He failed.

He doesn't apologize. He knows there is no use. There is nothing he can say that will bring my kids back.

Liesel walks over to him. I expect her to yell at him for failing. He deserves it. He deserves to be punched in the face and kicked in the balls. The suffering he's feeling is nothing compared to what Liesel and I are going through.

Liesel wraps her arms around him. "We'll get them back. It's not your fault. We should have known not to trust Phoenix or Maxwell. We'll get them back."

He rubs her back with his arm. "No, don't blame yourself. Blame me."

"We do," I say, answering for her.

She shoots me an angry glare.

"It's okay. I can take it. Hate me, not yourself," Beckett says.

She shakes her head and then pulls him into the living room. She chooses to sit next to him on the loveseat. Kai sits next to Enzo. I stay standing, looking down at them all.

"Tell me we already know where they took them. Tell me we already know where they are hidden. Tell me we already have eyes on them." I look between everyone sitting in this room moping, crying, and emotional. The only people who have the right to feel that way are Liesel and me; everyone else has a job to do.

"St. Kitts," Siren and Zeke say.

"Cancun," Kai and Enzo say.

"Atlanta," Beckett says.

I let out a breath. Thank god for them. They may have pissed me off and betrayed us before, but damn do they know how to do their jobs when we need them to.

I look to Liesel, who looks to be near tears at their answers. The question is, *who do we go with?* There are only two of us, and we have three kids to save. *How do we choose?*

"Good. Get a team and plan together to go with you. I want each of you to have a detailed plan in half an hour, then we move."

I storm out onto the back deck, suddenly needing air to breathe as I realize I'm one person, and I can't go after three kids myself at the same time. I'm not superman. I have to trust that others can do their jobs.

I hear the sliding door open and then close, and I know Liesel is standing out on the deck with me.

"How do we decide?" I ask her.

She steps next to me and then grips the railing like her life depends on it. She doesn't answer right away. *How could she? How do you choose between children?*

"We don't," she finally says.

"What?"

"We let our friends go. We let them do their best. And then we go help the one who fails."

The ocean crashes hard against the shoreline at her words. We both stare out at the sea, knowing that's the best plan. But it feels impossible to stay put when my kids are in danger.

My kids.

They will always be my kids. I don't care whose blood runs through their veins—they are mine. Just like the woman to my left, who is wearing my ring. She may have only married me because of a stupid quest, but I'm not giving her up.

I do know something that I can do while we wait to figure out which rescue team is going to need our help the most. I dig into my pocket and pull out the envelope that has the next task in it. I have to complete this task before we can head to Tokyo to get the final task and the location of the treasure. A treasure we can use to get the kids back if all else fails.

I open the envelop and pull out the note. Liesel notices me, but she's content to just stare at the ocean.

I read the note.

MAKE HER FALL IN LOVE WITH YOU SO DEEPLY THAT NOTHING CAN PULL you apart.

I READ THE WORDS TWICE THROUGH, TRYING TO ENSURE THAT I'M reading them correctly. Make my wife fall in love with me. I'm pretty sure she already is, even though she won't admit it. She won't say the damn words, not that I have either.

How do I prove we love each other so much that nothing will pull us apart? Especially if we won't even say the words?

I've spent my entire life hating her, and she hating me. Hating her is easier, but you can't hate someone without first loving them. The hate was more because we couldn't be together than because we truly hated each other.

This should be an easy task, but it won't be for so many reasons. Liesel is stubborn, and for whatever reason, she's scared to love me and for me to love her. She won't admit to loving me easily. Not only do I have to get her to admit it, but I have to be able to prove it to a stranger when we go to collect the next clue.

I fiddle with the edge of the crisp white paper before it slips through my hands. It dances high in the sky as the wind takes hold of it before dipping into the ocean.

Liesel and I both watch the piece of paper disappear into the water. Liesel could just as easily slip through my fingers.

Getting Liesel to truly love me is going to take everything I have. But that was my plan anyway from the second I said I do. There is no going back, not after she's mine. Fuck the consequences.

No—there are no consequences of her loving me. If Liesel gives me all of her love, I will protect it with everything I have. I will give her the world. I will kill any man or woman who stands against her. Being loved by her would be one of the greatest honors of my life.

I just can't love her in return. Not openly, not in the way she deserves.

The note didn't say that I need to love her, though. It just said that she needs to love me.

I can make her fall in love with me so hard that nothing will break us up. We can be a family once we get the kids back, along with the new edition that I feel in her womb.

"Do you know what you need to do?" Liesel asks, still not looking at me.

"Yes, I can do it easily."

"Good." She nods.

Get her to love me without falling completely in love myself, that shouldn't be too hard.

But I already know this is only half of the task. Last time she had to betray me, and I had to forgive her. So this time, I have to get her to fall for me, *but what will she have to do?*

CHAPTER 3

LIESEL

What did the note say?

I was dying to know as I watched it flutter into the ocean. Langston won't tell me, though. He can't tell me, just as I couldn't tell him that my mission was to betray him.

What pain is Langston going to have to inflict on me?

It won't be anything compared to the agony I'm feeling knowing all three of my children's lives are in danger.

Outside, rain starts as I stand in the living room hopelessly staring out a window, waiting for news. News that the teams have arrived at the locations, news that they've succeeded in getting through, news that my kids are safe.

I hate standing in Enzo and Kai's house doing nothing, but I know we need to wait. We need to be ready to go if one of them fails.

I hear Langston walking up behind me, but I don't turn around to face him. All I want is news that my kids are safe. Or news of which direction we should head—anything but doing nothing.

I count the raindrops as they run down the window. I grip the neck of my oversized white T-shirt, just needing something to grip onto.

I feel Langston's hand on my wrist, and he gently gets me to let go of my shirt before he laces his fingers with mine.

199

I go to pull away, not wanting to be with anyone right now, but he tugs me back. I finally glance at him. His pupils are dilated, his cheeks flushed, the vein in his neck is bulging, and his breathing is erratic.

"I'm just as scared to lose them as you are. We are in this together," he tugs me to him as his other hand strokes my back.

"I don't want to be comforted right now. I want to feel all the stress and anxiety. I failed them. I deserve to feel this way."

He shakes his head, obviously disagreeing, but he doesn't say anything. He doesn't let me go either.

"Let's eat."

I look at him like he's crazy. There is no way I can eat at a time like this.

"We need to have our strength if we have to go help. We are eating," he commands.

"No." There is no possible way I could eat right now.

He frowns. "Huntress, do you want to get your kids back?"

"Of course."

"Then eat."

"No, I'll just throw it up. I'm too nervous."

He narrows his eyes at me suspiciously, like he thinks I'm lying.

Finally, I yank my hand free of his grasp.

"Huntress," he says my name like he's begging me. "Trust me, if you want to do something to help the kids, then you need to spend time with me. Preferably eating, but we can also come up with something else to do if you don't want to eat."

I study him, trying to determine what he's not saying. My eyebrows jump up as I realize what he's not saying—this has to do with the note.

The note is the key to getting the treasure, which might be the only way we can get the kids back if our teams fail. *But what did the note say? What does he have to do?*

"Trust me, huntress. I won't hurt you," Langston says, brushing my hair off my shoulder as he leans in and tenderly kisses my neck. Shivers tingle down my body at the soft touch. It feels wrong to feel anything remotely near pleasant when my kids are in danger.

"It's not wrong to feel connected to me right now. It's not wrong to feel good when the world has turned bad. Don't ever feel guilty for feeling something for me, no matter what is going on, no matter who is in danger."

"All I feel for you is hate," I say softly as my thumb plays with the ring on my finger. The ring has started to disintegrate since it's made of stems and thorns.

Langston wraps his arms around me from behind and pulls me into a hug. "Have dinner with me."

I close my eyes as I lean against his hard chest, feeling calmer with his arms around me. I nod against him even though my stomach churns at the thought of food.

Langston leads me out onto the deck, and I gasp at the sight. The small circular table has a white table cloth, a bouquet of fresh flowers, two lit candles, two plates filled with food, and two wine glasses filled with red wine.

"Is someone else here with us? I thought Kai sent all the staff away so we could be alone?"

"She did. I did this; you were in such a trance you didn't notice."

He leads me over to the chair that has a better view of the ocean, pulls the chair out, and then waits until I sit. He's being such a gentleman. It's strange.

I smile weakly at him as he takes his seat across from me.

He flashes me a much more sincere smile in return. His actually reaches his eyes. It's meant to soothe my nerves, but it just makes me more anxious as I try to guess what it is he's going to have to do to me. *Betray me? Hurt me? Ruin me?*

He's the only man who has the power to do any of those things— the only person in the world outside of my kids who can hurt me.

His smile drops when he reads my mood, or maybe he can actually read my thoughts.

"I'm not going to hurt you," he says.

"You don't always get a say in whom you hurt."

Our eyes lock for a second in the pain that is our world before the smell of the food finally hits my nose, and I glance down at my plate. It makes me laugh.

"I made your favorite foods," he says, his voice full of pride.

I bite my lip to hide a smile. It's boxed macaroni and cheese with cut-up hot dogs. A giggle escapes despite how hard I tried to hide it.

"Don't laugh. Is macaroni and cheese not still your favorite food?" He says it so seriously that I laugh even harder.

"No, nowadays I prefer my pasta with some actual nutrients in it. Nothing with more chemicals in it than actual food."

He laughs finally. "I know, but Kai and Enzo's fridge didn't have much to make anything except what the kids like. So it was this or frozen pizza, and since I've already made you frozen pizza, I thought this would work best."

I shake my head with a smile as I pick up my fork and stab a piece of the macaroni before taking a bite. The smell overwhelms my senses and flips my stomach. I don't want to eat, but I need to try—Langston's right about that. I start chewing, but something is off.

"Um...it's crunchy," I say.

Langston's nose is curled up as he chews his own bite. He spits his food out into his napkin, which gives me permission to do the same without insulting him or insinuating that I'm pregnant or something.

"What did you do to it?" I ask, now inspecting the pasta to see that half of it looks completely undercooked, while the other half looks overcooked.

"I followed the directions on the box." He frowns before testing a bite of the hot dog.

I roll mine around on the plate and sink my fork in it, realizing that it takes too much effort to sink the tongs of the fork into the flesh of the hot dog. I put my fork down and watch Langston try a bite.

His face turns green, and he barely gets his napkin to his mouth before he spits it out.

"So I shouldn't be expecting my new husband to cook for me every night then?" I joke.

He runs his hand through his hair, and I notice some sweat coming through his T-shirt.

"I promise I'm a better cook than this. I've made boxed macaroni and cheese and hot dogs a hundred times for Rose and Atlas. I don't know what happened?" He stares at the food again incredulously, like it did something wrong to him.

His cheeks pink. He's sweating even more now. I don't know why he's so nervous, but I try to ease his mind by lifting my wine glass.

His eyes bulge as he watches me drink the wine. I know he thought for sure I was pregnant, but I'm not. Short of peeing on a stick, drinking my wine will have to convince him.

Except, one taste and I'm spitting the liquid out as I get a mouthful of cork.

"What's wrong?" Langston asks.

"Um...the cork disintegrated into the bottle. It's more cork than wine at this point." I put the glass back on the table.

Langston inspects his glass, takes a small taste, realizes I'm right, and then sets the glass back down in a huff.

"I'm sorry. I can order delivery."

I shake my head. "It's okay. I'm too nervous to eat much anyway. I'll eat once I know the kids are safe."

He nods with a frown. "What happens when this is all over?"

"What do you mean?"

"I mean with us. What kind of life do you want? Where should we live? What do you want out of life?"

I look out at the ocean. The sun has begun to set. We should get some news from how the missions are going. "I can't imagine this ever being over."

"It will be sooner than you think. What do you imagine our lives like then?"

Our.

That word sounds so nice leaving his mouth. We haven't had 'our' since we were kids. I'm not foolish enough to think that just because I have a ring on my finger that anything is going to change. I'll still live alone, and Langston will continue to be an incredible father.

Langston stands up then. It's clear he's not happy with whatever he sees on my face. He takes my hands as he kneels in front of me.

"Stop thinking that your life going forward is going to include anything but me and the kids in it," he says.

I shake my head. "You can't make promises like that, killer. You might hate me when this is over."

"I already hate you," he says with a wry smile.

"For real," I say. When he says he hates me, it means I love you, or as close to love as he can feel. "And nothing will change once the kids are safe. They aren't mine, not really. I'd make a terrible mother."

His eyes narrow as he clenches my hands tighter. "You'd make a wonderful mother."

I want to argue more, but there is no use doing that now, so I don't.

"Once this is all over, I see us building a house on a private island somewhere. We have more money than we need. We'll live on the island, the five of us."

I'd rather live in the house he already built—our dream house. I don't care that he and Phoenix lived in it together already—it's mine.

"We'll live happily ever after as we watch the kids grow up until they leave us to start their own lives. We'll get a dog, maybe some cats to fill the house while we wait for grandchildren. Maybe we'll start a charity for underprivileged kids."

He grips my hands tighter until they feel clammy. I don't know what the lead up is. He's about to drop the other shoe, something that will bring my world crashing down like always. I'm not ready for him to hurt me, even if he's doing it to get the treasure and help bring back the kids.

I see him reach for something in his pocket, but he misjudges and bumps the table. The plates rattle around, distracting me from the doom I'm feeling.

I watch as one of the candles twirls around before knocking over onto the table. A second later, flames dance over the tablecloth.

"Langston," I say, entranced by the flame.

"You love it?" he asks. "If not, I can get you a different one."

I have no idea what he's talking about; all I can see is the fire growing bigger behind him. He has no clue. He's focused on whatever annihilation of my heart he's supposed to be doing to me.

"Langston!" I shout, still frozen.

The single word is enough to get Langston's attention this time.

"Shit," he curses as he drags me away from the table before I catch on fire.

He drags me into the house before running back outside.

I don't watch him through the window. I don't care that our makeshift date or whatever it was Langston was trying to accomplish got ruined. I'm relieved that we didn't get to the hurting me part.

I walk into the living room, completely exhausted. I want the phone to ring to tell me that the kids are safe, but I'm more scared I'll get a call to find out one is dead. So I'd rather not hear the phone ringing. I'd rather just stay in this moment of fearful pain.

I lie down on the carpet in the middle of the room. I don't know why I do it. I just need to lie down fully, and I don't have the energy to walk to a bed.

I hear a commotion outside before Langston finally walks into the living room. His shirt is gone. His chest is glistening with sweat and dirt. His hair untamed on top of his head.

"That was a disaster," he says.

"I don't know. It kind of feels like all our dates should be like that. It would be more us."

His lip twitches as he puts one leg on either side of my hips before lowering himself until he's straddling me.

"Which is why I'm not going to try to be romantic, not anymore."

He was trying to be romantic? Why?

He grabs my left hand and pulls out a diamond ring. "This ring is yours forever."

He starts to push the ring onto my finger. He doesn't take the ring made of flowers off; he just pushes the new ring right on top.

"Just as I'm yours forever."

His eyes pour into me, vowing his love. I can't let him make such a promise. I can't let him fall any more than he already has. I can't destroy him any more than I already have. So I look at the ring instead.

My heart clenches when I see it. It's a simple oval diamond on a gold band. Timeless, elegant, and exactly what I said I wanted when I was a kid.

He remembered.

woman knows where Rose is. She might know where Atlas and Declan are.

I hit the bottom step and then flick on the lights. Knowing what I'd see didn't stop my heart from skipping a beat. Phoenix is beaten, bloodied, and crumpled on the floor with her wrists tied together. My jaw ticks in anger, and my body shakes.

I was once married to this woman—or fake married, whatever.

I thought she was the mother of my child. She acted like a great mother and stepmother. At least, that's what I thought.

My concern quickly turns to rage at this woman.

She looks up, her eyes squinting because of the abrupt change from dark to light. She may think I'm the light about to come to save her, but she'd be very wrong.

I grab her by the back of her neck, yanking her hair and forcing her onto her feet.

Phoenix stares at her feet rather than look at me.

I tilt my head, trying to force her eyes on me with just my glare.

"Look at me, Phoenix." My voice is low and sure. I won't be leaving this basement without answers. Phoenix is the one who will decide if she lives or leaves this basement in pieces.

She still doesn't lift her head to look at me, so I do it for her.

She groans, but I finally get to look her in the eyes. I want nothing but the truth from her, and the only way I can ensure that is if I look her in the eyes.

"Where is Rose?" I ask calmly. *How am I calm?* I have no idea. I just know I should start calm and collected. Then, if she doesn't answer, I can turn wild.

"Is that the question you want to ask me first?" she has the audacity to say.

"Yes," I growl.

Her eyes lighten, and a sly smile lifts on her cheek. "You're always asking the wrong questions. Always putting faith in the wrong people. I'll answer your question, but it will be the last one I answer."

I frown.

What other questions do I have? A million, but none seem as important.

My eyes roam up and down her broken body. I don't know how many bones Enzo broke; I just know that he did. Bile slips up my throat at everything this woman and I have been through together.

I married her.

Fucked her.

Thought she was the mother of my child.

I gave her my most precious possessions to take care of—my children.

I realize a question I need answering before she tells me where Rose is.

"Did you ever hurt them? Abuse them? Did you get your jollies off on hurting them?"

She looks me dead in the eyes. "I never hurt them."

A sea of relief floods me at her words. But why should I believe her?

"I don't believe you."

She shrugs. "That's up to you, but my conscience is clean."

She's baiting me. *But why?*

"I thought you loved me. I thought that's why you married me. Not to control me and get my children to trust you until the time came for you to take them."

"You're upset that I didn't love you? That our marriage was a scam? Our marriage would have been a scam whether or not I took Rose from you. You never loved me. It was always her."

She's not wrong.

"You lied to me! You tricked me."

"You lied to me. You tricked me," she says right back.

I want to scream. I want to rip her apart and then put her back together only to rip her apart again.

I don't trust her.

I don't know if she ever hurt the kids.

I don't even know if she's hiding Rose somewhere safe.

But I have one more question before I find out where Rose is.

"Why? Why start all of this? Why marry me? Why take the kids? Why is Liesel's treasure so important?"

She licks her lips and tosses her hair out of her face. "Now, you're finally asking the right questions."

PHOENIX

"What are you doing?" Corbin's voice makes me jump.

I turn, standing on the small step stool in the kitchen. "I'm trying to reach the mixing bowl. I'm making brownies."

He shakes his head like I'm crazy as he rushes over to me, worried my very life hangs in the balance. "Get down, right now."

He holds out his hand and helps me down the two steps. "Keep your feet on the ground. Or preferably, put your feet up."

I roll my eyes. "So, are you going to be cooking me brownies then?"

He climbs up the ladder and grabs the mixing bowl. "Waylon!"

I smile as my other brother runs into the room.

"What?" His hair is frazzled, and his eyes big with concern as he looks to my swollen belly and then up to my face, expecting some kind of emergency. I'm not due for at least another month, but my three brothers all treat me like I'm going to pop at any second.

"Do I need to bring the car around?" Maxwell darts into the kitchen.

I just laugh at the three idiots. I love them, but they are all too much sometimes.

"No! Nothing is wrong. Apparently, Dr. Corbin here has decided that I'm no longer able to climb the two steps up on a step ladder to grab a mixing bowl or cook myself some brownies," I say.

"Brownies, I'm on it!" Waylon says, grabbing the bowl from Corbin before flying over to the pantry to start grabbing ingredients.

I sigh. There is no use arguing with them.

"You. Couch. Now," Corbin says.

Maxwell runs to my side, taking my hand like I can't even walk without support. He helps me into the living room and onto the sofa.

"When is Martin getting off?" I ask Maxwell.

I know that Martin is working on his last deal before the babies arrive. It's a deal with a partner we've worked with a hundred times—a Mr. Dunn. Smuggling drugs is a dangerous business, but it's made my family infinite amounts of money. The business has made us all happy.

Until I fell in love.

Until I got pregnant.

Now, my fiancé and three brothers will stop at nothing to protect me and the babies I carry—including them giving up the business that has provided for us all these years.

What are we going to do once we give up smuggling drugs?

Be incredibly fucking happy; that's what.

We have more money than we need to survive.

We have three babies on the way that we can all give plenty of love to.

We all have hobbies we can spend more time enjoying.

My brothers can find time to date—to fall in love and fill this house with more babies, more happiness.

Just one more job, and then this is all over.

My eyes drift shut. It's exhausting work carrying around triplets.

I inhale sweet chocolatey goodness.

My eyes open just as Waylon brings me a plate filled with brownies.

I smile as he sets the plate on my stomach.

"Thank you," I say.

He glances at his watch. "Corbin and I have to go meet Martin to execute our sale with Dunn. You'll be okay with Maxwell watching you?"

I nod, my smile brightening. The sooner they leave, the sooner they finish the job, and we can get on to the next chapter of our lives. Selling drugs is a dangerous business, but my brothers and Martin are very good at it. I have no worries they'll make it back just fine.

"Yep, thanks to you, I don't have to eat any of his terrible cooking."

He grins and then leans down and kisses me on the forehead. "I love keeping my nieces and nephews fed." He leans down close to my belly. "Stay in there until we get back."

I just roll my eyes and watch as Waylon heads out, followed by Corbin, who just nods in my direction before taking off.

Maxwell collapses on the couch next to me. "So what are we watching while we stuff our faces?"

Maxwell's phone buzzes as we watch another house-hunting show.

I pop another piece of brownie into my mouth while Maxwell answers, assuming it's Corbin or Waylon calling to say the job is done and they are headed back.

Maxwell's smile immediately drops as he listens.

"What is it?" I ask.

He stands, not answering me as he whispers something into the phone.

My heart stops, which isn't good since it's supplying blood to not only me but the three babies growing inside of me.

I scramble to my feet, which is easier said than done.

I walk quickly through the house, each step forcing blood through my already breaking heart. I can feel the change, the shift. I know without any words that Martin is gone. I don't feel him anymore. I feel nothing but numbness.

No, that's crazy to think. He's not dead, just injured. He can't be dead.

I spot Maxwell out on the back deck, pacing, still on the phone. He's trying to protect me, but I have to know.

I waddle outside, moving as fast as my swollen feet will take me. I throw the door open and step out into the chilly air.

Maxwell drops the phone when he sees me.

"What happened?" I ask, using all my oxygen to get the words out.

He shakes his head. "You should be inside, sitting down." He rubs his neck. "No, maybe we should head to the hospital."

Head to the hospital?

"What happened to Martin? How bad is it?"

He closes the distance between us and takes my hands in his. "We all love you. We are all here for you. Whatever happens next, you will always have the three of us to love and protect you."

The three of us.

"What. Happened?"

He opens his mouth with tears in his eyes. "Dunn betrayed us. He took the drugs without paying. He attacked us." His throat catches, his tears fall, and the pain ricochets off him and onto me. "Martin—he didn't make it."

I feel myself falling, collapsing in his arms as my heart stops. My heart belonged to Martin. He was my everything. If he's gone, I don't want to live. I want to be gone too.

My body decides for me as I faint, my eyes roll back in my head, and I'm gone.

CHAPTER 6

LIESEL

I snuck halfway downstairs during the middle of Phoenix's story, but I heard enough for my heart to break. I heard enough to understand her pain. Enough that I can understand why she wants revenge, why the whole family does.

My father took the most important person from her.

He took the love of her life.

And the trauma of losing him caused her to lose the babies. She didn't explicitly say she lost her babies, but I can feel it in her tears. She lost everything, and her brothers, loyal to her above everything, shared her pain.

They want to make me pay for what my father did to them. That's why they took my kids, that's why they want the treasure as payback for what was stolen from them all those years ago.

I can't blame them for feeling this way. I'm sure I would react much the same if they had taken Langston or my kids from me.

When Phoenix finishes speaking, she collapses in Langston's arms. Just like she did in the story—like the trauma of retelling her experience brought her right back to those feelings.

I peer down to watch Langston hold a limp Phoenix in his arms. He hasn't spoken since she started telling her story, so I have no idea what's going on in his head. I'm also not sure if he knows I'm here or not. If he does, he hasn't said anything.

I watch him hold her in his arms, waiting patiently for her to come to. He checks her pulse with his fingers, but I can see from here that she's breathing. Then, he pulls a knife from his pocket and slices through the ropes binding her hands.

"I can't kill her," he says.

He knows I'm here.

"No, you can't," I agree.

"What are we going to do with her?"

"We are going to keep her here until we find Rose."

"And then?"

I have no idea.

Phoenix stirs, her eyes opening in Langston's arms. She takes her time sitting back up, but her eyes find mine. She's wearing black like always. I realize it's because she always in mourning. Every day she feels that loss because of my father.

As much as she hates my family and me, I don't think she would inflict the same pain on me. I don't think she'd hurt or kill any of my kids. She just wants me to suffer a small fraction of the pain she once felt.

That gives me hope that Rose is alive and untouched. It gives me hope that Maxwell and Corbin won't hurt my children either. Corbin may be the oldest and in charge, but Phoenix is the one they follow. She's the one who matters.

I walk down the rest of the stairs and over to where she is still in Langston's arms.

"Where is Rose?" I ask gently.

"My family owns three clubs; each of them is hiding one of your kids. The only way to get in is to play a game. Win the game to get into X, and you'll get Rose back. Pay with your sins and your treasure. Pay with everything you have."

"And if we lose?"

"Then I keep her forever."

CHAPTER 7

LANGSTON

Our kids are being held at three different clubs.

Jesus.

I remember the last "club"—the fucked up yacht masquerade weekend. I don't want to go through that again to get our kids back, let alone three more times. But I'll do anything to get them back, including playing some twisted game meant to torture us.

I feel for Phoenix, maybe because she pretended to be my wife. Maybe because I watched her with Rose and Atlas, and she was a good mother to them. You can't fake that. She cared about them, even if she only did it to hurt Liesel and me.

Maybe it was the story she told, the pain she felt, that has me feeling weak. But whatever the reason, I carry Phoenix upstairs to one of the bedrooms. She fell asleep in my arms, exhausted from telling me her story and from the injuries Enzo inflicted before we got here.

I lay her down on a white comforter with pink flowers on it. I grab a throw blanket draped over a chair in the corner and cover her before I close the door quietly behind me and head back downstairs.

All eyes are on me when I enter the small kitchen.

"Bring Phoenix some food and keep her comfortable," I say.

Enzo's eyebrows shoot up. "Why?"

"She's not a monster. She's just in pain," Liesel answers, giving me the smallest of smiles, letting me know she approves of my actions.

"Did you find out where Rose is?" Kai asks.

"The Brown family owns three clubs. The one on the yacht that we all went to and two others. The children are split between the clubs. We have to win the game at each club in order to get the kid being held there back."

"Well, they owe us one kid already then, since you won before," Enzo says with a growl.

"I need to call Siren," I say.

"I'll call Beckett," Liesel says.

I nod.

Neither of us thinks that any of them would hurt the children, not after Phoenix's story. It doesn't mean we are willing to stop searching and trying to get the kids back as quickly as possible.

I dial Siren's number.

"Hello," Siren answers out of breath.

"Phoenix told me where the kids are and how to get them back."

"Thank god," Siren exhales sharply. We've always been close; she's as torn up as I am about the kids being taken.

"The Browns own three clubs. One is here in Germany. The second is the yacht we were all on."

"Maxwell boarded the yacht this afternoon. We've been chasing him this whole time."

"Then, the third must be where Corbin is holding Declan. We are going to the club here to get Rose back tonight, and then we can come to the yacht."

"Why these games?"

"Liesel's father caused the deaths of Phoenix's fiancé and unborn babies. This is payback to make us suffer as much as possible. I don't think they will hurt them, though, thank god. But we need to get them back as quickly as possible, obviously."

There's a pause.

"We'll win the yacht game while you get into the club there," she says.

"Siren, you played the game last time. You know what it involves. There is no chance you'll win."

"I owe you. And those kids—" her voice cracks, and I can hear the pain in it.

"Siren?"

"Zeke and I will get Atlas back while you and Liesel get Rose. Has Beckett found Declan yet?"

"No, but Liesel is talking to Beckett now and letting him know to search for a club. That should help them narrow down their search."

"Good."

"Siren, are you sure? Liesel and I can come after we finish here."

"I'm sure. My heart isn't whole until yours is. I don't care who I have to fuck or my husband fucks or kills—we are going to get Atlas back tonight."

"Thank you," I exhale, able to breathe a little easier now that there's hope that two of our kids are going to be safe tonight.

I end the call at the same time Liesel does. Her face is so drained, her eyes heavy, her body frail. She needs sleep, rest, food, but all of that will have to wait until we get the kids back.

"Siren and Zeke are going to enter the yacht club by winning the sex game. They are going to get Atlas back tonight while we get Rose."

Liesel nods her head, tears watering her eyes with a tiny glint of relief.

I pull her into my chest, wishing I could do more to comfort her.

"Beckett said he would find the club. He said if he finds it, he'll enter it too. He'll do whatever it takes to get Declan back."

With Liesel in my arms, it's almost like I can breathe again. Almost.

"We are going to get them back," I say. I'm not sure why I ever doubted my friends. They are all going beyond what I would ever ask them to do to save my children. I automatically forgive them for anything they've done.

"We are going to get them back so they can be with their father," Liesel mumbles into my chest.

I grab her cheeks and force her to look up at me. "We are going to get them back so they can be with their father and mother."

A tear rolls down Liesel's cheek. There is so much pain in that single tear, so much heartbreak.

Heartbreak I won't let her go through alone.

Liesel doesn't think she's deserving of being a mother. She doesn't think she belongs in our kids' lives. She's wrong, and this time I'm not giving her a choice. When we get our children back, she's going to meet them. Then she'll realize just how much they need her in their lives.

CHAPTER 8

LIESEL

Beckett found the third club, so we're all going to try to rescue them at the same time. We have some really good friends willing to go this far to get our kids back.

I paint my lips with red lipstick as I finish getting ready in the bathroom. My dress is silver and sparkly as it clings to my curves and down to the floor, revealing plenty of cleavage as well. We don't know exactly what we are facing, but we have an idea after the yacht game we played.

It will be difficult and test our limits. Luckily we have none when it comes to getting the kids back.

I don't know if Beckett, Siren, or Zeke will succeed, but I'm beyond grateful that they are willing to try.

There's a light knock on the bathroom door. My stomach rumbles as I stand and open the door.

"You look beautiful," Kai says, standing in the bathroom door.

I smile at her, but it's fake.

"Do you need anything else? Food?"

I shake my head. I can't eat right now, but I don't want to draw attention to it. Langston will drive me crazy worrying about me.

"I wish there was more Enzo and I could do. Are you sure you don't want us to go with you?"

"You're doing enough staying here and watching Phoenix. Really, you have no idea how much your help means to me."

Kai hugs me. "We are going to get them back. And when we do, we aren't ever going to let them go again."

"I know."

Pain radiates through my body, but I don't let Kai know.

She steps back and holds out a silver mask. I take it from her, a familiar pang shooting through me from the last time I wore a mask like this.

We hear footsteps, and Kai steps back to allow Langston through.

"I'll just be downstairs if you need me," Kai says before leaving.

Then it's just Langston and me.

"Wow," he says as his eyes roam up and down my body. He takes in every curve, every inch of exposed skin, every contour of my face.

For a moment, all I feel is the heat of his eyes gracing my skin. I forget about how scared I am and how my stomach roars with pain and anxiety. For a moment, I feel wanted, desired, lured.

Langston must feel the change, too. Wordlessly, he takes two steps toward me, grabs my neck, and crushes his lips over mine. The kiss is needy and desperate. His tongue pushes into my mouth without asking for permission, without giving me time to think that I shouldn't be feeling any sort of pleasure when my kids' lives are at risk.

The kiss continues despite the tiny whispers of reason floating in my head, telling me I shouldn't enjoy this. All I deserve to feel is pain.

Langston's tongue disagrees with the thoughts in my head. He pushes them out with each stroke of his tongue until the thoughts flutter away. Finally, when the thoughts have vanished, does he stop the kiss.

"That's why you will make a great mother," he says.

"What?"

"Because you won't even let yourself enjoy a kiss. Your entire thoughts are on the kids. You love them without having met them. That's why you are going to make a great mom."

I take a deep breath. Now isn't the time to argue with him.

My eyes take him in for the first time. He's wearing a tux that I know he rented, yet somehow fits him like a glove. I can see his hardened muscles beneath the black fabric of his jacket and pants. His erection pushes against the zipper. My eyes shoot back up to his face, so he doesn't get the wrong idea and think I want to fuck him. But that's a mistake, too. His hair is tousled, and his face is clean-shaven, making me drool over the sharpness of his jaw. I know I can't go near his eyes. His eyes are a danger zone I'll get lost in.

He pushes his hands into my hair, not caring that he's messing up the curls I spent hours perfecting. He kisses me again—slower, gentler, reminding me that I'm his.

"Whatever it takes," he says, pulling my lips into his mouth once more.

"Whatever it takes," I say, agreeing to his promise.

Then, he locks his fingers with mine and leads me out of the house to the waiting car. We climb in the back, and one of Kai's employees climbs into the front. Langston holds my hand the entire thirty-minute drive to the club, but that doesn't ease the butterflies in my stomach.

The car eases to a stop.

"Look at me," Langston says.

I turn and look at him. He holds up my mask and fastens it around my face. "You're the fiercest, most beautiful, badass woman in there. Nothing will stop you."

"And you're the strongest, most handsome, cruel man in there. Nothing will stop you."

His eyes darken. "I hate you." There is a bite in his words that is meant to stir a reaction.

"I hate you, too." Every time I say the words, or he does, I no longer know the true meaning. I no longer know what the words mean when either of us speaks them, just that they mean a lot.

The car door opens. I step out, taking Langston's hand as he guides me down a sidewalk and inside the club.

We enter the building with blacked-out windows and no sign. There is nothing to indicate what takes place inside.

"Hello, welcome to X. Can I have your name and invite, please?" a gentleman in a tux asks with an iPad in his hands.

"Mr. Langston Pearce and Mrs. Liesel Pearce. Phoenix Brown is who invited us," I say.

Langston practically growls when I spit out his name as my last, making my insides tingle with what it does to him when I claim him as my husband.

"Welcome, Mr. and Mrs. Pearce. The games start in thirty minutes. I'll show you to the bar where you can have a drink while you wait."

He leads us down the hallway and stops at an open door. "Enjoy yourselves."

We walk hand in hand into the room. It's a spacious room, filled with guests in their most formal attire, all sipping various drinks as a woman sings at a piano in the center of the room. The bar is on the far side. All eyes turn to us as we enter. I suspect everyone does this with each new guest, trying to judge the new competition.

I roll my shoulders back, standing taller. Langston stares them all down. We make it clear we are here to win—anything less will not happen.

Together we walk over to a small circular booth in the corner of the room with a good view.

A waitress immediately comes over. "What can I get you to drink?"

"Two of your finest scotches," Langston answers.

I don't know if my stomach can handle a drop of alcohol, but I don't argue. I don't want to appear weak, and I don't want Langston to think something stupid like I'm pregnant or something.

"So what do you think this game is going to involve?" I ask.

"Fucking, pain, torture—the usual."

I nod.

"We are going to get her back. And if we lose, we'll try again and again until we win, or we'll find another way. I'm pretty proficient with a gun, you know."

His comment is meant to make me smile, but I find I can't.

The waitress returns with our drinks, and without thinking, I take a long sip, regretting it immediately as it burns all the way down to my anxious gut.

Langston stares at me curiously but doesn't say anything.

I set my drink down carefully and hold it in my hands while I peruse the faces in the room, trying to determine our biggest competition.

"No one is competition. No one is fighting to get their child back. We'll win," Langston says.

His words are meant to be encouraging, to douse some of my anxiety, but nothing but seeing Rose, Atlas, and Declan safely in Langston's arms will put out my fear.

We sit quietly until the man with the iPad re-enters the room. "The game is about to begin if you will all follow me."

People toss back the rest of their drinks before standing to follow him out. When I stand, I find my legs trembling. Langston notices, takes my arm, and leads me out. With his hand touching me, I'm calm enough to walk.

We are led into a smaller room containing four round tables, each with five seats. It's then that I realize there are twenty of us here, and I'm the only woman.

Chills race up and down my spine. Something isn't right. There is something that Phoenix didn't tell us, but I'm clueless. It feels like we've just walked into a trap.

Langston notices and stands a little in front of me, letting anyone in the room know they will have to go through him before they get to me. He'd take a bullet for me, not that I'd let him.

The host walks to the front of the room and begins explaining the rules.

"Welcome, gentlemen and Mrs. Pearce. Thank you all for coming. You all know what is at stake. Now for the rules of the game. They are quite simple. You will all be randomly seated at a table, and cards will be distributed to you, each containing a different...dares, shall we call them? Every dare has a point value, based on the card. Each round you will bet which dare, or combination of dares, you are willing to do. The highest bets stay in the game. The lowest bet must do their wagered dare, or dares, to stay in the game.

"Each round, you will have an opportunity to trade in your cards to be dealt new ones. You can trade in all or none of your cards, and you'll be dealt any additional cards to ensure you always have five cards in your hand. Once a winner has been declared at each table, the final round, or rounds, will decide our winner from the group of table winners. There will be a dealer at each table if you have any questions."

There are some murmurs, snide remarks, and grins from the men in the crowd. All of them stare at me like I'm a piece of meat to devour.

"I won't let anyone hurt you," Langston whispers.

"The only way to ensure that is if I quit right now."

"You should; I've got this."

"No, I'll play. We both stay, we double our chances."

"But—"

"I'm staying."

Names are called out as men are assigned different tables.

Then my name is announced; I'm at table two. I just have to figure out how to walk over there without Langston to lean on.

My legs shake as I attempt to strut with everyone's eyes on me, looking at me like I don't belong. I regret the stilettos with every step. One wrong step, and I'm going to fall and lose the game before it even starts.

Somehow I make it to my chair. I feel Langston from across the room. Unlike the last game we played, he's going to be more protective of me. He's going to have limits of what he can watch me endure. I just hope we get to Rose before that happens.

More names are called, and the rest of the men take their seats. Langston ends up at the table nearest to mine. It's nice to feel like he's a partner in the game this time, but I don't know how much good it's going to do.

Four men are eventually sitting at the table with me. All of their eyes are locked on me. I'm the outcast, and they are happy to destroy me. I really wish I knew why I was the only woman here.

I study my opponents as the dealers begin making their way to the tables. To my immediate left is a middle-aged man that must be a cowboy in a former life. He's decked out in boots, a cowboy hat, and handlebar mustache.

Next is a dark-haired man with slicked-back hair, a too-tight suit, and brown eyes. He's around my age and is wearing a wedding ring.

The third man is wearing a tux, but it does little to cover his rough exterior. Tattoos peek out around his wrists and neck. He has a nasty scar under his right eye that didn't heal properly.

My fourth table-mate is an older gentleman. What's left of his hair is graying around the bald spot on his head. He wears an expensive, ill-fitting tux that screams wealth.

"Good evening, gentleman and ma'am. I'll be your dealer for tonight. If anyone has any questions about how the game is played, then please let me know. Otherwise, let's begin," he says, shuffling what looks like an ordinary deck of cards. He looks around at the five of us, waiting to see if anyone speaks up. When no one does, he begins to deal us each five cards.

A couple of the men pick up the cards as they are dealt one by one and begin studying them. Me and the older man to my right wait until all the cards are dealt before picking up our hand.

"Point values are one for an ace all the way up to thirteen for a king. You can bet up to the full value in your hand or as little as one card. Remember, if you're the lowest bet, you have to do whatever you bet, so don't bet something you aren't willing to do. The deck is a standard 52 card deck, just with dares written on them. Take a moment to study your cards and decide your bet."

I look at my cards. I have two aces, a three, a seven, and a ten.

The aces are easy tasks. The three isn't bad. The seven starts to hurt. The ten I don't even want to think about. I don't want to know what's on a king.

"Mr. Wilson, you may start the bidding. The bidding will continue around until no one wants to bid any higher," our dealer says.

"Five," the cowboy, Mr. Wilson says.

"Seven," I say.

"Ten," the slick suit says.

"Ten," the tattooed man says.

"Thirteen," the older gentleman says.

"Eighteen," the cowboy says.

Shit.

"Twelve," I say, hoping that I won't have to play my ten and that someone else bids lower.

"Twenty-four," the slick suit says.

"Thirty," the tattooed man says.

"Twenty-five," the older gentleman says.

All eyes fall to me.

Shit.

"Mrs. Pearce, would you like to bid higher? If not, bidding is closed and you lose this round," the dealer says.

There is no point bidding higher. Even if I played all of my cards, it would still only be twenty-two, two lower than the next lowest bid.

I shake my head.

"If everyone would please lay down the cards they bid face down so I can check your bids," the dealer says.

Everyone places their bid cards face down, and he collects them one by one, ensuring the bet that was placed was in fact in their hands.

When the dealer collects my cards, he takes his time reading each of the tasks. He whispers into a microphone and then looks back at the table.

"To continue playing Mrs. Pearce, you owe a drop of blood, a kiss from a stranger, the removal of one item of clothing, and one lash of a whip. Are you willing to pay your debts?"

"Yes," I say, confidently. I didn't bet anything that I wouldn't be willing to do to get my child back. I would have bet everything I had every time if I had good enough cards.

He nods.

A woman in a slinky black dress walks over, carrying a tray of items stands behind the dealer. "The winner of the round gets to decide if he wants to inflict the debt." He motions behind him. "Or if Miss Kiff here will be inflicting the debt. Mr. Mullock, which will it be?" the dealer asks the tattooed man.

"I would love the pleasure," he says.

"Mr. Mullock and Mrs. Pearce, if you would follow Miss Kiff please," the dealer says.

I stand shakily on my feet. My head spins, and my stomach heaves, wanting to vomit, but not because of this stupid game. The men are going to try and gang up on me, but I have no doubt that I'll win.

We follow Miss Kiff to one side of the room, where I realize there is a small stage. This is part of the game—the show. I'm sure there are plenty of rich people watching our humiliation. There are people standing in line to the stage from each table. Langston isn't among them. I look back and find him sitting at the table, staring at me wide-eyed. The vein on his head is throbbing, and his eyes rage with pain.

Relax, I got this, I mouth to him.

He doesn't relax. If anything, the tension in his body tightens.

I sigh.

I can't worry about him. I need to find a way to win this game without having to endure stupid humiliation.

I don't pay attention to the first man. I hear laughter, then applause as he shrieks in pain. Then it's my turn.

I walk up the three steps onto the rickety stage, pleased with myself for staying upright. I really should have eaten something.

Mr. Mullock steps onto the stage behind me. Miss Kiff and her tray of evil things settles in front of me.

"A drop of blood," she says, handing Mullock the knife.

He takes it from her then encircles me, making a big show of running the blade of the knife over my breasts, then down my stomach.

I can sense Langston in the crowd, ready to jump to my aid at a moment's notice.

"Get on with it," I hiss through my teeth.

He snarls back and then slices the blade superficially across the top of my breast, causing more than a drop of blood to ooze out of my skin. The crowd hisses and snickers.

"So original," I say, not impressed at all by him.

He frowns, putting the knife back on the tray.

"A kiss from a stranger," Miss Kiff says next.

I don't wait for Mullock to take his time deciding how or where he's going to kiss me. I grab his cheeks and plant one on his lips before he even has time to realize what happened.

The crowd chuckles as Mullock growls. "I'm supposed to be inflicting the debt, not you."

I roll my eyes. "Then hurry up; we have a game to play."

"An item of clothing," Miss Kiff says.

I freeze. It's not that I really care if I'm naked in front of these men. I just don't want to have to play the rest of the game without my dress on, which is what I assume is the item he'll ask me to remove. I only have two items of clothing on—my panties and the dress. The low-cut front leaves no room for a bra.

Mullock studies me a moment, once again encircling me.

"If you want me to remove the dress, then you're going to have to unzip me."

"Your panties," he says, shocking me.

The crowd boos.

I'm thankful as I shimmy my g-string down and then fling it in his direction.

"I don't want to be distracted looking at your ugly ass body," he mumbles under his breath.

I smile and shake my head.

Mullock walks over and picks up the whip before Ms. Kiff even finishes her sentence. "And one lashing."

He whips the whip hard against my back before I have time to prepare. I stumble forward in my heels, but I refuse to show any more weakness. My body can't handle the sudden force, though, and I fall to my knees, my hands landing on the ground in front of me.

More snickers and catcalls as I finally stand up on my feet, watching Mr. Mullock and Miss Kiff walk off the stage.

As I scramble off, my cheeks flush even though I didn't have to do anything remotely embarrassing. I make it back to my seat before the next man takes the stage.

"I yield," he says before his punishment even starts.

"Me as well," the next man says.

I frown, realizing that may be how the games go. I may be one of the only people who will do any of the dares, debts.

The dealer begins shuffling the cards, and then he looks at me. "Would you like to keep your remaining card or trade it in?"

"Keep," I say, knowing it's a ten.

He deals me four more cards.

I pick them all up, reveling in the fact that they are all face cards. I don't read a single one. All I know is that my next bet is going to be a good one.

CHAPTER 9

LANGSTON

I stare at the men sitting around the table as the dealer gives us new cards. Three men now stare back at me after we lost one in the previous round.

Men.

Why are there only men in this game besides Liesel?

What didn't Phoenix tell us? What kind of trap did she set?

We both know this is a trap. That's the only reason Phoenix would tell us about it. She wants us to suffer since she blames us for her suffering.

I replay every conversation I've ever had with her. Every kiss. Every fuck. Every time I thought Rose was our child. I remember it all and realize how wrong I've been about Phoenix. How much I missed that I should have caught. I should have known that Rose was Liesel's and not Phoenix's. I think somewhere deep down, I did know.

What game is she playing? How badly does she want Liesel and I to suffer during these games? Did she just set them up just to ensure we endured complete agony? Are the others playing the game in on it? Are they all their employees, which is why they aren't doing any of the debts when they lose?

So many questions and no answers.

My eyes drift to Liesel across the room. She doesn't look back, but

I can see the hairs rise on her arms. Her body stiffens at the feel of my gaze on her. She's worried that I can't handle seeing her in pain.

She's right. I fucking can't.

Seeing her suffer is worse than any torture I could ever physically endure. I'd rather die than see her in pain.

But she deserves the same right I do to try to get our kids back. We are both willing to lose everything to protect them, as it should be. I have to put my feelings aside for now, but I hope to hell that we get Rose back before I have to watch Liesel endure more.

I take my cards as the next round starts. I don't have a single face card, which means it's going to be hard for me to win. At least the tasks won't add up to anything difficult.

The three men I'm playing against are all middle or upper aged. They all have gray hair, a well-fed stomach, and don more riches on their tuxes, watches, and rings than most people will earn in a lifetime.

I don't look at what the dares are on my cards. I don't care the pain I have to endure, as long as it doesn't hurt Liesel.

I smirk, thinking about my girl.

She might even slightly enjoy seeing me in pain for all the shit I've put her through over the years.

When it's my turn, I bet everything in my hand. "Twenty-three."

It's not enough. Every bet after mine is higher. It's my turn again, so I just lay my cards down, surrendering to the pain that I'm about to go through.

I look over at Liesel, who lets out a triumphant exhale. *Thank god her cards were better this time.*

A woman stands over me. "Mr. Pearce, right this way, please."

I stand up and follow her, my eyes still on Liesel. Her eyes grow wide, the corner of her mouth turns down, and the pink from her cheeks whitens. *Maybe I was wrong thinking that Liesel could somehow enjoy seeing me in pain, seeing another woman or man touch me? Maybe she feels more for me than I think? Maybe she already loves me?*

I walk onto the small stage, and the crowd grows silent, ready to watch the show. No one else is in line to the stage; the losers from the other tables walked right out of the room after they lost.

I'm right in thinking that only Liesel and I will be completing the debts. Only the two of us have enough at stake in order to be humiliated and in pain like this. For everyone else, this is just a silly game or an evil trap.

I find Liesel once again and give her a tight smile, trying to reassure her. I don't know what is about to happen because I didn't read the cards, but the only thing they could do to me that would truly hurt is attack Liesel or my kids. Since none of them are on the stage, the pain will feel nothing worse than a bee sting.

I wink at her.

Her frown deepens.

I hear the woman speak, but I don't register the words. My entire world is focused on Liesel, on figuring out how to get her to love me. Not just so we can get the stupid treasure, but because I want her to love me. I was wrong to run from loving her all these years. We can handle the consequences. I'm not even sure if there will be consequences of loving her.

I feel my jacket being ripped from my body. My shirt goes next, and I'm standing shirtless in front of the room.

Liesel's eyes water.

Why would they water? I'm just shirtless.

Then, I feel it. Not the pain, but the oozing of blood on my back.

I wish there was a way I could tell Liesel not to worry. With her safe in the same room as me, all I feel is her. My eyes plead with her not to worry, but I can see the concern marked on her face all the same.

A woman steps in front of me. I'm shocked when her lips land on mine. All I can think is when Liesel kissed that man. I turned feral as I watched another man touch what is mine, and I see the same look in Liesel's eyes now.

My eyebrows shoot up and wiggle in her direction. *I'm yours*, I remind her.

Liesel rolls her eyes at my antics, but then her face turns red. Her eyes almost come out of her head, and it looks like she's losing her mind as the woman licks her way down my body, groping me like her plaything.

I smirk, not because my body registers anything this woman is doing as remotely sexy, but because Liesel is jealous. I can work with jealous. Jealous can turn into love.

I hate you, I mouth to Liesel.

I hate you, too, she mouths back.

The woman who was licking my chest like her favorite lollipop grabs my chin and looks me in the eye. It's clear from the gleam in her eye that she's enjoying herself.

"I'm a sadist. I love this shit," she says as if there was any need to explain. Literal drool drips down her chin.

Her eyes look up at me as her tongue trails down my chest once again. "You sure you don't want to quit?"

Her hand rests on the top of my pants. It doesn't take much speculation on my part to guess what she's going to do next.

"I won't quit, no matter what you do to me. I can't."

Her eyes widen in realization. "The kid's yours."

I frown, my hand grabbing the back of her neck without thinking. "You know where she is?"

"As much as I'd enjoy the pain you want to inflict on me, you better let me go before they throw you out."

I let her go.

"Where is she?" I ask through gritted teeth.

She shrugs. "She's being kept as the prize."

"The prize?"

"Whoever wins gets her..."

They are trying to use my daughter as a prize for winning a fucked up game.

I can't.

My head snaps to Liesel, trying to let her know how important it is for us to win. We both knew it was important before, but now we know for sure. If we lose, Rose will be given to one of these men.

My heart.

I can't think about...

I just can't.

We have to win.

"Who—who are these men?"

"Most work for the Browns. The others are worse."

And then I feel her gripping my cock. I don't give a shit what she does. She can rip my cock from my body all I care.

Rose.

Atlas.

Declan.

We can't fail.

We won't fail.

If we fail, we have to fight to the death to get them back.

My eyes lock on Liesel, and her jealousy vanishes. She's no longer concerned that a sadistic woman is doing god knows what to my cock right now. She realizes why there are only men here—sick men who want our daughter.

Phoenix and her family were hurt more than we thought, and she plans on making us pay. All of these men know who we are, and they are going to do everything they can to destroy us, to hurt us. Humiliating us on this flimsy stage is the least of what they plan on doing.

They don't know who we are, though. There may be doubt about whether Liesel and I truly love each other, but there is no doubt that we love our children. They don't know the depths we will go to to protect them.

They're about to find out.

SIREN

I don't know how I didn't realize it before, but in a flash, a flip in my mind switches, and I realize what's happening.

Why there are only men in the room playing the game.

Why Zeke and I are the only ones completing the bets.

Why it's us versus them.

Atlas is the prize.

If we fail...no, there is no failing.

I felt that before, but I feel it even stronger now.

We won't lose. We won't back down. Even if the game is purposefully rigged against us, it won't stop us.

Langston may feel like I betrayed him before, but everything I did was out of love for him. He's like a brother to me, same to Zeke. We will do whatever it takes to keep his child safe.

That's what keeps me going round after round.

It's what keeps me walking up on the shady stage that feels like it will collapse under my feet every time I take a step. It's what keeps me removing clothing item after clothing item until I'm naked in front of a room full of men. Until I've bled all I can. Until I no longer feel humiliated from their stares and chuckles. Until I've given up all of myself.

It's a small sacrifice if it means I get to save an innocent child.

I look over at Zeke, who is now seated at the same table as me.

There are only three of us left: Zeke, me, and a man in a suit who miraculously has never lost a single hand. Zeke and I seem to lose every round, and with each one, more blood and clothes.

Zeke stares back at me with a heaviness. He's calmer than I've ever seen him as he sits naked except for dried blood. His blood coats his skin, his beard, his hair. There are gashes all over his body from being whipped, beaten, tortured. Pain should be oozing off his body in waves; it should be all I feel from him. Instead, he feels as calm as the ocean after a storm—my steady hulk of a man.

I smile with newfound determination in my eyes. This man that I chose to spend my life with, that I love with everything in my being, is proving once again that he will fight by my side no matter what atrocities we face. Somehow, Zeke has me falling for him all over again.

I've never met a braver man.

A stronger one.

A more selfless one.

I know how hard this is for him, watching me get hurt and not doing anything. Yet, I can see in the tenseness of his muscles that he's always ready to fight. One move too far from one of these goons, and he'll spring into action, sacrificing himself to save me.

If we die, we die together. We die protecting an innocent child who is loved by us just as much we love our own child.

I wish we didn't live in a world filled with so much evil. But I can understand the pain of a woman who lost the love of her life and her children. Just thinking about losing Zeke or Atlas in this game has me spiraling into a place I can't even think about.

How cruel would I be to anyone who took everything I loved away from me? As inhumanly as humanly possible. I would turn into a hurricane destroying everything in my path. I wouldn't be able to see past my hate because if I let it go for a second, the loss would overwhelm me. I would have no choice but to hate.

I can understand why Phoenix wants to hurt us and anyone associated with anyone who took so much from her.

I can understand, but it's why I'm willing to fight so hard to not lose those I love. I know who and what I would become if I did—a monster.

I nod to Zeke as I sit next to him.

It's time to end this.

Our cards are dealt between the three of us. At the start, it was everyone against us, but we prevailed, and now we have the upper-hand. We outnumber him.

I look at my cards. For a while, I didn't even read the dares. It didn't matter what the cards said. I would do whatever it takes to win.

But one look at Zeke, and I realized it mattered. If I won a hand, I would spare Zeke from having to see me tortured or undressed.

This is the final round.

Either Zeke or I win, or they do.

I see several face cards, and I see a new card I haven't seen before.

I hold that card closer to my face and read slowly.

To win, you must sacrifice a part of yourself—your voice. Play the card, sacrifice yourself, and you win.

I look over at Zeke. His head is buried in one of his cards as he studies it closer, reading the words over and over. He has a version of this card too. The other man must have a similar card too, but we already know he won't play it.

Give up my voice? What does that even mean?

My heart races, thundering rapidly like a drum pounding through my body.

What does Zeke have to give up?

What do we do?

The game begins as usual.

The other man at our table has higher cards. I'm out of anything but the sacrifice card. I look to Zeke, and from his gaze, it seems he's in the same position.

We have to win.

There is nothing left to do but sacrifice everything. We both play our cards and hope to hell it's enough to save Atlas.

CHAPTER 11

BECKETT

Finally, I've made it to the last table.

It's down to two—me and Corbin.

I was surprised he showed his face, even more surprised to see that he entered the game. And he, unlike the rest of his minions entered in the game, even did one of the dares he bet. It cost him his pretty face getting marred, swollen, and bloodied up.

It's that same face now that's dripping with blood that stands between me and saving Declan. He's the one remaining wall to possibly earning forgiveness for losing Rose and Atlas—not that I'll ever be able to forgive myself.

I'll win.

It's not about having the cards. It's about willing to bet everything. It's about being willing to endure the most pain, suffer the most without fear. That's how you win this game.

That's something I have plenty of. Losing an arm will teach you a thing or two about pain.

My concern isn't about how much more I can endure. Sure, there is blood dripping down my forehead and seeping into my eye, making it hard to see. And yes, my ears are ringing and haven't stopped for hours now. I have gashes all over my back. My cock doesn't want to be touched ever again. I'm pretty sure I can't have children after the beating my balls took.

But that's nothing.

My concern is what happens after I win. *Will I actually get Declan? Or is Corbin not going to keep his promise? Is he going to find a way to disqualify me? Is this all a ruse to keep us at specific locations while they move the kids to someplace we will never find them?*

The only way to find out is to finish the game.

Cards are dealt one by one to Corbin and me.

Neither of us looks at the cards. We glare at each other like this is a staring contest instead of a fucked up game where lives are hanging in the balance.

Finally, we both pick up our cards one by one. I have a few face cards, a two, and an ace. Then I pick up the last card.

This one is different than any of the cards I've previously gotten. 'Sacrifice Card' is written across the top.

I don't always read the bets, knowing there is nothing I wouldn't do to rescue Declan, but this card I read.

To win, you must sacrifice a part of yourself—your ability to feel and touch. Play the card, sacrifice yourself, and you win.

I look up at Corbin, who is grinning at me wickedly. No doubt he doesn't have a sacrifice card. That's what this has all been about—making us do the most ridiculous things, show how terribly we are suffering, then really make us hurt.

I'm afraid it's a trick. Even if we win, the kids might not simply be returned to us like they say. *What choice do I have, though?*

Corbin bets, then it's my turn.

I immediately go all in, including the sacrifice card. I'm tired of the games.

I either win and get Declan, or I lose and fight this motherfucker to the death. Either way is fine with me because either way, I'll win. I don't accept defeat.

I smirk at Corbin as I go all in, and his eyebrows jump up a second in shock. He didn't think I'd play the sacrifice card. He didn't think I'd be willing to go that far. He thinks pain scares me. He has no idea that losing my family is the only thing that scares me.

My ability to feel and touch—I'm not sure what that means, but I've lost a limb already. I can handle losing any physical part of my body. I have no problem adapting. Whatever it means, I'll give it up.

"Your loss," Corbin says.

"As long as I get the kid, I don't care what you do to me."

"I hate you," I say as I stand in the center of the stage, looking out at Langston.

The crowd chuckles, thinking I truly hate Langston. That couldn't be further from the truth. Even when I hated him, I still loved him. He's a drug I can't give up.

Right now, I wish he hated me. He could ruin everything if he prevents my sacrifice.

His limits have been pushed about what he can handle me enduring and what he can't. So far, he's stayed on the sidelines watching but not trying to stop the price I had to pay for losing each round.

I've seen every vein in his head pop, I've seen his muscles flex with the need to step in, I've seen his face redden as he held his breath to keep his ass in his seat instead of throwing me over his shoulder and getting me the fuck out of here.

This round will test him more than I think he can handle.

I'm standing naked on the little stage. I lost my clothes after the last round, as did Langston.

Anyone else standing in my place might be trembling in fear.

Goosebumps would have surely formed. Their hearts would have sped to an ungodly speed or slowed beyond detection.

For me, the only thing my body feels is Langston all the way across the room. His eyes sparkle with his love even from there. *How foolish was I to try and stop us from loving each other all these years? Why did I let him hate me? Why not demand his love all those years ago when we were five years old?*

Would we still be here now? About to lose everything to try and save our children?

Maybe, but at least if we'd spent those years loving each other, it wouldn't feel like we wasted so much time now.

I feel a hand start to graze my body, and Langston's body changes in the familiar way. His lips thin, his hand twitches, his eyes glaze over into darkness. He's fighting every nerve in his body to not save me. Saving me means losing Rose, and our kids will always come first.

"Stay," I half mouth, half say to Langston.

Another hand touches me. I try not to focus or think about where. It's easy to tune out when I'm so focused on not showing any signs of distress to Langston. I don't want him to suffer because he thinks I'm in pain—I'm not.

The debt I lost said that any man in this room could touch me where they want. So far, I've been poked and prodded everywhere— places no one but Langston deserves to touch. But the hand we've been dealt means we have to fight to get to that place. And when we do, I have a feeling our happily ever after is going to be short-lived. Even if we find happiness together, something will come along and take it away. The world always takes from us. It's why I've been so opposed to us being together.

I feel the man slide his grubby finger inside me. I don't react. I'm not in pain, not really. This will all be over soon, so fucking soon.

Langston looks like he's about to combust. But if I could stay in my chair while that sadistic woman almost cut off all the blood supply to his balls, then he can sit in his chair for this.

Langston can't put up with it, though. He rushes onto the stage. The man who was fingering me steps back, probably because he thinks

Langston will punch him. Langston takes a deep breath as he stands in front of me, shielding me from the rest of the men.

"Langston, I'm okay. I promise," I say, making my voice sound as strong as possible.

"I know you are. I'm not."

"We have to play the game. We have to win. There is no other option."

"I know."

"Then, what are you doing? Go back to your chair."

He tilts his head as cocky grin spreads. "I'm having my turn."

I frown, confused, just before his hand cups my sex.

"Oh."

I bite my lip to keep the sex noises that are begging to leave my body as Langston rubs a thumb around my clit before slowly pushing a finger inside of me.

God, it feels like no other man. I could be blindfolded and fucked in the exact same way by every man here, and I'd be able to tell the difference between Langston and everyone else. He may have just recently become my husband, but he's been my everything for so much longer.

My breath speeds up as he touches me. My cheeks flush, and my toes curl on the stage.

I prepare myself for the inevitable—someone is going to yank him off of me.

Langston leans into my body, his lips resting on mine. My eyes are closed as the pressure builds inside me. My mind begins to soar above all the wickedness of the room. Vile creatures walk among us every day, only to haunt our dreams later. I float above it all.

"Come, my wife."

I do.

Langston's mouth closes over mine, keeping all of my noises to himself. His body blocks the crowd so they can't see my face as I come apart, as Langston claims me in front of everyone while protecting me in the only way he can.

"They can touch you all they want, but you're mine," he says loud enough for the whole room to hear.

"Leave," I breathe out.

"What?"

"Thank you. I hate you. Now, leave. It's easier for both of us. Go take a break in the bathroom or grab a drink at the bar."

He frowns.

It's my turn to help him.

He doesn't like it, but eventually, he walks out of the room.

I exhale, feeling a weight lift from me.

More touching me, defiling me, trying to make a claim on me, but all I feel is Langston. His touch still tingles everywhere, and when they touch me, it ignites his touch once again.

I don't know how much time passes. I'm blissfully ignorant to it all until Kiff finally tells me I can step down.

One step, then two, then...

I fall.

The room breaks out into laughter.

I don't care.

My head spins. I must have gotten lightheaded from how long I was standing upright.

"We are going to take a twenty-minute break and then start the next round of games," the host says.

Twenty-minute break.

My stomach heaves, and I know how I'm going to be spending my time.

I force myself up before I race to the bathroom.

I clutch the toilet as I dry heave. My stomach churns, but nothing comes out. Sweat forms and mixes with the blood seeping from my wounds before making a small puddle on the floor underneath me.

I expect Langston will burst through the stall door at any moment. This is the women's bathroom, but that wouldn't stop him. I expect him to search me out the second he realizes there is a break.

He can't find me here. He can't find me crumpled on the bathroom floor, a complete mess.

I flush the toilet and then use the seat to push myself up. My feet wobble, and the world spins around my head. I hold my arms out by my sides, trying to keep my balance. They flail a bit as I walk over to the sink and wash my hands. I try to wash some of the blood and sweat from my body, but it's no use. All it does is smear.

I decide to focus my attention on my face, thinking I can at least wash enough off, so my eyes no longer sting.

"I said macaroni and cheese, not cheese pizza," a soft voice says.

I turn the water off, my ears perk up, and my eyes search the three stalled bathroom for the source of the voice.

I throw open each of the stalls, but the room is empty.

Speak again, I beg the silence.

Did I just imagine that sweet little voice in my head?

"You are so incompetent. When I get older, I'm going to get you fired," the sassy voice says again.

I grin as I look up at the vent directly above me.

Rose.

She's here.

Right above me.

My heart flutters, coming alive again with true hope I didn't know I could feel anymore. Rose is here. She's alive, and from the sound of her voice, it sounds like she's giving them hell.

This all won't be for nothing. We will be able to get her back. *Maybe sooner than we think?*

I consider my options to get to Rose. Leave the bathroom, find the stairs, count the doors to her room, and then try to sneak in. That's a lot of things that would have to go perfectly for me to be able to find her.

Or?

Or I climb up through the vent.

My time to make a move is running out. We only had a twenty-minute break. This could all fail miserably, but my gut tells me I have to try.

I can still hear Rose's voice, but it's softer now. I can't make out her words.

I have to try.

I run to one of the stalls and climb up on the toilet. I look around for my next move and decide the best option is to climb up onto the wall of the stall. I stand on my tiptoes, barely able to reach the top of the wall while I balance on the top of the toilet.

I grab hold of the top of the stall, and then I clamber up. I slip and slide, but somehow I manage to hang on until I can hike my leg up onto the top of the wall.

The ceiling is tiled, so I push up on one of the tiles. It pops open. I grab onto the cheap ceiling tile and toss it to the floor. Finally, I pull myself up into the opening.

I take a deep breath. Climbing up into the ceiling won't help if I can't get into the ducts and up to the floor above me.

I crawl across the ceiling to the vent I saw. When I get to it, I pop the opening off before sliding up inside. I hold myself up with my arms and legs bracing against the sides of vents.

"I asked for milk, not soda," Rose says.

"We don't have milk," a man's voice grumbles back, clearly annoyed.

I smile. Rose has this man wrapped around her finger.

"The least you could get me is water. Soda is so unhealthy."

"Fine. I'll get your damn water. I'll be right back."

He's leaving.

My eyes widen, and my heart pounds. This is my chance.

I scramble up as fast as I can until I get to the top of the vent that leads into the room where she's being held. The lid is stuck. I push as hard as I can, but it won't budge.

"Rose," I whisper through the vent.

"Who is that?" she asks.

"I'm a friend of your dad's. I'm Liesel."

Her eyes peer down at me through the slats.

"Liesel? That's a funny name."

I smile at how truthful she is. She's not afraid to speak her mind.

"It is, isn't it? I wish we had time to talk more, but I'm here to take you back to your dad."

"Thank god. These people are idiots."

I laugh.

"Rose, can you help me try to get the top of this vent off before that man comes back?"

She nods and kneels down, her small hands gripping the edge of the vent cover while I push up.

It starts to budge.

"Almost there," I say, pushing with everything I have.

It pops open, and I'm face to face with my daughter. I'm bloodied, naked, and my head is peering out from the top of a floor vent. Of all the ways I imagined meeting my daughter, this isn't one of them. And yet, seeing her smile at me like I'm her savior makes it all worthwhile. Seeing that she isn't injured or hurt is the miracle I've been praying for.

"Why are you covered in blood?" she asks.

"I'll tell you someday, but for now, we have to go."

She nods.

I hold out my arms, and to my surprise, she lowers herself into my arms, no questions asked. She's either very naive or a good judge of character. Carefully, I lower us down into the vent, then I pull the lid back so, hopefully, her guard won't realize how she escaped.

Then I help her down the vent.

I carry her down until the duct turns, and then she can start crawling on her own. She's much faster than I am. I see stars when I open my eyes, and my muscles shake with each movement. I'm naked; I have no weapons, nothing to get her out of here. This was a terrible idea.

"Rose, wait a sec," I say.

She stops. Her head looks back at me as her blonde curls hang down her back.

"I need you to listen to me carefully, Rose."

"Okay," she says quietly.

"I have to go back to where I came from now. I have to tell your father where to find you."

"You're not coming with?"

"Not right away. I'll meet up with you both later, but I need you to keep crawling as quietly as you can in the ducts here. You can go straight or to the right, but try not to go to the left or back the way we came unless you have no other choice. Your dad will know where to look for you."

She nods slowly, her eyes big and yet so strong. She's the strongest little girl I've ever seen.

I smile at her, trying to reassure her. "You've got this. Your dad is the smartest man in the whole world. He'll find you no matter which way you go."

My hand reaches out before I realize what I'm doing. Her small hand reaches back, and I give it a squeeze of encouragement. Or maybe she's giving me encouragement. Either way, touching her small hand flips a switch inside me. I thought I was protective of my kids before. But now, there is nothing that will stop me.

"You've got this, Rose. Trust your instincts and try to be quiet as a mouse."

"Mice aren't quiet," she laughs.

I chuckle. "I'll see you soon, Rose. And your dad will find you sooner."

I wink and then watch as she starts crawling again before I turn around and head back to the bathroom.

I'm not as graceful returning to the bathroom as I was climbing up. I fall to the floor.

"Ow," I say, trying to rub my sore neck as I get back onto my feet.

Quickly, I run out of the bathroom, hoping I run into Langston before the next round starts. As I exit, I see the other men walking leisurely back into the game room. My time is up.

I head to the entrance and poke my head inside, but I don't see Langston.

"Where have you been?" Langston says from behind me.

I exhale, my eyes closing in relief.

I turn and face him as his eyes search mine, trying to understand why he couldn't find me for the last twenty minutes.

"Lose the next game. Don't complete the debt," I say as quietly as I can between clenched teeth. Hoping to god no one else hears me.

"Why?" he asks.

"If you will all take your seats, the game will resume."

"Search the ducts on the east side. I'll keep playing and give you as much time as I can."

Then I turn and head inside, hoping Langston got my message loud and clear.

CHAPTER 13

LANGSTON

The ducts?

What the hell?

Liesel walks away from me back into the room. I follow after her calmly, even though I actually want to run after her and force her to tell me what the hell that was all about.

I don't have too much time to think about it before I'm sitting back at the table, and cards are being dealt out again.

There are only two other players left at my table. We are nearing the point where they will combine us all to one table.

I glance at my hand. It's mediocre at best—one face card and the rest in the single digits.

Liesel wants me to lose on purpose and then quit when I get to the stage. She wants me to look in the ducts on the east side of the building.

Why?

Did she find where they are holding Rose? If so, what do the ducts have to do with it? Is that the only way to get to the room where they are holding Rose? Or is this some elaborate way to convince me to quit so she doesn't have to see me in pain anymore?

I peer at Liesel over the top of my cards at the next table. She is looking right at me, not bothering to look at her own cards. Her eyes are wild and desperate.

Trust me, she mouths.

Trust her.

I close my eyes, trying to listen with my heart. My heart wants me to throw Liesel over my shoulder and run as far away from this place as my feet will take us. My heart wants me to save Liesel and then find another way to save Rose.

Trust her.

I love Liesel. I know that. Part of loving her means trusting her. It's not something I'm good at, but if I love her, maybe I should start trying.

I'm the first at my table to bet. I bet everything, which only gets me to nineteen points. It won't be enough.

It's not.

Liesel wins her hand, knocking another person out of her table.

My eyes lock with hers as I stand up and walk to the stage area. They never leave hers. That's not unusual; my eyes are always on hers when I'm suffering.

This time is different, though. This time I look at her to make sure she hasn't lost her damn mind. Or she's not trying to sacrifice herself to save me. I look for any sign that she's changed her mind.

But she looks completely at peace when she sees that I'm going to do what she asks.

I don't know what my dares are, but I feel a slash land on my already ripped apart back. I usually try to keep the pain inside, but this time I let out the wince. Then another, louder groan with the second beating.

I fall to my knees on the third.

The fourth—tears are falling down my face.

And by the fifth, I'm holding my hand up in surrender.

The room gasps as I give up, collapsing in a heap on the floor, completely defeated.

The room is silently watching and judging me. Then they turn their attention to Liesel. I lift my head enough to see tears falling down her face.

Drip.

Drip.

Drip.

Each drip is a mark on my soul. I feel like I failed her, even though I'm doing what she says she wants.

The room may think the tears burning down her cheeks are a sign of defeat, fear, and heartbreak.

Only I can see the truth behind the tears. I see the absolute relief and the hint of a smile she holds back, so the others don't get suspicious.

Eventually, I'm lifted onto my feet by two men. I'm walked off the stage and led out of the room, away from Liesel.

That's when my heart starts losing its shit. I just left her in a room full of dangerous men to fend for herself while I go in search of our daughter that she thinks I'll be able to find if I use the ducts. Liesel's lost it. *What the hell was I thinking leaving her?*

I should go back, change my mind. I can't leave her.

The men continue to drag me by my arms. I don't know where they are taking me; I just know they need to turn around and take me back to Liesel.

Suddenly, I'm falling face-first onto a tiled floor. I catch myself at the last second.

"Here, clean yourself and get dressed. You can either wait in the bar, or we can call you a car ride home," one of the men says before the door swings shut.

I realize I'm in a bathroom, and the heap of fabric that was tossed at me is a towel, pants, and shirt.

I quickly stand up and use the towel to wipe some of the blood off. Without a shower and closing some of my wounds, nothing will get rid of the blood.

I put the plain clothes on. They are a little big, but the pants stay up when I walk, so they're good enough. Then I go in search of the ducts on the east side of the building. I'm not sure exactly what I'm going to find, but I hope I find Rose. Rose is the only thing that would be worth me leaving Liesel alone in that room.

I exit the bathroom and assume those idiot guards are going to be waiting for me. They aren't.

There is no one in the hallway.

I glance up, sure that there are cameras monitoring me. People who work for the Browns are watching me and will attack me if I go somewhere undesired.

I move quickly, headed toward the east side of the building. My ears perk up, and my eyes glance around every turn, trying to figure out where Rose might be.

The ducts?

Rose must be a floor above us, but still, *why would Liesel tell me to search the ducts? Is that the only way to get to the second floor?*

There is another bathroom on this side, so I decide to duck inside, hoping there aren't any cameras in here while I figure out a plan.

I pace inside, trying to figure out what Liesel isn't telling me.

I hear a clank, and I look up.

"Shit," a soft voice curses through the vent.

My heart—my heart leaps at that sound, a sound I wasn't sure I'd ever hear again. My precious girl is in the ducts.

"Rose?" I say hesitantly.

"Dad?" her voice returns.

Oh my god.

The ceiling is low, so I jump with everything I have and grab hold of the vent cover. It falls off easily with my weight. Then I jump again and pull myself up the sides of the vent. I poke my head inside to see my favorite smile in the whole world staring back at me.

"You came for me, just like the woman with the funny name said you would."

I smile. I don't think I'll ever stop smiling.

"Liesel?"

She nods.

"Did she help you get in the ducts?"

"Yes, she told me to crawl straight or right, not left. To be as quiet as possible and that you would find me. I'm so glad you did."

"Me too."

I feel myself slipping. I can't hang on much longer.

"Rose, I'm going to drop back down. After I do, I'm going to need you to jump down, and I'll catch you. Can you do that?" I already know my adventurous girl will have no problem jumping.

"Of course, I can do that," she says in her sassy little voice.

I let go and land back on my feet.

"Okay, Rose, I'm ready."

I watch as her feet scoot to the opening, and then she falls down into my arms.

I squeeze her tight to me the second she lands in my arms. I'm never letting her go again. I hold her tighter against my body.

"Dad, you're squeezing too hard."

I chuckle, but don't let her go. Based on how tightly she's squeezing back, I don't think she wants me to let her go.

Liesel found her. She protected her. She knew she couldn't get Rose out of here safely on her own, so she sacrificed herself to ensure Rose and I could escape.

How could I have ever hated Liesel or thought she was a monster?

"I need you to climb onto my back, Rose."

She nods, and I help her onto my back.

I don't have a gun or any other weapon, but that won't stop me from getting Rose out of here.

A part of my heart grieves as I leave Liesel behind, though. It's the right thing to do. Liesel chose to make this sacrifice, but it feels wrong to leave her behind for any amount of time.

"I'll come back for you," I whisper, and then I get Rose out of this hell hole.

There's a shift in the air. Goosebumps form on my arms. My heart stops. My breathing slows. The world changes for the better.

I purse my lips and let out a long exhale as my entire body relaxes.

Langston found Rose.

"If you will all move to the table in the center," the host says.

There are only three of us left, so we're moved to the final table.

Rose is safe.

But what about the others?

I thought I only had one child to worry about, but now I know I'm a mother of three. My heart is split three ways, trying to ensure they are all safe. I'm not going to survive worrying about all of them.

I wish I had a better connection to them so I would be able to feel the shift like I did when Langston found Rose. The only reason I felt it is because of my connection to Langston, not my connection to my children.

Our dealer starts handing out cards, and I try to focus. It doesn't matter now if I win or lose, but I need to protect Rose and Langston by giving them as much time as possible to get away. And if I win, they'll have no reason to go after her. She would belong to me either way.

So I'll win—to protect her.

Whatever pain they want me to endure now is nothing compared to the pain I've felt in my lifetime. Now that Rose and Langston are safe, there is nothing they could do to me here that could hurt me.

Cards are dealt one by one, and I feel an icy chill curl around my spine, taking hold. I stare at the extra card that was passed out. *Why is there an extra card?*

I hesitate to pick up the cards, knowing that whatever is on that card is about to change my fate once again. For once, I'm desperate to know what my own future holds.

The other two men at my table have both picked up their cards. They scan them quickly before staring me down, trying to intimidate me.

I've come this far. I won't be intimidated.

I grab the cards and slide them toward me before picking them up. I scan the first five cards quickly before getting to the new card—the card that will change everything, as usual, with my life.

'The Sacrifice Card' the top reads.

I smile; how ironic. My whole life is one big sacrifice. My life has never been my own. First, it was about protecting Langston. Then, it became about saving my kids. And after this is all over, it will always be about Langston and my kids. That is my entire purpose for living— to protect them.

I read the card quickly, knowing it doesn't matter what the words say. I'll do whatever it takes to protect those I love. I always have.

The words sink in. They envelop my body. The sacrifice I will have to make. It's the same one I always make.

The first two men bet.

I look down at my cards. Without the sacrifice card, I'll lose. I can't lose, so I do the only thing I can. I sacrifice everything to protect those I love.

CHAPTER 15

LANGSTON

I got Rose out. I only had to punch a couple of guys and shoot another, but I got her out. I was afraid she'd be traumatized when she saw me with a gun. Instead, she beamed like I was a freaking superhero or something.

I don't deserve her. I don't deserve any of my kids. Still, once this is all over, I'm taking them somewhere safe. I'm quitting the business. I don't want to have to look over my shoulder every day for the rest of my life wondering if today is my last day or not. My kids deserve better.

Enzo met me about thirty minutes after I left. Thank god, he'd been monitoring my location and started driving as soon as he saw us leaving. He took Rose somewhere safe. She fell asleep as soon as I put her in his arms. I don't know what she's been through, but she looks physically safe. *Psychologically, who knows what she went through?* She's tough, though, and I'll do everything I can to help her heal and move on from this.

Until I can get back, I trust Enzo and Kai to keep Rose safe and to keep her away from Phoenix. I don't know what we are going to tell Rose and Atlas about Phoenix, but for now, keeping them away is for the best.

Now, I'm driving like a maniac to get back to Liesel, to get her the fuck out of there.

I run every red light. Take every turn too sharp. Speed as fast as the car will go through the straightaways. But none of it is fast enough. Every second that I'm away is another second of pain for Liesel. Another second of agony that she has to heal from. Another second something could happen that she won't be able to get over. It's another second of me hating myself. Another second that could be our last together.

A tear springs to my eye just thinking about life without Liesel. Our entire life has been about each other. I can't lose her now that I've finally gotten her. Now that I'm so close to getting her to love me like we should have all those years ago before life fucked us both.

I slam on the brakes as I pull back up at the club. I open my door and jump out, running to the entrance. Nothing can stop me now, except...

"Liesel."

She's standing in the doorway in gray sweatpants and a loose-fitting white T-shirt, an angel casually walking away from hell. Blood clings to her skin, littered with cuts and bruises. She actually doesn't look much, if any, worse than the last time I saw her.

And she's alive.

She's free.

She's mine.

I pause for a second before my brain works again, and I race to her. I force myself to stop just in front of her, my hands reaching out but not touching her. Just because I don't see any new injuries doesn't mean she wasn't hurt worse. And it doesn't mean the injuries I saw happen don't still hurt like hell. I won't make her suffer more.

"You got Rose?" she asks.

I nod.

A happy tear rolls down her cheek as she smiles and then jumps into my embrace.

Once she's in my arms, I can't help but hold her tightly. My arms extend around her and hold onto her like vice grips. I'm never letting any part of my family go again—never.

Her head nestles into my chest, and her tears soak through my shirt.

"We need to leave," I say, wanting to get her as far away from this vile place as I can. Once we are safely away, we can talk more.

She nods as I lead her to my car. We both jump in, and I drive just as hard and fast as I did to get back to her. My hand finds hers, and we hold hands, not speaking, letting the car engine do all the talking.

After speeding away and seeing no cars following us, I pull over into an alleyway and park the car.

Then I look over at Liesel.

"What happened?" I ask.

She shrugs. "I won the game. I told them I had already taken my prize and then I left. They have no reason to come after Rose now. I won."

I nod. There's a heaviness in her eyes. *What isn't she telling me?*

"Rose is safe with Enzo and Kai. I didn't see any injuries, and her spirit hasn't changed. I don't think they hurt her."

"Thank god."

I grab the base of her neck and rub my thumb over her swollen cheek. I want to know everything that happened, and yet I'm not sure my heart can take it. She can't keep putting herself last. She can't keep taking all the pain while shielding the rest of us. She has to let some of us take on the danger too.

I'm about to ask her more questions when my phone buzzes in my pocket.

I can feel Liesel's heartbeat in her neck skip when I reach for my phone.

"It's Siren," I say before I answer. "Hello."

Liesel grips onto my hand so tight that my knuckles start turning white.

"Hey," Zeke says.

"Did you win the game? Did you get Atlas?"

There's a long pause. Too long of a pause.

"What did they say?" Liesel asks.

I shake my head. "Zeke? Siren?"

I hold the phone out, thinking that the call must have dropped, but it still shows that we are connected.

"We won the game. We got Atlas," Zeke says, his voice sounds strange when he should sound happy.

"Good, let's all go to my island house. Meet there. We can protect ourselves there." I look to Liesel, who nods her head in agreement.

Another long pause before Zeke answers. "See you there soon."

The call ends. That was strange.

"Atlas is safe?" Liesel asks.

"Atlas is safe."

More tears water her eyes as she almost collapses with relief against me.

Two down, one to go.

We are back to where we started.

"I—"

Another phone call.

We both stare down at my phone in disbelief as Beckett calls me.

Our hearts thump in unison. This could be the call that changes everything. The call that means we finally have all of our kids.

"Didyouwin? DoyouhaveDeclan?" I ask, rushing my words out so quickly I'm not even sure Beckett can understand me.

"I won—"

"Thank god, meet us at my island house. Okay?"

The line cuts out, but it doesn't matter. I blink back my own tears, but there is no use. For the first time, all three of Liesel's kids are safe and on their way to meet her.

"He's safe?"

I nod, grabbing her cheeks and resting my forehead against hers. "They all are."

Our tears mix together, as do our smiles and laughs. Too many happy emotions flood through us. I can't remember another time when I've been this happy.

"What does this mean? What do we have to do?" Liesel asks, completely dumbfounded.

"It means we're safe. We'll make sure Corbin and the rest of them are no longer a threat, but it's over. We are safe. We won. It means we only have to keep pursuing the treasure if you want to. If you don't, we can tell people we found it, and it was only a million dollars or something; not worth anyone coming after us. No one will know. We're safe. I won't let anyone hurt you or our kids ever again."

Her lips slam down on mine as I say my last word.

I groan into her lips, partly because moving fucking hurts, but more because she tastes so damn delicious. I've wanted to kiss her every second since we started all of this. And now—now it feels like we can finally kiss, fuck, be together in every way. There is nothing stopping us now, not anymore.

I run my hand under her shirt, needing to feel her skin. I stop when she moans as my fingertips encounter the sticky warmth of her blood.

"I'm sorry. I didn't mean to hurt you. I—"

"Shut up." She grabs my face, stares down at me, and starts climbing across the seat toward me. "You didn't hurt me. You couldn't hurt me. When you touch me, all I feel is mind-blowing pleasure. You overwhelm me, Langston. Now hate fuck me like you want to." She rips her shirt off her body, revealing too many bruises, cuts, and blood stuck to her skin.

My eyes sadden.

"Hate fuck me," she repeats, pushing her breasts into my face. Her hand tilts my head back while she pushes her nipple against my lips.

Hate fuck her?

I don't hate her; I love—oh, she wants me to make love to her. Hate means love. *How could I have forgotten?*

"My pleasure." I lick over her already hard nipple and am rewarded with soft, gentle moans. They're the kind that hits me straight in the groin, making me instantly hard.

She notices and rubs her sex against me through our clothes. I'm so wound up that I'm going to come way too quickly, which is probably a good thing considering we are in a cramped car in an alleyway and not entirely safe. Phoenix's people could find us here.

But it's not what Liesel deserves, and I plan on only giving her what she deserves from now on.

I take my time teasing her first nipple, then her second, careful to listen for any sound that I might be hurting her. She moans with every lick of my tongue, but now that I'm listening more carefully, I realize her moans are of pleasure.

I won't hurt her ever again. And I'll spend the rest of my life making up for all the hurt she's had to go through. And I'll start right now.

My fingers dive into her pants, between her folds, finding her clit as I tease her nipple with my tongue.

I rub over her sensitive nub in slow circles, knowing there is no way I'll fuck her until I've made her come. I don't know what torture she's just endured, but I want this to take it all away.

Her hands grab onto my shoulders, her eyes close, and her body shakes as I continue to bring her closer to ecstasy.

"I need you inside me," she whispers.

I slip a finger inside, pumping gently into her while my thumb circles her clit, moving faster, applying more pressure.

"That's not what—aww—I meant," she says as I slide two fingers inside her.

I kiss my way up the curve of her chest and neck until I can nip the edge of her earlobe with my teeth.

"I know," I growl.

She tremors at my words, and it pushes her into a spiral of pulses that race down her spine all the way to her toes. She climaxes hard on my fingers, soaking me and making me fall even harder for her as I watch her come so undone.

Liesel's body may be broken, but her soul is not. Her soul is more alive than ever. And I want it—her soul, her heart. I want it all.

Right now, she wants my cock. She's grabbing at my waistband, trying to push my pants down to get to me. When I don't immediately rush to help her, she snarls at me.

"Help me get these pants off you, now."

I grin at her bossiness, her neediness. I love it all.

I shove my pants down until they are a heap at my ankles. Before I have time to even stroke myself, she's already on top of and pushing down on my cock like she owns me, which I guess she does. I love that even more.

She starts sliding up and down on my cock. She's going to make me come way too soon, and all I can do is look up in her eyes, knowing that I want to look into her eyes every second of the rest of my life. For the first time, I feel like that's a real possibility.

"Stop looking at me and hate fuck me," she says, moving faster over my dick. I can tell it's exhausting her and that she wants me to take control soon.

I grab her hips and drive into her, keeping some restraint so I don't hurt her. The devil in her eyes tells me to fuck her harder. She doesn't want to be treated gingerly; she wants to be fucked hard.

The next stroke is harder. It rattles her body, but her moans only heighten. It drives me to fuck her rougher until I can't hold back any longer.

"I hate you," I moan as I come.

"I. Hate. You. Too," she screams as she comes on my cock.

We pant into each other's mouth; both of us still consumed by everything we just went through. Liesel eventually rests her head against my shoulder. She must be completely exhausted and starving.

I grab my phone and text out a quick message to Enzo, letting him know to get us a jet and that we are all flying to my place.

"Liesel, baby, as much as I want you, you have to get in your seat so I can drive."

"No," she says softly, wrapping her arms tighter around my neck.

I can't let her go either, even if I wanted to, so I don't. I hold her in my lap as I carefully pull back out on the road and start driving us to the airport.

I'll never let her go.

CHAPTER 16

LIESEL

I fall asleep against Langston's shoulder. I know sleeping on his lap while he drives isn't the safest thing, but I decided we might as well tempt fate after everything we've been through. For now, I just need to be with Langston to not overthink everything.

He says this is the end; everyone is safe.

I know the truth.

The end is when we can finally say, 'I love you.' It happens when we get a happily ever after or we die tragically.

We didn't say, 'I love you.' We didn't celebrate as one big happy family. And as far as I know, I'm not dead, *but who knows? Maybe I am, and I've died and gone to heaven?* That's what it feels like lying on Langston's shoulder.

What comes next, though?

Do I tell him everything that happened; how I won the game?

Do I finally get to stop hunting for the truth?

"Huntress, we're here," Langston says, kissing my forehead. He doesn't realize I'm already awake.

I open my eyes and smile at him. The sky is dark, but I spot the plane behind us.

Langston pops the door open and then lifts me out of the car. He carries me honeymoon style on the tarmac and then up the stairs to the private jet.

"Daddy!" Rose's voice screams happily as we walk into the plane's cabin.

I think Langston is going to set me down so he can scoop Rose up, but instead, he somehow scoops up Rose until she's lying on my lap. She gives Langston a big hug.

I can't hold back my own smile.

"Liesel!" she yells happily when she recognizes me and throws her little arms around my neck.

My first hug.

Thump, thump. Thump, thump.

All I can feel is the beat of her heart against mine. A strange, wonderful feeling I never thought I'd get to feel.

"Thank you for saving me," Rose says when she leans back.

"You did a pretty good job of that yourself, but gladly. I'd save you any time." I will save you every time.

Rose smiles brighter. "Good, I'd save you too."

I smile. "I know you would."

Her bright eyes look between Langston and me curiously. I don't know what she sees when she looks between us, but I can see the wheels turning in her head.

I give Langston a worried look. I'm not ready to tell Rose that I'm her biological mother. I'm not ready to tell her that we're married or make any commitment to stay in her life.

"Have you eaten, Rose bug?" Langston asks, trying to change the subject.

She nods. "But I could use dessert."

Langston laughs. "Let's see if we can find you dessert."

He sets her down and then puts my feet back on the ground while keeping a hand at the small of my back. We both could use a shower, change of clothes, food, and sleep. But first, we need to take care of Rose.

We find Enzo and Kai sitting on one of the tan couches in the back of the plane. They both stand when we come back. Kai walks over to me. "You okay?" she asks quietly.

I give her a quick nod. "We'd be better if we found some dessert."

Kai smiles down at Rose. "We have a couple of different flavors of ice cream. Which is your favorite, Rose?"

She thinks really hard.

"How about one of everything?" I say.

Rose nods happily.

Kai winks. "One of everything coming right up."

Rose hops up on one of the couches. She seems completely normal, so I'm glad this doesn't seem to be phasing her.

"Where is Mom? Is she meeting us on the island like Atlas?"

The room quiets.

Langston halts mid-step. He looks to Enzo as he realizes that Phoenix could be hidden somewhere on this very plane.

"Your mom had an important job she had to do. I'm not sure if she'll be able to get away from work to come to the island or not," Enzo answers.

Well, at least that means Phoenix isn't on the plane, but I don't know what we do about Phoenix long term. Rose thinks Phoenix has been her mom her entire life. We can't kill Phoenix, but we can't just let her go back to being Rose's mother either.

Kai returns with a giant bowl of ice cream and several spoons.

Rose holds out her hands, and Kai places the bowl in her lap. Rose's eyes light up so big when she sees the mountain of ice cream.

"Dad, Liesel, you need to help me eat this. It looks like you both have been starving like me," Rose says.

Langston and I exchange worried glances as we join Rose on the couch, taking a seat on either side of her. "Did they not feed you, the men who took you?" Langston asks casually as he takes one of the spoons and a bite to satisfy Rose and probably some of his own hunger.

"They tried to, but everything they kept feeding me was gross like a cold pizza and sodas. I know I'm not supposed to drink sodas, so I didn't drink any," she answers.

I laugh, my eyes meeting Langston's as we relax, knowing that Rose was at least offered food.

We all eat in comfortable silence for a little bit before I've had enough sweets in my stomach.

"Is there a shower on this plane?" I ask no one in particular.

"There are always showers on the planes we fly. And pajamas too! You should try the fluffy pajamas. They're the best," Rose says mid-bite.

"I'm going to go shower and try to find the fluffy pajamas then," I say.

I stand and head to the back of the plane. As I close the bathroom door, I hear Langston tell Rose he needs to make sure I find the pajamas and he needs to shower after me. I leave the door unlocked as I turn on the water in the small shower and strip my shirt just as Langston pushes in.

"Rose is smart, you know. If you keep showering at the same time as me, she's going to figure out that we are together."

"What's wrong with her knowing that we are together?"

I place my hand on his chest. "I'm just not ready yet."

He shakes his head. "I think we are way past time, Liesel. You don't have a choice any longer. It's time whether you are ready or not. The kids deserve to know you. They deserve to know who you are, and we deserve to live happily ever after. Preferably with you spending lots and lots of time naked." He smirks.

I smile back, but a part of my smile is fake. I don't know how he thinks we can live happily ever after when we can't even say we love each other.

Instead of saying anything else, he just pushes us into the shower, clothes and all.

He catches my bottom lip and kisses me before I can say anything.

"I vow to make you feel good every chance I can, which means I owe you an orgasm."

I shake my head. "You made me come less than an hour ago. You don't need to make me co—"

I stop mid-word as his fingers press against my clit.

Holy cow.

A million tiny fireworks light up in my body when he touches me.

He flips me around until my back is pressed against his front while his hand continues to tease my sensitive nub. My pants are yanked to the floor, and the showerhead hits the front of my body, beginning to wash the blood away, along with the remnants of the other sacrifice I made.

Langston sweeps the hair off my neck as he kisses my bare skin. His fingers circle around my clit as more water bounces off my skin.

"I want—"

"No. This is about you—your pleasure. I'm tired of taking anything from you. You have to get at least double the amount of gratification as I do."

"But—"

There is no way I can finish that sentence, though. All I can see are stars as I come once again. It's different than in the car. In the car, I was desperate. I needed to feel alive again—in control, connected to Langston.

This orgasm rips through my body, releasing all the feelings I've been hiding. All the feelings of pain I was holding back explode. Agony, despair, fear, loss—it hits me all at once.

"Let it all out, baby. I've got you."

It's at Langston's words that I realize I'm crying, trembling, shaking. I'm only standing because Langston is holding me up.

The water mixes with my tears and blood as it all goes down the drain. Everything we've been through—I let it all go. It's no longer my burden to bear.

We stay in the shower so long that we run out of water. At some point, we collapsed onto the floor, so I'm sitting in Langston's lap.

I look back. "You never took your clothes off."

"No, I was more concerned about making sure you were okay."

I kiss him softly. "I don't know what I would do without you."

"Me neither."

I am finally able to stand. I hold out my hand. He takes it, and I help him up. He's soaking wet and still covered in blood.

"I'm not sure the shower helped clean you that much," I say, looking him up and down.

He peels his shirt off. "Sure, it did."

I take a washcloth and do my best to clean off the rest of the dried blood from his body. He slips out of his pants, and I get a better view of the pain he went through with a large gash in his thigh.

I brush my hand over it. If I hadn't already cried out all the pain, I would start in again.

He takes my hand and kisses it. "We are all going to be okay now. I promise."

I smile at his empty promises. He doesn't mean them to be empty, but he can't promise me the world when the world doesn't belong to me.

"So, where are these fluffy pajamas?" I ask.

He laughs. "I think Rose means the fluffy white robes."

He grabs one on the hook behind me and drapes it over my shoulders.

I slip my arms through it and then wrap the sash around my waist. "Rose is right; these are fluffy."

Langston wraps the other robe around him.

He opens one of the drawers in the bathroom and pulls out two pairs of boxers for us both to slip on underneath our robes. Now we're decent enough to go back out with everyone on the plane.

"Ready?" he asks with his hand on the doorknob.

I nod.

He kisses me one more time, opens the door, and we walk back to the plane's main cabin.

Rose is talking animatedly to Enzo and Kai, who just nod along, encouraging her.

"Much better, now you don't look all icky anymore," Rose says as we sit on either side of her.

I yawn.

"I think it's time for us all to sleep," Langston says, giving Rose a stare that warns her from arguing with him.

She yawns. "Okay, fine."

"Is it okay if Liesel sleeps with us too?" he asks.

Rose nods. "She saved me. I don't want her to be afraid if she sleeps alone."

Langston motions for us all to stand, and he converts the couch into a small bed. Kai gathers some blankets and pillows for us.

"We're going to sleep up front," Kai says, and then she and Enzo leave.

Langston climbs into the bed in his fluffy robe. Rose climbs in next. I'm slow to move, too busy watching the beautiful sight.

"Liesel, get in the bed. I'm cold, and your robe will keep me warm," Rose says.

I climb into bed and snuggle up next to Rose. Langston's arm wraps around us both. My eyes grow heavy, but I fight sleep as long as I can, wanting to memorize this incredible moment forever. I can't wait to have this moment with all of my children.

CHAPTER 17

LANGSTON

The plane lands with Rose and Liesel snuggled up against me. We slept the entire flight, and it still doesn't seem like enough. I feel like I could sleep a month, and it wouldn't satisfy me. That's why we are all going to my private island—to rest, recover, and end our enemies once and for all.

Snuggling with my two girls was amazing, but my heart isn't full. It won't be until Atlas and Declan are both here.

We have a lot to figure out. *How do we introduce Liesel to the kids? What do we tell them about Phoenix? How do we ensure the Browns and the rest of our enemies don't come after us? What are we going to do about the treasure?*

None of that matters right now, though. In a few short hours, we are all going to be together. And once we are together, nothing will rip us apart again.

Kai walks into our section of the cabin, carrying a pile of clothes. "I found these for you guys to wear."

"Thanks," I say before waking Liesel with a kiss on the forehead. I can't bear to wake up Rose.

Liesel stirs and takes the clothes wordlessly back to the bathroom to change while Rose sleeps.

I put on the T-shirt and then slip into my pants while Rose continues to sleep. Carefully, I shift my arms under her body and then carry her off the plane to one of the waiting cars my staff drove over.

Rose murmurs something but stays asleep as I lay her in the backseat of the car. Liesel is right behind me. I motion for her to climb into the front seat as I jump into the driver's seat.

Enzo and Kai ride in another car with the staff behind us.

We don't speak as I drive us to my house. But I know we are both thinking about the last time we were here—me taking her, making her hike through the forest, threatening her life.

"I'm sorry," I say, knowing it's not enough.

"Me too," Liesel says back.

"You have nothing to be sorry for," I say.

She smiles thinly at me and then looks out the window, not responding.

As soon as we stop in front of the house, a switch flips in Rose, and she pops her head up.

"We came back here! This is my favorite home!" Rose says, throwing the door open and racing out.

"Her happiness is infectious," Liesel says.

"It is, but she knows how to use it to get what she wants," I say, raising my eyebrows as Rose throws open Liesel's door, grabs her hand, and drags her into the house, excited to show her around. She doesn't realize that Liesel has already been to the house before, back when I was a jackass, married to the wrong woman, and thought Liesel was the devil.

Kai and Enzo walk up behind me. "Our kids and Siren and Zeke's son are getting flown here as well. We want to be all together."

"Good," I say, gripping Enzo's shoulder. It's about time we were all together as a family.

Then I walk inside to look for my girls.

At first, I don't hear them, just the eery silence of a house that I haven't lived in for months, but then I hear Rose's giggling from upstairs followed by Liesel's laughter.

I decide to head to the kitchen to make coffee and breakfast, letting them have time to bond.

Rose is a good judge of character and outgoing, so it doesn't surprise me that she instantly took to Liesel. She knows Liesel is a good person instinctually, but Atlas isn't so trusting, and Declan is a mystery. We have no idea what he's been through or where he's been his whole life. Whatever has happened, we will figure out how to heal together.

Enzo walks into the kitchen as I start filling the coffee machine with grounds.

"Siren and Zeke's plane will be here in thirty minutes. The kid's plane about twenty minutes after that. And Beckett's plane will land in about an hour and a half."

"Good. After everyone is settled, we can all talk about what to do next."

Kai enters the room. "I have most of our fleet surrounding this island, protecting us. No one gets through unless we want them to."

"Thank you," I say.

She nods stiffly. "Phoenix is being held on one of the yachts just offshore. Just tell us what you want us to do with her."

I let out a long sigh. Deciding what to do with Phoenix is going to be difficult. Instead of thinking about it, I make coffee, eggs, bacon, toast. I mindlessly cook while people come in and out of the kitchen.

Rose, eventually drawn by the smell of bacon, brings Liesel down from playing tea party in her room.

I hand Liesel a cup of coffee, knowing she needs it to regain her energy after what we've been through. To my surprise, Liesel also makes herself a plate of eggs and bacon.

I smile, happy to see her finally eating something.

"Can I have some of your coffee?" Rose asks Liesel. I watch from the door as they sit out on the back deck, looking out at the ocean. Rose is an expert manipulator, and I want to see how Liesel handles her.

"Are you allowed to have coffee?" Liesel asks her.

"I am if an adult says I can," Rose bats her eyelashes.

Liesel tries to hide her laugh, but she can't. "You should ask your dad."

"But I don't want to run all the way inside," Rose whines.

"You can have some," I say as I walk over to them. Although I wish Liesel would feel like she can decide for herself what Rose can or can't do, she is her mother after all.

Liesel holds her cup up to Rose with a sly, knowing grin, but she doesn't say anything as she lets Rose take a drink. Rose, being Rose, takes a sip, doesn't like it, but won't say she doesn't like it because she wants to act like a grown-up.

"Do you like it?" Liesel asks.

"Dad doesn't make the best coffee. I like it better from Starbucks."

I frown. "When are you drinking coffee from Starbucks?"

She shrugs. "It tastes more chocolatey from Starbucks."

I laugh. "That's because I order you a hot chocolate from Starbucks, not coffee."

"Oh, well, I like that better."

I shake my head at her.

"So, do you live here now?" Rose asks Liesel.

Liesel looks to me for help, but I'm not going to help her.

"Would you like that?" Liesel asks her.

Rose pulls on the end of her shirt and decides to change the subject. "When is Atlas coming?"

I glance at my phone to check the time. "Any minute now."

"Good," she says, closing her eyes and letting the sun hit her face.

We relax, enjoying the sun and watching the road until two black SUVs roll up. We all jump up and run to the driveway as the cars come to a rolling stop.

Rose gets to the SUVs before Liesel or I do.

She throws open the back door and sticks her head in to find Atlas.

"Atlas!" I hear her happy cry as she wraps her arms around him.

"Okay, Rose, let him breathe," I say as I step up behind her.

She doesn't listen. She lifts him out of the car, still hugging onto him.

I shake my head, but I feel the same urge, so I wrap my arms tightly around them both. There was a time that holding them both in my arms made me feel whole, but not anymore.

Not without Liesel.

Not without Declan.

Right now, I feel the parts of me that are missing.

I don't know how to introduce Atlas to Liesel. He's more timid and cautious than Rose, and this is all a lot for Liesel.

"Liesel, come here," Rose says in a frustrated tone.

Liesel rushes over. "What's wrong?"

Rose lets Atlas go long enough to take his hand. "Atlas, this is Liesel. I know she has a funny name, but she saved my life, so she's one of us now."

Atlas falls into Liesel's arms, shocking the hell out of Rose and me. Liesel collapses her arms around him. They don't speak; they don't need to. Apparently, they already have a strong connection.

Finally, Atlas lets go of Liesel.

Rose's jaw has dropped to the floor. "How did you do that? Who are you?"

Liesel brushes Rose's cheek. "That's a question for another day."

Rose blinks rapidly and then takes Atlas' hand again. "Are you okay? Did they hurt you?"

"No, I'm not hurt. Uncle Zeke and Aunt Siren saved me. Are you hurt? I should have been there to protect you," Atlas says.

"No, I'm good. And that's okay; Liesel saved me," Rose says.

The two run off toward the house hand-in-hand.

We should get them some therapy and make sure they don't have lasting effects, but for now, they seem like they are going to be okay.

Zeke and Siren are both standing to the side of one of the SUVs. Liesel and I walk over to them.

"Thank you," we both say at the same time. We both hug each of them.

"Are you okay? We can never repay you for what you did," Liesel says.

Siren opens her mouth but doesn't speak.

Zeke is staring at Siren like he's trying to read her thoughts.

They both look like we do—exhausted, worn down, bruised, and cut up. It wouldn't surprise me if they are slow to answer or process what we are saying, but they aren't talking at all. Something's wrong.

I walk up to Siren, my eyes searching for an answer. I touch her arm. We've always shared a connection that I don't understand.

Somehow all three of our families are connected through a bond different than the ones we have with our spouses. My connection is with Siren. Zeke has a connection with Kai. Liesel has a connection with Enzo. It's a strange circle, but it's our family.

When I touch her, I know something is wrong. My eyes search hers; I can feel loss inside of her.

"Siren lost her voice. I lost my hearing," Zeke says.

Siren nods, once again, not speaking.

I grab her head and pull her tightly to my body, needing to comfort her in some way. Once I've tried to take away some of her pain, I look to Zeke.

"Explain," I say as slowly as I can, mouthing my word to him.

He knows what I'm asking, though, even without looking.

"The game. In order to win and save Atlas, we both had to play a sacrifice card. The card made us sacrifice something. They poured liquid in my ears and Siren's throat, burning my eardrums and her vocal cords. We think the damage is temporary. My ears are already starting to ring, but we should have a doctor see if there is anything they can do to speed the healing up," Zeke says. His voice is shaky and tentative as he speaks since he can't hear himself talk.

"You shouldn't have given up your voice or your hearing," I say, completely speechless at the sacrifice they were both willing to make.

Siren tries to speak, but I can see how much pain stabs into her throat when she tries. She frowns and shakes her hand at Zeke, who pulls out a pen and paper from his pocket and hands it to her.

She starts scribbling furiously and then holds it up to me. Liesel looks at it over my shoulder as well.

It was our choice. We wanted to make the sacrifice to save Atlas. He's like a son to us. It was just my voice, just Zeke's hearing. Both can heal, and even if they don't, it will still have been worth it. Saving Atlas' life was worth it.

She's scribbled three lines under the last sentence.

"I'm going to find a way to heal you," I look at Siren, then Zeke. "Both of you."

Siren rolls her eyes and huffs.

"I understand that it's not about that. Thank you. You did your part though, let me do mine," I say, hugging Siren again.

I'm so consumed by my concern for Siren and Zeke that it takes me a minute to realize what this means. To win his game, Beckett also had to sacrifice something in order to save Declan. *What did he have to sacrifice?*

And then my heart drops even further as I look at Liesel; she's watching me carefully. She said she won her game to ensure they wouldn't have a reason to get Rose back.

What did she sacrifice?

CHAPTER 18

LIESEL

Langston figured it out. He knows that I sacrificed something; he just doesn't know what.

Langston looks at me as Zeke rests his arm around Siren's shoulders, and they start walking together toward the house.

I freeze. I'm not ready for this conversation. I'm tired of lying to Langston, but I'm not ready to tell him the truth yet either.

He walks toward me, presumably to ask me what I sacrificed. Instead, he kisses me tenderly on the lips.

The kiss tells me everything I need to know. He's here when I'm ready to tell him. I take his hand and let him lead me back inside the house.

"I'm headed back to the airport to get the kids," Enzo says.

We are so close to all being safe, so close.

"I need to make a phone call," Langston says, kissing my hand before stepping away.

I notice Rose and Atlas watching me closely from the living room. They both have their suspicions about me, about this whole situation. They deserve answers, but we need to wait until everyone is here before we talk. There is no use in having this conversation twice.

So instead, I walk into the kitchen, open the freezer and pull out a pint of ice cream. I grab three spoons and walk over to where the kids are sitting on the couch and hand them each a spoon.

"More ice cream?" Rose asks incredulously.

"Atlas didn't get any the last time."

We sit together and eat ice cream. They deserve to know who I am. They deserve the whole truth. Honestly, I'd just be fine if I was the ice cream lady to them.

ENZO RETURNS WITH HIS TWINS AND CAYDEN, ZEKE AND SIREN'S baby.

The twins run to Kai, and Enzo joins them.

Siren scoops up Cayden, who has just started walking. She goes to speak to him, then stops herself when she realizes that she can't. She catches me watching her and smiles before kissing Cayden all over his face, which makes him laugh hysterically.

"We missed you, little man," Zeke says, grabbing him up and swinging him around, making him laugh more. Zeke smiles brightly at him, not showing any outward sign at all that he's upset he can't hear his child's laughter.

But it breaks my heart.

It shouldn't be this way. Their family shouldn't pay because of something my father did.

"We're going to fix it," Langston says, coming up next to me.

I look at him.

"I called some doctors that specialize in hearing and vocal cords. They will be out here tomorrow. We are going to get them fixed."

I nod, hopeful but unsure if it's as easy as that.

We hear another car pull up; Langston and I exchange worried glances.

The last car is here, early.

Beckett.

Declan.

"Kai, watch Atlas and Rose, please," Langston shouts as he tries to catch up with me. I'm already running outside.

We don't know the tortured state Beckett could be in. He already went through so much when he lost his arm. I can't imagine what else he could have lost.

More importantly, I need to see Declan with my own two eyes. I need to know that he's alive and that he's here—safe.

Beckett throws open the passenger door. He walks over slow and steady to us. He's covered in blood. His shirt and pants are ripped like he was just attacked by a mountain lion. And his hand has a shirt wrapped around it.

But none of that is what has me concerned. My heart is beating a thousand miles a second because of the look in his eyes—complete sorrow.

"I'm so sorry," Beckett says.

"You lost?" Langston snaps a little too harshly.

I put my hand on Langston's shoulder and shake my head, trying to remind Langston that even if he did lose, it's not Beckett's fault. He did the best he could.

But I don't think that's what Beckett is saying.

It's clear he fought.

He played the game and did the dares, based on the injuries he has. He played the sacrifice card, and from the looks of it, he sacrificed his other hand. He already told us that he won.

"Corbin didn't give you Declan even after you won, did he?" I ask.

"He gave me a child, but that child wasn't Declan. I'm sorry."

"How did you know he wasn't Declan?" Langston asks.

"I know Rose and Atlas. I know their features, their mannerisms, their size. This child was bigger, older. His skin was tanner. He didn't share any of Rose, Atlas, or Liesel's features. I have some of his hair if you want to run a DNA test, but the child isn't yours, Liesel."

A tear starts to roll, but I wipe it away quickly.

"Where is the child?" Langston asks, still not convinced.

"He's with his parents. I did a quick search of the missing child reports. There was one from a few months ago that matched his description. He has a sister with reddish-brown hair that matches his."

Langston looks at me like he needs my assurance.

I sit down, right in the middle of the driveway. I don't have the energy to stand anymore. I just need a minute to process all of this.

"We should run the DNA test just to confirm, but it doesn't sound like that child is mine," I say.

"Then, where is Declan?" Langston asks.

Dead?

Missing?

With Corbin?

I don't know the answer, but we have to find out. Until I know for sure where Declan is, I have to keep searching, hunting. I'm the huntress, after all, and I won't give up. Corbin and Maxwell are still out there. They could still have him.

Langston sits down next to me on one side. Beckett slumps down on the other.

Seeing his bandaged hand breaks me. "Oh my god, you went through all that pain for nothing. You lost your other hand for nothing."

Beckett shakes his head. "It wasn't for nothing. I saved that kid. I don't regret it." He unwraps his hand, revealing boils and burns all over his skin. "And I didn't lose my hand, just my sense of touch and attractiveness until this heals."

Langston whips out his phone. "I'm going to call for a doctor to look at those ASAP. I already have specialists flying out tomorrow for Siren and Zeke."

He stands and walks a short distance away to make the call.

"Siren and Zeke are okay?" Beckett asks.

"Yes, Siren sacrificed her voice; Zeke, his hearing."

"And the kids?"

"Rose and Atlas are safe and sound. They aren't injured in any way we can see. I think Langston has a pediatrician and psychologist coming out to check on them just to be sure, but they seem perfectly fine. When I left them, they were eating a tub of ice cream."

He smiles at that.

"Thank you, Beckett. You have no idea how much your sacrifice means to me, even if it didn't turn out the way we planned."

"It was the right thing to do—no regrets."

We both turn and look out at the ocean. The sun is already beginning to set. Where did the time go?

"What happens now?" Beckett asks.

Langston returns, standing over my shoulder.

I turn to answer Beckett. "First, we talk to the kids. We tell them the truth or as much of the truth as they can handle. Then we make a plan to find Declan and protect all of us from Corbin, Maxwell, and Phoenix."

Langston lowers his hand to me. I reluctantly take it.

I'm not sure I'm doing what's best for Rose and Atlas by telling them the truth. A large part of me still feels like I should hide the truth from them to protect them, but the other part wants to love them openly.

That part can't be silenced any longer.

CHAPTER 19

LANGSTON

"They are going to love you. There is nothing you should be nervous about," I tell Liesel as we walk back into the house, Beckett trailing behind.

I can tell she's nervous, her hands are shaking at her sides, and she doesn't respond.

"Or we can go with the whole hate me thing we got going on. They'll think that's a hoot," I joke.

I tilt my head, hoping she'll crack a smile—she doesn't. She's a woman on a mission, and I have no choice but to go along with it and hope she's ready to tell the truth. *Maybe after she tells the kids the truth, she can start talking to me?*

We head back inside, and Liesel freezes. I'm guessing she's having second thoughts, but I'm not going to let her think too hard about this. She needs to tell the kids who she is. It's the only way we can be a family again.

"Rose, Atlas, you want to go for a walk on the beach with Liesel and me?"

"Yes!" Rose says immediately.

Atlas nods, and they both pop off the couch.

Beckett walks in behind us, and Kai runs to him, engulfing him in a

297

hug. They all have a lot to talk about, so I take Liesel's hand and lead her out the back deck, then down the stairs toward the beach. Rose and Atlas chase after us.

As we get closer to the beach, I find a quiet spot and sit down. Liesel doesn't sit immediately, so I tug on her hand until she takes the hint and sits.

"Are we building sandcastles?" Rose asks.

I shake my head. "Maybe later. We both wanted to talk to you about something first. Liesel is..."

Jesus, it's harder to tell my kids their whole world has changed than I realized. And if I tell them Liesel is their birth mom, do I have to tell Rose that I'm not her biological father?

I rub my neck, unsure of what to do next when Liesel speaks.

"I'm your birth mother."

Both Rose and Atlas snap their head to Liesel.

"Whose? Mine or Atlas'?" Rose asks, staring at Liesel in awe.

"Both. See, once upon a time, I was a young woman, and I got pregnant with three special children."

"Three?" Atlas blinks.

"Yes, three. I was young and scared, but I loved my three babies more than anything in the world. Those babies were you, Rose." She smiles at Rose. "And you, Atlas." She turns her smile to Atlas. "And another baby named Declan."

Neither of the kids ask questions anymore. They are entranced with Liesel's story.

"The day came that you three were finally ready to leave my belly. I got sick and fell asleep when you were born. Someone took you three away before I got a chance to see you or hold you. You were split up and given to different people to live with.

"Rose, you were given to your mother, Phoenix, and your father, Langston. Atlas—eventually, Phoenix and Langston found you. They didn't know that you and Rose were biological brother and sister at the time, but they knew you belonged to this family all the same."

He smiles up at her.

"Now, we are looking for your brother, Declan, to complete the family."

"We really have another brother?" Atlas asks.

Liesel nods.

She reaches forward and takes both of their hands. "What you need to know, though, is that even though I wasn't around, I still loved you and tried my best to protect you all your lives. Langston, your father, is your father in every way that matters. Phoenix—" She takes a deep breath.

"Phoenix is still your mother. She loves you desperately, and she's helping us find your brother. We all love you. Your mom, dad, me, and all your aunts, uncles, and cousins inside. We all love you."

I'm not sure about telling them that Phoenix is still their mother and loves them, but everything else is spot on.

"Do you have any questions for your father or me?"

"Can we call you Mom?" Rose asks.

Liesel smiles. "You can call me whatever you want."

"What do we call Mom, though?" Atlas asks, confused.

"You can call your other mom, Mom, too. You can have two moms."

"I like that idea," Atlas says.

"Are you two dating?" Rose asks, looking from Liesel to me.

"That's a complicated question, but yes, we are," Liesel replies.

"What about our other mom? Do you not love her anymore, Dad? Where is she?" Rose asks.

"She's looking for Declan, but I have a feeling she'll be back soon," Liesel says, stepping in before I can answer, forcing me to follow her lead.

"I love both of your moms very much in very different ways. We still have a lot to figure out as a family, but we are all a family. All of us in our own complicated way, okay?" I say.

All three pairs of lips smile and nod at me while I get a queasy feeling in my stomach. I trust Liesel with my life; I just hope she knows what she's doing.

We put all the kids to bed, and then it's just the adults sitting in the living room.

Kai sits on the floor, leaning against Enzo's knees. Siren and Zeke sit snuggled together, a large legal pad and pen lying on their lap so Siren can communicate.

Beckett sits in a single chair with his hand in a new bandage. He has a smoothie with a straw, so he can lean over to get some calories until a doctor looks at his hand.

Langston and I sit on a loveseat with Langston's arm around my shoulders, just as much a couple as the rest of them. I twirl my ring around my finger. We talked to the kids. They know almost everything and took it surprisingly well, even though it's ridiculously complicated. Now we all have to decide what we do next.

There would have been a time when I thought it was just my and Langston's decision. I thought everyone in the room betrayed us, but now that everyone has sacrificed so much, I know differently. We are a family, no matter what happens.

"So, what do we do next?" Kai asks, starting the conversation.

All eyes fall on us.

"We talk to Phoenix," I say immediately, even though I know the whole room will disagree with me. There is no immediate outrage, at least not from anyone except Langston, who looks at me like I'm off my rocker.

Siren jots down what I said, so Zeke is up to speed. I get no protest from them either. I do need to remember to pause after I speak, so they can get caught up.

"For now, we have to assume Corbin and Maxwell have Declan. Phoenix is likely to confirm or deny it, so let's start there," I say.

There's some nodding from the room.

"Phoenix won't tell us the truth. We will gain nothing from talking to her," Langston says, removing his arm from behind me.

I miss the loss immediately.

"She told us the truth about the clubs."

"No, if she did, then we would already have Declan."

"We have Rose and Atlas because of the information she gave us. And they didn't hurt the kids. If she truly wanted to hurt us, then they would have hurt them—they didn't. They just want more from us. We need to talk to her."

"Or we could attack Corbin and Maxwell. Kill them and their team, extract Declan ourselves, if they even have him."

"And what would you do with Phoenix?"

"She doesn't deserve to live after what she's done," Langston says.

I sigh. He's just being a protective father. He feels betrayed by her. But every person in this room has hurt and betrayed people, often-times betraying others in this room. We're all human, and we have all fucked up when we were hurting or trying to protect others. Everyone deserves a second chance.

"It's no longer just up to us to decide, so let's put it to a vote. Should our next step be talking to Phoenix or not?" I ask the room.

Langston stares them down, trying to persuade them to his side. It wouldn't shock me if they took his side, simply because they are closer to him than they are to me.

"Enzo?" Langston asks.

"I don't trust Phoenix, so no, I don't think you should talk to her. I agree with Langston—we should attack Corbin and Maxwell, then find Declan once we've destroyed them," Enzo says.

Kai looks at me with sympathy in her eyes and says, "I agree with Enzo."

That's two for Langston and none for me. It's not looking good.

We all turn our attention to Siren and Zeke. Siren is writing furiously on the paper, and Zeke is studying every word closely. He looks at Siren, who nods at him.

"Siren agrees with Liesel. We should get every bit of information we can from Phoenix. And for the kids' sake, she deserves a second chance," Zeke speaks.

That makes it two to one, but Zeke and Beckett will take Langston's side.

Zeke thinks for a moment and then speaks. "I also agree with Liesel."

I blink rapidly, not sure I heard him correctly. Two to two.

Everyone's attention turns to Beckett.

"You're the deciding vote, Beckett," Langston says.

Beckett stares at his injured hand. He's lost the most. Sure, Siren lost her voice and Zeke his hearing, but they can rely on each other to make up for the losses.

And I lost...

But Beckett has no one to help him. He was already at a disadvantage, and now that his other hand is injured, he's going to struggle without a lot of help.

"We have to do what gives us the best chance to get Declan back. Talk to Phoenix, find out what she knows. Then, you can decide what the best course of action is to get Declan back."

Langston stands in a huff. I think he's going to storm out, frustrated with the group's decision. He holds his hand out to me instead.

Carefully, I place my hand in his.

"Fine, let's get this over with," Langston says.

CHAPTER 21

LANGSTON

I *got outvoted.*

That's why I'm currently climbing on board a yacht instead of planning a tactical mission to take out Corbin and everyone who works for him. Being on the ocean like this used to be my sanctuary, but now it's my nightmare. Anywhere my kids aren't is my nightmare.

Liesel stands next to me on the top deck as we ask one of the employees where they're keeping Phoenix. He gives us her room number and the code to get in before walking away to continue his duties.

We head downstairs to her room. My hand hovers over the security keypad outside her room.

"You sure?" I ask Liesel.

She nods. "Phoenix is not a bad person. She's done some horrible things because she's hurting, and she doesn't know how to deal with the pain. She'll help us."

I'm not sure if I agree with her, but I enter the code and open the door. I step inside first; I'll do anything I can to protect Liesel.

Phoenix is sitting on the bed, staring out a window, looking out at the ocean. She doesn't glance over at us as we enter.

"So, you failed and are begging me to convince my brothers to give you your kids back, huh?" Phoenix asks.

I'm about to yell at her, attack her, squeeze her until she pays for everything she's put us through.

"No, that's not why we are here," Liesel says, stepping out from behind me.

Phoenix snaps her head to Liesel.

I grab Liesel's hand, trying to keep her back. Phoenix is going to try to attack her.

Liesel shakes me off. She walks over and sits on the foot of the bed staring at Phoenix.

"We won the games," Liesel says.

"You got the kids back?" Phoenix asks.

"We got Rose and Atlas back," Liesel says.

Phoenix exhales, her shoulders visibly relaxing, acting relieved. But then she looks Liesel in the eyes with concern. "You sacrificed? All of you?"

"We did," she says quietly.

Phoenix nods.

"We did our part. We felt the pain. We hurt. We won, but we only got Rose and Atlas back. We didn't get Declan. Corbin gave Beckett another kid, not Declan," Liesel says.

Phoenix looks down as she picks her nails.

"Phoenix? Does Corbin even have Declan?"

She nods.

"How do we get him back?"

"I'm sorry," Phoenix says, looking from Liesel to me. "Truly, I am. I never wanted the kids to suffer. I only wanted to hurt you."

"Will Corbin hurt Declan?" I ask. If he would, I'm not waiting. I'll fight Corbin to the death right now. I'm not going to wait for whatever games.

"No, he just doesn't think you all have suffered enough."

"What do you think?" Liesel asks.

Phoenix exchanges a glance with Liesel. "I think once you finish the games, you'll have paid me back for the pain your father caused me."

"So, how do we finish the game?" I ask.

"You get the treasure. You give it to Corbin. You set me free, and you promise to never attack my family again."

That's not something I can promise.

"Can I ask for something?" Phoenix asks.

"No," I say, at the same time Liesel says, "Yes."

"I'd like to say goodbye to the kids. I know you don't think I deserve it, but I want to explain to them why they won't be seeing me anymore when the time comes," Phoenix says.

"No," I say, walking out the door. I'm done with her. I don't trust her. She's manipulative and did the one thing I view as unforgivable—hurt my children.

I'm nearly out the door before I hear Liesel say, "He'll come around. He's just hurt. We'll figure something out when it comes to the kids."

I head up to the top deck of the yacht and lean over the edge of the railing, looking out as the moon rises over the ocean.

Liesel stands next to me.

"Are you upset with me?" she asks.

I inhale a deep breath. "No, I can't be upset with you, even when we disagree—not anymore."

"You can be mad at me and still care for me. I'm sure you get mad at the kids sometimes, but that doesn't mean you don't love them."

I shake my head. "I'm not upset with you. I just disagree with you. And I'm upset with myself that you don't trust me enough to tell me what you sacrificed so I can help you heal."

She sighs as she leans further over the edge of the railing.

"What if I told you the sacrifice I made didn't matter because I already lost that part of me years ago? The reason I don't want to tell you is that nothing has changed. I don't want you to think I was suffering and you weren't there to stop it when it's not true."

I frown. "I'd say that whatever you went through, no matter how small, I want to know. I need to protect you. I need—"

"No, you don't. Sometimes, it's better if you don't know."

We are both silent a moment.

"What do we have to do to get the next clue to the treasure?" she asks.

"You really think finding the treasure, and playing their games, is the best way to get Declan back?"

"Yes, I do," she says.

God, help us.

"What is it? What aren't you telling me?" Liesel asks.

Fucking everything.

"Nothing—it's nothing."

She folds her arms and faces me. "Tell me the truth, killer."

"You go first."

She frowns.

"Fine, we both keep our secrets. If it means we're protecting each other, then I agree we shouldn't tell each other."

"Fine."

"Fine."

"Now what?"

Now, I make you admit you love me instead of hating me while trying to keep my own feelings hidden so I don't destroy us all.

How do I make her fall in love with me?

Romance.

I've tried it before and failed, but I don't know what else to try. Maybe a day away from all of this will make her admit her feelings. One day where we aren't thinking about the kids or how to protect our family and friends.

"One day," I say.

"What?"

"Give me one day where you don't ask any questions. We forget about the past, our future, the kids, the danger—everything. Give me one day where it's just us. Can you do that?"

She bites her lip, and I expect her to say I'm crazy, but then she says, "Yes."

LIESEL

I know something is up. There is a reason Langston wants to spend a day together. A day where I just go along with whatever he has planned and not ask any questions. A day where I forget that I still have a child in danger and that my other two children are on an island, still in danger as long I keep waiting to finish this ridiculous treasure quest.

But I trust Langston.

I trust him too much.

So when he calls his team to bring us his sailboat, I climb on, no questions asked.

We are as safe as humanly possible. Kai has her entire team out on boats surrounding and protecting us, but it still feels strange to be on a boat by ourselves.

I sit on the side of the boat as I watch Langston work, pulling on ropes and getting the sail into the position he wants. At one point, he loses his shirt, giving me an exquisite view of his rippling muscles.

Finally, he must be satisfied with the work he's done on the sail. He reaches into a cooler and pulls out a bottle of champagne and a couple of flutes.

"Come here," he says, sitting and patting the spot in front of his lap.

My stomach does a little flip as I sit in his lap. If he were truly mine, then sitting between his legs under the stars while we sip champagne would be the most romantic thing in the world. Despite the fact that we are legally married, despite the fact that we care deeply for each other, have said that we belong to each other, it's not true.

He's not mine.

I repeat those words to myself as I lean back against his bare chest.

He hands me a glass of champagne, which I take, even though I don't want any alcohol tonight. I have a feeling I'll be replaying this night forever in my head, and I don't want to forget a single detail.

His arms wrap around my stomach, pulling me tighter against his chest until we can both look up at the stars.

Then Langston starts softly singing John Legend's 'All of Me.' My heart stops beating as he sings the first verse, wondering what's going on in my mind. Next, my breathing stops as he nears the chorus. I wait to hear the words I've been dying to hear from him since I was seventeen, maybe even longer.

"...*hates* all of you," he sings, changing the lyrics.

I chuckle. It's what the moment needs, but god, does it sting to not hear him sing the one word that's missing from my life.

But if he were to say he loves me, it will end up killing him. It's for the best.

Tell that to my lovesick heart.

He continues to sing the rest of the song, and every time he says 'hate' instead of 'love,' I wince. He must notice, but he doesn't say anything.

Finally, when my heart can't take anymore, I get up from his lap and walk to the other end of the boat. Maybe I should have drunk some of that champagne after all?

"You okay?" Langston asks.

I nod, not trusting my voice.

His hand slides up and down my back. "You're tense. How about a soak in the tub and massage?"

I nod again.

I feel his breath on my neck; I hiss because he feels so good without even touching me. I can't fight giving him my heart anymore. It's his—it's always been his. Now to decide if it's fair to tell him or not.

He walks away from me, removing the cover of the hot tub. He presses a button to turn it on, and bubbles come to life.

I smile. Only Langston would have a sailboat with a hot tub on the top deck.

Silently, he walks back to me. We haven't spoken much since he sang his song. He grabs the hem of my shirt and pulls it up and over my body. Then he moves to my pants, taking his time sliding them down my body until I'm in nothing but boxers from the plane.

He sucks in a breath as his eyes rake over my bare chest. He hooks his fingers into the waistband and pushes them down too.

"Are you going to undress me, or do I have to do that too?" he asks with a smirk.

"You seem to be doing a pretty good job yourself."

His grin turns vicious. He shoves his pants and boxers down in one push before yanking us backward into the hot tub.

The water engulfs us, warmth soothing my aching muscles, but his body against mine is cruel. I want him forever, instead of just this one fairytale of a day.

We surface, and I'm once again sitting on Langston's lap. He starts working my shoulders, and I melt. I try to push out my fears and do what Langston said—just enjoy tonight. His touch helps. I can't help but relax.

"Where should we go on our honeymoon?" Langston asks suddenly.

I turn my head to look at him. "What honeymoon?"

"The honeymoon we are going to go on after we get Declan."

"But—"

Langston kisses my lips, shutting me up. "Where?"

When I still don't speak, Langston says, "Humor me. Do you want to go somewhere warm? Another beach? The mountains?"

When I don't answer, he continues throwing out ideas. "Paris? The Maldives? Sydney? San Diego? St. Lucia?"

"Stop."

"What? I need to imagine a life after this—a month-long vacation that's just the two of us. I love our kids, but I want to do very dirty things to your body to make up for lost time, and I can't do that with them around. We'll make it up to them with a trip to Disney World or something afterward. And they'll have fun playing with Kai and Enzo's twins."

I scoot off his lap, wanting to look him in the eye when we talk.

"Does it bother you that our kids aren't biologically yours?" I know it doesn't, but it heals my heart to hear him talk about the kids, to know he will always be their father, no matter what else happens.

"No, it doesn't bother me. They're mine," he growls.

I smile.

"Even if their father wasn't a dead motherfucker, they would still belong to me."

Then another thought pops into my head that I can't dismiss; I have to know its answer. "I know you already think of Atlas and Rose as your kids and that you will feel the same way about Declan, but..."

"But what?"

"Do you want biological kids? Kids that look like you, share your mannerisms, your blood?"

"Rose already looks like me with her blonde hair and adventurous spirit. And Atlas mimics every behavior of mine that he can. The other day I caught him trying to use my razor to shave his face," he chuckles at the memory.

His laughter stops when he sees how serious I am. I need to know the truth.

His eyes drop to my stomach beneath the bubbles. He still thinks there is a chance I'm pregnant, that I can be the one to provide him with a biological child.

I should tell him the truth, but I can't—not yet. It could ruin his whole world, and not when there is still a tiny fraction of a chance that—

"No, I don't need a biological child. I have Rose, Atlas, Declan. I never thought I'd make a good father with the example I had as a father."

"Langston, you're a good father."

"I know. I'm not perfect, but I do my best, and our kids know I love them. Being loved by them, having you in my life, it's more than I could have ever imagined. I don't need a kid that shares my blood to make me happy, but if one comes along, I'll love them too."

Can't. Feel. My. Heart.

"Is something wrong?" Langston asks.

I shake my head.

He snickers knowingly. "Something you want to tell me?"

I shake more furiously.

He laughs and relaxes his arms over the edge of the hot tub, seemingly at ease with wherever this conversation is going.

"I always knew we'd end up married," he says.

"You did?"

"Of course. We both fought it because we are both so independent and stubborn, and we believed the lies. But I always knew you were it for me, huntress." I can't tell if he's glad that I'm the person for him or tormented that we are stuck together.

He notices my change. "Tell me something I don't know about you. Tell me a wish, a dream."

I run my tongue over the front of my teeth. There is a wicked gleam in my eyes. I don't have a wish or a dream for some far-off future other than ensuring that our kids are safe. I can't think or plan for our future. That's not something I want to imagine. It doesn't warm my heart to plan a honeymoon or pretend that our marriage can survive what's coming.

"I've never had sex in a hot tub under the stars," I say.

"Really? I thought everyone had," he teases.

I shake my head slowly, keeping my lust-filled eyes on him.

I'm tired of talking.

He's obviously trying for a romantic night, but I'm tired of it. I want dirty, filthy sex. That's the only thing that can get me out of my head right now.

I inch toward him; his arms stay on the edge of the tub. His eyes are already attacking me, roaming over every part of my body he intends to kiss, lick, tease. A rush of excitement spreads between my legs at the look.

I inch forward until I'm as close as I can get without touching him. Still, he doesn't try and touch me. When I glance at his hands, I see his knuckles are turning white. He's gripping onto the side of the tub to control himself.

"What are you doing?" I giggle at his ridiculousness.

"Trying to take my time so I can memorize every face you make. How you sound when you breathe versus when I'm touching you. How you feel."

"You can't know how I feel if you don't touch me."

"If I touch you, I'm going to get caught up in fucking you and miss the glow you have, the fire in your eyes."

"What's wrong with getting lost in me?"

"Nothing—I just want to take my time with you."

I straddle his lap as I hold onto the tub on either side of his shoulders and let my body sink down on top of him.

"We only have one night. You don't get to take your time with me."

He frowns, but my comment finally makes him touch me. He grabs my hips as his pelvis tilts his hard length between my legs. He tilts his head forward, taking my bottom lip into his mouth. His growl rattles through our bodies.

"We are pretending the outside world doesn't exist for one night, but you are mine forever," he promises.

He lifts me up and then drives me down onto his cock, claiming me in one stroke.

"So much for going slow," I tease.

He responds by driving into me harder, shutting me up until I can no longer speak.

My body responds to his every thrust. My lips kiss his over and over. Our tongues collide and slide over each other.

Langston wants to take this slow to ensure we remember every second. I'd prefer to spend the night fucking over and over again until my body and brain can't forget how Langston feels inside my body.

"I belong in your body," Langston says.

"Yo—" I can't get any words out. He's fucking me so hard; he's rattling my brain cells. Shocks of emotions pulse through my body.

I don't know how he does this. I love sex; I've had plenty of good partners over the years. But with Langston, it's not about where we are, the mood, the scenery, or the position. Just being with him—kissing, licking, fucking, any of it—takes me to a different place. My body is overcome with some emotion I haven't felt before. I don't care if I come or how good it feels, as long as Langston and I are connecting.

"Come, baby," Langston growls.

He can sense how close I am. That growl thing he does, low and vibrating through my whole body, is all I need to come. I explode, and my eyes are seeing shooting stars in the sky above me. I still can't form coherent syllables, let alone words.

Langston is kissing my swollen lips slowly before he scoops me into his arms. "I hate you so much, Liesel. I hate you so much."

CHAPTER 23

LANGSTON

The sun wakes me as it begins to rise over the ocean. We slept on the top of the sailboat with a comforter snuggled around us. Liesel is still asleep on my shoulder.

I don't want to move her, but I failed last night. Liesel didn't admit she loves me. I'm going to have to try something different. We fucked three times last night. Each time was rough and frantic. It was all either of us could manage, but slow, romantic lovemaking is what this task needs; not feral, animalistic fucking.

I inch myself out from under Liesel. She continues to snore as I stand up. Then I run to the small kitchenette to make coffee and omelets.

After whipping up a quick breakfast, I return with a tray of food and coffee to where Liesel is still sleeping. I don't want to wake her; she looks so peaceful, and in our life, you sleep as much as you can. But every second we fail to get the treasure is another second our son is in danger, so this can't wait.

I slip under the covers next to Liesel, and then I hold one of the cups underneath Liesel's nose as I kiss her cheek.

"Good morning."

"Mmmh," she moans but doesn't open her eyes. "Am I dreaming, or is that coffee?"

"It's coffee."

Her eyes snap open, and she smiles at me with flushed cheeks.

I frown. There's a chill in the air; she shouldn't feel warm.

I brush my hand over her forehead—she does feel warm.

Her lips lean up to kiss mine, and I forget about her feeling warm.

"Sit up," I tell her.

She moves into the crook of my arm and leans against my shoulder. I hand her the cup of coffee and then move the tray across our laps so she can eat her omelet.

"Wow, I've never had breakfast in bed, but I'm not sure I can call a comforter on the deck of a boat a bed," she says.

"Is that a thank you?"

She grins. "Thank you."

"You're welcome."

We both drink our coffees and pick at our omelets. Liesel doesn't eat enough, but I'm not going to try to get her to change her eating habits now. She sets her almost empty coffee mug down on the tray.

"Why are we really here? I know you are doing this, so when you do the fucked up thing the task requires, I'll have some good memories to pair with it. But we are running out of time. Can we get to the hard part now?" Liesel says.

She's right; that's what this whole night and morning have been about. As much as I enjoy sitting here eating breakfast with her, it's not going to get her to admit she loves me. Hopefully, it is giving her warm and fuzzy feelings that might help her get there faster.

I set the tray to the side wordlessly. Yes, this is all about the stupid treasure, but I'm not treating her sweetly because I plan on hurting her. It's the opposite. I want her to love me as I love her.

I grab her neck and lay her back down as my body moves over her. She's naked underneath the comforter, as am I. The feeling of our naked bodies touching overwhelms my senses, and I'm immediately hard again.

"What are you doing?" she asks, her bottom lip trembling just slightly.

Leaning down, I close my eyes and kiss that lip tenderly.

She gasps at the impact.

My intention is to worship every inch of her body. I want to make her know how much I love each part of her and that she's safe with me. I'll love her forever, no matter what happens. I want to flood her with feelings so that the words just fall out of her.

She can't take it back because once she speaks the truth, she's not going to be able to stop speaking or feeling it. I'm guessing that's why she hasn't spoken the words so far. She doesn't want to love me. She wants to go back to her independent life by herself and get visitation of the kids or some shit like that. She's scared; everyone she has ever loved has hurt her, left her, or been taken away from her.

She needs to know that I won't hurt her.

I won't leave her.

And I won't be taken from her.

I start at her forehead. I leave a kiss there and then move to each of her cheeks.

"Your eyes have captivated me since we were five, and we hunted a spider together," I say.

She smiles, her face heating.

My lips find the spot behind her ear that causes her breath to speed. Then I move to her earlobes, my tongue flicking the lobe until she gasps.

"I want to worship your entire body forever. Will you let me?"

"Mmmh," she moans.

I grin. "I'll take that as a yes."

I kiss her lips gently, trying not to get carried away and fuck her too fast.

"Every time I kiss you, your lips hold me captive. I get swept away in your delicious lips. Your taste. Your moans. It's everything I've ever dreamed of."

I kiss down her neck until I'm licking down her clavicle. She shifts underneath me as I move closer to the upper curve of her breast.

"And your curves drive me wild, Liesel."

I find her first nipple with my teeth, teasing it gently as I swirl my tongue along the tip. When I move to the second, she arches her back and sinks her hand into my hair, becoming even more breathless.

"You still with me?" I smile around her other nipple. I want her to feel amazing, but I also need her able to talk. It's a fine balance.

She groans.

"I'm going to need an actual answer, or I might have to stop." I flick her nipple with my tongue.

"Fuck," she curses.

"That's better, baby."

I continue my way down her body, kissing over her stomach. I take my time here, still not convinced she's not pregnant. Her questions from earlier about wanting a biological child of my own pop into my head. My hopes of her being pregnant have nothing to do with my own feelings. Although, it does make me possessive as hell to think I put a baby in her belly. I hope she's pregnant because she missed out on so much with the kids' early days. She should get to experience that.

She notices that I spend extra time on her belly.

"I hate you," she says, once again avoiding saying the real words. I almost regret starting the hate you line.

We are getting close, baby. Just say the actual words.

"You're the most incredible mother. This whole time you've been protecting them, loving them. Just fucking amazing."

I spread her legs, deciding she's earned my attention on her most sensitive area—the part she's been trying to push me toward with her hand in my hair and the arch of her back.

I lick up her slit.

"Jesus, Langston."

There's my girl.

I hold her legs apart as I find her clit with my tongue and swirl around it. She bends her knees, and her legs fall further open, giving me better access. My tongue pushes inside her, finding her soaking before I lick her clit again and again.

"You taste so sweet. And yet, you are the strongest woman I know."

I slide two fingers inside her, intensifying her pleasure before I make her come. I barely push inside her before I feel her clenching around me. Her nails dig into my skull as she grips my hair. She moans and screams my name, but nothing for her feelings for me.

Before she's finished her orgasm, I settle between her legs, and my cock slides inside her contracting pussy.

Her eyes roll back, but I kiss her lips calmly as I stop after one thrust inside her. I'm going to move slowly, so she feels everything. I want her to have time to feel every emotion and articulate them before I have her losing her mind.

"Look at me," I say.

She takes her time, but eventually, her bright eyes are staring into mine.

I rock into her gently.

"You're mine."

She bites her lip at my words. I'm not sure she truly believes me.

"Say it."

"I'm yours."

I nod, kissing her again as I slide through her slick walls again.

"And you're mine," she says, unprompted.

Good girl.

I rub my thumb over her clit in slow circles.

"You're intoxicatingly beautiful."

"You're frustratingly handsome."

Yes, this is how I get her to say 'I love you.' She'll follow whatever I say, but can I tell her that I love her? Can I tell her and protect her at the same time?

My heart pounds wildly in my chest until I'm sure she can tell how nervous I am. I've never told a woman I loved her, but I know without a shadow of a doubt that I love Liesel. I always have; I've just been looking for any excuse that I can to not love her. Now, I can't stop loving her.

"You were the first person to have a nickname for me," I kiss her.

I rock into her as slowly as I can muster, trying to draw this out, but damn, is my cock obsessed with her. I won't last nearly as long as I want.

"You are the only person to ever have a nickname for me," she says against my lips.

I thrust harder.

"Only your kids could feel like mine."

"Only you could take care of my kids like they were your own."

More—more of everything.

"Only your fierceness could be enough to tame me."

"Only your strength could be enough to own me."

SO. FUCKING. CLOSE.

"I hate you," I kiss her, trying to hold our orgasms back for a couple more seconds.

"And I hate you." She nips at my bottom lip.

It's now or never.

Say it!

NOW.

"I—I lov—"

Her lips press against mine, hard.

Our tongues swarm each other. Our breaths combine. Our bodies slam together as we reach our climaxes.

We shake from the aftermath, tremble in each other's arms.

Our lips are still locked together, so I gently pull them apart.

I failed.

I didn't get her to say 'I love you,' and I didn't say it myself.

She smiles up at me, and the moment is over. Her brain is working again. If I say 'I love you' now, she'll just think I'm crazy, and she won't say it back.

I have to find a different way.

She's expecting the worst, not for me to tell her I love her.

She's prepared for the nightmare, not the dream.

I consider my options. Liesel is a stubborn woman who will refuse to admit her love for me. She's scared, and I'm not even sure she realizes what her feelings are for me. She says she's not capable of falling in love with anyone.

"What?" She frowns up at me, her eyes searching mine for what's going on in my head.

I lick my lips, trying to buy myself time, trying to think of another way—I can't. I've tried everything else. I promised I wouldn't hurt

Liesel, but sometimes the only way to reveal the love in a person's heart is to cause their heart to bleed.

"I'm sorry," I say, knowing what I must do.

"Do your worst," she says, and then she kisses me hard on the lips.

Oh, huntress, you have no idea what my worst is. You call me killer for a reason. I'm about to murder your heart and hope that when you are picking up the pieces, you realize your true feelings.

CHAPTER 24

LIESEL

We just made love.

That's what Langston was going for—a romantic night filled with hot, dirty sex. Then breakfast in bed, followed by slow lovemaking and a declaration of his love.

It was beautiful, magical. I could feel his love in every kiss, every touch, every breath.

He poured everything he had into showing me with his body just how much he loves me. I just couldn't let him do it with his words.

For years I've managed to keep him hating me for real. I just have to keep him from loving me for a little bit longer.

I told him to do his worst, so I'm preparing for it, even as his naked body still lies on top of mine. Even in the afterglow of what just passed between us, I know what comes next is going to hurt like a motherfucker. It's going to hurt worse than anything that happened to me in that game, on that yacht, when I was raped—all of it combined because Langston is going to be the one hurting me.

He thought it would make it easier on us if he said he loves me, easier to heal after he's done the terrible task he has to do for the treasure. We would be more connected if he said the words, but I know that's not true.

Words said or not; I've already fucked up. I already let us get too close. I'm just hoping that whatever way he has to torture me now will break both of our hearts enough that we can't possibly stay together.

For once, I hope my father came up with some wicked game to ruin us.

I run through all the things that Langston could do to prepare myself. If I could force my heart to break first, I'd do it, but I can't. Langston is the only one who has that power over me. And once he does destroy my heart, I have to be careful not to let either of our hearts break again.

Could he fuck another woman in front of me?

Could he break up with me, divorce me?

Take my kids away from me?

Physically hurt me? Rape me?

Each image plays in my head. I feel the pain; I feel my heart expanding in each instance, pushing it to its limits. I see it getting stabbed, ripped, cracked, but it never fully breaks.

Because I love him unconditionally; I love him wholly. Despite what he does, he's doing it to save our child, not because he wants to hurt me. There is nothing he can do that will make me stop loving him.

Fuck, if this is how I feel, I'm sure Langston feels the same. I don't know what it's going to take to get rid of our love, but I'm going to figure it out.

Langston closes his eyes as his body continues to pin me to the deck of the sailboat. When they open, there's a wicked fire. He's flipped a switch inside. Before, he was a man; now, he's the devil.

I purse my lips and try to breathe to control my heartbeat, not that I've been able to control my fucked up heart before. I already know I'm a goner. *Is dying by love a real thing that can happen?* If so, I'm going to die from loving Langston too much.

I'm rambling in my head, trying to process this moment to keep it separate from what happened earlier tonight. Maybe whatever Langston has to do will break him hard enough that he won't be able to be in the same room as me. He will stay away from me, and distance will make our love fade.

I bite my lip as he rubs himself against me.

Nope, I don't think there is anything that will make me stop loving him. The only way our love is dying is tragically, without the words ever being said out loud.

"Stop trying to guess what I'm going to do, huntress. You don't have a clue." The sinful gleam in his eyes tells me I don't.

He leans forward and whispers in my ear, "And to make sure you don't fuck up my plans, I'm going to tie you to the mast."

"You shouldn't have told me your plan."

"I didn't even tell you half of my plan."

"You told me enough." I squeeze my legs tight, trapping his junk before I knee him hard.

"Jesus," he groans as he rolls off me.

I grin and run.

I'm just delaying the inevitable, but I want him to do whatever he has to do with my arms and legs free. I don't think I can handle giving up so much control in my moment of torture.

There aren't many places to run on this boat. My choices are to jump overboard or head down into the below decks. I decide to head down, knowing he'll catch me if I jump into the water.

There are six steps down that lead down to a short hallway and one door. I pop the door open and then throw it shut, slamming my body against the door as I flip the lock. I press my ear against the door, listening carefully.

I listen for his footsteps down the stairs or in the hallway, but I hear nothing.

Strange.

I hold my breath, thinking the sound of my breathing is affecting my ability to hear, but I still hear nothing. Then again, Langston can move silently.

I expect him to start kicking down the door any second now, but he doesn't.

He's messing with my head, I think, after twenty minutes have passed, and he hasn't made any attempt to come after me.

I slink to the floor and pull my knees to my chest as I continue to rest my ear against the door, waiting.

"Waiting for me?" Langston says from behind me.

I jump.

It's too late—Langston has me pinned to the door.

"How did you get in here?"

"I have to have some secrets," he winks at me as he growls and pins my hands above my head. My hips are trapped against the door with his.

"Don't even think about trying to knee me again."

He leans in close, and I bite at his lip. "How about if I bite?"

"I can handle the biting," he gruffs.

Kiss me, I think.

Our naked bodies are pressed against each other, and even though we fucked all night and again this morning, I can't get enough. Maybe it's because I know our time is running out, or maybe it's because it's him.

He possesses my body as he breathes into me. His nostrils flare— maybe in anger, or maybe in preparation for another attack.

I feel the familiar wetness drip between my legs. I can't believe I'm getting turned on from him manhandling me, even knowing that what he's doing now is just the tip of what's to come.

He steps back and yanks me away from the door before he kicks once hard against the door. The door falls easily. If only our hearts broke as easily.

He grabs my wrists, but I'm able to slip one out.

He pulls.

I pound on his back with my free fist and dig my heels into the ground, making it almost impossible for him to drag me out of the room.

He murmurs something in a gruff voice I can't make out.

Then he yanks me to him in one jolt.

I move my punches to his head, determined not to let him tie me up. If he wants to hurt me, he's going to have to do it while I'm free.

He shakes his head. "You'll never learn. You're mine, huntress. You hunt while I go in for the kill. Tonight, you're the one I kill."

He lets go of my wrist, and I know what he's going to do. It's too late, though. He's faster than me.

I try to run back into the room, but he grabs my calves and flips me over his shoulder.

"Langston! Put me down!"

I flail my arms, pounding into his back, his ass, anything I can reach. He doesn't let go. I dig my nails and teeth into his back, but no amount of pain that will make him put me down. He's decided how he wants to do this, and for some reason he thinks it will be easier if I'm tied up.

I have to think of another way.

I stop fighting, saving my energy as he carries me up the stairs.

The sun hits my back, and once again, I hear the waves of the ocean as the boat rocks gently. He's going to have to set me down to try and tie me up, so my only other choice is to jump into the ocean.

I take slow, deep breaths, trying to prepare my lungs for a long shot. If I can swim back to the island or to one of the other yachts, then maybe Langston will give up on trying to tie me up. He'll feel like we are running out of time and just get on with whatever horrible thing he has to do.

"If you are going to hurt me physically, you don't have to tie me up to do it. I can take it."

"I know," he says as he sets me down. By the tone of his voice, I know he's not going to change his mind. He still thinks he has to tie me up first.

So the second that my feet hit the ground again, I run as hard as I can in a straight line toward the side of the boat. I dive under the water, holding my breath for as long as I can. I pretend I'm a dolphin free in the ocean, even though I'm as far as you can get from being free.

I pop up finally when I run out of oxygen, but I can already feel Langston behind me. He knew what I was going to do.

He catches me in two strokes, wrapping his arms around me so I can't swim anymore. I'm relying on him completely to keep us above water.

He leans down and kisses me, sweeping me away. We're floating away in the ocean, away from all the heartbreak that awaits us.

He kisses me harder, his tongue rocking like the waves in my mouth. My heart thaws, my body relaxes. My mind tries to remind me of something, but I can't think why my brain would need to interrupt me right now.

And then I'm being hauled up. My body is no longer in the ocean, but my lips are still locked against Langston's as we both breathe hard into each other's mouths.

His eyes are filled with guilt. Finally, I feel it—the rope around my wrists. He's tied them together without me even realizing. He used his kisses as a weapon to control me, and I fell for it.

I swear I see a teardrop as he lifts my arms above my head and ties me to the pole.

"Killer," I plead in a whisper, but I stop fighting. He's already won.

He ties each of my ankles with a rope until they are spread apart.

My body reacts immediately, thinking that we are going to fuck instead of whatever horrible thing is going to happen next. My nipples pucker, wetness spreads between my legs, and my body heats.

He steps in front of me like he's trying to decide what he does next. He doesn't have any sort of weapon in his hand, which is a good sign, but I have no clues as to what dark sin he's about to commit.

"One more time," he brushes his lips against mine. "I just need you one more time first."

One more time until what?

I can't ask because his lips are against mine again, and his fingers are cupping my sex, spreading my wetness over my sensitive nub. I should keep my wits about me. After all, him kissing me last time was how I lost, but I don't care. I can't not kiss him, so I put everything into the kiss.

I don't know why Langston feels like this could be one of our last times, but he does, and I'm not going to let one time go to waste.

I can't move, being tied and naked to this pole, but it doesn't matter. Langston is the master of my body. He knows how to turn me on, how to bring me to the edge, how to slow me down, so I don't come too fast. He knows everything—even how to make me forget that I'm supposed to be fighting him, that I can't love him.

When he kisses my lips, I moan.

When he teases my nipples, I groan.

When he pinches my clit, I see stars.

"I could listen to the sound of you coming forever."

"You should."

He kisses me tenderly again, sucking on my bottom lip. "Maybe I'll keep you tied up naked forever, so I can always have my way with you, whenever I want you."

"Maybe," I say in a daze.

Then he steps back away from my body until the sun hits me in my face, reminding me that something sinister is about to happen.

I look at Langston standing naked in all his glory. His cock is hard, but he ignores it. He made me come, but he didn't fuck me. The one more time thing was about getting me riled up, giving me one more gift before he hurts me.

He walks over to a bag I didn't notice before. He digs inside with his back turned to me.

I hold my breath, waiting to find out my fate. *What horrible crime do we have to overcome?*

When he turns back to me, he's holding a knife.

I tense.

I can handle a knife, though. *Cut me, slice my skin, mark me. I'll still love you.*

Langston's eyes darken.

"I wish we had more time," he whispers.

"Me too," I whisper back.

My eyes look down, then up. "Do what you have to. Hurt me; I already forgive you."

"You won't forgive me for this."

He paces back and forth a second. He doesn't want to hurt me, just like I didn't want to hurt him, but we have to save Declan.

"Whatever it takes," I whisper.

His eyes meet mine again. They're dark orbs; I can't see any of the whites of his eyes. A hurricane of feelings roars in his eyes.

He could say it.

I love you.

I can't stop him. I can't shut him up with a kiss. I can't throw my hand over his mouth. I could try to talk over him, but he would still say it.

Suddenly, I'm panicking again. I struggle against the ropes, but they're bound so tightly. Langston himself taught me how to escape bindings, even his own, so I don't give up. I glance up, and I see a stray end of the rope. *Maybe if I can tug on it, I'll be able to get free?*

Langston says something, and it draws my attention back to him. He's twirling the knife around in his hand.

"The next location to find the treasure is Tokyo."

"Okay," I say. Now, stop stalling and do the thing so you can untie me, and we can get out of here.

"Tell the kids I love them," he says.

I frown, confused. "Sure, do you want me to stay here while you go? I don't think they'll let you get the treasure by yourself. I'm pretty sure I have to be there, too."

He shakes his head.

"I'm sorry," he says again.

"It's okay. Stab me or whatever, and then we can go."

That's when he turns the knife around and directs it toward his own heart.

"Langston....what are you doing?"

"Have Enzo cut out my heart. It's going to be too hard for you to do it. Then take it to Tokyo. The exact address is in the bag."

"Langston, no!"

"I love you, huntress. I always have." Then he jabs the knife into his chest, directly into his heart.

He collapses to the floor, away from me.

"Langston!" I yell.

I wait, looking for any signs of life.

He groans.

He's still alive.

But then I see a puddle of blood on the ground underneath his body.

I can't tell if his chest is rising or falling.

"Langston!" I shriek again.

My yelling does nothing. This is why he tied me up. This is why he was so heartbroken. He knew he had to die, and he knew I would try to rescue him unless I was bound.

I reach for the rope that's hanging down. My fingertips just barely touch the bottom of the rope.

"Don't you dare die, Langston!" I yell through my tears. They're flowing uncontrollably down my face. I'm going to have to get used to the tears because if Langston is really dead, there is no way I'm ever going to be able to turn the tears off.

I cling to the end of the rope and pull with everything I can, but nothing happens. I try to jerk my wrists free, but somehow the ropes tighten. I can barely see through my tears.

"Help! Help!" I scream at the top of my lungs, knowing there are yachts nearby, but I don't see any headed our way.

I tug again, and again, trying to free myself. Nothing happens. I can't move.

"Langston!" I cry out again, desperate for him to get up, for him to not die, but that's not my life. He's gone. I can sense it. He would do anything to save Declan, even die.

He just didn't think through the whole tying me to the mast, so I can't escape thing. Hopefully, he texted someone to come here, because if not, who knows how long it's going to be until someone comes to look for us.

My stomach flips, and I think I'm going to puke. My entire body trembles as saltwater sprays my face.

I want to collapse into a ball. I want to grab onto an anchor and drown myself, so I can be with Langston, but that's not fair. The kids need me if they can't have their father.

Tell them I love them.

Fuck you, Langston.

Fuck you.

I hate you.

I sob again, uncontrollably. A wail leaves my body that I'm sure rattles the entire earth in a massive, global earthquake.

I hate you so much, Langston.

I feel the ring on my finger.

He married me.

He protected me all the way to the end.

He *loved* me.

I take it back—hearing those words meant more to me than I real-ized. Hearing him actually speak the thing I've known all this time out loud proves that we should have been saying those words to each other since the first time we felt them, fuck the consequences and the broken heart. Knowing we've loved each other for years and not having said anything now that he's gone is ruining me.

"I love you, too," I whisper.

I squeeze my eyes shut as another heart-wrenching scream leaves my body. My heart is shattered. I will never love again. There is no way to repair the millions of pieces of my heart.

Say it again, Langston's voice says.

I open my eyes and see a hallucination. *Maybe it's his ghost already haunting me?*

Whatever it is, he's floating in front of me with a glow around him.

Say it again.

"I LOVE YOU!" I scream at the top of my lungs. "I've always loved you," my voice breaks. "Why did you leave me?" Then my voice leaves me; I open my mouth, and nothing else comes out.

"Only you would wait until I die to tell me you love me. But if death is the only way you'll tell me you love me, then so be it," Langston says.

My brain must have finally lost it because I'm pretty sure Langston is standing in front of me, very much alive.

"I'm going to kill you," I murmur as my heart finally beats again.

CHAPTER 25

LANGSTON

I chuckle through my own tears.

Hearing her shriek and cry over my fake death almost broke me. Lying on the ground, covered in fake blood, trying not to move was the hardest thing I've ever had to do. I've never heard such pain. It was like a pack of wolves tore into my own heart as I felt her heartbreak ooze off her, knowing that the only way to save her is to be patient and let her feel everything.

If my plan hadn't worked, I would have felt horrible forever. There would be no way that either of us would forgive me for causing her so much pain.

Thank god, it worked. She finally said the words, and she can't take them back.

Despite the agony we were both in, hearing her say she loves me was the most magical sound I've ever heard. I would die a thousand deaths if that is the only way I get to hear that she loves me.

Liesel's face is covered in tears, snot, and sweat. Her hair is matted to her head. Her body glistens with saltwater still clinging to her body. Or it might also be tears, snot, and sweat.

I'm not sure she has fully processed that I'm alive and not dead. I'm not a figment of her imagination; I faked my death.

I cup her face. "Huntress? Talk to me."

"No, get the hell away from me!"

She struggles with the ropes, trying to wiggle free. Seeing her naked body shimmy in front of me stirs my cock to life. Damn, do I want to fuck her senseless now that I've heard her admit that she loves me. Although I'm pretty sure when she gets free, she really will kill me given how angry she seems to be.

"I'm alive. It was all fake. I had to get you to admit you love me—"

"And pretending you were dead was the only idea you could come up with? You're a monster!"

I grab her face, and she jerks her head away.

"Untie me," she says.

I inhale her scent. "Not yet."

Her eyes shoot back at me with fire. "Untie. Me."

"Not until we finish talking. My task was to get you to admit you love me."

"I don't—"

"You do. You have this entire time, same as me, but you wouldn't admit it. I did a night of romance and a morning of lovemaking. We've already been through hell together, and you still wouldn't say the words out loud. Why? Why didn't you want to tell me?"

"Why didn't you?" she snaps back.

Touchè.

We stare each other down. I need to untie her and let her release her wrath, but I'm not ready just yet.

"How did you get the supplies? The knife? The fake blood?"

"That's what I was doing while you locked yourself in the bedroom. I had my team bring me Rose's toy knife and blood from her Halloween costume last year."

"What did she go as?"

"A prince who had just slain a dragon. The knife was her sword. Atlas went as the dragon."

Her lips lift in a smile at the mention of our kids. When she sees me notice, she immediately glares again.

"Untie me," Liesel tries again.

"I will, but first, say it again."

She shakes her head. "You've heard those words leave my mouth for the last time."

"No, I've heard them for the first of a million times. Say it again."

"No. I'll say it in front of the person who will give us the next clue, but that's it. I'm not letting you hear me say those words ever again after what you put me through."

"You can hate me all you want. You can punish me and make me pay for my tactics, but it worked. And you can't take it back now; I know how you feel. There is nothing to be afraid of anymore."

Her eyes drop in guilt, scared of some unknown fear. I consider telling her why I never wanted to admit to loving her, but it's my burden to bear.

I lean in close until our lips are just grazing each others. "I love you," I say against her lips.

My hands reach up to untie her. I can't be greedy and expect to hear those words again until we reach Tokyo.

"I love you," she says back.

I grin the widest smile I ever have before.

"I love you, you fucking bastard," she says.

That makes me grin more.

"Now, untie—"

I release her arms.

She gasps.

Her hands fall to her sides as I kneel down and untie each of her legs. Then I stand in front of her. We are both naked. I'm covered in fake red blood.

Tentatively, her hands reach out and touch my chest where I fake stabbed myself. Her fingertips roam over my body as if she still needs to confirm I'm really here and not dead. I let her explore my body. She runs her hands over my pecs, my abs, and then she dips lower.

I hold my hands at my side, letting her do whatever she wants with me. She should be able to do whatever she wants—I'm an asshole.

Her nails dig into my flesh.

I hiss but still don't move. "Whatever it takes, remember? I had to do whatever it took to ensure Declan's safety."

She nods, but she won't just let this go.

She grips my cock in her hands.

I freeze.

I want to stop her before she does something she regrets, like cutting off my cock or balls for hurting her, but I won't. I will endure whatever punishment she thinks I deserve.

She slides her hand roughly up and down my length.

I suck in a ragged breath. My body shudders in delight as her nails skim over my sensitive flesh, but I doubt what she has planned has anything to do with pleasure. I try to calm myself down, to get my cock to settle, but when she's touching me, there is nothing I can do that will stop me from getting hard.

She strokes me again.

I about come undone.

She smirks, enjoying the control she has over my body. Then she kneels—fucking kneels like the goddess she is.

"What are you doing?" I ask, too quickly.

"You don't get to ask me that after what you did."

She strokes my cock in her hands as she wraps her lips around the tip. Flashes of what she did to that poor guy on the sex-game yacht, where she practically bit off his cock come to mind. And I would deserve it if she did.

I try not to let myself enjoy it as she pushes her lips down my length. My cock hits the back of her throat, and she extends her tongue to lick my balls with the entirety of my shaft inside her mouth.

I hold back a groan and hold my breath waiting for her to turn vicious, but she just keeps sucking. Until I can barely stand, until my eyes roll back in my head, until I become dizzy with desire, she sucks. I can't hold back much longer.

Just when I'm starting to let my guard down, I feel my feet knocked out from underneath me.

I fall hard on my back.

Liesel climbs on top of me.

"I hate you," she growls as she straddles me.

"I know, but I'll never hate you again," I say.

She shakes her head stubbornly, and then she's pushing herself down on top of me. My cock sinks into her. She doesn't move initially; she just lets my cock stretch her.

Her eyes close, and a tear rolls down her cheek.

"Hey," I say, brushing her cheek. "I'm sorry. You're not going to lose me."

My words cause more tears, which makes me frown. I try to sit up. I'm not sure fucking is the right thing to do now, but then her hand is at my throat, and she's pushing me back down onto the floor. Her hips move over me hard. When she finally opens her eyes, there's a fierceness to them that shines through the tears.

She bounces on top of me, hard and fast. There isn't anything gentle about it—no long, loving strokes, caresses, sweet nothings. This isn't about lovemaking. This is her telling me how much she hates me.

I test the waters, meeting her thrust as she slams down on me. The look in her eyes turns more feral, so I take that as an affirmation that she wants me to fuck her, just as she's fucking me.

She pushes down harder on me, losing complete control in her thrusts. There is no way she's going to come if she keeps fucking me wildly like that.

Her grip on my throat loosens in her frustration, so I flip us over until I'm on top and in control.

I fuck her, slowing our strokes down so I can rub her clit and make her come.

She growls at my slower, more purposeful strokes. Her nails dig into my ass as she begs me to speed up. She leans forward and sucks my lip into her mouth, biting down hard.

I groan at the taste of blood in my mouth.

She pushes me hard in the chest, causing me to lose balance enough for her to roll us once again, so she's on top. I reach for her face, but she grabs my wrists and pins them overhead as her body fucks me furiously.

I could easily get out of her grasp, but the look in her eyes tells me if I try it, she will murder me—so I don't.

My hips meet hers thrust for thrust.

She arches her back, but her eyes stay locked on mine.

"I hate you," she spits out again.

"I love you," I say back.

Her eyes sparkle at my words like she's been waiting all this time to hear them, same as me. I'm pretty sure if I told her, 'I love you' enough, she would come from the sound of my voice alone.

"I love you, Liesel," I say as she drives her body down on me.

Her arms move down to my chest to get a better angle as she continues to fuck me, bruising our bodies with each thrust.

"I love you, huntress."

Her mouth falls open, her breathing faster. She's losing control, but she still spits out, "I hate you, killer."

I smile, loving her saying she hates me almost as much as I love hearing that she loves me. I just wish she would say the loving words easily and freely, that she didn't feel she has to keep them to herself.

My cock is drenched in her wetness, and I feel myself losing the fight to keep my orgasm back until she orgasms.

"Come, baby," I plead.

"Don't tell me what to do," she groans.

I try to move my hand to her clit to ensure she comes, but she swats my hand away.

"Liesel, I'm going to come. I need you to come with me."

She shakes her head, not stopping her movements. I'm not even sure if my words registered with her.

"Liesel, I—fuck!"

My dam bursts, and I come inside her.

Unexpectedly, she comes along with me.

I smile, my head falling back in complete exhaustion. There is no way to describe what we just did other than a hate fuck. But the fact that she did fuck me, instead of ignoring me or hurting me, says we can get past this. She won't hate me forever.

She falls against my chest, completely spent. Her hand strokes my chest where the fake blood is for a long time as the sun burns our bare skin.

"I love you," she whispers.

I close my eyes feeling those words stronger than ever. She loves me. I love her too. *What could tear us apart?*

"I love you, too."

CHAPTER 26

LIESEL

I don't know why I resisted saying 'I love you' for so long. Saying it even when I'm pissed at him is fucking incredible.

We lay in the sun, my head on his chest. As good as it feels, neither of us understands the danger that saying 'I love you' has caused; I can only guess.

Neither of us will take it back now, though.

The damage has been done, and our fates are set.

"We should get up and go have dinner with the kids before we take off," Langston says.

"Mmmh," I say, knowing he's right, but after thinking I lost him, I can't tear myself away from his body.

The anger at him faking his death returns; he put me through hell. I can't really be mad at him for long, though. He did it to get my stubborn ass to admit the truth and save Declan. Not to mention, I had Siren fake killed, and it almost destroyed him. Nonetheless, I let the anger fill me enough that I can unclench my claws from his body.

I sit up and smack him across the cheek. "Don't ever scare me like that again. I can't handle losing you."

He sits up, chuckling, and then crosses his heart like we are five again. "I promise."

"No more tricking each other. No more hiding. My heart can't take it."

"Neither can mine."

We kiss, but I don't let his tongue in my mouth. If we start that again, we will never leave this boat.

Langston scoops me up in his arms, then grabs his duffle bag before carrying me to the back of the boat.

"There are clothes in the bag to get dressed," he says as he sets me down and begins getting the sail back up.

I find yoga pants and an oversized shirt. I put them on and watch as Langston works, still completely naked.

Finally, he finishes his work and digs through the bag to find his own clothes.

"I think you need a bath before you get dressed. You have your guilt all over you," I say as annoyed as I can muster. Honestly, I'm just so happy that he's alive that I don't care he was the reason for thinking he was dead.

He shrugs a shirt on over the dried fake blood and pulls up his pants before sitting next to me. He doesn't speak as he kisses me on the forehead, but I know he's apologizing. He would spend the rest of his life apologizing if I let him. We both could.

That's not the life we want, though. I vow to myself that the second we step foot back on the island, I'm letting this shit go. I can't live my life mad at him forever.

Langston ties off the sailboat at the small dock on the island, and then he helps me off.

We start walking up the beach to the house. Our hands tangle together, and Langston looks at me.

I smile deliberately back. "I forgive you."

"What? You can't. I—"

"I forgive you. I love you." I kiss the back of his hand. "Now, let's go enjoy time with our family and friends."

I tug his hand, and he walks with me. I can tell he wants to talk about it more, but I'm not going to let us. Our time together is too precious.

Atlas and Rose see us as we approach the house. They run out and jump on us like we've been gone for months instead of just one day. That's what I regret the most—loving them, knowing the life we lead. There is always a chance we won't come back. A chance they will go through what I fake went through—losing Langston.

Langston frowns as I lift Atlas up into a hug. He seems to sense the turmoil going on in my head.

"Are you guys hungry?" Langston asks.

"Yes! I want pizza," Rose says.

"Me too," Atlas agrees.

"What are Uncle Enzo and Aunt Kai fixing?" Langston asks, assuming they are the ones doing the cooking.

"Pizza!" Rose yells.

We all laugh as we carry them inside. We stop in the kitchen and see that Enzo and Kai are, in fact, making pizza.

Cayden cries in Zeke's arms; both Atlas and Rose turn concerned. "We need to go cheer up baby Cayden. He cries if we aren't around him," Rose says.

Atlas nods.

We put both kids down, and they race over to Zeke to have a look at baby Cayden. To our surprise, Zeke lowers him to let him get a look at Atlas and Rose, and Cayden seems to stop crying. He reaches out to Atlas and touches his face.

But then I frown when I realize that Zeke can't hear any of the exchange the kids are having. He can't hear, and it's all my fault.

"It's not your fault," Beckett says from behind us.

Langston and I turn around. Langston is gripping my hand again.

Beckett walks closer and holds out his bandaged hand. "The doctors you sent took a look at all of us. Because you got us medical help so quickly, we are all going to heal; good as new."

I frown. That's not possible. Nothing is as good as new.

"Zeke's hearing has already started coming back. The doctors are extremely hopeful he'll get his hearing back completely within the year. If not, they can fit him with hearing aids that will get him to one hundred percent."

I look at Zeke in surprise.

"My hearing is already coming back," Zeke says. He either heard part of the conversation or guessed what we were talking about.

I nod, giving him a small smile.

"The doctors looked at Siren's vocal cords, and they're mostly infected at this point, not really damaged. It's painful, but Siren can already make small sounds. She's on painkillers and antibiotics, so she should heal quickly and be able to talk. Singing might take longer to come back, but it will return."

I stare down at his heavily bandaged hand. "And what about you? You lost the most. Without the ability to use your hand, life is going to be hard—way harder than it should be."

Beckett smirks. "I've lost a hand before. The body is amazing at adapting. If I lost this hand, too, I'd learn how to use the residual limb or my toes. The doctors gave me a salve to apply to the burns, though. I should heal, but if I don't, it's mostly cosmetic. My fingers still function even if I can't feel what I'm touching."

I wrap my arms around him. "It's still too high a price to pay."

"I just wish I had been able to save Declan," Beckett says.

I pull away from him and pat him on the shoulder.

"You're going to get the treasure to use to get Declan back, aren't you?" he asks.

Langston and I nod. "Let me go with you," Beckett pleads.

"No, you need to stay and watch the kids."

"Yea, cause I was so good at it the last time."

Atlas runs over to Beckett at that moment. "Come help make the pizzas. Uncle Enzo doesn't know what he's doing and is going to burn it."

Beckett nods and starts to follow Atlas.

"I think you do more than just 'good' with the kids. You're great and will do everything in your power to protect them. Stop blaming yourself," I say.

He heads into the kitchen after Atlas but stops just short. "You too."

I nod silently.

"I'm going to go check and make sure they know how to use the pizza oven, you okay?" Langston asks.

"Yep, go."

Langston reluctantly leaves my side and grabs one of the pizzas on the kitchen counter. He heads outside to the pizza oven on the far side of the deck with Atlas and Beckett in tow.

My stomach rumbles at the sight of the food, and a wave of nausea pulses through me. I race to the bathroom, thankful that Langston isn't nearby to question me.

I try to hurry in the bathroom, quickly rinsing my mouth out with mouthwash. When I open the door, I find Siren standing in the doorway.

Her eyes search mine, and I know she heard me puking my guts in the bathroom.

She rests her hand on my stomach with a knowing twinkle in her eye as she raises her eyebrows in question.

"No, just sick," I say, answering her question.

She frowns and moves her hand to my forehead. I'm sure it's hot and sweaty from being sick.

"I'm okay, just an upset stomach with everything going on. I'll be better once we get Declan."

She nods.

"Can you do me a favor?"

She tilts her head waiting for me to ask my question.

"Can you get Phoenix brought here to the island? Langston and I are leaving tonight, and although the kids are getting to know all of you, they trust her. She loves them, and she deserves a chance to say goodbye."

Siren frowns. It's not fair to ask her to do something like this when she can't really argue back. She can only either say yes or no.

The look on her face tells me she's going to say no, but she eventually nods.

"Thank you," I say as she pulls out her phone to text.

I'm not afraid of Phoenix hurting the kids again. There will be more people here this time to watch her. She already knows we have suffered and paid for causing her to lose her kids. Once she sees them again, she'll want to spend time with them. She won't hurt them. She loves them.

And the kids need as many parents as they can get, as many people who love them as possible. You never know when one of us might be taken away from them.

CHAPTER 27

LANGSTON

"Mom!" the kids yell and jump up from their seats around the fire pit. They toss their empty plates to the side as they run down the beach.

For a second, I thought they were talking about Liesel, but then I turn and see Phoenix running up the beach.

She kneels down and hugs each of them. Her hugs and smiles seem genuine, but I know the wickedness that lies underneath.

My blood boils that she's near the kids.

I stand up and start storming down the beach to Phoenix with Liesel hot on my heels.

"Langston," Liesel warns from behind me. I snap my head to her, knowing she's the reason Phoenix is here.

"They love her. She loves them. We can't keep them apart; it's not fair."

I growl and then start down the beach again without speaking to Liesel. She continues to follow after me, I assume, to make sure I don't do anything stupid.

"Mom, have you met our other mom?" Rose asks Phoenix.

"I have. She's pretty awesome, isn't she?" Phoenix asks Rose.

"She is! I'm so excited. I get two moms! How lucky are we?" Rose grabs Atlas' hands and jumps up and down. He just rolls his eyes at her.

Phoenix stands and nods a thank you to Liesel before she turns to look at me. Without looking at the kids, I say, "Atlas, Rose, how about you race back to the house?"

"Are you going to race us?" Atlas asks.

"Us adults will race after you."

The kids take off.

I stare Phoenix down. "I'm doing this for them, not for you."

"Of course," Phoenix answers.

"If you hurt them, try to take them away again, do anything—I will kill you, your brothers, and anyone you've ever met. Do you understand?"

"I won't hurt them. I would never hurt them."

"You hurt them when you took them away from me, their father!"

"I'm sorry."

"Just say goodbye to them," I say.

Phoenix walks toward the house, and then it's just Liesel and me. We exchange glances but not words. I can't believe that Liesel trusts Phoenix. Trusting other people is what got us into this mess.

"Let's go say goodbye to the kids before we head to Tokyo," Liesel finally speaks instead of arguing with me.

I nod.

♡

THE PLANE RIDE TO TOKYO IS LONG, BUT I ENJOY EVERY MINUTE of it.

We alternate between fucking and sleeping naked in each other's arms.

The car ride is more nerve-wracking as we think about what we are about to face. We pull up at the address and step out of the car.

The small temple sits on the edge of a river, covered in moss, bushes, and trees. The walls of the temple are barely visible through the overgrowth.

We approach the entrance and knock softly on the door.

A woman opens the door.

"I've been expecting you." She opens the door, and we enter. In retrospect, the tasks we've been given so far to prove we love each other were pretty easy. I shouldn't be upset with her father for this wild goose chase, but I am. I don't know what games he's playing from beyond the dead. If he weren't dead already, I'd kill him myself.

The room we enter is simple. You can see the beams holding up the roof, and there is a small, low to the ground, circular table with four small chairs around it.

"Sit, sit," the woman says.

We both take a seat at the table. The woman leaves the room, leaving Liesel and me alone. We both smile at each other, knowing this is almost over.

"Don't move," the woman suddenly says.

We both freeze, not sure what the hell is going on.

My eyes scan the room and find the woman has a gun pointed at my head. She's across the room, so I can't just yank the gun free from her hand. I have no idea how good her aim is.

"Do you love him?" she asks Liesel.

Liesel is sitting next to me with big eyes. I can hear her heart beating from here. After what I put her through, I know she's not going to let this woman shoot me without a fight.

"Yes, I love him," Liesel says.

"Would you die for him?" the woman asks.

"Yes," Liesel says at the same time I scream, "No!"

The woman turns the gun on Liesel. "If either of you moves, I'll kill her."

I freeze, even though I want to protect Liesel with every ounce of my being. I rock my feet under the table, preparing myself to jump on Liesel to protect her from any bullets if I need to.

"Do you love her?" she asks me.

"Yes, with everything I have," I say.

"Would you die for her?"

"In a heartbeat."

"No," Liesel says with tears in her eyes. She quickly wipes them away. I'm guessing the only reason she's not bawling right now is that she knows she has to remain strong for whatever happens next. She's going to need her sight to be able to fight or run.

The woman shakes her head at us.

"She loves me, and I love her. If you want us to prove it, we will. You don't need to kill either of us," I say.

The woman laughs. "You think you completed the task successfully?"

"Yes, I did what was on the card. I made her fall in love with me. Liesel loves me, and I love her."

"That was what was on the card, but that was not the actual challenge. Your task was to resist falling in love. You were told years ago what would happen if you fell in love with Liesel, now you will pay the price," the woman says.

Shit.

"What is she talking about?" Liesel asks.

I should have told Liesel, but I didn't want her to worry. Her father's dead; I didn't think he'd know or have any way to carry out his threat. I guess I was wrong.

"Go on, you can tell her, we have time," the woman says.

I should be figuring out how to get out of here, not tell Liesel a story about how horrible her father is. She already knows that, so I try my best to search for ways I can get Liesel out of here safely while I tell her the story.

"Your father saw us rip his letter to you in half. He knew you had half the clues, and I had the other half. So he looked me up, found out that I worked for Enzo Black, the son of one of his rivals who betrayed him. He approached me. It took me a minute to realize who he was, or I wouldn't have taken the meeting. He threatened me."

Actually, his men beat me to within an inch of my life.

"He told me he'd rather his daughter be dead than loved by a man like me. He saw already how much I wanted you, how I loved you. He made me promise before he'd let me go that I would never fall in love with you or let you fall in love with me. If I did, he'd kill one or both of us. At the time, I knew you hated me and didn't think you could ever love me, so I didn't see the problem with making that promise. I fell in love with you, anyway. I'm sorry for the danger it's put us in."

Her father was a snake. He set up this game and ensured that we failed. The only way she would have had a chance to win is if she had chosen someone else to marry.

"Your father left very clear instructions, Liesel. If you fell in love with Langston, then only one of you survives. Only one of you will be walking out of this temple alive. It doesn't matter which one of you it is. Either the two of you decide, or I do," the woman says.

I've found all the exits in this room. It's one woman against the two of us. I have a gun in the band of my pants. I just have to reach for it and shoot her dead faster than she can pull the trigger. More importantly, I have to ensure that Liesel doesn't get shot.

Liesel seems to be trying to read my mind as I plan out our escape. I don't know if she gets the message or agrees with it, but when I whisper, "Now." Liesel takes the hint and dives as hard as she can underneath the table.

I dive after her as I grab my gun and aim at the woman.

I fire.

The woman fires.

"You okay?" I ask Liesel.

She nods.

"We have to get out of here. Crawl behind me toward that back door. Understood?" I ask.

She nods.

I fire rapidly in the direction of the woman as Liesel starts crawling. I use my body to shield her, but the woman hasn't fired at us since I aimed my gun at her. She seems to be hiding behind the wall.

"Go!" I yell.

Liesel runs; I run after her.

We throw open the back door, exit, and find ourselves on a garden terrace.

It's eerily quiet out here. We have to trek around the temple to get to our car. I don't spot the woman who was shooting at us, and I don't know if she has anyone else working for her, so I keep Liesel behind me as I hold out my gun, and we start creeping around the outside of the temple.

We don't make it a step before we are being fired upon. We duck down behind a pillar as I return fire.

"Oh my god," Liesel says as she catches a quick glance of the garden before she hides behind the pillar.

My eyes scan the garden. There are at least thirty men approaching us in tactical gear.

Fuck.

"We need to get back in the temple."

"We can't. They have us surrounded. There are men coming out of the temple now."

I glance behind us and see she's right—more men storm out of the temple.

I have a gun with limited bullets. I don't think Liesel even has a gun. We have no backup team coming to rescue us. It's just the two of us, and as good as I am, I can't take down this many men. We need a miracle.

And if someone has to die, it's going to be me, not her.

CHAPTER 28

LIESEL

There are so many guns pointed in our direction right now. We are crouched behind a pillar. Langston has a gun with a limited number of bullets left. I don't see a way out of this.

And yet, all I can think about is how much of an asshole my father was. It would've been terrible enough for the fact that he wasn't around for most of my life. He ran a criminal organization and destroyed other people's lives. And instead of simply letting me inherit whatever this treasure is, he created an elaborate game that I have no chance of winning.

My father wanted me dead.

He didn't have the balls to do it himself, though. So he invented this game to ensure my death, but not after he thoroughly tortured me first.

Hiding the treasure had nothing to do with love, as he said in his letter. That story about him and my mother breaking up because the sheer quantity of the treasure sprouted greed was made up. They got divorced because he was a criminal, and my mother was an addict.

This is about control. My father wanted to control me even from death. He didn't want to give me any money unless I earned it. He wanted to choose who I married, who I loved. He thought Langston was unworthy.

I look to the man crouched next to me, protecting me, knowing that he'll probably die doing it. We could have loved each other so much sooner if my father hadn't intervened. I have no doubt the reason why Langston tried so hard to hate me all these years is to save me. Loving me was dangerous.

I understand now why he was so hesitant to say the words. Not because he didn't love me, but because he was afraid of getting one of us killed. I'm not going to let that happen. I just have to figure out what my dad's endgame was.

Is this it? Is this where he expected us to die? He set a trap for us, letting us get so close to the end only to kill us instead?

Maybe, but it doesn't make sense to me.

I rack my brain through all of the clues. I try to think of my father as the monster he is. The only monster I knew to be similar was Enzo's dad. He, too, set up ridiculous games in order for his son to inherit his company. He, too, tried to control his son's life.

This is no different. I just have to outsmart my father.

I'm beginning to think there isn't even a treasure to be found. *Then how are all these people getting paid? Why are they still loyal to my father after he's dead?*

There has to be a treasure. But what is it? Why hide it? Is it a reward or a way to punish me further?

My father was an evil man, so I lean toward punishment.

Suddenly it hits me all at once; I know what the treasure is! Still, it doesn't help me figure out how to get out of this mess alive.

I grab Langston's bicep. "Don't you dare sacrifice yourself. You saw what happened the last time I thought you died; I died right along with you. Don't sacrifice yourself."

Langston takes a deep breath. "I won't let you die. I have to protect you."

"No, you've done that, and this is where we've ended up. Whatever happens next, we do it together."

He nods.

"Promise me," I demand.

"Only if you promise the same."

"I promise," we both say at the same time, looking into each other's eyes. I can't lose him, and he can't lose me. We have no other option than to live or die together.

"What ideas do you have for getting out of here?" I ask.

"Not many. We are obviously outnumbered, so we have two options left, really. We try to fight our way out and get shot and killed, or we surrender and hope that gives us enough time to find another way out while they decide what to do with us."

"I don't love either of those options."

"I don't either."

"We surrender together. We call their bluff," I say.

"You don't think they'll actually kill us?"

"No, I think they will, but they will want to play with us first. They'll torture us until the brink of death and then kill us. We can both survive the pain. That gives Kai, Enzo, Siren, Zeke, Beckett—any of them—time to come save us. Or as you said, it gives us time to come up with a better way to escape or convince them to let us go."

His lips meet mine in the briefest of kisses, but his kiss tells me everything I need to know. Then his lips say it, "I love you, huntress."

"I love you, killer."

He grabs my hand, interlocking our fingers, and then we both stand with our hands up. Langston makes a show of dropping his gun.

"We surrender!" we both shout over the gunfire and yelling in our direction.

The gunfire almost immediately stops. The muffled shouts draw quieter.

"Don't move!" someone yells at us.

We don't. We feel two guns pressed against our backs, our arms are yanked behind our bodies, and our wrists are tied together with rope. Our eyes meet in a show of solidarity. If his eyes are the last thing I see before I die, I'll die having loved and been loved, which is more than I ever expected out of my life.

The men shove us into the center of the terrace until we are surrounded by the entire squad pointing guns at us.

I glance at Langston, realizing we might have chosen the wrong course of action to get us out of here. This doesn't feel like they are about to torture us. It feels like we're facing a firing squad.

The woman from inside comes out with a smirk on her face.

"Have you decided?" she asks.

When we don't answer, she tries again. "Have you decided which of you is going to die and which is going to live? Only one of you has to die; the other gets to live a long, happy life."

Langston looks at me, and I know it breaks him to not try and save me, but I shake my head, and he nods. We are star crossed lovers destined to die together.

"Either both of us live, or both of us die; there is no other option," I say.

The woman smiles. "Fine, it makes no difference to me. I get paid either way."

"Look at me," Langston says.

I turn my head and stare deeply into his eyes.

This is the moment when it all ends; we die.

I should be terrified.

Shaking.

Crying.

Begging.

I should be afraid of death. I'm not.

I smile. Langston smiles back.

We love each other. I have no regrets. If I only got to love Langston out loud for a day, it was enough. We got our one day. That's more than most people experience after a lifetime of searching. Our love was real; it was all-encompassing. It was enough.

"Fire!" she screams.

I hold onto Langston's eyes for as long as I can, but eventually, the hits of the bullets are going to knock me dead. I hold onto his eyes until the darkness comes.

The darkness comes too soon; Langston is gone, and I'm in hell.

CHAPTER 29

LANGSTON

Dying—what does it feel like?

Immense nothingness.

The darkest of darks.

I didn't feel any pain, which shocks me. Death should be the worst pain, but all it feels like is a final end—an eternal end, an erasing of memories.

And yet, I remember her—Liesel, my huntress.

I may have forgotten everything else, but her love can't be taken from me, not even by death.

My mind clings to the memory of Liesel.

Where is she? Is she dead too? Is she floating in this darkness with me?

I dip down, my stomach drops.

How is that possible?

Am I an angel? Am I flying?

Voices register in my brain.

What is that?

I move my fingers. *I still have fingers!* They barely operate at first, but the more I wiggle, the more control I have over them.

Finally, I'm able to move them enough to feel my face. There is fabric covering my head. I push it up, and light blinds me. I try to close my eyes, but my lids move too slowly. Everything moves too slowly.

I'm not dead.

I'm on an airplane, by the looks of it.

Liesel is sitting down the aisle from me in a chair facing Corbin and Maxwell. She's not dead, either. She's very much alive.

Did they save us?

"Why did you save us?" Liesel asks them.

"You know why," Corbin answers.

Maxwell looks annoyed and tired by this conversation, like they've already been talking for a long time.

She frowns. "The treasure."

Corbin nods.

Liesel considers. "I'll find the treasure, just leave my kids alone."

Corbin smiles; it's what he wants.

"No!" I say, but nothing comes out. They don't look at me. *Am I really here? Maybe I am dead?*

"You will help me find the treasure; otherwise I'll kill you and Langston, and all three of your children will grow up parentless. But first, I need proof that you've paid your sacrifice. I saw Beckett's hands. Maxwell saw Siren and Zeke's sacrifices. None of us were there to witness your sacrifice, however," Corbin says.

"How do I prove it?" Liesel frowns.

"We'll go to a hospital to get an ultrasound."

Ultrasound? Do they think she's pregnant too?

"That's a waste of time. We need to go, now," she insists.

"You need to pay your dues first."

"Do you have a knife on you?"

Corbin frowns and looks at Maxwell, who reluctantly pulls out a knife. She snatches it from their hands, and then I watch in horror as she lifts up her shirt and plunges the knife into her lower belly.

"No!" I try to scream again. I try to kick, to fight, but in my drugged-up state, I can't do any of those things.

She removes the knife, then takes off her shirt until she's just in a bra and wraps it around her fresh wound. "Does that satisfy you? I sacrificed my ability to get pregnant. I injected the poison you gave me at the club, and I just stabbed myself in the uterus. There is no way I'll ever be able to get pregnant."

Corbin grins, pleased.

"That will do."

My stomach twists, aching to go strangle the man to death.

Liesel speaks again. "Now I want something first. Take Langston back to his private island and ensure he gets medical help right away. Don't hurt him or my kids ever again."

"Very well. Maxwell, take Langston to his island and see that he gets medical help. Assure him that we won't hurt or take his kids from him ever again."

I lose consciousness. The next time I awake. I'm on a new plane, alone with Maxwell.

"Don't worry, Corbin won't kill Liesel," Maxwell says. "He won't kill her."

The darkness pulls me under once again.

CHAPTER 30

LIESEL

Now that Langston, Rose, and Atlas are all safe, I'm able to focus on what comes next.

"What happens when we find the treasure?" I ask.

"You've realized that Langston isn't going to be able to help you get the treasure on his own. The way your father set up the game was to make sure you'd fail if you chose to find it with him."

"Yes, I realize that," I say.

Corbin sips his whiskey. "Good, so let's talk. I want the treasure. You'll help me get it, and then I'll let you go free. You'll be free to live your life with the man you love and two gorgeous children."

My heart sinks thinking about what that life would be, but it doesn't matter. That would never be my life, no matter if Corbin intervened or not.

"No."

Corbin frowns.

"Take me instead. Langston gets the treasure; you get me."

He looks at me slowly. "You figured it out, didn't you?"

I nod.

"Tell me," he says.

"In my father's story, the one with my mother, I was the treasure—

the treasure that ruined their marriage, the treasure that wasn't worth it. The treasure isn't money or jewels. The treasure is a child, my child. The treasure is Declan."

Corbin nods for me to continue.

"You never had Declan. You tricked me into thinking you did so I would go after the treasure for you. You just want to hurt me. You want to take all of my kids away from me so I'll feel the pain Phoenix went through. The pain you all went through because of my father."

"Very good. So you see, I can't give Langston the treasure. I already caved to Phoenix and Maxwell, who both have big hearts and wanted me to give you the kids back. I won't cave when it comes to Declan. We find him; I keep him. You go free and unharmed to return to what remains of your family—that's the deal."

I shake my head. It's a horrible deal. It means I'm trading one kid for the other two. I can't do that.

"No, take me instead. Take me and give Declan to Langston. You want to hurt me? This is how you do it. You separate me from all of my kids, not just one. You separate me from the man I love."

Corbin doesn't want to kill me; that would be too easy. He just wants me to suffer as his family did and continues to suffer to this day.

Corbin considers my proposition for a minute. For several long seconds, he doesn't speak. He just sips his drink, thinking it over and looking at me. I don't know what I'm going to do if this doesn't work. What other options do I have?

This has to work.

"I know your secret," he finally says.

I freeze.

"How?"

"It doesn't matter. What matters is that I do know, so I also know your deal is not a fair trade."

I understand what he's saying, but it's all I have to offer—my life for Declan's. I was put on this earth to save my family. I'm not going to fail at my one mission.

"All you've ever wanted to do is make me pay for the atrocities of my father. Take the deal. Me for Declan."

More time passes. He considers his options. I consider mine.

"If you don't take this deal, then you get no deal. You don't find Declan without me. He stays hidden forever. This is the only way you get what you want."

Another second passes before he holds out his hand.

"Deal."

ENDLESS LIES

ENDLESS LIES

PROLOGUE
CORBIN

Revenge.

It's all I can think about. It's the only thing keeping me sane, keeping me breathing, keeping me alive.

The amount of loss my family has endured is too much. The pain destroyed us all. It turned me into a hollow shell, with nothing but a black heart left beneath my ribs. It turned my brother into a fighter intent on killing. It turned my other brother into a hardened soul who will never let anyone in. And my sister has become a woman whose only wish is for death.

I have no doubt that my actions will do little to heal any of us, but that isn't my intention. We are all broken souls, all heartless. There is no fixing people who have been touched by the absolute worst darkness in the world.

Revenge isn't about us; it's about destroying those who unleashed the darkness onto the world, but who we can stop from causing further carnage.

As I take a step into blindingly white hallways filled with people rummaging about in and out of hospital rooms, I know this is the first step toward getting our revenge.

The bastard thinks I'm working for him because I'm a greedy

asshole who will do anything for money. He thinks I'm broke and need to get in his good graces to rebuild my family. He doesn't realize I'm working for him to gain the tools to destroy him.

There is a nurses' station that I'll have to get past before I can reach Liesel's room. I play my options in my head. Pretend to be the father or other family member. Pretend to work here. Flirt my way through. Or use the threat of danger.

It turns out I don't have to use any of those strategies. As I approach the nurses' station, an alarm sounds.

"Code blue!" someone yells, and everyone scatters to the room on the far end of the hallway.

Quite convenient—unless it's the room I'm here for.

I scan the board behind the desk and find names attached to rooms. Liesel Dunn is in room 302.

I snag one of the hospital bands for guests and slap it on my wrist. I begin to make my way toward room 302, but I immediately stop.

There is a man outside the room pacing back and forth.

The father?

No, this man is barely more than a boy. The man who raped Liesel is much older. This boy's brow is covered in sweat, his eyebrows are raised in worry, and his entire body is tense and flustered.

He's muttering words to himself and doesn't notice my presence.

There's a scream coming from the room that draws his attention to the door. He stops abruptly like his heart just stopped at the sound of the woman's screams.

I hate to admit it, but my heart flutters too. The sound the woman is making is not that much different than Phoenix's wail of agony the day her triplets were born lifeless.

Is the woman losing her baby?

I want to run inside to see. If she is, then my plan is ruined. But this damn man is standing in the way. I could take him. He's nothing but a scrawny boy, and in his state, I doubt he'd put up much of a fight. But I don't want to draw any unwanted attention.

Suddenly, a doctor and a nurse push past the boy, not giving him a second look as they enter the room. Their voices are quick as they explain what's happening.

C-section.

Perfect, it will be easier for me to take the baby if Liesel is unconscious. They will have to move the baby to the nursery. The plan continues to form in my head.

The boy's face is white as a ghost. He's terrified. And yet, he's too afraid to go into the room. What he's afraid of, I don't know, but it's clear he loves the girl in the room.

You shouldn't—I'm about to destroy her world, just like she and her father destroyed mine.

Suddenly, the doors to the girl's room are flung open, and her hospital bed is being rolled out.

The boy jumps back, turning down the hallway before she can get a glimpse of him.

She's writhing in pain in the bed. Her large belly is shifting even though contractions are no longer needed to get the baby out. She's gripping the railing of the bed so hard that her fingertips have turned white. She lets out a low, guttural growl as another contraction sweeps through her.

Her eyes glare at me as I realize I'm standing in the middle of the hallway in the direction the doctors are turning her bed.

I jump out of the way.

No one questions my presence here. They are too worried about getting her to surgery.

I watch as they begin to turn the corner with her, and I look back at the boy. I expect him to be staring at her, to be running after her, but he's gone—vanished.

Strange.

I watch as the doctor uses a badge to get through the doors to the surgery wing.

I glance in the other direction toward the room at the far end where all the commotion was. Nurses and doctors have started to file back out of the room and head back to their usual stations. They all look exhausted but relieved. Whoever was in that room is still alive.

But they are distracted.

I walk purposefully toward them until I knock into one of the women.

"Sorry," I mutter.

She smiles at me and then turns abruptly when she gets a look at my eyes. She sees the wickedness in the way they gleam at her, and she's smart enough to know that despite my good looks, she shouldn't get involved.

I cling her stolen badge in my fingertips and head toward the waiting room.

I don't know how long it takes to deliver a baby via c-section, but I suspect I have a few minutes. I need the baby alive, so I need to let the doctors do their jobs.

After sucking down coffee and seeing some of the nurses that headed back with Dunn reemerge, I decide the baby must be born.

I walk through the door, quickly scanning the nurse's badge. Past the surgery door, I see Liesel still lying on the operating table. I notice the boy is looking through a door's glass on the other side of the room.

Interesting, maybe he's smarter than I thought.

The boy is focused on the girl, not the baby. He doesn't see the nurse rolling the baby out of the room and into the hallway.

Here's my chance.

The woman turns the small incubator, and I gasp at the sight.

There isn't just one baby.

There are three babies.

Plural.

I glance around, looking for the source of the other babies. *Did another woman deliver her babies recently as well?*

But they wouldn't put all three babies together if they weren't siblings, would they?

The nurse stops when she spots me with my jaw dropped on the floor.

She smiles sweetly at me.

"You must be the father," she says.

"Uh-huh," I say back.

"Follow me, and I can take you to a room where you can meet your new babies."

I don't move, so the woman walks over to me and takes my hand. "I'm Anne."

I nod.

Then she's holding my hand while pushing the cart of three babies.

Three.

Babies.

What the hell am I supposed to do with three?

The woman leads me into a small room.

"Liesel needs to go to recovery first, and then she'll be brought in, probably in about an hour. I can take the babies to the nursery for you, but I thought you might like a private room to be introduced."

"The babies—are they...?"

"They are all perfectly healthy. Usually, with triplets, we expect at least one or more to have to spend time in the NICU, but Liesel did an excellent job keeping these babies safe."

Three babies. I still can't wrap my head around it.

The woman must be used to shocked dads because my expression doesn't even phase her.

"Sit down on the bed," she says.

I don't know why she wants me to sit on the hospital bed in the room. Maybe she thinks I'm going into shock?

I sit on the edge. "I'm fine, really."

She smiles, shaking her head. "Get all the way in the bed."

I frown but do as she says.

I watch as she picks up the first baby and walks over to me, placing the baby in my arms without question. Then she does the same for the second and the third until I'm holding all three babies.

"See? It's not so hard. You got this, father. You've got two strong boys, and your baby girl has one hell of a pair of lungs on her."

I look down at them—two boys, one girl.

"I'll leave you alone to get acquainted with your new babies. I'll be back in twenty minutes to do another health check on them, but press the call button on the bed railing if you need any help."

And then she's gone.

My eyes are wide as I look at each of the tiny infants in my arms. All of them are in various states of sleep. Thank god, because I don't know what I'd do if they started crying or begging for food. I know the nurse thought she was giving me a sweet moment alone with my babies, but how ignorant of her to think that I would know what to do. She didn't even check my bracelet; she just assumed that since I was a man outside of surgery that I must be the father.

"What do I do with the three of you?" I say, looking at each of them.

I remember Mr. Dunn's words. *If the baby is a girl, kill her. If it's a boy, bring him to me.*

I stare at each of them as a plan forms in my head. *Maybe one of us can heal after all? And sooner than I think.*

Carefully, I stand up, balancing the three babies in my arms. I lay them down on the bed. I don't know much about babies, but I don't think they can move or roll much at this age, so I'm not too worried about them falling off the bed.

I walk over to the computer in the corner and use my badge to scan in. I want to make Liesel and her father suffer, and the best way to do that is to kill them—all of them.

But since I have no intention of actually killing the babies, I'll just make them think they are dead.

I pull up Liesel's chart and start typing furiously in, trying to sound as medical and objective as I can so my ruse will be believed.

I type out the babies died just after birth. The funeral home already received them for cremation.

Now, to get out of here without being seen.

One baby would be hard enough to sneak out, but three? It's going to be impossible.

I unzip my jacket before snuggling two of the babies inside. The third I scoop up and hold in my hands.

My objective is to exit the building as fast as I can. I saw an emergency exit stairwell at the end of the hall—that's my goal.

I run out into the hallway, jogging fast and determined—so fast I don't notice the boy rounding the corner. I smack into him. The baby in my hands falls into his arms.

He catches the baby, completely confused.

I make a rash decision. The boy doesn't know there are three babies. I can still get out of here with the other two.

"Congratulations on becoming a father," I say, and then I run out the exit door and down the stairs, cradling the two babies beneath my jacket.

I burst through the final door and out into the bright sunlight before jogging to my truck.

No sooner have I climbed into the car do I hear him.

"Did you do it? Do you have the baby?" Mr. Dunn asks from behind me.

Fuck.

Of course, he didn't think I was loyal to him. He needed to be here to ensure I behaved and did as I was told.

Both babies are somehow still asleep beneath my jacket.

I consider my options carefully.

I can still get away with keeping one—the girl.

I can give him the boy.

I don't have a choice.

Reluctantly, I reach into my jacket and spot the blue blanket surrounding the boy. I pull him out and hand him to the dangerous man behind me.

"You—you aren't going to kill him, are you?" I ask, even though I know it's not my place, and he probably won't answer me.

"Why would I kill such a perfect boy? He's going to ensure my name lives on."

Then he climbs out of the car with the boy I had no intention of giving up.

I'll get him back, I vow. The kids are all innocent. Mr. Dunn and his daughter are not.

Liesel has the other boy.

I'll get them all back.

I'll get my revenge.

For now, my sister has a child to raise. A child who might help her heal.

CHAPTER 1

LANGSTON

My body bounces harshly in the front seat of the truck. My body thumps into the window as my ass rises and falls with the truck taking the bumps too quickly.

"You still with me?" Maxwell asks from the driver's seat.

"Like you give a damn if I live or die."

"I do, actually, since it's my job to keep you alive long enough to deliver you back to your friends. After that, I don't give a damn what you do."

"Turn us around and go back to the airport. I need to get back to Liesel."

Maxwell laughs. "If I turn this car around or slow down in the slightest, you won't be breathing long enough to get back to Liesel. Your only chance of ever seeing her again is to get back to your friends and hope they have a surgeon ready like I told them to."

"I'm fine. I'm not in any pain; the wound can't be that bad."

"That's because we pumped you with so many pain meds you're high as a kite and can't make decisions for yourself. That's why Liesel had to rescue your ass, again."

I curse under my breath but stop arguing with him. It's not going to do any good. I can barely feel my toes, let alone do I have the energy to attack Maxwell and take control of the car to get back to Liesel. I need to spend my time thinking, preparing for when I regain control of my body.

I think back to being on the plane, to the conversation Liesel and Corbin had. *What deal did Liesel make with Corbin? What did she trade in exchange for my life? For our kids' lives?*

She already gave up her ability to have future kids. Both by taking some kind of poison and then again with the knife she forced into her lower abdomen. She wasn't pregnant. Liesel is a lot of things, but she would never kill her own child to save another. She wasn't pregnant like I thought.

I need to go back to get her, to tell her to hell with the treasure. It's not worth it. We need to kill all these motherfuckers. The people who are still loyal to her father even though he's dead. If we kill them, everyone will think we got and safely secured the treasure. They will stop attacking us, and our kids will be safe. That's all that matters.

Liesel seems to know more than I do, though. She's smart—that's why I call her the huntress. She's always searching, hunting, figuring things out long before I do. I'm the muscle, the killer, the one who finishes what she starts. She should know that she can't kill all these people by herself, though.

Maybe killing them isn't her plan? It's already clear she thinks Phoenix deserves to live. She's going soft and going to let them all live after what they've done. That's why she needs me to do the work she can't, and shouldn't, do herself.

"Take me back," I say again, as firmly as I can.

"I can't," Maxwell says, not looking in my direction. I can see the vein in his neck bulging, the shape of his brow dipping, his jaw clenched. Something has him stressed. *Is it the fact that he's on my island and about to be vastly outnumbered?*

"You can. I promise to make your death quick if you take me back. Otherwise, I'm drawing out the torture for years before I kill you."

He shakes his head. "Trust me; you don't want to go back."

"Why not?"

"Do you love Liesel?"

"Of course."

"Then, you can't go back. You don't have all the facts. Liesel does. Or she will shortly. You can't go back."

"Why not?"

"For one thing, she'll hate you, and all of this will be for nothing." Maxwell looks at me now. "Shit."

His eyes bulge as he looks at me, and he turns the wheel of the car sharply, driving us off the edge of the road.

I turn my head looking out the window behind me, expecting to see someone attacking us. But I don't see anything but darkness descending around us.

Maxwell throws his seatbelt off, and then he's reaching behind my seat and pulling a bag into his lap.

"Take some slow, deep breaths for me," Maxwell says.

"I'm fine."

"You're not fine. Your face is blue, and I'm pretty sure you have some internal bleeding causing havoc. If I don't do something to stop it, you're going to bleed out in my fucking truck. Which, as I told you earlier, is not going to fucking happen on my watch."

He leans over and examines my head more closely. Then he reaches behind my neck.

"Shit," he says again. He pulls a couple of items out of his bag. "I think the first problem is the back of your neck. I don't know how I didn't notice the blood spilling out from the back of your head."

"I'm not bleeding."

"You're delusional."

If I really am bleeding as badly as Maxwell's eyes and tone of voice are telling me, then I'm fucked. There is nothing Maxwell is going to be able to do to fix it.

Maxwell's mind whirls as he tries to think about what to do to stop the bleeding. A piece of gauze isn't going to work, and neither is stitching it up.

"This is going to hurt," is the only warning he gives me before he jabs something into my neck.

"Fuck!" The pain finally registers, rattling through my whole body and reminding me how nice it was to feel nothing before. "You stabbed me."

Maxwell ignores me, studying my neck where there is now a blunt object protruding.

"Don't move your head. Don't rest it on the headrest. Don't fucking die. Sound good?"

"Why are you helping me?"

He doesn't answer. He just starts driving again. Now, I think there really is more that he's not telling me.

"You shouldn't have fallen in love with her," he says.

"I know. I should have hated her, but she's too easy to love."

Maxwell shakes his head. "Just don't die."

"After I'm fixed, then will you take me to where Corbin has taken her? Or are you going to make us torture the location out of you?"

"Neither. You can't go to her. You know that. Her father's men will attack you and kill you both if you continue on with her. And you wouldn't dare risk her life."

"Then I'll send Enzo, Zeke, and Beckett."

"No, you won't, because they'll do the same thing to them."

"And you don't think they won't do the same thing to Corbin?"

"No."

"Well, he can't help her anyway. Only the man who married her can help her get the treasure."

I stare at Maxwell. "Don't tell me Corbin's plan is to get her to divorce me and then marry her himself."

"No, that's not his plan."

"Then, how does he think he'll be able to help her?"

"He just can. You don't need to worry about the details. Liesel already understands, and she agreed. If you won't listen to me, you need to listen to her for once in your life, or your kids are going to end up completely parentless."

I growl at the mention of my kids.

"Your kids are safe as long as you stay with them and let Liesel keep her end of the bargain. She doesn't need your help. She's got this. Loving her will just put her life in more danger."

"I can't un-love her. It's not possible."

"Well, it would help her most if you could figure out how to un-love her and prove it to the world. That's the only way to help her now."

I frown.

I'm going to get more information from him. As soon as I don't have to have a knife sticking out of the back of my neck in order to keep me alive, he's a dead man. So are his sister and brother and anyone else who has threatened our kids' lives.

We pull up in front of my beach house. All of my friends start running from the house toward us.

I smirk at Maxwell. "You better start talking, or they are going to kill you. You're the reason Siren may never talk again, Zeke may never hear again, and Beckett may never touch again. They aren't a forgiving bunch. And as you said, I'll be in surgery and not able to convince them to keep you alive until you tell us where Corbin and Liesel went."

"They already know. I already told them."

"What?"

My door is thrown open, and Enzo and Zeke are grabbing me, trying to figure out how to move me without injuring me more so they can take me to a room I'm sure they've set up for surgery. But I need more information from Maxwell before I'm put under. I implore Maxwell to talk to me with my eyes as my jaw is currently on the floor from what he just said.

Maxwell leans over so only I can hear his next words. "You want me and my family dead, but you shouldn't. Just maybe, we are all on the same side."

Then I'm whisked away by my friends, away from my ability to question Maxwell further. Darkness overcomes me before my brain can even process how there is a possibility that we are all on the same side.

Stop loving her. If you want to save her, then never love her. The words her father spoke to me all those years ago are the last thing in my brain before I'm unconscious.

CHAPTER 2

LIESEL

We check into a hotel in Singapore. It's a penthouse with dozens of rooms, modern appliances, a jacuzzi tub, and a hundred-inch flatscreen in almost every room. You wouldn't want to be in a room where you couldn't not soak and fill your brain with constant television.

Corbin and I have an uneasy truce, so it's shocking to not see any of his security team in the hotel room and in the hallway.

"Where is your team?" I ask.

"I don't need a team. It's just you and I."

"You don't think I'll run?" I say, running my hand over the leather of the couch in one of this suite's two living rooms.

"No, you won't run. You know I'm your only hope of finding Declan and keeping those you love alive. If you run, our deal is off, and I'll go after your kids, as was my initial plan. Alas, I've gone soft. I want you to suffer, not your kids."

"You do realize your beef is with my father, not me, right? I've only met my father once."

Corbin puts his hands in the pockets of his black jacket. "I know, but your father is dead. It's only fair that you pay for his sins."

I shiver as he stares at me.

"So once this is all over, you're going to keep me as your sex slave until I eventually die?"

"Would it be so bad? If I remember correctly, you were the one who willingly sucked my cock."

"I did that to get the next clue. To find my child! Not because I enjoyed it, you fucking pig!"

He smirks, enjoying seeing me rattled up. "I don't want you as a sex slave. I have other plans for you."

He walks over to his suitcase and pulls something out before handing it to me. It's a first aid kit and a change of clothes. My clothes are bloodied, and I still have an open wound from where I stabbed myself.

I take the clothes and head into one of the six bathrooms in the penthouse hotel. I don't know why Corbin decided to get us such an expensive hotel for the night. It makes me nervous about what is going to happen next.

I shower, tend to my wound, and get dressed quickly. Every second we waste is another second my son is in danger.

He could be dead, that voice in my head says. If he is, everything we've all sacrificed for would be for nothing.

He's not dead. I refuse to believe Declan is dead.

I step back out into the living room where I left Corbin, but I don't find him.

"Corbin?" I ask, shouting down the hallway, and my ears turned up trying to listen for him. I half expect him to have brought his entire team up to the floor while I was in the shower. Instead, I find him out on the large patio that overlooks the city with a drink in one hand.

His eyes scan me up and down, but not in a hungry way. It's annoyed, more in a way that tells me I interrupted him deep in thought.

"What were you thinking about?" I ask.

He motions for me to sit, and he takes the chair opposite mine. Most outdoor furniture is stiff and scratchy, but this chair feels like I'm sitting on a cloud.

"Your father," he says. He finishes his drink, once again staring off into the distance. I don't think he's going to tell me whatever he's thinking about, but then he turns back.

"I think it's time you and I tell each other everything we know."

"You go first," I say.

"I will because you need to realize that we aren't on different sides, you and I."

"I sold my soul to you in order to keep my children and husband safe. I think you and I are on as far of opposite sides as we can possibly get."

"You're wrong."

"Tell me about my father."

"When I first met your father, I thought he was a nothing. I thought he had a few connections to drug dealers, but I didn't think he was much more. He didn't seem that powerful. Honestly, I thought he was an addict himself. He was always a bit on edge, twitchy, with red shot eyes. Realizing I misjudged him cost me everything." He balls his hands into fists, full of anger and frustration at himself as much as my father.

He's silent for a while and then nods his head in my direction. I realize he's expecting me to tell him what I know about my own father.

"You know more than me. He didn't raise me. I only met him once, and it was to tell me about the fucking treasure, the bastard. He's the one who took two of my kids from me, wasn't he?" I don't know why I expect Corbin to know, except that he actually knew him. They worked together.

"Yes, he took Rose and Declan."

"Why only take two and not all three?"

"Because your father wanted an heir to his operations. He knew no daughter of his would ever be strong enough. And after you were born, he suffered an injury that prevented him from having kids after you. So he waited until you had kids of your own. He took Declan because he was the strongest, the healthiest, and he thought he could raise him to become his heir."

"So my father's people have Declan now?" I ask, although I already know this. I just need Corbin to confirm it for me again.

He nods once solemnly.

"Why take Rose? He obviously didn't keep her?"

"Because daughters were weak. He didn't want you to raise a daughter. He ordered his men to kill her, but evidently, that was a line that even his men couldn't cross."

"And Atlas? Why let me keep him?"

"He was the smallest, weakest, most fragile. I think he figured he'd die, but if he didn't, he'd have a backup heir to come after."

I tremble in my chair.

"You hate my father. You hate me. Why help me get Declan?"

Corbin fidgets in his chair as his eyes water.

"Wait...how do you know all of this about my father?"

"Because I worked for him. After the death of Martin and Phoenix's children, I signed up to work for him. I was the one who took your children with plans to kill them all. I couldn't, so I made a plan to give them to Phoenix to help her heal and get her revenge for what she had lost. Your father intervened before I could enact my plan."

"You saved Rose instead of killing her?"

"Yes."

I frown. *Maybe we are on the same side after all.* No, he still demanded my body and soul in exchange for helping me. He still blames me. *But why does he blame me?* It has to be more than he's telling me.

And then it hits me.

"You want me separated from the kids so Phoenix can have them. You think with me out of the picture, she can be their mother instead of me. She can heal."

His eyes glaze over, but I know it's the truth. He feels guilty about her losing her babies, and this has always been about trying to remedy that.

Finally, he speaks again. "Falling in love was stupid. You could have gotten Declan back if you hadn't fallen in love. Now, I'm your only hope."

"I know falling in love was stupid, dangerous, cruel. I tried preventing myself from it almost my entire life. And even more, I tried to keep him from falling in love with me, but neither of us could help it. I think we fell in love when we were kids, the first time we met. Our hearts fell. Each one belonged to the other. It took years of fighting it before either of us admitted it out loud."

A tear rolls down my cheek. "What do we have to do next, or do you not know?"

"You're going to have to give him up, for real. You're going to have to stop loving him and get him to stop loving you. That's the only way to get Declan back."

I wipe my tears, not sure if he's answering my question or reacting to my comments from before.

"I know," I say because I want Langston to give me up. It's the only way to save him from so many terrible things.

His eyes search mine, sliding slowly back and forth like he's questioning if I'm strong enough to do it. Apparently, he's satisfied, and then he speaks words that send chills down my spine.

"Your father is alive. Declan is with him. We find your father; we get Declan back."

CHAPTER 3

LANGSTON

I open my eyes but don't feel anything.

Am I dead?

It would make sense if I were. I remember being whisked into a back room of the house where a surgery room had been set up. Bright lights shone down on me before I became unconscious. Some might think it's a sign that I'm in heaven, but I know better. If I'm dead, I'm definitely in hell.

I can't feel anything, though. I'm numb. I'm not in hell. If I were, I'd be in burning pain. Instead, the only thing I feel is an erratic heartbeat as I wait to find out if Liesel and my kids are safe. I haven't been here to protect them as I should. I have no idea how long I was unconscious; anything could have happened.

I feel a presence in the room but don't hear anything.

I turn my head and see Siren sitting next to my bed; a window that looks out to the ocean is behind her. It's a dreary looking day. The sun is barely poking through the clouds, and there is a light drizzle soaking the sand.

Siren takes my hand as we both take a deep inhale and exhale, both settling now that she knows I'm going to survive. I suspect nothing bad did happen while I was out since Siren is here and not trying to get someone else to come in and help her explain some atrocity that happened.

Even though Siren can't speak much right now, I don't need her to. And she doesn't need me to speak either. We've been through too much together. We share a connection that transcends the ability to speak. Right now, I'm thankful for that. I know I can use my voice, but I don't really want to speak.

"Safe," Siren finally speaks out. The one word is enough to confirm that everyone is safe. No one has been hurt while I was out.

I nod.

Her eyes scan over my body, taking in all my injuries, bandages, and scars. I let her, but I don't follow her gaze. I don't want to know all of my injuries. It makes no difference. All I really want right now is to talk to Maxwell and find out what he was talking about before I became unconscious. I want to find out why he thinks we are on the same side. But I don't know if he's even still here or if he's dead. I wouldn't put it past Enzo and Zeke to kill him. He deserves it.

Siren pats my hand again, drawing my attention back to her. Then she's hugging me tightly. I don't feel that either. I don't feel anything but my aching heart that's longing to be with Liesel. I don't care if we have to face a firing squad again; I'd rather be facing death with her than be without her.

Siren's eyes flick left and right over mine, searching for what I want. She sees whatever it is without having to ask. She holds up one finger and then walks out the door. I don't know what she saw or who is going to enter my room next. I expect a doctor to come in and examine me, to tell me the extent of my injuries. If it was Kai who was sitting next to me when I woke up, I would have no doubt that that is what is about to happen.

But the door opens, and Maxwell steps in instead.

I grin; Siren always knows me as well as I knew myself.

"You look like hell," he says as he walks near the queen-sized bed I'm lying in.

"It's your fault I look like this. You could have just left me for dead," I say.

He grins. "I could have, but then that would be breaking a deal. That's not something I do."

"A deal you made with Liesel to save my life?"

He nods.

"Why did you say we're on the same side when clearly we aren't? You're holding Liesel hostage. You tried to kill my family. You took my kids from me. You took Siren's voice, Zeke's hearing, Beckett's touch, Liesel's fertility. You've taken so much from all of us. Do you really think we can just forgive you and work on the same side?"

Maxwell doesn't take Siren's seat. He walks over to the window and looks out at the ocean, taking his sweet time. It's time we don't have. I want to jump out of this bed and force him to talk to me, but the numbness in my limbs hasn't vanished. There's an IV still in my arm pumping me with drugs, so I'm at his mercy.

"Have you figured out what the treasure is yet? Have you pieced it together?" he asks me.

I frown and shrug. "I assume an insane amount of money or gold or something stupid like that."

"No." Maxwell snaps his head back to look at me. "The treasure is Declan."

"What?"

"The treasure is Declan. We never had him; we just knew the way to get Declan was to solve the puzzle, the clues that Liesel's father left."

That's why Liesel made the trade—not only for my life but to ensure she saved Declan. All the more reason I should be by her side doing whatever it takes to save him with her.

"Her father is still alive," Maxwell says next.

"What? That's not possible. I buried that motherfucker. I stood at his grave. I—"

"It was an imposter—someone her father hired to pretend to be him. You've never actually met her father. Neither has she."

"That's not—I have to go to her. I have to help her! I can't stay here. If her father's alive, I—"

"Need to stay away from her. Her father hates you. Hates what you represent. He thinks you'll destroy his daughter and everything he built. If you go to Liesel, he'll attack you again."

"Fuck!" I yell, not sure what to do. I should try to contact Liesel at least to figure out what her plan is and how we can help. But I'm not sure how to contact her or if Corbin will let me talk to her.

"Corbin won't hurt her," Maxwell says.

"He has before."

"He won't now. He wants Declan as much as you do. He wants to take down her father as much as you do. He won't hurt her until that's done."

"And after? What then?"

Maxwell's silence answers for him. Once they save Declan and kill her father, Corbin will finish his revenge. Liesel saved my life in exchange for working with Corbin to get Declan back. *But what else did she trade? What else did she have to sacrifice?*

"What do you think I should do?" I ask.

Maxwell's brow furrows. "You do whatever it takes to keep Liesel safe while getting Declan back. You protect your family. You don't cower. You fight. But you don't let her father know that you're helping Liesel."

The corner of my mouth lifts; he's right. Maxwell seems to be the kind of man who will help me. We have an uneasy truce that I still don't understand or trust, but I'm going to need his help.

"I'll tell your friends that you're awake," Maxwell says, exiting the room.

When the door opens again, Atlas and Rose come running inside and jump on the bed before Phoenix can corral them.

I glare at Phoenix, who stands in the doorway. "Be gentle with your father. You don't want to hurt him more."

"Sorry," both kids say at the same time.

I smile at both of them sitting on my lap. "Don't be sorry. I missed you both so much."

I try to move my arms to squeeze them both, but they are so heavy I can barely lift them.

"Guys, give your dad a hug," Phoenix says, noticing that I can't give them one as I want.

The kids don't have to be told twice. They cling to my neck as my arms lift enough to pat them on their lower backs.

"You're going to be okay?" Atlas asks.

"Yes, I'm going to be just fine. I just had a car accident, so I'm a little beat up, but I'll survive."

"Good," Rose says.

"Do you want ice cream? Ice cream always helps," Atlas says.

"I'd love some ice cream or anything else you two make me."

"Come on, kids, let's go make some ice cream with Aunt Kai, and then we can let your dad rest," Phoenix says, letting me know that she's not been hanging out with the kids unsupervised. It's then that I spot Kai just outside the doorway, keeping an eye on Phoenix.

"What about our other mom? Is she coming back soon?" Rose asks.

I take a deep breath, stalling as I try to figure out how to answer.

"Your other mom is with your brother right now," I start. I hate calling Liesel their other mother when she is their mother and has sacrificed so much for them, while Phoenix has done nothing but use them. But I know it's what's for the best for the kids right now. They barely know Liesel, and Phoenix has done nothing but love them in their eyes.

"When will they be back?" Rose asks.

I squeeze them both. "I don't know, as soon as they can. They want to be with us very much but it's safer for them right now to not travel. As soon as they can though, they'll come here. I promise."

CHAPTER 4

LIESEL

My father is alive.

For most people, hearing that a parent you thought was dead is, in fact, alive might bring joy. It might raise their spirit. They might race to go find them and regain the lost time.

Not for me.

For me, hearing my father has been alive this entire time and that I've never actually met him sends shockwaves through me.

The man I met, who gave me the letter, wasn't my father.

The man I buried wasn't my father.

I've always known my father was a cruel man. I just didn't realize he was worse than the devil.

My father is responsible for every horrible thing in my life. For the loss of time with my kids. For their kidnappings. For my enemies. For my pain. For the loss of Langston, I will surely endure. He's responsible for all of it.

I don't know why my father decided not to be in my life and yet ruin it entirely. *Why take my children from me? Why refuse me to love the only man in the world I ever could? Why control me without ever getting to know me?*

Because he's a wicked, evil man.

A man I now want dead.

I stare at Corbin across from me, still not sure if I should trust him or if I should run from him. But he seems to have information that I desperately need to find the last of my children. To kill my father and ensure my family's safety.

"What is the next clue?" I ask Corbin. My throat creaks as I speak.

Corbin studies me a moment before he speaks. "Are you ready to help me?"

"Since I have no information about where my father is, I don't know how I can help."

He pulls a card out of his pocket and hands it to me.

I take it carefully to ensure our fingers don't brush. I read the card, and it doesn't make sense. It might as well be gibberish or in a foreign language.

"What does this mean?"

"I was hoping you had the rest of the clue. I've spent the last few years trying to figure it out, but I haven't been able to."

I read the card over and over, trying to piece together what it could mean. I think back to the note that my father, well, the man pretending to be my father, gave me.

It hits me all at once.

"Moscow," I say.

Corbin's eyebrows jump up. "Moscow? Do you have more than that? Moscow's a big city."

I study the card again. "No, but I know who might."

Corbin narrows his eyes like he's not sure he believes I don't already know.

"Langston?" he finally asks.

I nod.

"Shit," he curses under his breath.

We are going to have to involve Langston in this. At least call and talk to him. Something I'm desperate to do anyway because the last time I saw him, he was pale and rapidly deteriorating. But I don't want him involved. Even calling Langston could decide his fate, and I won't allow him to die. He has to live at all costs. He has to be there for our children. He has to take care of them.

Before I contact him and get more information about our next step, putting his life in danger, I need more reassurance from Corbin that we are on the same side. If I do speak to Langston, I don't know if I can keep him from coming if he knows the location. I'll only work with Corbin if I know that Langston will be safe.

"I'll call Langston. I will figure out the rest of the clue, but I need some reassurances first."

Corbin cocks his head. "What makes you think you are in any place to negotiate?"

"You need me to get your revenge. You've had years to figure it out on your own, and you failed."

Corbin smirks. "As I said before, we are on the same side."

"Prove it." My eyes dig into his skin, threatening to end him.

Our eyes lock as he thinks about how he can prove his loyalty to me. I don't think he can. I don't think he will. I'll have to figure out how to save Declan, kill my father, and keep Langston alive by myself.

Corbin leans forward and reaches into his boot, pulling out a knife.

I don't recoil. I stay strong as I face my enemy, now holding a weapon he can use against me. I've been tortured enough to know that nothing he does to me will matter.

Corbin twists the knife around in his hand, taunting me with how he'll use it on me. It makes no difference. I always knew I would die a horrible death. Today is as good a day as any, especially if it means Langston is safe. My father will have no reason to go after Langston if I'm dead.

"You sacrificed, your friends sacrificed, so I too shall sacrifice."

My eyes darken, not understanding what he's going to do. Suddenly, he plunges the knife into his stomach in a very similar spot to where I did.

He doesn't make a sound as the knife pierces his flesh. Nor does he moan as the blood oozes out after he's removed the blade. His piercing eyes remain on mine, judging if I'm happy enough with his sacrifice. His eyes tell me that if I'm not, that he'll do something else. If I asked him to cut off his own arm, he would.

If we really are going to be on the same side, then I need him as whole and uninjured as possible.

"Are you satisfied, or should I cut off an ear? An arm? A testicle?" He smirks at me, daring me to tell him to do more.

I've given him my life when this is all over. The more pain I inflict on him now, the worse he'll make my life later, I have no doubt. We are on the same side now with the same mission, but that won't always be the case. Although, watching him cut off a testicle could be entertaining.

"I'll go get the first aid kit," I say, accepting his sacrifice. His is small, a wound to the stomach, but for now, it's enough.

CHAPTER 5

LANGSTON

axwell and I just landed in Singapore and are driving into the city. We don't know if Liesel and Corbin are still here, but this is the last place Maxwell knew, so this is where we'll start.

Saying goodbye to Rose and Atlas was heartbreaking even though they were happy to play with their aunts and uncles in their favorite place in the world. But every time I walk away from them, I don't know if I'll be going back. I don't know if it will be the last time I ever see them. It's the right thing to do; they deserve a mother. They deserve to have their brother. My risking my life is worth it, but it's still hard.

Watching them with Phoenix was harder. They still think of her as a loving mother, and she still acts like one. I don't know how I'm ever going to be able to remove her from their lives without destroying them, but that's a conversation for a later date.

Right now, Maxwell and I are headed to Corbin's house to see if they are still there.

My entire body is sore. After my medication wore off, the pain set in everywhere. My muscles ache, my head pounds every time I have a thought, let alone move it, and my every breath burns up my throat. I

397

can't move without hissing. I can't think without wincing. I don't know how I'm going to be any use saving Liesel, but I'm going to try and hope that Maxwell is truly on my side this time.

I glance over at Maxwell, who is driving in the seat next to me. He saved me when he could have just let me bleed to death. He brought me to Liesel when he didn't have to. It seems that for some reason, he's on my side, but that doesn't mean I don't have questions for him.

"Why does Corbin blame Liesel? Why not just her father?" I ask.

Maxwell's jaw ticks, and I know he doesn't want to answer. He starts to open his mouth, though, and I hold my breath.

"Corbin—"

My phone buzzes in the cupholder of our rental car, interrupting what Maxwell was going to say. Liesel's name flashes on the screen.

I grab it and press answer before the second ring.

"Hello," I say with a shaky voice.

"Langston? You're alive," her voice trembles, and I can hear her sniffles through the phone.

"I'm fine, huntress, thanks to you. You're always saving me."

She sobs a sigh of relief.

My heart clenches hearing her cry.

"Huntress, stop crying. I'm okay. Are you okay? Did Corbin hurt you?"

"No, he didn't hurt me. I'm fine."

"Where are you?"

That question she doesn't answer.

Maxwell studies me carefully; his ear perked as he tries to listen. *We are on the same side*, I remind myself. He can listen.

"Tell me, Liesel. I'll come to rescue you this moment. We can get Declan back without his help."

"You know about Declan? Do you know that my father is alive?"

"Yes, Maxwell told me."

Her voice strengthens. "You have to stay with the kids. You have to keep them safe. If my father finds out about them, he'll take them away from us or kill them. You have to protect them. Promise me."

Fuck, I don't want to promise her anything that I might break. I might not be with the kids in person, but I do know they are as safe as it gets.

"I promise to keep them safe," I say, hoping she doesn't realize my omission.

"Thank you," she sighs. "Can you put one of them on? I miss them."

Shit.

I glance at the time. It's after nine at night at my beach house. "Sorry, they're asleep."

"Oh, right. Of course, they're asleep. How is everyone doing? How are you feeling?"

"Everyone is good. I'm good. Liesel, tell me why you called."

She hesitates as if she's deciding better of it.

"If I tell you, you have to promise me to stay there with the kids. You can't come. I've got this."

"I know you've got this. You're the strongest woman I know. Now, will you tell me so you can go rescue Declan?"

"Corbin had the final clue. I was able to put it together with my half of the letter to figure out the location."

"Where?" I ask too quickly.

"Well, that's the thing. I only have part of the information. I think you have the other half."

"Okay, I don't think there was much left on the letter that we haven't already used."

"Anything that might have a clue about Russia?"

"Russia?" I say out loud.

Maxwell's eyebrows jump.

"Yes. But we don't know where exactly. Moscow is a big city, and we don't know where to start."

"Moscow," I say, thinking about the note while letting Maxwell know where we are headed.

He nods and turns, driving us back toward the airport.

I read through the note in my head, trying to figure out anything that could help us.

"There were numbers written at the bottom—352. I don't know what it means, but hopefully, it helps."

"It does, thank you," Liesel says, not explaining more.

"So you're going to Moscow with Corbin then?"

"Yes, we have a deal. Don't worry; we are on the same side at the moment."

I frown, not liking that she's trusting Corbin. "Don't trust him. Do what you have to do, but don't trust Corbin."

The line is quiet.

"Promise me."

"I promise. You promise me that you are going to stay with the kids?"

"I promise," I lie.

We end the call.

I look to Maxwell. "We need to hurry and get to Moscow. If I know Liesel, they are already there. We are running out of time."

CHAPTER 6

LIESEL

I wipe my eyes, still moist with the tears at hearing Langston's voice. I hadn't realized until now just how much I worried that he wouldn't survive.

"I have the info we need," I tell Corbin.

Corbin nods stiffly, cleaning his gun. "Do you think he'll follow us?"

"Yes."

"I figured. Maxwell thinks too fondly of you and couldn't just tell the bastard to stay the hell at home." Corbin stands suddenly and walks across the living room to me. "That complicates things. Langston can't be there. He's only going to make it harder for us to kill your father."

"I know."

"Then why did you tell him the actual location?"

"So I can save him."

Corbin squints his eyes, not understanding.

"Trust me. This is the only way to stop Langston and to keep him from coming after us."

"As long as we are on the same side and still have a deal, that's all that matters."

"We do."

"Then, let's go to Moscow."

♡

WE WALK INTO OUR ONE-BEDROOM HOTEL ROOM IN THE CENTER OF Moscow. We used our real names to travel first class and, when booking the hotel, purposefully booking a room with one bed.

"You sure this plan of yours is going to work? I'm pretty sure it's just going to get me killed once Langston thinks we are sleeping in the same bed," Corbin paces.

I smirk. "Well, if he doesn't come to try and rescue me tonight, you'll be sleeping on the floor."

He groans. "I haven't slept on the floor since I was a kid."

"Well, you might tonight, so you better hope Langston comes."

Corbin unpacks his computer.

"Any movement on his tracking device?" I ask. Corbin had Maxwell put a tracking device on Langston when he dropped him off.

"Not yet, which means he's probably in the air."

We both stare at the screen, waiting for Langston's dot to appear to tell us he's in Moscow. We order room service and go over our plan again while we wait.

"You sure this is going to work? I'm not sure you have it in you to hurt him," Corbin says.

I laugh. "After everything that Langston and I have done to each other, this is nothing. I fucking sucked your cock remember?"

His eyes darken, telling me he does, in fact, remember.

I swallow hard.

I fucked up.

He laughs at my reaction. "You're so easy to mess with."

My heart slows, but it just goes to show I still don't trust this man. And as Langston said, I probably shouldn't.

"Look." Corbin points to the screen. He sits in the desk chair looking at the screen, while I stand behind him, looking over his shoulder at the dot that just appeared.

"He's here," I say, my breath catching.

"He is. You sure about this?"

"Yes, will you stop asking me that? This is the only way to protect him."

"If you say so."

I roll my eyes, snatch the laptop, and bring it to the bed where I can watch Langston's every move. The dot spends several minutes at the airport before it starts moving again.

Come find me. Come find me, killer.

"Is he moving toward us?"

I stare at the screen as the dot moves.

"Yes."

"Good, I don't want to sleep on the floor."

"You're such a baby."

"And you are a twisted, dark soul."

We both stare at each other. I suspect there is something we aren't telling the other, but that will have to wait. I have a husband to deal with.

Husband—I still can't believe I married him. It was the best and worst decision of my life. But if I die being married to Langston, it will have been worth it.

"He's here," I say, not believing he found us that fast. "Did you tell Maxwell where we are?"

"No, I should have, though. Your boy's good."

"Now what?" I ask.

"Don't 'now what' me, this is your plan."

I close the laptop and jump up off the bed to go listen at the door. A few minutes later, I see Langston pacing outside my door. He doesn't enter. He doesn't say anything. Then, he presses a hand to the door, and I know he's decided not to come in. He's going to just watch and wait, then follow us to the next location.

"Fuck," I whisper.

"What?" Corbin whispers back.

"He's not going to come in," I whisper.

"Oh, yes, he is."

Corbin marches toward me. He swoops me in his arms and lands a kiss on my lips.

"Corbin! Get off me!" I scream between kisses. "Stop, Corbin!"

The door pops open, and Langston stands there with a gun in his hand.

"Shit," Corbin says under his breath as he uses me like a shield.

I roll my eyes and pop him hard in the nose, knocking Corbin unconscious with a thud as he falls to the floor. Corbin and I had planned on him faking his unconsciousness, but I'm pretty sure I just knocked him out for real. It serves him right for kissing me instead of just letting me fake it.

Langston takes me in his arms like I'm a fragile piece of glass he's afraid he's going to break.

"Are you okay? Did he hurt you?" His eyes search up and down my body as his fingers caress my cheek, looking for clues that Corbin hurt me.

"I'm fine." I tremble in his arms all the same. Feeling Langston's hands on me again drives me wild with hunger and need. It doesn't matter that every second we are in Moscow, so close to my father, we are in imminent danger. My body craves Langston.

Langston's lips crash down on mine, devouring me in stark contrast to how gentle his hands are still holding me. Clearly, he feels the same way. Luckily, I can use both of our weaknesses to my advantage.

"I missed you," I say, grabbing his neck and tilting his head to deepen the kiss.

"If you wouldn't have sent me away, you wouldn't have had to miss me at all."

"If I didn't, you'd be dead."

I bite the bottom of his lip, drawing blood.

He pulls back.

Our eyes snap to the other's, daring each other.

Langston whistles, and Maxwell enters.

"Remove Corbin," Langston says to Maxwell.

Maxwell nods and then scoops Corbin up under his arms. "I'll have him in the room next door. Let me know if you need me."

I'm silent as Maxwell removes Corbin from the hotel room. I don't know if Corbin is conscious enough to take on Maxwell, but I hope he is. I don't have a plan for seducing Maxwell.

The door shuts, and I turn to Langston, glaring at him. "So you can trust Maxwell, but I can't trust Corbin?"

He frowns. "Maxwell is on our side."

"So is Corbin."

"He was trying to rape you. If I hadn't come, he would have."

"No, I had the situation under control. I knocked him unconscious. Corbin and I have a deal. When he awakes, he'll realize his mistake. You should go."

"Go?" Langston cocks his head at me like he can't believe his ears as I stomp toward the door.

"Yes, it's not safe for you here. You shouldn't have come."

Langston walks toward me. The prowl on his face shoots through my body. If I didn't already plan on seducing him, my insides would be melting for him.

But the fear of losing Langston is what keeps me firm in my plan.

Langston takes my lips in his again, kissing me sweetly so as to seduce me. To shut me up with comments about how it isn't safe.

I grab his neck, and I feel him wince. My eyes draw large. "Are you hurt?"

I remove my hand, but Langston catches it, putting it back on his neck.

"I feel better when you touch me."

I hold my hand gingerly on his neck. "What happened? What surgery did you require?"

Langston smiles down at me. "The surgery doesn't matter. The injuries don't matter. What matters is that I'm here because of you. You saved me, and now it's my turn to save you."

"We can't—" I gasp as he kisses down my neck. "You can't rescue me. I have to save Declan first."

He grabs the hem of my shirt and lifts it over my head before kissing me again.

"We will, but I'm not letting you put yourself in danger again. We do this together, not with Corbin."

My eyes heat. I try to push our conversation out of my head because we won't be facing the danger together. Langston won't be saving me. I'll be the one saving him.

CHAPTER 7

LANGSTON

I told her we'd do this together. We'd take down her father and rescue Declan together.

It was a lie.

I can't have her anywhere near her father. I can't go through what I went through last time we faced her father's men. I won't let her face a firing squad again. She has to be safe, so that's what I plan on doing. I'll get her the hell out of here and back to my island with the kids. Back to where I can keep her safe, while Maxwell and I meet with her father to end this.

You might think I need a big team with lots of men to approach her father, but sometimes sneaking in with as few people as possible is better than a full-on attack with a full team. The dozens of people he can see coming and protect against, but with one or two, it's harder to know my next move.

Tonight though, I'll be enjoying my wife before I send her on the first plane out of here. It might be the last time I ever fuck her, so I plan on making the most of it by giving her a night that neither of us will forget.

Her sultry eyes and luscious lips pull me toward her.

"I want to fuck you slow and sweet. Make love to you like a husband should."

She smirks. "I don't want you to make love to me. I want you to fuck me."

Jesus Christ, this woman is perfect. How did I ever manage to stay away from her? To hate her?

Because I wanted to avoid losing her at all costs.

I can't lose her.

She has to stay alive. That's all I care about.

Me—I know I'm as good as dead. I'm not invincible.

Our lips join once again, crashing hard as our tongues swell and sweep through each other's mouths like a tornado. I'm dizzy from the first kiss. I could blame it on the blood loss I endured, but it's because of her. Everything I ever feel is because of her.

I've wasted so much of my life not having her. The second my hands touch the smooth skin just above her hips, I grow frantic. I can't wait to have her.

I grab her jeans and yank; they slide down her hips without even unbuttoning them. She's lost weight. With everything we've been through, food has been the furthest thing from her mind. The anxiety and stress make it hard. I'll have to send her back with orders to Kai and Siren to put some weight back on her.

But that isn't what has my eyes transfixed. My eyes are glues to the still fresh knife wound over her stomach. She's applied a gauze bandage to cover the spot, but I still mourn what she lost. *Did we lose a child? Did she lose the ability to have more children?*

She unhooks her bra and slides her panties down her body while I watch, speechless, still lost in thought.

She smiles a seductive grin as she hooks her fingers into my jeans and jerks me to her, breaking me from my worried trance.

"Naked, now," she purrs.

I don't have time to undress. "I have a better idea."

I invade her space as I kiss her again, consuming her thoughts. That's my goal for tonight, for her to completely lower her inhibitions. For her to give herself to me. Let me make the decision that's best for all of us. She may think she's trying to do the right thing in saving me, but she doesn't realize the only way to save me is if she stays alive. I won't be truly alive if she's not breathing.

I back her up against the window behind her. She gasps as her ass hits the cool glass.

"I want to fuck you so everyone can see. I want everyone to know that you're mine."

I flip her around so her breasts are against the window, and her ass is pressed against my crotch.

"I'm tired of hiding." I suck her earlobe.

She gasps. Her hands splay across the glass as she pulls her bottom lip into her mouth.

I undo my pants and kiss her neck.

"I'm tired of pretending I hate you."

I slap her ass before I shove my pants down enough for my cock to spring free. It slides between her ass cheeks and then between her legs as I feel how wet she already is for me.

"The world should know how much I fucking love you."

My cock slams inside her.

"Langston," she pants.

"That you're mine."

I fuck in and out of her against the glass for the entire town to see. There is a world of people below going about their business on this chilled night. Snowflakes are starting to fall down on their heads. A few of them look up.

Liesel gasps. "Can they see me?"

"All they see is that you're mine," I growl into her ear.

She tilts her head back and moans as I hit deeper inside her.

The lights are dim in our room; there is no way they can see much if they look up at us, but the thought that they could turns her on even more.

"My dirty huntress."

I fuck her harder.

"I need—"

I move my hand around her front, finding her clit, knowing that's what she was begging for. She's so responsive that I've been afraid that as soon as I touch her clit she's going to explode. I wanted my cock inside her when that happened.

I stroke her once, and then she comes undone.

"Killer!" she shouts. It's probably not the best thing to scream in a hotel room in the middle of Moscow, but I don't care. I'll fight anyone who comes to our room for a chance for my girl to feel good and be free to scream how she wants.

I pump into her once more, chasing my own orgasm. As I do, I feel her growing weak in my arms. I catch her.

"Make love to me in bed?" she asks, still wanting more.

I smile at her, afraid if we get into bed, our night will end too soon. The drugs pumping through my body combined with her exhaustion will cause us to drift off to sleep as soon as I fuck her again. I can't have that yet. I need more.

I shake my head as I scoop her up in my arms.

I'm still dressed, so as I lean down to tangle our tongues together again, she fights my shirt off my body.

I carry her toward the bathroom. I need to have her on every surface in this hotel room—the desk, the sink, the shower, and then finally the bed.

She reads my thoughts as I bend her over the counter of the bathroom, and our eyes meet. She reaches behind her and yanks my jeans and underwear down until they are a pile on the floor.

"Fuck me, show me I'm yours."

I sink into her body once again, feeling at home as soon as her tight walls surround me.

Our eyes meet in the mirror before I kiss down her back.

"Mine," I growl as I thrust harder into her.

Her body quakes as I do. It doesn't matter how many times I've had her; every time feels incredible—like I'm experiencing the greatest pleasure for the first time. And every time we finish, I think I imagined how good it felt. Being with someone couldn't possibly feel that good. But being with Liesel isn't like being with anyone. Being with Liesel is the only way I know how to exist.

I show her that she's my entire world as I fuck her against the bathroom counter, fuck her in the shower with her in my arms and the water pouring down her back, devour her on the desk with her legs spread and my face buried between them as her wet hair drips on me.

When she comes for the fifth time, and I look into her lidded eyes, I know that I have to let her rest. I can't keep pushing her body any further.

It's then that I know we must fuck in the bed so that when her body hits her wall of exhaustion, she can fall asleep in my arms and wake up on the island with the kids.

If I succeed, Declan will be on his way before she even wakes up. I have to succeed because of all the times I've failed her.

"Come here," I say, grabbing her hand and pulling her off the desk. She falls forward into my arms, too weak to even stand.

She grins up at me. "You've made me weak in the knees."

"And you thought I wasn't romantic."

I fall back and yank her with me as we land on the bed. She doesn't have the strength to be on top right now, so I flip us over, inching us closer to the top of the bed. My cock is already hard and pushing between her legs that she lets fall open for me. Her pussy is still drenched with our combined cum.

"Please," she begs as her eyes begin to flutter closed. She can't stand to keep them open any longer and yet can't not have me inside her again.

I glance at the clock on the nightstands. It's after three in the morning. No wonder she's so tired.

I slide inside her in one slow stroke. This time fucking her is going to be about rocking her to sleep.

"I'm never going to let you go," I whisper against her lips as I push inside her.

"I'm never going to want you to."

There's a sadness in her voice, though. One that says we have to let each other go. I refuse to believe or accept her words. I will not be letting her go. She's mine. And I will fight every day to keep her.

"I love—"

She doesn't let me finish. With renewed energy, she flips us over until she's on top, riding me with much more vigor than I thought she had. I let her take control because she's a beautiful sight riding on top of me. Her breasts bounce up and down, and her gorgeous eyes shine down on me.

Our fingers tangle together as she rides me faster and faster. Our breaths turn to pants, our voices turn to moans, our hearts flutter so fast that I'm afraid I'll have a heart attack. None of that stops us.

"Fuck, I love you!" she screams as her orgasm pulses her pussy, milking me until my own orgasm spills from my cock.

She collapses on top of me like I expect.

I stroke her back with one arm as the other is still gripped by hers.

Within seconds I hear her breathing slow, and she's drifting off to sleep. I consider moving her, so she's snuggled up against me instead of on top of me, but I'd rather have her draped over my body for as long as possible.

I close my eyes, relaxing even though I know I won't be able to sleep.

And then I feel the clink of metal around my wrist.

My eyes fly open, afraid that someone has infiltrated the room and Liesel is in danger. I fling her hard off my body to my side so I can use my body to protect her as best as I can.

I yank my arm, which is now handcuffed to the bed, but it doesn't break free. I try again, but the metal bed frame doesn't shift.

"Liesel, stay behind me. I won't let anyone hurt you."

I sit up, trying to push her behind me.

My eyes scan the room, but I don't see anyone.

"Who is it?" Liesel asks.

"I'm not sure. My gun—"

"Is in the bathroom with your jeans," she whispers.

"Don't!" I try to grab her, but she's already running toward the bathroom to retrieve my gun. I search the room, but I still can't spot who's in our room.

"Here," Liesel says from the other side of the bed. I reach out to grab the gun from her while keeping my eyes on the floor near my bed. I assume whoever is in our room is beneath the bed and trying to figure out how to shoot us before I shoot him.

Clink.

I never feel the gun in my hand. Instead, my other wrist is attached to the other side of the bed with another handcuff.

I look up at Liesel's big eyes as she stands naked before me.

"Liesel, what are you doing?" I ask, realizing that no one else is in the room with us. It's just Liesel and me. She's the one who restrained me.

"I'm sorry," she says with tears in her eyes.

"What. Are. You. Doing?"

She doesn't answer me. Instead, she looks to the door.

It opens.

"Took you long enough," Corbin says as he enters.

"How did you...?" I say.

Corbin smirks at me. "Maxwell and I have been brothers for a long time. I know his weaknesses."

"You killed him?"

"No, I just made him see reason."

I frown and then yank on my cuffs, put on me by the woman I love.

"Excuse me," Liesel says suddenly and runs to the bathroom.

I hear her vomit.

Corbin looks as distressed as I am as we listen. For a moment, we both seem concerned about the girl in the bathroom. Me because I can't live without her. Corbin because he can't succeed on his mission if something happens to her.

A few minutes later, Liesel reemerges with a robe wrapped around her.

"Liesel? What's wrong?"

She shakes her head. "I've been a nervous wreck about doing this to you all day. I wish it didn't have to be this way."

"What way? Liesel, uncuff me. We have to fight your father together."

"No. Don't lie to me. Don't tell me you didn't have the same plan to drug me and send me back to the island where your friends would hold me captive."

"Huntress, you can't kill; you need my help."

"I'm sorry."

Then she nods at Corbin, who I realize is here to do the thing she can't.

I don't look away as Corbin approaches and places the needle into my neck.

A single tear rolls down her cheek as the drugs take hold of me, knocking me slowly unconscious.

I fight the drugs as long as I can.

"I'm sorry, killer, but I have to protect you. I love you too much to risk losing you."

And then I succumb to the darkness once again.

CHAPTER 8

LIESEL

Langston drifts off, and then Corbin checks his pulse, but I can tell from here that he's still breathing. The sedative Corbin gave him shouldn't hurt him.

"You okay?" Corbin asks.

I nod. "Just a little queasy."

"I wasn't talking about that." He hesitates, running his hand through his hair. "This is for the best. If Langston steps one foot inside your father's club, then he's a dead man. If you want Langston to live, this is the only way."

"I know." I grip the edges of the robe, tightening it around my body. My eyes peer up at Corbin in a shy way.

"Get dressed. I'll be right outside when you're ready." Corbin walks out of the hotel room, leaving me alone with a sleeping Langston.

The tears start falling freely now. I'm not sure if this will be the last time I ever see him. I'm going to face my father to do whatever it takes to get Declan back, so it very well could be.

I wipe my tears and then quickly shower and get dressed. I pull my hair up in a high ponytail after quickly blow-drying it. I know I'm just stalling, taking as much time as I possibly can to prolong the goodbye.

Langston is already unconscious, so the goodbye should be easy.

But for some reason, I linger in the bedroom, feeling so deep in my bones that I have to make this goodbye count. I have to pull every bit of joy I can from this moment because this goodbye is going to be our last.

No, don't think that way. I'm going to go kill my father, get Declan back, and I'll be back with Langston on the island in a couple of days. This isn't goodbye.

I lean over a motionless Langston and kiss his lips. "This isn't goodbye."

I can feel the tears welling again. I have to leave before I change my mind and stay.

"I love you."

And then I walk out the door.

Corbin is leaning against the wall. He looks up when I exit.

"Ready?" he asks.

I nod. "He's going to be okay, right?"

Corbin walks toward me. He puts my head in the palms of his hands, cupping my face gently. "You're doing the right thing. The drugs will wear off in twenty-four hours. Maxwell's will wear off a couple of hours earlier, and I've given him strict instructions to get Langston out of here. With any luck, we will have already killed your father by then."

"Where is Maxwell?"

"In the hotel room one over. I have cameras on both rooms." Corbin pulls up his phone to show me the feed. "If they wake up early, we'll know."

"Let's go."

I pull out of Corbin's grasp and walk downstairs to the taxi waiting for us.

We climb in and don't speak on the way to my father's club. There is nothing left to say. We have a plan, and we are going to do it. For now, we fight on the same side. We both want my father dead.

The car stops, and we climb out.

Snow is still falling as we enter the single unsuspecting door that leads to the unnamed club.

There is a guard at the door who scans us with a metal detector.

Corbin offered me a gun, but I knew I'd never get it in. My scan is clean. The man turns to do Corbin's scan, but before he can, Corbin removes his gun and two knives and hands them to the security guard.

The man looks from me to Corbin. "Mr. Dunn has been expecting you. I'll show you to a room where you can wait for him."

My heart rate spikes, but I don't let it show. I don't know how my father was expecting me to show up tonight, but it seems that he has eyes and ears everywhere.

Corbin tries to take my hand as we follow the guard, but I swat his hand away. I don't need any help, and I don't want him to try to give me strength—I've got this.

The guard opens a door after we've walked down two sets of stairs and turned at least a half dozen times through various hallways. Wherever he's taking us, it's deep underground and not going to be easy to escape from.

He motions for us to step inside, so we do.

My eyes widen at the number of people in the room. More than a dozen men stand with guns strapped across their chests like we are the most dangerous terrorists they have ever met.

The man slams the door shut behind us. Suddenly, I'm back with Langston facing the firing squad. Except for this time, I'm with a man who is still more or less my enemy, even though we are facing a greater enemy.

I scan the room, looking for my father, but I don't see any man old enough to be him, nor do I see any man who appears to be in charge. They are all wearing the same bland outfit of camouflage pants and a dark shirt meant to look menacing.

"Coward!" I yell, knowing my father must be listening. How cowardly of him to have his men kill us without even facing us.

Corbin grabs my hand again. "I'm sorry." He knows we've failed. This is how it ends. Our plan failed.

I shake my head and release Corbin's hand. I refuse to go down like this. This is not how my life ends. I know my fate, and this isn't it.

"You've been hiding from me my entire life! If you're going to kill me, at least be man enough to do it face to face. Don't send your men in to do your dirty work for you," I say, looking into the camera in the corner of the room I guarantee my father is watching.

The room is silent after my outburst. None of the men train their guns on Corbin or me. Maybe I was wrong or a bit overdramatic to immediately think we were about to die.

We both wait.

And wait.

And wait.

We wait so long that Corbin and I end up sitting back to back in the center of the room, resting our backs on each other because there isn't anywhere else for us to sit.

Finally, a door opens, and a man in a suit enters. He has peppered hair and my eyes. I know instantly he's my father.

"Thanks for waiting. I don't do business before six in the morning," he says with a smirk.

Corbin and I both jump to our feet. I immediately feel the urge to attack him, so I start running toward him without thinking. Luckily, Corbin grabs my arms and holds me back.

"I take it you didn't enjoy waiting."

"I've waited my entire life for this. I can wait a few hours," I growl back.

"Well, let's begin," my father says, snapping his fingers.

His men start rearranging the room, bringing in a circular table, three chairs, a bottle of whiskey, glasses, and a tray of cigars.

"Please, have a seat." My father motions for us to take our seats.

Corbin and I sit across from my father. I don't know what game he's playing, but whatever it is, I'm ready. He doesn't realize how strong I am, how much pain I can endure. When you lose a child, nothing affects you anymore.

My father smiles at Corbin. "It's good to see you again, Corbin. I'm glad she brought you instead of that schmuck she's married to."

Corbin stares my father down. I'm happy to see for a fact that Corbin is on my side in this.

"Why?" I ask, knowing it's the only question I care to know before I kill this man.

"Why? I built an empire. One grander than the one your husband belongs to. Mine is more secretive, more dangerous. It has made me a very wealthy man. I had plans to pass it on to my son, but then I had a daughter. Your mother wasn't strong enough to have another. So I looked elsewhere. It turns out, I took an injury to the groin that left it impossible for me to have kids either. That left you as my only option." He snorts, laughing at the ridiculous idea of depending on little, pathetic me.

He's right. It is ridiculous. If I took over his empire, I'd just purposefully burn it to the ground.

"You're weak, just like your mother. I knew it from the moment I laid eyes on you and watched you play with the boy across the street. I knew who he'd grow up to be—our enemy. And I knew you wouldn't see it that way. So I ensured he stayed away, that he hated you. But I should have killed the bastard when he was a kid."

I want to jump out of my chair and attack my father, but Corbin slips a hand onto my thigh, steadying me. I know I'll have an opportunity to kill this man; I just need to bide my time.

"And then you got pregnant."

"I didn't get pregnant like a horny teenager who didn't know how to use a condom. I was raped."

"I know. I was thankful that the father of your children wouldn't be that boy from across the street. Your children would still be of the blood of my enemy, though."

Our eyes lock in a battle. *I'm going to kill you*, my eyes say.

I already destroyed you, his eyes say in return.

"So I had Corbin take your son so I could raise him and prepare him to take over my empire."

"Where is Declan?" I ask.

My father smiles. "He's safe. He's already turning into quite the young boy. I have every confidence that he's strong enough to take my place."

"That's because you brainwashed him."

"No, it's because he's strong."

"Why send me the note? Why fake your death? Why have me seek out my son?"

"That's the question, isn't it?"

I frown. He's not going to tell me.

"What do you want from me? I'll give you whatever you want. You want money; I'll give you money. You want my body; you can have it. You want my soul; it's yours. You want to watch me burn; I'll tie myself to the stake. Just release my son."

"But you haven't played the final game yet. I can't just give you Declan. You have to earn him. And since you brought Corbin instead of your husband, I'll let you play."

I stiffen in my seat. All of my rage floods my heart. I'm ready to play whatever stupid game he has planned. I wasn't bluffing earlier; I'll do whatever it takes to get him back.

"I'm putting my money on you losing, though. You can't get Declan back while you still love that man. Love is weak. You're weak. And soon, you're going to realize it too."

CHAPTER 9

LANGSTON

I open my eyes, but I wish I was still asleep. My head is pounding, my mouth is drier than a desert, and the light in the room is irritating my eyes.

And then I remember.

"Liesel!" I yell. I try to jump up, but my arms are still tied to the bed.

"Woah, easy there. You don't want to cause more damage," Maxwell says.

I stare at him.

"Where is she? What happened?"

"I presume she's fine, and she's with Corbin going after her father. After I dragged Corbin's lifeless body out of this room and into mine, he attacked me. I'm strong, but Corbin has always been the better fighter. Plus, he had the element of surprise. He knocked me out, tied me to the bed, and drugged me. I woke up about an hour ago."

"You've been awake for an hour? Does that mean you know where they went? Did they go to the address?"

"I know where they went."

"Untie me, let's go." I yank on my wrists, the metal cutting through

421

my skin. The pain barely registers. Liesel went after her father. She's in danger. I have to help her.

"No."

"What do you mean, no? Untie me! That's why we came here, to go after Liesel. To keep her safe."

Maxwell frowns. "We also came here to rescue Declan."

I know he's right. "We can get him after we get Liesel out of here."

"Can we? Do you really think two men sneaking into his lair is going to end well? He's had years to prepare for this moment. He's got dozens of men, security systems, a plan."

"We can do it. We can defeat him."

Maxwell looks me in the eyes like he's trying to understand something. "Do you think Liesel isn't strong enough to get Declan back? To kill her father?"

"She's strong enough."

"Then why not do this with her? Why send her home?"

"Because I can't risk losing her."

Maxwell pauses for a beat, understanding washing over him. He looks at me with a sadness that says he never wants to fall in love. In his eyes, love makes you weak. He doesn't realize the truth is the opposite. Love makes you incredibly strong. But losing that love—that's the only weakness.

"I'll untie you."

Maxwell walks over to the corner of the bed and begins to work on unlocking the handcuff. I could get out of the handcuffs, but it would take me a lot longer, and I'd fuck up my shoulder to do it, so I'm thankful for Maxwell's help.

Five minutes later, he has both of the handcuffs off my wrists.

He tosses clothes at me.

"Get dressed, and then we can go."

"You're still going to help me go after Liesel?"

There's a pause. "Yes."

I pull on my jeans then have my arms pushing through my shirt. "Did they go to the club?"

"Yes, but then they moved to another location. I have the address, and our rental car is waiting. Let's go."

My heart thumps wildly. I'm terrified of what we are going to find, but I have to help Liesel. Maxwell is right that if she's already with her father, it's going to be hard to get her to leave. That doesn't mean I won't try.

Most of all, I will do everything I can to ensure she lives.

CHAPTER 10

LIESEL

I'm so sick of games. I'd rather just fight this out. Let's all pull our guns out and duel rather than go through another game. I'm tired, and I want this over. My exhaustion is multiplied by the pressure—I have to win. That's my only purpose in this world—to be my kid's protector, not their mother. I save them; I just don't get to love them.

If my father wants to play more games, then let's play. I never lose a game.

"If I win the game, I get Declan?" I ask, needing to understand the terms. I can't trust my father, but I at least have to know that winning will give me a shot at getting my son back.

"No. If you win, then you take his place. You become the heir to my empire, and he goes free to live with whomever you want," my father replies.

I suck in a breath. This is the second time a man has wanted to take my life in exchange for freeing my son. I now owe my life to both Corbin and my father. It doesn't matter, though. They don't realize it isn't a good trade; my life isn't worth much.

"Let's play," I say.

"Igor, please bring out the game," my father speaks to one of the men I forgot were in the room. My eyes roam around the room to the still-standing guards with guns strapped to their chests. Not only do I have to convince my father, but I have to convince these men to let my son go.

It hits me all at once—why my father sent me the note, why he's using my son as bait, why he wants to play these games. He doesn't think Declan is cut out to be his heir. He's manipulating me into becoming what he wants. His games are meant to brainwash me into being the monster he is.

So I'll show him how evil of a monster I can be. He'll see I truly am the devil's daughter. It's the only chance I have of winning.

Igor brings a box out and sets it on the table.

Corbin and I eye the box carefully. I don't know how helpful Corbin is going to be, but bringing him as a backup was better than Langston. If Langston were here, these men would be shooting at us.

My father opens the box and pulls out a board before handing me a bag of my game pieces.

"Chess?" I ask dubiously.

"Chess will test your mental strength and strategy."

I open the bag and find that I have the white pieces, while my father has black. I've never played chess before, so I'm not holding my breath at being very good.

"I beat you at chess, and Declan goes free?"

My father snickers. "No, you beat me at chess while completing tasks that test your physical and emotional strength, then Declan goes free. Every time one of us captures a piece, you must complete a task to continue the game."

"And Corbin?"

"He can help you. You need to learn to rely on a man who can actually assist you, instead of a man who works for Enzo Black and could betray you at any moment."

"Actually, Langston used to work for Kai Black, not Enzo. And he quit."

"We all know Enzo is the real leader of that empire, not his wife."

I laugh. "You have no idea what you're talking about."

"Prove me wrong. Prove that a woman is strong enough for a life like this."

I don't know exactly what my father does, but I can guess. He sells drugs, weapons, women—anything that can make him money. It's a life I've always been running from, but it seems like my destiny.

"Who goes first?" I ask.

My father smiles. "White always goes first. Do I need to tell you the rules?"

"No, I'm a fast learner." I know enough, and the rest I'll learn. It's not really about the game of chess anyway. It's about the tests he's about to make me endure. He wants me to win. He needs me to win. But he needs me to prove I'm strong enough first. When it comes down to it, if I succeed in his tasks, then he'll forfeit the game to me.

I move one of my center pawns two steps forward.

"Good, I was afraid you had no idea how to play the game." My father counters with one of his own pawns.

The only experience I have with chess is from watching a movie once. They played the opening sequence, and so I start by trying to mirror it and get a feel for how each piece moves.

I move my knight next.

So does my father.

I move another knight.

My father moves a bishop.

I move a bishop.

He moves another pawn.

I move another bishop.

We both castle.

We've developed our pieces—moved them into strategic places in the center of the board. It feels like a dance, moving our pieces together without attacking. In the movie I watched, the game cut away at this point, so I don't know how to move next.

My eyes cut to Corbin out of the corner of my vision. He's studying the board carefully. I don't want to ask him for help so soon, but if he has any idea how to play the game, I'll take any help I can get.

On the other hand, this isn't about winning the chess game. It's about being willing to complete any task, sacrifice anything, show him I'm strong enough to do what needs to be done to run his empire.

Now isn't the time to ask Corbin for help.

I move my pawn clearly into a spot where it can be captured.

My father grins, taking my pawn.

One of his men walks over and hands him a folder. My father nods and opens the folder. He slides the contents across the table to me.

Corbin strains his head to read the papers as I pull them toward me.

Divorce papers.

"You know if I sign these, it doesn't mean I'm divorced? Langston also has to sign, and a judge has to agree. This takes time."

"I understand how filing for divorce usually works. In your case, let's just say the divorce will be approved at an expedited speed."

I run my thumb across the ring on my finger. It's not giving Langston up exactly. Being divorced doesn't mean that we've stopped loving each other. When this is all over, we could get remarried. This is an easy sacrifice to make.

"Hand me a pen," I say firmly, showing no emotion. Signing some divorce papers means nothing to me.

My father slides me a fancy pen with engraving on the side. I turn the pen open and sign my name across the bottom line. Then I slide the papers back, raising an eyebrow in defiance of my father's weak test.

Then my father signs the other side of the document where Langston is supposed to sign.

I admit that I can't fully hide my emotions seeing my father so easily dissolve my marriage.

His man returns to take the papers and leave the room, while my father pulls his cell from his pocket. "Judge Hider, it's Dunn. I have a divorce I need your sign-off on ASAP." My father hangs up before the person on the other end can reply.

It doesn't mean anything. It's just a piece of paper. It won't stop me from loving Langston.

I follow my father's gaze to my hand on the table, and I realize I'm fidgeting with my wedding ring.

I pull my hand into my lap.

"Now that you will no longer be married within a matter of hours, take off your wedding ring. I'm sure I can get you a good price for it."

My father's gaze is a challenging one. He expects me to protest, put up a fight, and force him to have one of his men physically remove the ring from my finger. He doesn't know that by taking a physical object from me, he's taking nothing. This piece of metal on my finger is meaningless. It doesn't make my heart stop loving Langston.

I slide the ring off my finger and place it on the table between us.

"Good girl," he says.

I wince inside, hating being treated like a dog.

"Now that you're one step closer to being free of that man let's continue."

It's my move, but I understand the game a bit more now. I understand what game my father is truly playing.

I move a pawn.

He does too.

We continue to move pieces back and forth before I finally have an opportunity to take one of his pawns.

Igor walks back over with a laptop in his hand and gives it to my father.

"Every time any piece is captured, you have to complete a task or forfeit the game." He slides the laptop in front of me. "This task should be relatively painless. Transfer any money in your bank accounts to me. All of your assets will be mine."

I quickly make the transfers and then slide the laptop back to my father.

"Satisfied?" I ask.

"Well, you've proven that you can follow orders and make sacrifices, but there's more to being me than that."

"You mean like being an ass who abandons his daughter to go kill people?"

He shakes his head. "Play."

He moves a piece, then I do, and he captures one of my knights.

Fuck, I didn't even see that move.

Igor comes over, not carrying anything this time, which somehow scares me more. Before, it was about paperwork, now it's about to get physical—I can feel it.

My father whispers something in his ear. Igor nods and then steps to the side of my father.

"You've endured emotional suffering, but now it's time to see if you can endure physical pain." By the coy smile on his face, I already know what he's about to say. It doesn't terrify me at all.

"There's nothing quite like the sting of a bullet as it pierces your skin."

"Really? Are you going to shoot your own daughter? How does that prove anything? How does it prove how strong she is? If you want to know how strong she is, just ask, I've seen her endure plenty of physical pain. She stab—" Corbin says.

"It's okay, Corbin. If my father wants to shoot me, then let him shoot me. I couldn't possibly hate him more than I already do, and I would enjoy using it as added motivation when I eventually kill him," I say.

My father lights a cigar and then leans back in his chair as he puffs on it. "I won't be the one shooting you."

"What?"

"Igor will shoot you."

"Coward."

He shrugs. "I don't get my hands dirty for anyone who isn't worth it. So far, you haven't proved your worth."

Somehow, the fact that he isn't going to be the one to shoot me pisses me off even more.

I move to stand; I won't cower in front of this man. Corbin grabs my arm.

"Shoot me instead," Corbin says, holding me in my chair as he looks to my father.

My father takes the cigar out of his mouth, and Corbin continues. "Liesel and I are on the same team; shoot me instead."

My father snickers. "So you got two men to fall in love with you. Is your pussy that good?"

I spit in his face. I don't care that he's my father. I don't care that he has my son; I can't believe he spoke to me like that.

"There's that fire. I knew you'd eventually fight back. But only her husband could take a bullet for her."

"Marry me then first," Corbin says.

I wasn't sure if Corbin was on my side, but I'm sure now. He's willing to do anything to keep me from getting shot, including taking the bullet himself and marrying me.

Maybe he's after my father's empire, and taking a bullet for me seems like his best shot? It doesn't matter because I'm only going to let Corbin help when it's absolutely necessary. I can take being shot.

"No," I say before my father can speak. "I'll take the bullet. This is my fight." I turn to my father. "But Corbin is the man I brought here. I just signed the divorce papers for my marriage to Langston. For all intents and purposes, Corbin and I are married. We are a team, and you are going to accept that."

My father dusts off the end of his cigar into a dish. "I'll accept your terms. Igor, shoot whichever one of them they decide."

"Me," I say, pushing Corbin back into his chair.

"But—" I can see the pain in his eyes. *Maybe he does care about me more than I thought? Or maybe it's because he knows my secret and is afraid of what will happen?* He's never spoken the truth of the secret to me, but I suspect he already knows. However, he can't speak it out loud, or my father will know, and that would change everything.

"I'm fine. I need to do this." I need to prove to my father that I'm strong enough. I'll only let Corbin help when I can't do the task. This one I can do.

Reluctantly, Corbin lets go of my arm.

I stand. "Where do you want me?"

"Where you're standing is fine," Igor answers.

I notice that the men behind me have moved out of the way.

I hold my arms out casually to the side, unsure of where he's going to shoot me or what's going to happen afterward. Am I going to get any medical assistance? I doubt it. I doubt I'll get any painkillers either, another reason I should take the bullet instead of Corbin. I need Corbin's muscle, his ability to fight and shoot. I don't need him physically impaired. I'm not much of a shot, so getting shot myself won't matter.

I don't say anything as Igor takes his time readying his gun. My instinct is to close my eyes to keep from flinching, but I refuse to show that I'm scared.

I won't show fear.

I won't show pain.

I'm a rock. I'll do anything for my kids. This is just another step to prove it.

And then his gun is aimed at me. I'm not good enough with a gun to understand exactly where he's aiming.

Without warning, he fires.

I blink, the only reaction I allow myself.

At first, I feel nothing. I'm guessing with how close he shot me and how quickly the bullet sped through my body that it stopped the pain. I don't even know where he shot me.

Suddenly, I feel the damage.

The middle of my thigh. I'm surprised I haven't fallen to the ground or doubled over from the pain.

Screamed.

Cried.

Succumbed.

The pain hits me again and again in waves crashing through me. It started in my leg but quickly spreads everywhere.

I feel my father's eyes on me, and I refuse to give in. I will not let any pain show in my appearance.

I'm not sure if I can really walk on it, but I take a step all the same. When I put my foot down, I realize that bearing weight on it isn't a good idea. Instead, I hop on my left leg back toward my chair.

Corbin can't stand it and jumps up, putting my arm over his shoulders.

I open my mouth to speak.

"If you protest me helping you right now, I'm going to drag you out of here right now."

I shut my mouth and let Corbin help me to my seat.

I continue to glare at my father.

I'm going to kill him.

Me.

Not Corbin.

Me.

"Can you get me a first aid kit?" Corbin asks Igor.

"No," my father says.

"Really? Do you want her bleeding all over your chair and carpet? That's going to be a bitch to clean," Corbin tries again.

My father frowns as he sucks on his cigar and then lifts a glass of whiskey to his lips in his other hand.

"I'm not going to give her any medications, just something to keep the blood off your floors and her conscious enough to finish this game," Corbin pleads.

I take deep, steadying breaths as I stare down at my father. I don't care if he lets Corbin tend to my wound. I don't care if I bleed out on the floor right here. All I care about is saving Declan and ensuring this man dies.

My life doesn't matter; I will succeed either way.

CHAPTER 11

LANGSTON

Maxwell stops the car in the middle of a field, and my heart sinks. I know before I step out of the car that Liesel isn't here. That doesn't stop me from jumping out of the car and running through the field, yelling her name over and over.

Birds squawk as I run.

The wind howls.

The thick brush stabs into my leg through my jeans as I run, searching for any sign of Liesel, Corbin, or her father.

I find nothing.

And yet, I keep running.

I need to have hope that she's here. I need to have hope that I can do something to help her, to protect her after all the times I've failed.

I search every place as far as I can see, but this place looks untouched by people.

Maxwell said he tracked her cell here. *Does that mean…?*

My heart sinks.

Is she dead? Is she buried out here?

I turn and get a good look at Maxwell, who is leaning against the outside of the car, waiting.

He's not searching.

He's not frantic to find his brother.

He knows he isn't here.

Fuck.

He tricked me.

I thought I could trust him.

I thought we were on the same side, but of course, he's still loyal to his brother.

I stomp back toward him calmly, trying to settle my anger and focus it on how to find Liesel. That should be my focus, not this asshole.

But I can't let his action go completely unnoticed.

"Didn't find her?" he asks.

My jaw ticks, but I don't answer.

"I've been looking at a map, and there looks to be a small town a couple of miles from here. I think we should search—"

I hit him square in the jaw, shutting him up.

I intend to only hit him one time. Getting into a scuffle with him won't help anything.

"What was that for?"

I turn, glaring at him. "You brought me to the middle of nowhere knowing Liesel isn't here. Where. Is. She?"

Maxwell's facade drops. He looks away for a moment, unable to hide his guilt.

I don't have time for his apologies.

I march over to the driver's seat and throw the door open.

As I'm climbing inside, Maxwell grabs my arm and throws a punch.

I duck just before his fist can land on my eye. Then, I wrap my arms around his waist and tackle him to the ground.

I throw another punch, hitting him hard in the head.

He punches me in my gut until I'm gasping for air.

I fall back as he punches, but I have too much rage to let him get the upper hand, even for a second.

I throw another punch.

Then another.

And another.

I no longer remember who I'm fighting. In my vision, Maxwell morphs into Liesel's father.

I'm going to kill him; nothing will stop me.

"Put your hands where we can see them," a deep voice says.

Those words break me from my spell.

I release Maxwell, and we both carefully put our hands in the air as a dozen armed men approach us.

I look over at Maxwell out of the corner of my eye and see his eyes dilated. This wasn't part of his plan. He brought me here to get me away from Liesel.

I smirk because I know these men will take me to her. I'd rather be in chains, facing death near Liesel than safely away from her.

CHAPTER 12

LIESEL

I feel the pressure in my thigh with every breath. Corbin wrapped gauze and a bandage tightly around my leg to stop the bleeding, but that was all he was allowed to do. Bloodstains cover my jeans and the carpet below. Pain radiates through my body like a stampede of horses.

How can a bullet wound in my leg affect my ability to breathe? For some reason, my chest feels tight.

I'm dying.

I have no doubt about that, but then again, I've always been dying—slowly, torturously. It's why I should have never had kids, never married, never fallen in love.

I'm dying faster than I first thought. The wound in my leg has quickened the death I knew was to come.

I can't stop myself from dying, but I can ensure those I love are safe before I die—that I vow. I will not allow myself to die until my father is dead. Until my kids are safe. Until Langston is safe.

"It's your move," I say to my father, now on his second cigar and third glass of whiskey.

"You look pale. Are you sure you don't need a break?" He puffs smoke directly in my face.

"Move," I say, gritting my teeth to keep from jumping across the table and strangling him.

Corbin shifts uncomfortably in his seat next to me. He wants this to end as badly as I do, kill my father just like I do. He, too, knows my time is limited. If I'm going to kill my father before I take my last breath, then I need this to move faster.

My father takes his sweet time moving a piece. He studies the entire board like he hasn't already decided on his move. Finally, he moves a bishop into the center of the board, seeming to sacrifice it, but I can't see why.

My head is spinning. My eyes are glossy. I'm not going to be able to think clearly when it comes to the game.

I don't know what my father has planned next, but if it's physical torture, anything could finish me off. I'm not sure I should be sacrificing or taking any chess pieces that aren't absolutely necessary for me to win.

I reach my hand forward, but it shakes.

Corbin grabs it and gives it a squeeze next to me, reminding me he's on my side.

"What do you think?" I say quietly. I'm sure my father will see me asking for help as a weakness, but I don't have a choice. My choice is to lose on my own or ask for help and win.

Corbin takes my knight and moves it forward. I have no idea what he's doing, but at least we didn't capture any pieces, so I don't have to do any challenges to keep playing the game.

Corbin stands up, releasing my hand. *Why is he letting go of my hand? Doesn't he know that holding his hand is the one thing keeping me alive?*

My father once again takes his sweet time moving. Not because he's not an expert at this game, but simply because taking his time draws me closer to death.

Corbin sinks back down into his chair next to me, and then he shoves something else into my hand. It's cold and wet.

I glance down. A glass of water rests in my hand.

It takes all of my focus to lift it to my lips, but as the cold liquid slips past my lips and down my throat, I realize how life-giving water is. The small glass of water ensures that I'll live for another hour instead of dropping dead shortly.

My father moves, and I have no choice now but to take one of his pieces, but I glance to Corbin out of the corner of my eye to see if he agrees.

He gives me a tight nod.

I move my queen, taking one of his bishops.

Fearlessly, I stare at my father. I'm not afraid. Do your worst. Death doesn't scare me.

My father must think that I'm not capable of standing. Instead of forcing me to do something physical, he goes for my heart. He slides some papers to me.

Three papers, to be exact.

As soon as I see Rose's name, I know what these are.

It doesn't matter. Soon they won't belong to me anyway. Soon they will be safe with Langston. Signing over my rights as a mother is meaningless. A piece of paper doesn't make me a mother any more than a piece of paper stops me from being a mother. I've never truly been their mother, just their protectors. Phoenix has always been their mother, and Langston, their father. It doesn't matter that neither of them gave their blood to my kids; they loved them all the same.

I quickly glance at the papers. They don't give my kids to anyone, just relinquish my rights.

From my father's smug expression, he doesn't think I'll do this. He thinks this will be the thing that breaks me, the thing that ruins me.

"Give up. Surrender, and you'll live, my daughter. You'll get medical treatment just as soon as you lose. You can go back to living with your two children, but I keep your third to raise as my heir. Give up, and you still have a chance to be happy."

He doesn't know I'll die either way. And I refuse to know any one of my children isn't safe.

"Pen," I demand.

He picks up a pen and slides it to me. His eyes narrow slightly as I take the pen.

I have no time to waste. Every second I stall is a second closer to death.

I sign all three quickly, somehow managing to not let my hand shake. Then I shove the papers hard across the table.

"Your move," I say.

My father's eyes widen. Instead of puffing on his cigar, he puts it out. He sits straighter in his chair. For the first time, he seems proud of me. Of course, a man who gave up his only daughter would think me signing away my children makes me strong.

He moves faster this time.

I move.

He moves.

Again, I'm forced to take another piece. He sees it, I see it. Actually, I see a way I can win, but I'm going to have to take two pieces and sacrifice another to do it.

I can tell by the gleam in his eye that he sees my path to victory too. He won't let me win this game easily. He still may not let me win at all. And surviving three more challenges is not a given.

Three.

More.

And then Declan is mine.

Then I can fight back.

Then I can find the perfect time to kill my father.

I gather all my strength as I take his rook.

His eyes shine brighter, prouder.

"The next challenge is simple. Prove that you don't love Langston. Prove that your heart is open to being with another man."

I frown, guessing where he's going with this, and it makes my already uneasy stomach twist on itself.

"You want me to fuck someone who isn't Langston?"

My father laughs in my face. "Why would I want you to do something that could just result in you having more bastards? You have plenty of those already."

I frown. "Don't talk about my children that way."

"Except they aren't your children anymore. They aren't your anything."

His words don't have the effect he intended them to. Instead, I smile at him like I have a secret he will never know. I've already won. Keeping my kids safe is all that matters, not my legal parental rights.

"You're going to have to be more explicit with what you want from me."

"People forgive their spouses fucking another all the time. Fucking a man won't prove that you stopped loving Langston. Kissing another man. Letting him touch you in an intimate way while his lips are pressed against yours. That is much harder to forgive."

Why is he talking about forgiveness?

"Who will I be kissing?"

My father looks to my left. Corbin.

I look at him, and he has a pained expression on his face. I've sucked his cock. We've threatened to kill each other. And yet, kissing him does seem harder than fucking him. I don't understand why, but somehow my father has realized this truth.

I don't have a choice, and neither does Corbin. He has to kiss me. I have to let him. And I have to prove that I'm enjoying the kiss, giving part of myself over while Corbin's lips are pressed against mine. I have to open my heart during the kiss and encourage Corbin's hands to wander over my body like I'm his.

I stand, deciding that I need it for courage. Standing will make me more lightheaded and more likely to lean on Corbin, making it seem like I'm falling just a bit for him.

Corbin stands wordlessly next to me. I know he's in this just as much as I am. He's just as willing to do whatever it takes to win, same as me.

I don't let myself think.

I don't let my father win.

I lean in and let my lips brush against Corbin's while I open my heart and let it bleed.

LANGSTON

My arms are tied behind my back, as are Maxwell's behind me.

We've been led into a small, dark room. I assume it's our prison until they decide they have a need for us, but I sense Liesel is close. If she's here, Maxwell and I will escape. We'll find her; we have to.

I'm sure the men who led us into this room think keeping the lights off will dull my senses, and I'll be less of a threat. They don't know I thrive in the darkness. I can see better here than in the light.

I'm not sure about Maxwell, so I can't signal to him the moment we should fight back. I'm sure he'll catch on, though. If not, I have no problem taking down the six guards in the small room with us.

I hear the thud of the door, locking us inside with our enemies. This is the moment to attack.

Before I can spring into action, a bright light draws my attention. A screen has been turned on in the center of the room.

On the screen, Liesel is standing in the center of a room, face to face with Corbin.

I should scan the room behind her to figure out where she might be. I need to figure out what danger she's in and how to save her, but all I can focus on is her.

I can't take my eyes off her.

Her face is pale as a ghost. Her pink lips are parted. Her hair is in a messy bun on top of her head.

I continue down her body that has somehow thinned in the hours since I've seen her. When I scan further down, I see why. Blood soaks through a bandage wrapped around her thigh.

A low growl escapes my throat at the sight of her in pain.

"What the hell happened?" I say out loud, but I get no answer.

I step forward, the hands gripping my biceps allowing me. I forget about the men in the room with me. I forget about Maxwell or a plan to escape.

Liesel is in danger. She's been shot, and the wound is not properly closed. She's slowly bleeding to death.

My time is running out.

Her father says something, drawing my attention away from her to the rest of the room. Her father sits at a table with a chessboard in the middle. I don't have any doubt that this man is her real father. The man I met before had dark hair and soft eyes; this man has the same shade of blonde hair as Liesel and cold eyes.

There are a dozen men with guns surrounding every wall in the room. Any one of them could be the one who shot Liesel. Whoever it is, I'm going to find him and kill him, but not after spending weeks torturing him for hurting the woman I love.

Liesel moves, and my eyes cut back to her just in time to see her lips pressed against Corbin's.

What.

The.

Hell.

My brain immediately replays the images of her sucking his cock, but seeing them kissing is worse.

It doesn't make sense.

But when you're in love with someone, your feelings never make any sense.

I'm sure she's kissing him because it's the only way to get Declan back. But it doesn't stop my heart from seizing at the sight.

The kiss starts off simple, a tentative brush of their lips in the same way you might kiss a stranger for the first time, but it quickly evolves into so much more. She's the one who initiates, her tongue sweeping over the seam of his lips, begging for entry.

Corbin hesitates for a moment like he doesn't want this kiss any more than she does.

I narrow my eyes as I study him closer, trying to figure him out. His body is stiff and unmoving. His face isn't flushed, he keeps his eyes open, not closed, and I see no signs of an erection.

As Liesel's tongue pushes between his lips, he stills even more. He can't stand to participate in the kiss.

She pulls back, realizing what she's doing and regretting it.

I don't know why they were told to kiss, but I suspect it has something to do with proving that she no longer loves me. Her father hates me. He wants me dead. He doesn't want me as her husband or lover.

He thinks he can make them kiss, and somehow, her heart will simply start fluttering for another man. He thinks love can be controlled and changed simply by putting two people together and forcing them to hump.

He doesn't know what love is. Love is like jumping off a bridge into the ocean with no idea if it will give you the greatest thrill of your life, kill you on impact, or drown you under the surface. It's a beautiful, magical place that can carry you around the world or destroy you. There is no in-between.

I have no control over whom I love, neither does Liesel. If we did, we wouldn't be together. We would have chosen someone else, someone whose life wouldn't be at risk because we loved each other.

Just as Liesel is about to pull away and decide she can't play this game, Corbin comes to his senses. I know he has to in order to satisfy Liesel's father's twisted demands, but it feels like a betrayal.

He grabs her hips and yanks her to him as their lips clash together. Her mouth is open at the abrupt change, and his tongue slips into her mouth.

She moans like she's trying to convince her body to accept his. At least, that's what I tell myself. She can't possibly be enjoying the kiss.

Their eyes close, and they angle their heads, allowing for a deeper kiss. Their tongues dart in and out of each other's mouths. Liesel's hands grip his shirt, holding him firmly to her, while Corbin's hands slide up and down her hips.

Every move, touch, kiss is like a paper cut to my skin. Tiny little stings singe all over my body, but none of them are deep and merciful enough to finish me off. Watching the woman I love with another man, pretending to care for him, is the worst kind of torture.

I want to run in and save her, but I realize the best way to save her is to watch from a distance. I won't let her die or bleed out, but she's strong enough to do whatever it takes to get her son back. I have to let her take the lead. I have to support her. That's what loving her means right now.

Eventually, I close my eyes, blocking out the sight, but the sound... god, the sound is so much worse. The moans, the sighs, the smacking of their lips together produces worse images in my head than the actual sight.

Suddenly, the sounds stop.

I blink my eyes slowly, allowing them to open.

They are taking their seats back at the table, and her father has a calculating expression. I don't know what he saw when he looked at the two of them together. *Did he see the lies, what they pretended to show him? Or did he see the truth as I did?*

There is no way for Liesel to fall for another man as long as I walk this earth. Even if she wanted to, our love holds us captive. We are in a prison together with unbreakable walls.

I don't know what he sees, but whatever it is, he's pleased with it.

"Let's continue," he says.

He moves a piece on the board.

Then she does.

I'm not much of a chess player. I have no idea who has the advantage or how much longer this will take for her to win. But I have complete confidence she will be victorious.

I want to break out of this room and run and find her. I want to drag her out of here to a safer place. For once, I don't listen to what I want. I don't give in to my protective urges to save her.

Instead, I work on the ropes tying my hands behind my back. I loosen them enough so I can easily slip out of them, but not enough to arouse suspicion from the guards.

Then I watch the screen and wait. I wait for her to win, for her to get her son back. I wait for the moment I'll get them all out of here, praying it comes soon because I'm not sure I'm strong enough to wait very long.

CHAPTER 14

LIESEL

That kiss felt like a dream. No, a horrible nightmare. It stirred nothing inside me. My body didn't flush. I didn't grow wetter. I didn't come alive in his arms.

In fact, I was bored as hell kissing him. I had to remind myself of the motions, the mechanics of kissing. I had to remember to make the sounds, to tilt my head, to open my lips wider to allow him in.

It made me realize that if I were to somehow survive my fate, but Langston didn't live on, living without him wouldn't be worth it. I would never again feel alive.

Good thing I won't be surviving then. I'll never have to suffer living in a world without color, a world without Langston. I don't know how I'd endure for even a day.

But Langston will have no choice. I should have been focused on helping him to fall for another woman because not loving me won't be enough. I can't just make him hate me; I have to make him love another woman before I go. Unfortunately, there is very little time to make that happen.

We return to the game, and once again, I'm faced with having to take another piece in order to win the game.

My father notices my hesitation. "From this point forward, we

451

finish the chess game first. Then, you complete all the final challenges at once."

His voice is dripping with wickedness. I don't know what he has planned for me next, but I suspect if he showed me the next challenge now, I wouldn't take another piece. I'd find a way to win without capturing any piece beside his king.

I try to take the possibility of an evil grand finale into account as I continue to play, but I still find myself taking two pieces before I can check his king.

"Check," I say.

He studies the board.

Corbin lets out a breath beside me. I think he's been holding his breath since we kissed, but now his shoulders slump in relaxation.

It's Corbin's reaction that tells me what I already suspect —*I've won.*

"No," my father says.

My heart stops. *Maybe Corbin and I are wrong? Maybe I just lost?*

"Not check; checkmate," my father says with a grin.

I didn't expect him to be so happy that I beat him, but it seems to be what I suspected all along. He wants me to win. He wants me to be strong enough to take over in my son's place. I'm finally close enough to prove it, *but at what cost?*

"Where is Declan?" I say, not trusting my father. I still don't even trust that Declan is truly alive until I lay eyes on my son myself.

"You're right. I think you've earned the right to see your son." My father turns his head to one of his men. "Bring Declan here."

My heart stops. I'm going to see my son.

Time slows as we wait for the guard to return. I don't know what condition Declan will be in. *Will he be well taken care of? Will he be frail and weak? Scared? Thriving? Sick? Will he think of my father as his own?*

Suddenly, the doors open behind me. I only have to turn around to see him, but I'm terrified of what I will find.

Corbin finds my hand under the table and squeezes. Then together, we both turn and look.

The boy standing in the entryway has my hair, my eyes, my coloring.

I have no doubt he's my child, and yet, he looks so much older than Rose or Atlas. He's probably an inch or two taller than Rose, and his hair is gelled back much like my father's. He looks like a small man instead of a boy in dress pants, a gray buttoned-down shirt, and a jacket.

There isn't a speck of dirt on him, nor smudge of food. His clothes are perfectly tidy, like he hasn't played a day in his life.

I don't have to ask questions to know that he's had a strict childhood. Although he's been fed and physically taken care of, he hasn't had a good childhood. It's going to take time to deal with whatever trauma he's experienced since he's been here.

I feel tears watering my eyes, but I blink them back. I can't give in to my emotions. I have to stay strong.

"Declan, come here, boy," my father says.

Declan walks over, easily obeying. His tiny feet glide quickly, not running. He stops at my father's side, and he looks to the table. His eyes grow big at the sight of the chessboard.

"You lost?" he asks my father. "You never lose."

My father puts a hand on Declan's shoulder.

My instinct is to rip his hand clean off for daring to touch my son, but I'd never get away with it.

Patience. Just a little bit longer, and my son will be free of this world.

"I did lose to this woman here."

Declan puts his hand out to me. "Well done. My father is the best chess player I've ever seen. I never beat him. I'm Declan."

I take his hand, and he shakes mine with surprising strength for such a small person.

"I'd love to play against you sometime," he says.

I can't hold the tears back. I let one fall—one drop of everything I've lost and everything I'm about to lose.

"I'd like that," I say.

I quickly wipe away the tear as I see my father studying me for weakness. "What do I have to do?" I stare into my father's eyes.

"Kill."

I glare at his vulgar in Declan's presence. He's too young to be listening to talk about killing, but I also can't bear to have him leave the room. I want to keep my eyes on him, but I have to think about what's best for him, not for myself.

"Declan, would you mind taking my friend Corbin on a small tour while your father and I have a chat?" I ask, deciding it might be best to address Declan directly rather than asking for permission from my father.

Declan looks to Corbin and nods.

We wait until they have left the room before we speak again.

"That was very smart of you to ask Declan instead of me."

"Why? I'm sure you could have told him not to go."

"No. I'm raising a leader, not a follower. I don't give orders. I let him make his own decisions. He knows the world he's in. He's seen danger and death. If he's going to be my heir, he has to learn how to make the right choices."

"He won't be your heir for much longer."

My father leans back in his chair, folding his arms across his chest as he smirks. "You still have two challenges to complete. Two challenges I doubt you are strong enough to endure."

I'm sure he's right, but he underestimates what I'm willing to do for my child.

"What are they?"

"The first is to prove that you can kill."

"Who is my target?"

"Anyone, you can kill anyone. But good luck killing my men; they fight back."

I frown as my eyes circle the room. They all have guns. I have no weapon. I'm outnumbered. It's going to be impossible for me to kill one of them.

"They will, however, have no problem helping you round up Corbin for you to kill him."

I won't kill Corbin. With any luck, he's found a way out of here and has taken Declan with him. But if he hasn't, I have to finish the rest of the challenges.

I have to come up with a plan, a way to kill one of his men even though they have weapons and I have none.

Suddenly, his words resonate in my ear—*prove that you can kill.*

He didn't say to actually kill. He might have meant that, but after I've proven that I can kill, I'll argue the point later.

I take inventory of what I have on my body that I could use—a hair tie, a shirt, jeans, and boots. I don't have much that can be used to kill a person. I need a weapon, *but how to get one?*

I stand from the table and circle the room, looking for my target as a plan forms in my head. I limp a little with each step, exaggerating the appearance of my pain.

I make eye contact with every guard as I circle. Most meet my gaze with a stoic expression, unfazed by the heat in my eyes or the way I puff out my chest. After walking by four, the next man's eyes linger on my chest before giving me a wink.

"You," I say. "I'll kill you."

He laughs, and then the whole room breaks out in laughter. They all see me as a weak woman incapable of harming them. Luckily, that's exactly the attitude I need to be able to gain a weapon and the upper hand.

"Fight me fairly, and we'll see who's stronger," I say.

The man taps his fingers on the outside of his gun strapped across his chest. "We don't have to fight to know."

"I know. I'm stronger." I wink at the man to his left, who laughs at me.

The man I've decided to challenge growls at me. He doesn't like me teasing him. His ego is too small for that, which means I chose my target well. He's just lucky that the first man I plan on killing isn't him. I don't like the idea of killing people, even men who work for the devil. Killing the devil himself; now that's a different story.

"You wouldn't last ten seconds fighting against me, especially not now that you're a cripple."

"Prove it, then."

"What do I gain? Everyone here already knows I can beat you. You're nothing but a weak bitch with an injured leg."

"You get the honor of killing me, of getting rid of me." I look back at my father. "I'm sure my father would look highly on the man who finally got rid of the thorn in his side."

My father nods sternly.

"Fine." The man unhooks his gun and hands it to the guard next to him. As he moves, I get a glimpse of my target. I don't want the big gun. I want the one at his hip, the handgun I've practiced shooting before. He's too much of a coward to remove all of his weapons. I suspect he also has a couple of knives on his body. He won't play fair, which is exactly what I want.

I take a step back as he takes a step forward. I watch as he walks. He's a hulking man, so his movements are slow but forceful. He doesn't think before he moves; he just barrels his way through, used to his size intimidating his foes. That's exactly how he attacks me—barreling forward, throwing his entire body into me as he tries to knock me to the ground.

I let him, not expending energy unnecessarily.

We fall hard to the ground, and I land on my hip.

The men cheer and laugh at how quickly I was knocked down. They think he's going to squash me like a bug.

The toe of his boot hits me hard in the side, kicking me while I'm down. I'm sure it's painful, but I don't feel it with adrenaline flowing through me.

Still, I moan like he's just defeated me with one blow.

More laughter fills my ears.

"Get up, bitch."

I try to get up and then collapse, putting on a good show of weakness.

The man grows impatient. He grabs me by the collar of my shirt and lifts me up until I'm face to face with him. He swings his arm back, ready to hit me hard in the face, but he isn't prepared for me to fight back.

I duck just as he swings. He misses, causing him to stumble forward. We both fall, him on top of me. His body crushes me, but it gives me the access I want. I grab his gun and fire into his shoulder.

I roll out from under the now moaning guard and jump to my feet. I fire in the direction of the man I really want to kill—my father.

The second my bullet whizzes by my father's head, the entire room stops laughing. They grab their guns and aim them at me.

I continue to point my gun at my father.

"Shoot me, and you die," my father says.

"I'm dying either way. At least this way, you die too."

"You have terrible aim. You missed when you had the opportunity to kill me."

"No, I missed on purpose. I want Declan to be completely free of you before I kill you. I don't want your men coming after him his entire life. But if I have to, I'll kill you. Or you can admit that I could if I wanted to and move on to the final challenge."

My father grinds his teeth together. He's furious that he's been outsmarted, but then his face softens. "I accept your terms. You have proven that you can kill. Now it's time for you to actually do it. Bring him in."

I don't have to turn to know who the 'him' is—the only man I've ever loved. The only man who has ever existed for me. The only man I refuse to kill.

CHAPTER 15

LANGSTON

The men in the room grab me as soon as Liesel's father gives the command. I don't put up a fight as they hurry me out with my arms still tied behind my back. I look behind me and don't see Maxwell being dragged in. They left him in the dark room with fewer guards. He'll escape. I've worked my bindings enough that I can get out of it too.

They pull me into the room with Liesel.

Our eyes meet.

We've been in similar situations countless times. Somehow we've survived each time, but this time I don't feel like we are going to be so lucky.

Liesel's standing in the center of the room, holding a gun in her hand. I can see the bandage around her thigh more clearly now. The blood is barely trickling out, which either means the bandage is doing its job, or she's already lost so much blood that there isn't much left to bleed.

I won't let her die.

She has to live.

Whatever it takes.

I tell her that with my eyes. She looks away, not accepting my promises.

I hope Corbin has found a way to get Declan out of here. Maxwell will break free soon and meet them. They'll run far away from here and hide until Liesel gets free.

I never thought I'd want one of the kids to be taken by Corbin and Maxwell, but she can easily defeat Corbin and Maxwell later; we've done it before. Defeating Liesel's father is going to take more sacrifice than we are willing to make.

Liesel's father stands and walks over to her. He puts his hand on her shoulder, a thinly veiled attempt to control her.

"Your final task is simple. You want Declan to go free and inherit my empire? Then you have to prove that you put my organization and my men first. You have to prove you are strong enough to do the job. You won't allow yourself to love. You won't be selfish or weak. You'll be strong."

Liesel looks at her father, refusing to look at me.

"Prove that you no longer love him and your son goes free. Kill him, and I'll make you the leader of my men."

I don't believe he's just going to let her have control, but I do believe he'll let Declan go. It's clear he doesn't think he's up for the job or he's much too young to take over for an older man. He wants Liesel, and this is how he thinks he's going to get her.

"I need more assurances that Declan will go free. That he's safe," Liesel says sternly.

"Bring in Declan and Corbin," he says.

A few minutes later, they enter. They look well and unhurt. Declan looks sharp in his tailor-made suit. He has stern eyes and stands proudly with his shoulders back. Corbin looks on cautiously. His fists clench, and his pupils dilate. It seems he wants to say something but can't.

Liesel's father walks over and hands Corbin a set of keys and a security card. "The keys are to the black SUV parked behind the building. The security card will gain you access through the building to the back door. It will take you ten minutes to reach the car. The card will only work if Liesel has completed her part of the bargain. If not, you'll be trapped inside."

Corbin looks to Liesel, trying to tell her something. I hope she can read him better than I can because I don't have a clue what he's saying.

"Take the boy and go," Liesel's father says.

Corbin takes the boy's hand, and they leave.

"The clock is now ticking, Liesel." He pulls up his phone with the access code. "If they reach the door and you haven't killed Langston yet, the door will explode when Corbin goes to use the security card."

"No," Liesel gasps.

"Then kill Langston. Kill him, and they go free. Don't, and they die."

Liesel continues to stare at her father instead of me. It takes me a moment to realize why. She finally turns her head my way, and I see the fear in her eyes. Not fear of killing me, though, because I can see in her eyes that she's working on a different plan. Rather, fear that I'm going to try and convince her that she should shoot me.

And she's right.

I will do anything for her—even die for her.

I'll give her a minute to think, but that's it. I've already thought through our options. I can't take on all the men in this room and get to Corbin in time to tell him not to use the security card. We can hope he's smart enough to check for explosive devices before he opens the door. We can hope Corbin will find another way out, but I suspect Liesel's father has already planned for all outcomes. He knows Corbin is in this world. He knows he'll see a trap a mile away.

That only means he's set the trap perfectly. Liesel's father has ensured that Corbin won't get away with Declan unless he allows him to.

There is only one way Declan is getting out of here alive—Liesel has to kill me.

I just don't know how she's getting out of here alive.

She bites her lip, trying to hold back tears. She has a plan to save Declan. She has a plan to save herself.

I smile. Of course, she has a plan. It was my mistake to ever doubt her.

My entire body relaxes and accepts that she's going to live. She's going to live a long and happy life with her kids, with our friends. Someday she'll find someone else to love. Nothing else matters. My death is meaningless because she's going to live.

Shoot me. It's okay. Save him.

She can't help the tear rolling down her cheek, but I just smile at how strong she is. She may not think she's strong enough to survive this, but she is. I wish I could save her from having to be the one who kills me. I'm her killer; she's my huntress. She hunts; I kill.

But I can't kill for her this time. She's always been strong enough; I just wanted to protect her from the pain.

I love you, I mouth.

Then I close my eyes, trying to make it easier on her. I won't feel the pain. I'll just slip off to death.

"Five minutes until they reach the door, possibly less. What will it be?" I hear her father's words.

She's strong. She'll do what she has to.

A bullet hits me. I don't know where on my body because I don't feel a sharp pain. I do feel the wind knocked out of me as I fall backward, though. I don't open my eyes. I don't want Liesel to see me in pain. I don't want her to watch the life leave my body. I want her last memory of me is how much I love her before I drift away.

CHAPTER 16

LIESEL

I watch as Langston falls back against the two guards behind him. I don't know if everyone realizes what I did, but I don't have time to wait and see. I have a plan to enact, and time is running out.

I turn the gun on my father. "Deactivate the bomb so Corbin and Declan can get out."

"Not until I'm satisfied that Langston is indeed dead. You'd be surprised by what people can live through." My father is determined to check Langston himself.

As my father walks by me, I pick the cigar lighter from his pocket. Quickly, I grab the bottle of whiskey on the table, pour out its contents, and ignite the liquid—the table bursts into a wall of flames.

The men on the other side of the fire are trapped. They yell and scream as they scramble to attempt to put out the flames and get out of the room.

My father turns and smirks at me. "I didn't think you had it in you. It'll cost you your son's life."

I point the gun at my father. "Deactivate the bomb, or I'll kill you."

He tosses his phone at me; his security app still open on the screen.

My eyes shift to the phone in the air, and I catch it. When I look up again, my father is gone.

One of the men next to Langston is starting to stir. I fire at him before running to Langston.

"Langston! Get up!" I yell.

He opens his eyes, confused as to why he's still alive.

"I didn't shoot you. I shot the guard holding onto you knowing he'd fall backward and bring you with him."

"You're incredible," Langston says wide-eyed before grabbing my neck and pulling me into a kiss. I want this kiss to last forever, but there's not enough time to enjoy even a second of his sweet lips.

"We have to stop Declan and Corbin from using the security card until we've deactivated it," I say. I hold up the phone, and Langston quickly looks it over.

"The app is asking for a passcode. It could take hours to figure out how to hack this," he says.

"We have three minutes, maybe less."

"Shit." Langston jumps up, his mind spinning what to do next.

The fire spits and bursts behind us as it spreads toward us.

"Go," I say, knowing my injured leg will only hold him back from reaching them in time.

"I won't leave without you. I'll stop them, and then I'll come back for you."

I grab his shirt and kiss him quickly one more time. "Go."

Langston jumps up and takes off to find Declan and Corbin.

I start fidgeting with the phone, trying to figure out how to deactivate the bomb, but I don't have a clue.

I cough as the smoke from the fire hits me hard. I need to get out of here. I run out through the door and run smack into a chest.

"I've got you," Maxwell says. He looks at the fire behind me and coughs. "We need to get out of here."

I shake my head. "We have to deactivate a bomb that's going to go off when Corbin and Declan try to exit the building."

I hand him the phone. "Shit. I'll see what I can do while you find a way out of here."

"Deal."

I lead us down the hallway, following the direction that Langston went after Corbin and Declan. I need to know that Langston got to them in time. I need to know that they are safe.

CHAPTER 17

LANGSTON

I run as fast as my feet will carry me. I won't fail Liesel. I won't fail Declan. I have to run faster than I've ever run before. The hallways are long and winding, but thankfully there aren't a lot of choices of direction to be made. The only way I'll fail is if I don't run fast enough.

I run faster.

I can't feel my feet as I run. Sweat covers my brow and starts soaking through my shirt. My lungs burn from the exertion, but I only run faster.

I expect to run into some guards, but they all must be back in the room where I left Liesel. Hopefully, the guards are all burning in the fire.

I can't believe Liesel found a way not to kill me. She found a way to save us all. When I started running, I saw Maxwell coming out of the room we were held in and told him to get Liesel out safely. I don't know where her father went, but I'm sure he's running from the fire and carnage. He's a coward. He won't go back to fight his daughter. He's long gone.

Right now, the only fight we have is against the bomb that might explode, the fire inside, and any of the remaining guards.

We won't fail.

We can't.

We've come this far. We are all going to get out of here alive, and then we are going to live happily ever after together on my island away from all of this.

I don't know if I believe in the powers of manifestation, but I'm willing to try anything.

Run—faster.

Somehow, my body picks up speed, and I see the exit door at the far side still intact, but I don't see Corbin or Declan.

Shit, where are they?

Suddenly, a hand sticks out into the hallway from what seems like a wall, and I come to an abrupt stop. A panel in the wall fully opens, and Corbin appears, a boy I assume is Declan behind him.

"The door is...boobytrapped," I say, breathing hard, barely able to get the words out.

"We know; that's why we are hiding here," Corbin says.

I let out a big breath. "We have to get Declan out of here. The building is on fire, and Liesel's father took off."

Corbin nods. "Know of any other exits? Or do we need to deactivate the bomb?"

"Run!" I hear Liesel yelling from behind me.

"Shit," I say when I see guards running behind her and Maxwell, followed by flames.

It seems our decision is made for us. We don't have time to deactivate the bomb. I look at Declan.

"Do you know a safe way out of here?" I ask him.

"Why should I tell you?" Declan puffs his chest out.

"You're going to die if you don't."

"I'm not afraid of death."

"I believe that, but I have a secret. I know who your brother and sister are, and they'd very much like to meet you."

"I don't have any siblings."

"Their names are Rose and Atlas. You can meet them if you show us how to get out of here."

Declan considers. "This way." He slips past Corbin and me and starts running away from the flames.

Liesel and Maxwell are catching up, but they are still a good thirty seconds behind us. "Run!" Liesel shouts.

I want to stay with Liesel, but we need to get Declan out. That has to be the priority, and he's already taken off through another hidden panel in the wall that leads to a tunnel.

"Here," Corbin says, tossing me a gun.

I catch it as we continue to chase after Declan. The tunnel is dark, but it doesn't stop Declan from running full speed ahead. The boy isn't afraid of anything; I'll give him that.

I hear footsteps behind us, and I know Liesel and Maxwell have made it to the entrance of the tunnel; thank god.

Then Declan is at a door at the end of the tunnel.

"Wait!" I yell.

Declan stops.

"Step back, Declan. Let me see if it's got explosives rigged to it," Corbin says as he's closer to the door.

Declan doesn't move, so I yank him back as Corbin inspects the door carefully. "It's clear. Let's go."

Corbin pushes open the door, and streetlights shine on us. I grab Declan just as bullets start raining down on us from outside.

I turn him around, so my body shields him from the gunfire. Corbin and I start returning fire out the door.

The gunshots are limited, which means only one, maybe two, people are shooting at us.

"There's an SUV parked to the left," Corbin says as he tosses me some car keys.

I have to get Declan out of here, then come back for the rest of them.

"Go, I'll cover you," Corbin says as I inch toward the exit.

We both pop out onto the street at the same time. Corbin fires, and I run with Declan in my arms to the car.

The SUV is nearly a block away, but Corbin's fire is enough to get us there safely. I unlock the car with the key fob, hop in, and gently toss Declan into the backseat as I turn the car on.

"Stay down," I tell him as I drive the block back to collect everyone else. Suddenly, there's an explosion, and the entire building erupts up in flames.

"NO!" I yell as I watch the building burn.

Declan sits up in the backseat and looks out at the building in flames. I suspect this building has been his home his entire life. It's gone in a second; everyone he knows—gone.

Carefully, I drive toward the exit from which we just escaped. There is a body burning; I suspect Corbin's.

I grab my gun. I can't go without knowing for sure if Liesel is...

I can't even think it.

"Declan," I say.

The boy looks at me with big eyes. He's in shock.

"Look at me. I need you to keep your head down. I'll be right back, you hear me? I'll be right back. Stay hidden."

I wait until he crouches down on the car floor, then I run into the flames.

The smoke hits me first, and I cough over and over. There is no oxygen here, but I have enough left in my lungs to yell for Liesel. "Liesel!"

I get no response.

The flames flicker around me. I crawl down low to try to avoid the smoke, but it's everywhere.

I open my mouth, but it lets in too much smoke. I cough relentlessly, trying to get the smothering fumes out of my lungs. My hands reach out and make contact with a body—a body that is more ash than human flesh at this point.

"Liesel?" I beg.

Please, it can't be.

But then I see the strands of blonde hair.

"No," I whisper as my heart shatters. "Please, god, no."

But it's her. I know it's her—*Liesel's dead.*

"I'll protect them. I'll love them as my own as I loved you. As I'll always love you."

It takes all the strength I have to move away from her body, but I do. I have to. I have to get back to Declan before anyone who survived discovers him.

I run back out of the still-burning building and jump into the car.

Declan is still in the backseat where I left him.

I cough, unable to speak. I start driving. I can't think of where I should drive; I just know I have to drive away. Once we're a safe distance away, I'll call for someone to pick us up.

The boy in the backseat shakes as I drive, but I don't know how to comfort him. I don't know how to explain to him that he just lost his mother. And although I want to be his father, I just failed him.

A car pulls out in front of me, and I slam on the brakes. We stop just short of hitting the car, but Declan isn't buckled in and flies forward. I put my arm out to stop him from flying through the windshield.

At that moment, my heart flips. He becomes my son in an instant. Being a father is the most natural thing in the world to me. I wrap him in my arms and pull him onto my lap.

I may have failed Liesel, but I won't fail him.

"You're safe. I've got you. I've got you, Declan. I won't let anyone hurt you. You're safe."

She's dead.

I still can't accept it.

Liesel is gone, burned in the fire.

The feel of her charred flesh is seared into my memory. The singed ends of her blonde hair turned black will haunt me for the rest of my days. It's not how I want to remember her. In some ways, it's better that I saw her body. I'm not sure I would ever believe she is really dead if I hadn't seen her myself.

Still, my heart still can't process that she's gone. Once again, I failed her.

I haven't stopped crying since we left the shattered building. I continued weeping the entire flight home with Declan in my lap. You'd think my tears would dry now that we've landed on my island, but they still fall just as freely. I can't imagine a time when I won't be crying. From now on, I'll see the world in shades of black, white, and gray. My world will be void of color.

The only love I'll ever feel again is for my children. I'll never remarry. I'll never fall in love. I'll never have my soul be connected to another woman ever again.

My heart wishes I were dead. The loss is suffocating. It's the worst pain I've ever felt. I don't know how I'm going to endure a lifetime of it.

Then I look down at my lap, where Declan has fallen asleep with his head on my thigh. I stroke his hair. This is how I'll survive the pain —by taking care of the children she gave her life to protect.

I'll remember Liesel in Rose's hair and bravery, in Atlas's eyes and intelligence, and in Declan's strength. She'll never really be gone as long as they live.

The plane comes to a stop. Carefully, I lift Declan up in my arms. He doesn't stir. He's too exhausted from the day he's had. I wish I could sleep as easily as him. He can sleep away his pain, while nothing will be able to push my own heartache away.

I carry him off the plane and see a car waiting with Siren standing outside. I wasn't able to tell them much, just that I had Declan and I would arrive tonight, but it's not surprising they figured out what my lack of mention of Liesel meant. They sent my best friend to help me.

The second I step foot on the ground, Siren runs toward me and pulls me into her arms while I'm still holding Declan.

I sob into her shoulder, unable to bear the anguish of what I've lost. She helps me collapse to the ground, careful not to disturb Declan as she holds me in her arms. I don't know how I'm ever going to find the strength to stand again.

Siren starts humming. I don't recognize the tune, but it sounds sad and lonely. I don't know why she's humming such a sad song. Maybe she thinks it will soothe my soul to hear something that so clearly matches how I'm feeling. Instead, it drives me further into sadness.

More tears fall.

My body shakes.

Her arms wrap around me tighter as her voice gets louder.

I want to tell her to stop singing, that it's not helping me, but I don't want to upset her. I glance down and am surprised that Declan hasn't woken up with how loud she's humming now.

Her voice changes from hums to words. The song speaks of slipping away, of missing her. It takes me a minute to place the song before I realize she's singing 'Slipped Away' by Avril Lavigne. It's a fitting song I feel down to my bones. I don't know how Siren was able to conjure up a song that fits my feelings so clearly, but I can't take much more of the sadness. There is no escaping my agony right now, but I can't handle it flooding all of my senses at once.

Wait.

Siren. Is. Singing.

My eyes widen as I stare at Siren. She's not struggling to sing. Her voice is back better than ever. There is no sign that singing is bringing her pain. She's healed. She's regained what was lost.

I realize then that her singing isn't to put my heart's emotions into words; she's singing to remind me that not all is lost. I should have hope.

Liesel is dead; there is no hope.

But my heart clings to the tiniest bit of hope as I listen to Siren sing. She shouldn't be able to sing like this, not so soon after her injury. The doctors weren't sure if she would ever speak again, let alone sing. And yet, she's singing.

Siren grabs my elbows and helps me stand while I continue to hold Declan in my arms. She walks me to the car, still singing. She helps me into the front passenger seat as I hold Declan in my lap. Then she climbs into the driver's seat.

She never lets there be a moment without her humming or singing on the drive back. I realize now how comforting it is. I can't speak, and nothing she could say would bring me any comfort. She fills the silence with her songs—all sad, melancholy songs about love and loss.

As we get closer to the house, though, she speaks.

"Everyone knows already. They want to be there for you, but if your grief is too much to handle being around anyone, let me know, and they'll give you space until you're ready."

I don't know what I want. I should do whatever is best for Declan, Rose, and Atlas, but I don't even know what that is. Declan has just been ripped from the only world he knew. Rose and Atlas barely even knew Liesel. I don't know if any of them need to deal with the pain of her loss today.

Siren doesn't ask again. She studies me carefully after stopping the car in front of the house.

Everyone is standing on the porch, looking at us with somber expressions as we pull up. My heart bleeds as they walk over, not ready to face what happened but knowing I don't want to push them away either. The only thing worse than facing my grief is facing it alone. Luckily, I won't have to do that.

I'm engulfed with hugs as I step out of the car with Declan in my arms. I'm afraid he's going to wake up with everyone hugging us, and I'm going to have to introduce him to everyone. I'm going to have to talk—that's not something I'm capable of at the moment.

Declan sleeps through it all, and it makes me wonder what he went through before to be this exhausted.

As we all walk into the house, I know I need to make some decisions—where I want to sleep, where Declan should sleep, if I want Rose and Atlas to come to greet me. Yet somehow, I never have to make a decision.

Enzo leads the way, opening doors and speaking solemn commands to Zeke and Beckett. Kai and Siren walk on either side of me. Siren strokes Declan's hair, soothing him when he starts to stir until he falls back asleep.

I don't know what's happening until I enter the house and see the living room has been turned into one giant mattress. All the mattresses in the house have been brought down, along with pillows and blankets thrown everywhere.

"We're going to all sleep down here together. No one has to be alone tonight," Siren says.

It feels right.

For the first time, I truly look into the eyes of all of my friends. All of them are dripping with tears. They were Liesel's friends. They felt the loss too.

The men start carrying the kids down the stairs. It's past their bedtime, so they're all groggy. If they wake up, they probably won't remember moving downstairs.

Enzo and Zeke lie their kids down on one of the mattresses on the side, and then Kai and Siren carry down Atlas and Rose. Atlas stirs awake in Siren's arms.

"Dad?" he says, but his eyes are still closed.

"I'm here. Sleep, we can talk in the morning." I kiss his forehead.

"Okay," he yawns.

I walk over to Kai, who is holding Rose. I kiss my daughter's forehead as well.

They place both of the kids on one of the center mattresses. I walk over and sit down next to them with Declan still in my arms. I'm not sure I can let him go tonight. I don't want him to wake up afraid.

Then I spot Phoenix on the outskirts of the room. She searches the room for her brothers, but she's not going to find them. I need to tell her what happened.

I lie Declan down next to Atlas, careful not to wake him, before walking over to Phoenix.

We stare at each other, unsure of how to act. Our relationship is strained; I'm not sure if it will ever be repaired.

But right now, we both lost the most important people to us.

"I'm sorry," I say.

"I'm sorry, too," she croaks back.

Then we collapse in each other's arms, both grieving enormous loss. Everyone else is crying, but not like us. We each lost a piece of our souls, not just a close friend. There is no consoling us; I don't know how we'll ever stop.

Somehow we have to stop. I'm the kids' father, and as far as Rose and Atlas are concerned, she's the only mother they will ever really know. We have to find a way through this pain. We have to find a way back to them.

Someone must have moved us both to a bed because the next thing I know, I'm cocooned with my kids on one side, Phoenix next to them, and Siren on my other. The rest of my friends, my family, sleeping on various mattresses around us.

Despite my grief, the strong pull of slumber eventually pulls me under, granting me a moment of relief, at least until the morning comes and I have to endure all over again.

LANGSTON

"Are you dead?" Rose asks, pulling one of my eyelids up.

I wince at light hits my swollen eye.

"No," I reply.

She's sitting on top of me, tilting her head to the side as she studies me. "Sick then? You slept past lunchtime."

I frown.

I should have woken up earlier. I should have been there to explain to my kids what happened the second they woke up. Instead, it's day one without Liesel, and I'm already failing.

I grab my pounding head as I sit up and look around. The room is quiet, despite how many people are in it. Everyone is sitting on the various mattresses holding scattered plates with a few bites of food, hard liquor drinks, and used tissues.

Rose is sitting on my legs, *but where is Atlas? Where is Declan?*

Siren must realize my alarm because she lifts Atlas up over her legs, so he's sitting right next to me. Then, she nods silently for me to look to my other side.

Declan is snoring next to me.

My heart relaxes. All the kids are safe.

"So you're sick?" Rose asks again.

"Yes, I'm heartsick."

She scrunches her nose. "What does that mean?"

"It means my heart is broken. You remember Liesel? Your other mother?"

Both kids nod.

"She..." I can't say the words. Why can't I say the words?

She's dead.

Just say it. Tell them. They deserve to know that their mother is dead.

But I can't say it. Not yet. I can't. I just can't.

"She wasn't able to come back with us, and it makes me sad."

Rose takes my hand. "I miss her."

"I miss her, too."

Siren gives me a smile. None of the adults in the room argue with me about my decision. It's too hard for them to talk about too.

Then Rose looks down at Declan. "Is he dead?"

"No, he's sleeping. He had a long night."

"Who is he? He kind of looks like Atlas but with neater hair and slightly bigger," Rose says.

This draws Atlas' attention, and he peers over at the sleeping boy as well.

I open my mouth, so not ready to have this conversation. *How do I explain everything to them? How do I explain everything to Declan when he wakes up? What is he going to be like when he wakes up?* He trusted me last night because he had no choice. I'm not sure if he'll feel the same way today. I'm a complete stranger to him.

Luckily, I don't have to worry about that. It seems that the kids will solve those problems on their own.

"I'm Declan."

"I'm Rose, and this is my brother Atlas."

They all stare at each other a moment, and then Atlas says, "You're our brother. We're triplets. We are going to be best friends, and you'll learn to love Rose."

"Hey, don't act like I'm hard to love," Rose says.

Atlas laughs.

Declan looks back and forth between them. His eyes are big, entranced by them.

"Come see my room, Declan. You can sleep there until dad gets you your own room," Atlas says, grabbing Declan's hand. Then they all run upstairs.

Just like that, they become siblings.

I'm not sure Declan fully understands what's going on, but he didn't protest when they dragged him upstairs. We'll talk more later.

"Here." Siren hands me a shot glass after the kids run upstairs.

"Should I be drinking at a time like this?"

"What else should you be doing? It will numb the pain."

I throw the shot back, not even registering what kind of liquor is in it. Siren pours me another shot, and I take that one too.

"Do you want any food?"

I shake my head. Alcohol is the only thing I can stomach. I don't think I can chew food. I grab the bottle from Siren and start working on it.

"I know now isn't the time for talking, but if you need us to do anything, we're ready," Enzo says. I notice he has his own bottle of whiskey, and his eyes are already bloodshot.

I nod as I lift the bottle to my lips before I realize the answer. I put the bottle down abruptly.

"We have to go back."

"I thought the explosion killed everyone?" Enzo asks.

"It did, but I need to make sure…" I can't say Liesel's name. "I need to make sure her father is dead and that he has no successors to take over whatever is left of his organization."

"When do you want to leave?"

All eyes in the room are on me. Everyone in this room will do whatever I want. They won't judge me. There is no judgment in watching someone grieve. We all grieve differently. Whatever I need, they'll do.

I hear laughter from the kids upstairs. For the first time since my world ended, I smile. They will never have to experience my grief. I can protect them from the worst. What's most important now is to ensure they are completely safe. Ensure the man who took their mother is dead. Ensure they are safe forever.

I take another sip, knowing I'm going to have to stop drinking soon. I need to be sober enough to do what I need to do.

"Tonight."

CHAPTER 20

LANGSTON

Siren and Enzo agree to go with me back to Moscow, the rest deciding they should stay to protect the kids. Siren insisted she come, and Enzo didn't even give me the option. But of course, they would be the ones I would choose to come with me. They had the closest relationship to Liesel. They are the closest to me.

My head pounds on the flight back.

"Here," Siren says, handing me a bottle of scotch.

"I shouldn't drink. I'm going to need to be sober if I have to fight."

"You won't survive the flight if you don't drink." She nudges the bottle at me. "Enzo and I are sober enough. If he's alive, we'll kill him. There is no one here you need to protect. Drink; stop feeling."

I take the bottle and do as she says. She's right—it numbs the pain. My hands stop trembling. My heart settles. It's almost like I need the drug in order to be sober.

I can't live like this forever, but for today the alcohol is necessary.

"Do you want to talk?" Enzo asks, staring at me.

Everyone here has thought they lost the person they loved most at one point or another. I'm the only one who actually has lost that person.

I don't want to talk.

483

And yet, I do.

The words spill out of me.

"The first time I met her, she was hunting for a spider. I called her huntress. She hunted but couldn't kill, so I had to kill the spider for her." I smile, thinking of the memory. It seems that when you reach the end, your mind decides to go back to the beginning.

"I became her killer. We lost so much time we could have spent together. Somehow, even in that lost time, I have the best memories of her. We hated each other. We loved each other. We tried to kill each other, and we protected each other."

Tears well again, but I continue.

"I'll never find another woman so infuriating and so wonderful. I'll never love again like I loved her. And I'll take the pain. I'll take it all after tonight because I want to remember her. I don't want to be afraid to talk about her. I want to remember everything. I want my kids to know their mother. We have to tell her story. We can't be afraid of the pain."

Enzo smiles at me, reflecting on his memories of Liesel.

"She was the biggest bitch. She wanted me for my money and to fuck with you. I hated her. And yet, when she thought no one was watching, she would do something so kind, so incredible that I thought she had a twin sister who was an angel.

"I remember one time, my father caught me with stolen drugs. She took his wrath. She paid the price so I wouldn't have to," Enzo says through his tears. He holds up a bottle. "To Liesel."

We all clink our bottles and then take a sip.

"She hated me because she thought you loved me more than her. At least, at first, she did. She knew we were soulmates and best friends, and yet, she was so convinced she was the right woman for you, not me. She knew. She always knew, even when she pretended to hate me. We may be best friends, but you and she were two halves of the same heart," Siren says.

"I could only be friends with you because of her love for you. She loved you enough to not be jealous of our friendship. She knew that she had captured your entire being when you were five years old, so it didn't matter that we were friends. Us being friends wasn't a threat; I couldn't steal your heart even if I had wanted to. It already belonged to Liesel."

She clinks her bottle with ours again. "To Liesel," she says with a smile.

"To the only woman I hated and loved in equal measure. I love you, Liesel—my huntress, my wife, mother of my children, my everything. I'll carry you with me always so I can't miss you. I'll never let you leave me."

I clink my bottle one more time to theirs, and we all drink.

Then we change our focus to what we're going to do when we get back to Moscow. We discuss the layout, the likely scenarios. We prepare for war, knowing we are probably only going to find the remnants of an explosive fire that burned the building and everyone inside to death.

We reach the compound as dusk settles over the city. There is still smoke billowing from the building even though it's been over a day since I left.

There are no signs of life.

No people digging through the rubble. No squatters. Nothing but death.

I lead Enzo and Siren back to the spot where I last saw Liesel's body, but we find nothing.

"Are you sure this is where you last saw her?" Siren asks.

I nod and kneel down to get a better look. I find a few strands of her blonde hair, just like before. But this time, there is no body attached.

Enzo and Siren pick up pieces of fabric, threads of shirts similar colored to the ones Corbin and Maxwell were wearing, and hand them to me.

All signs that they are indeed dead.

"The fire must have raged so intensely that it burned their bones," Enzo says.

I nod. It's still hot.

"We need to find Liesel's father. We need to make sure he's dead."

We walk through the debris, spreading out to look for any clues as to who lived and who died.

We don't find any bodies, though. They all burnt up.

I walk to the far edge of the wreckage when I finally spot a body.

The body is badly burned. I can't make out any facial features, but once again, there's a clothing thread. I pick it up, adding to the collection of other items we can test for DNA and bury to give our lost ones some type of burial. It's the thick dark fabric of Liesel's father's coat.

"Did you find him?" Siren asks.

I nod.

"We should go back home," I say.

I hold all the items in my hand—the three pieces of fabric and a lock of Liesel's hair.

I scan the debris one more time, but these are the only personal items we find. A strange feeling overcomes me.

Strange that in a field of debris, we only found items belonging to the four people whose living status we need to know.

Strange that we found no bodies.

Strange that we found no evidence of anyone else.

Strange that it feels like this evidence was planted.

Strange.

And hopeful.

I don't think Liesel's father is dead. I don't think Corbin or Maxwell is dead. I don't think Liesel is dead.

I stare at my friends. They won't believe me. They'll think I'm delusional and I'm inventing theories because I can't handle my grief. I need more proof.

I grin. I'll do whatever it takes to find the truth. I'll search to the ends of the earth. My huntress is alive. She lived. Now it's my turn to hunt for her, to survive long enough to save her like she's saved me.

CHAPTER 21

LIESEL

I have no question who set off the explosion—my father. He'd rather see us dead than let us escape.

I cough up blood and soot after the explosion knocks me to the ground.

Declan.

Langston.

I don't process the damage done to my own body. All I care about is whether or not my boys made it out. I force my head up to try to look to the door, but I can't see anything through the billowing smoke.

They had to have made it.

I remember the last thing I saw was them exiting through the door. It was several seconds before the explosion happened. They are safe.

My head collapses, and my face hits the ground with a thud. I don't feel the sharp pain of the rocks sticking into my face. I don't feel anything.

I'm dying.

Even before this happened, the wound in my leg was a death sentence unless I got medical attention fast. Whatever damage added to my body will just quicken my death. All I can wish for now is confirmation that Declan and Langston made it out alive before I slip away.

As if the universe decides to answer my wish, Langston appears before me. I must be hallucinating, but then I feel his touch against my hair.

I don't move.

I don't breathe.

I beg my heart to stop beating.

He can't know I'm alive. I have to stay here to ensure my father is dead with whatever little time I have left, and he needs to get Declan out of here.

Langston stays for a moment. I can hear his sobs and feel his pain emanate off his body as he continues to touch my hair. He must think I'm dead. I don't want to imagine what the rest of my body looks like for him to assume that so easily without checking for breathing or my pulse.

I could put Langston out of his misery. I could speak, move, let him know that I'm alive. But it would only ensure he suffers more pain when he eventually lost me anyway, when he couldn't save me.

It's better for him to let me go now.

He touches my hair one more time, and then he's gone.

Feeling Langston gone is what gets me. The tears start, but not because I lost him. I got to love Langston before my life ended, and that was worth everything it cost me. He's the father of my children. I don't care that he isn't theirs by blood; he's theirs by love.

Once I'm convinced he's gone, I try to stand up. I need to kill my father. I need to destroy the last threat against my children. My body refuses, but I've never listened to what my body wants. My heart is the only thing that matters, and my heart isn't injured. My heart is strong, strong enough to stay alive long enough to destroy my father.

I don't know how I get to my feet, just that I do.

I see bodies lining the hallway, but I don't linger to look at them. I quickly see the blood, the ash, the carnage. I don't know if any of them are alive or dead, friend or enemy. I just know that I have to find my father and kill him.

After walking down a few hallways, I begin to lose consciousness again. I succeed in finding my father, just not in killing him.

I WAKE IN A DARK CELL COMPLETE WITH BARS, A DAMP FLOOR, AND A thin mattress on the floor. I don't remember how I got here. I remember finding my father and then nothing.

I failed.

I don't know how much time I have left to succeed.

"You're finally awake," a deep voice says.

I look in the direction of the voice, but the room is too dark to make out who is in the cell next to me.

"Who are you?"

"You don't recognize my voice?" he chuckles.

It takes me a second but then I place it. "Corbin?"

I race over to the side of the cell he's on. I reach my hand through the bars, and he takes my hand in his. I can't believe I'm thankful that Corbin is in the next cell over.

I have so many questions to ask, and I don't know which is most important to ask first.

"How long have I been out?"

Corbin opens his mouth to answer, but I'm already asking the next question.

"Where are we?

"Where is my father?

"Have you found a way out yet?

"What about killing my father?

"Are you hurt?

"What about Maxwell?

"How am I still alive?

"What about Langston? The kids?"

Corbin reaches through the bars and squishes my lips together to shut me up.

"If you'll stop talking, I'll tell you everything I know."

I nod.

He lets go of my lips.

"You tried to attack your father after the explosion. I don't know what you thought you were going to be able to do in the physical state you were in, but I saw you hunt for him, and I followed you. You got a good punch in before he knocked you out with some drug."

That's why my head is spinning.

"His men did the same to me, and I suspect Maxwell. He's in the cell on the other side of you, but he's in really bad shape. He hasn't woken up yet."

"What about you?" I ask.

"My left leg is badly burnt, third-degree if I had to guess. I suffered a concussion and a few broken ribs, but nothing I won't recover from. I've been in here for over two weeks. You just arrived here yesterday."

"Where have I been all this time?"

"The hospital. You had surgery. You got skin grafts for the burns, a cast for your broken wrist, and pain medication. A nurse came in this morning and injected you with some drugs. Your father wants you to live, unlike Maxwell and me. He gave us the minimal amount of medical attention to keep us alive."

I study my body. I have on loose-fitting pajama pants, a cotton shirt, and slippers on my feet. My body looks clean, and I feel several bandages on my legs and arms. There's a cast on my left wrist. I feel a dull ache, but nothing too intense, which means pain medicine is still pumping through me.

"Is Maxwell going to make it?" I ask.

"I don't know. From what I can tell, he's been torched all over his body too. He has an IV providing him nourishment, but that's all I can tell until he wakes up."

"Let me see what I can see." I start to move away, but Corbin grabs my arm.

"Langston and the kids are safe."

"How do you know?" I can hear my heart pounding in my chest. I saw Langston escape with my own eyes before everything went dark, but I need all the evidence I can get.

"Your father talks about them. He doesn't want them; he wants you. But it won't stop him from trying to use them as leverage to get what he wants from you."

"Where are we?"

"Not sure. We were all unconscious and woke up down here. We could still be in Russia or a thousand miles away."

"We have to kill him."

He nods. "I agree. We need to come up with a plan."

"I'm going to check on Maxwell. We need to know how many people we have on our side."

I slide across my small cell. It can't be more than ten feet by ten feet. "Maxwell?" I ask through the bars.

No answer.

I'm able to see what Corbin described—burns cover his skin, and there's an IV in his arm. I watch his chest rise and fall and compare it to my own.

"His breathing is slightly slower than mine, but he's alive and unconscious. I don't know what we could do to help."

"Nothing. Either he'll wake up on his own, or he won't."

I sigh as I sit back on my bed and lean against the wall. I'm about to ask Corbin if he has any ideas for an escape or how to kill my father when he speaks.

"I'm sorry."

"Why? This isn't your fault," I reply.

Corbin leans against the same wall next to me, with the bars separating us. He lets out a large sigh, seeming to relax.

"No, but I assumed the reason you were going after your father was because you wanted his power for yourself. I knew the men you're friends with. The Black family seeks power and money at all costs. At least, that's how it used to be before Kai took over. I thought you were working with your father to gain their trust and overthrow my family before taking over for your father. I thought you were playing us all."

"And now?" I ask cautiously.

"I know you love Langston. You love your kids. You hate your father for what he's done to your family. I know you just want him dead. You want to watch his business burn. You're not your father's daughter."

He takes a deep breath. "I'm sorry for my part in hurting you. After this is all over...when we kill your father and escape, I won't punish you. I won't take you hostage. And I won't come after your kids. I—"

"No," I stop him.

He frowns. "No? I'm telling you that our deal is off. I'll help you kill your father, but I don't want you as my hostage. You're free of our deal. If we survive this, then you get to live your life with the man you love and your kids."

"No, I don't think I'm going to survive this. Even with the best medical care, we both know my destiny. I can't let Langston love me again. He thinks I'm dead. We can't let anything change that. I can't let him go through my death twice."

"So, what do you want from me?"

"If we somehow manage to survive this, then I want you to take me as your hostage."

"You can live with me, of course, but I'm not so cruel as to take you hostage."

"You have to. If I live long enough, I'll want to run straight into Langston's arms once I'm free. You have to stop me from doing that; make it so I can't get to him. Promise me."

Corbin runs his hand through his hair before his head falls back. I know he's trying to think of another solution, a way he doesn't have to keep his promise, but he can't think of one. And he owes me.

"I promise," he finally says.

I relax, knowing that I won't have to put Langston through my death again. I have a plan. I'll only have to break his heart once.

And for now, that's enough.

♡

THE DOOR TO MY CELL POPS OPEN, AND THE CREAK IT MAKES PULLS me out of a dreamless sleep.

I sit up and come face to face with my father.

"Brave of you to come into my cell on your own," I say, noticing he's brought no men into the cell with me.

"It is brave of me. I know you'll try and kill me any chance you get. Lucky for me, the nurse just gave you another shot of pain medication while you were sleeping to further sedate you. You don't have the strength to fight me."

He's right. Simply sitting up like this is taking all of my energy. I'm not even sure I have the strength to stand.

"What do you want?"

"I just want to have an honest chat, you and I." He sits down on a folding chair he's brought into my cell.

I glance over at Corbin, who is either asleep or pretending to be.

"I'll make this simple for you, my daughter. Do as I say, and I won't go after Declan or either of your other kids."

"I already won the game. I did as you say. The deal was Declan went free, and I got your empire, not locked up in a cell."

"Don't pretend like you completed the final challenge. We both know Langston is still alive."

I swallow. Would my children be safer if Langston were dead? No, I refuse to accept that. I won't kill Langston, no matter what my father says he needs from me to not go after my children.

"What do you want?"

"The same thing I've always wanted—to know you are strong enough to be the leader my men need. I need to know you'll put them and the power that comes with it before anything else. You can't still be in love with that man and do this job."

"Why is it so important you have a successor?"

He stares but doesn't answer.

"You're dying, aren't you? You don't have much time left. You don't have time to wait for Declan to grow up. You need someone to take over now."

"It doesn't matter why. You will do what I say, prove that you can do the job, then I'll let your kids live."

"So you want me to kill Langston?"

He nods. "Prove that you no longer love him."

"No," I say, knowing that Langston has all three kids on his island with our friends and their resources. My kids are safe. I don't care what torture my father inflicts on me. I'll survive long enough to kill him or watch him die from whatever illness he has.

"I'll let you have some time to think about it." He stands up and stops at the door. "Stop loving him, or I'll go after your children. I'll kill the other two, who aren't up for the job, and hand everything I own to Declan when he turns eighteen. I'm a patient man. I can wait for your answer. You have a year until I go after your first child. Two years until I go after your second. And over a decade before I go after your third. Is loving him really worth sacrificing your children? I'd stop loving him now if I were you and save us all some time."

He clinks the door of my cell shut.

"If you want me to consider it, then ensure Maxwell and Corbin live. Give them proper medical treatment. If either of them dies, then I won't consider your offer at all. Call it a good-faith gesture."

My father glares at me, grinding his teeth together so hard and loud in his rage. Finally, he gives me a curt nod.

I saved Corbin and Maxwell. My children are safe with Langston. Now, if I could only find a way to kill my father while saving myself.

CHAPTER 22

LANGSTON

One Year Later

I hold my cup of coffee in my hand, drinking it quietly on the deck while Atlas, Declan, Ellie, and Cayden eat their breakfast. Rose and Finn aren't early birds and won't be up for another hour. Most of the adults are milling about in various parts of the house. I'm the only one who has been up for hours. I don't sleep, not anymore. Not while I'm separated from Liesel.

I've taken the duty of feeding the kids breakfast in the morning. The house I originally built as Liesel and I's dream house has become our safe haven. Everyone moved here. Siren and Zeke are building a house nearby. Kai and Enzo sleep on one of the yachts parked just off the shore. Phoenix sleeps in the part of the house I designed for her. Beckett sleeps in one of the guest bedrooms, and all the kids sleep here in the main house with me more often than not.

It works.

We're safe here on our own private island. We control who comes and who leaves. The seclusion does make it harder to search for a man who doesn't want to be found, though.

He's haunted my dreams to the point that I think I must be

deluding myself into thinking he's still alive. He must have burned in the fire just like everyone else. That's why we haven't found him.

But if that's true, if he's really dead, then that means Liesel is too. If she were alive and her father was dead, she would have come back. She would have been free.

He has to be alive. I can't handle him not being alive. I can't face the reality that Liesel is probably dead, and that's why I haven't found her either.

Either way, I won't stop searching until I have definite proof. I can't stop searching, not if there is a chance she's alive.

"Go for a run with me?" Zeke asks as he steps foot on the deck.

I nod, knowing it's better to answer without words. Zeke's hearing still hasn't fully recovered, although he is healing. Or he's getting better at reading lips.

Kai takes over watching the kids while Zeke and I quickly stretch and then start running down the beach. Every morning I run with Zeke. Every evening I run with Enzo. Every afternoon I swim with Kai. And every evening after I put the kids to bed, I drink with Siren. It's become a bit of a routine. Beckett is the only one who doesn't have a specific task in taking care of me and ensuring I don't have a moment to think about Liesel. His focus is more on security, but he tends to fill in whenever someone needs a break.

Running with Zeke on the beach is just a normal morning here. Occasionally, I take a small team to go follow a lead when we think we've found Liesel's father, but otherwise, we are here, living a dream life on our own private island.

"Did you follow that lead in India?" I ask as we jog, our bare feet hitting the sand with each step.

"Yes, it was a dead end."

I sigh. "Beckett thought he had something in Chile that he wanted to follow up on. Hopefully, that will lead to more clues."

"Can I be honest with you?"

This can't be good. "Sure. You've upended your whole life for me. I think you have the right to be honest with me."

He stops running.

I take a couple more steps before I stop too. *This really can't be good.*

He puts his hands on his head like he's struggling to breathe, but really he's struggling to get his words out. "It's been over a year. We have everyone searching for any sign of them. His organization has gone silent. His money is tied up in banks, motionless. Every clue leads to him being dead."

I know he's right, but I can't accept it.

He puts his hand on my shoulder. "I'm sorry. If I were in your shoes, I wouldn't stop looking either. I'd never stop looking for Siren. I shouldn't have said anything."

"No, you should have. Don't be afraid to speak what's on your mind. I need to hear what you all are thinking. It's not just me I have to worry about. I have to think about the kids too."

"Race you back?"

I grin, taking off, knowing I'm much faster than him. He's almost twice my size. He can beat me at lifting weights, but not this.

It feels good to run this fast. It makes me feel alive when I mostly feel lost, dead, empty. I don't know what I'd do if it weren't for everyone ensuring I eat, drink, and shower every day. If they didn't plan every second of my day, I'm pretty sure I'd be homeless and wasted away to nothing. It's these little moments that keep me living.

I beat Zeke back to the house easily when I spot Siren walking down the steps leading to the beach.

"Looking for your husband? He'll be back in another five minutes. You know his slow ass can't keep up with me."

She smiles. "Actually, I was looking for you."

"Wanting to get a drink early? Or are you swapping your time for Kai's?"

She laughs. "I guess we have established a bit of a babysitting routine, but no. Actually, we found a clue. We think we found Liesel's father."

My eyes go wide. Usually, when anyone brings me any evidence, they try to say it in the most subdued, pessimistic way as to not get my hopes up.

"Where is he? What do we know?" I ask too excitedly. I know no one likes talking to me about Liesel's father. They all know that I think she's still alive, and no one has the heart to tell me differently.

"He's on a yacht." She doesn't say it excitedly. There's something she's not telling me.

"Where?" I move closer to her, getting in her face trying to read her mind and hesitation.

"Here. The yacht is less than ten miles away. He stole one of our ships and has been moving it around the Pacific Ocean, getting close occasionally, but not so close that we would suspect him. Until now."

"It's a trap?"

She nods. "He wants us to find him. That's what's changed."

Shit.

I stare out into the ocean. I can't see any yachts except for Kai and Enzo's, but he's here. He's been taunting us this entire time with how close he is—something's changed.

"What do we do?" she asks.

"We go kill him." And we find Liesel alive.

CHAPTER 23

LIESEL

"Bishop to the second white square from the right," I say.

"That's bishop to F5," Corbin sighs, exacerbated with me for once again not using the actual names of the squares. In the months we've been playing chess with each other in our heads, I've learned what the squares are called, but I like annoying him.

"It doesn't matter what the name of the square is; that's check," I say.

"Actually, that's checkmate," Maxwell says, throwing a ball he made out of aluminum foil and catching it.

"It's not. It can't be," Corbin goes through the position of all my pieces in his head, trying to figure a way out of it. I don't think there is a way. My queen and bishop are positioned perfectly, and I have his king stuck in a corner. I think I've won.

"Dammit," Corbin finally curses. "You win again."

I grin as I lay on my cold mattress with my arms behind my head, staring up at the ceiling.

"Your turn to play me, Max."

"Nope, I'm not playing chess with you. You know how much I hate using my brain that much."

"We could play checkers?"

"No."

"Tic-tac-toe?"

"No."

"Fine, push-up or pull-up challenge?"

"Push-ups," Max grins.

Corbin and I roll my eyes. While Corbin prefers to work his brain, Maxwell prefers to be entertained with games of physical strength.

We all roll off our mattresses to the floor. We get in position to start our push-ups, and then Maxwell shouts, "Go!"

We don't have a timer or any sort of clock to measure how many we can do in a set time. Instead, we just go until one of us can't anymore, then we count. In the months we've been doing this, I've only won the pushup contest once. And that was only because Maxwell was sick with a cold, and Corbin let me win.

I don't expect to win, but it is fun to watch the two brothers compete.

I move quickly, doing as many push-ups I can before I exhaust my arms. I love how it feels to have my blood pump fast, and my lungs burn with exertion.

I get lost in how my body feels. I forget my pain, how I've failed to kill my father. I forget about everything. If I'm honest, I think doing the physical games take my mind away from everything better than the mental games with Corbin. But I wouldn't ever tell Corbin that. Both brothers are trying their best to take care of me and distract me.

My arms continue to push my body up off the floor before lowering myself back down—again and again and again.

Finally, I collapse. My arms no longer have the strength to lift again.

The boys notice and stop their push-ups.

"One hundred and five," Corbin says.

"One hundred and thirteen," Maxwell says and then looks to me. "Liesel? Are you alright?"

I can tell by his voice that I don't look good. I'm sure my face is pale, my breathing shallow and erratic. "I've been waiting for death for a long time; it never comes. I'm not going to die because I did too many push-ups."

"Still, you should take it easy," Maxwell says.

"This is why we should play mental games, not physical ones," Corbin says.

I sit up to prove that I feel fine. "I'm fine. See, perfectly fine."

I feel my stomach twisting, and I suspect I'll be sick soon. I take a couple of slow breaths, trying to ease my queasiness. I try to hide how I feel from them, but they notice.

"Come here," Corbin says.

I inch myself closer to the bars on his side. He wets a cloth and presses it to my forehead before lifting a bottle of water to my lips.

"Drink."

I take a couple of small sips, but it's all I can stomach.

"How are you feeling?" Maxwell asks.

There's no use lying. "My stomach is burning and wants to eject everything inside it."

Corbin and Maxwell exchange worried looks.

I don't know how I'm still alive, honestly, except that I have unfinished business. My father is still alive; still a threat to my children and my body refuses to die until my father is dead.

Speaking of the devil, my father makes his almost daily appearance.

"You don't look so good, my daughter."

"I look better than you," I say, forcing my body up. I won't look weak in front of him. Just like my father won't look weak in front of me.

We both know the other is dying; we are both sick. We're playing a game of chicken, trying to appear braver and healthier than the other. My father thinks I can be saved. As soon as I do what he says, he thinks he can give me the drugs to save me. But if that were true, he'd use them on himself and live.

I don't know what his game is exactly. He knows I'm dying, that I can't take over for him, and yet he keeps trying. Every. Single. Day.

"Don't you have something better to do with your day than annoy us?" Corbin asks.

My father ignores him.

"Today is a very special day."

"The day you finally keel over dead?" Maxwell asks.

"It's been one year exactly. It's time to decide."

"Decide what?" I ask.

"Decide who I'm going to kill first—Rose or Atlas?"

I frown. Nervous energy zips through my body before I blow out a breath, letting the anxiety go. He can't get to Rose or Atlas. They are completely protected. I don't have to worry about him killing them.

"Neither."

"So confident in your beau to protect them. So stupid of you to think that I can't kill them."

"You can't," I say defiantly.

He pulls out his phone and starts a video. It's of Langston playing with the kids. I become transfixed by the video. They've all grown so much. Rose now towers over her two brothers. Declan has grown his hair out, while Atlas has gotten a recent buzzcut. They look happy, content, safe. My eyes drift to Langston. He's lost weight, but not muscle. His eyes are hollow and slightly red. I'm guessing from lack of sleep or excess alcohol.

I touch the screen with my fingers, wishing I could send him my love and comfort. I wish I could let him know that I'm alive, but that would break him. He's strong but in a fragile state. I won't be the reason he breaks.

The video ends, and I hand the phone back to my father. "This means nothing."

"It means I have a spy on the inside. Did you see the angle this video was taken from?"

"Who?" I can't believe anyone there would spy for my father. Not any of our friends. Not any of the employees.

"Phoenix."

I gasp.

"Phoenix wouldn't risk the kids' lives. She loves them," Maxwell says.

I agree. She would never hurt them.

"Maybe, but then she would do anything to save her brothers' lives."

"You bastard! I'm going to kill you," Corbin says.

My father smirks. "I'm going to win. The sooner you realize that, the better. There is no use in you rotting your life away in this cell."

"Just because you got Phoenix to take a video for you doesn't mean she'll help you get to one of the kids. You won't get anywhere near the island."

"Oh, child, how you underestimate me. Where do you think we are?"

He pulls up another video. This one is a security feed from the yacht we're on, apparently. It's staring straight ahead at Langston's island.

He turns the phone off and then turns, walking to my cell door. He pauses.

"You have until midnight to decide which child dies."

I squeeze my eyes shut. I can't take the chance that he could get his hands on one of my kids. I have no doubt if he got close, he'd kill one of them. He doesn't need all three as a backup. He just needs one.

"Wait!" I scream.

My father stops.

"What do you want me to do?"

CHAPTER 24
LIESEL

"Kill him," my father says.

"I would, except you won't let me out of this cell, and he's too smart for you to catch." I'm not sure if that's true. Phoenix may easily give Langston over in exchange for her brothers getting to live. She'd definitely prefer to hand over Langston than one of the kids.

"The time will come when you will have the opportunity to kill Langston. Until then, in order for me to not head to the island tonight to kill one of your children, prove that you've stopped loving Langston."

"How?" I ask, even though I know I'm going to regret asking.

A sly grin forms on his vile face as he looks from Corbin to Maxwell. "Have your pick."

"Fuck one of them, you mean."

"Yes, fuck them, want them. Show me you've forgotten all about that stupid boy. Show me you're strong enough to do what it takes to be a leader."

I take a deep breath. Fucking another man doesn't mean that I've stopped loving Langston. He would understand and forgive me for cheating. He has before.

I look at Corbin and Maxwell out of the corner of each eye. They are frozen in place, trying to figure out how to kill this devil. Maybe this is our chance. He hasn't let us out of these cells in a year. This might be our first opportunity.

"I assume if I do this, you'll at least allow me a proper bed. I'm not fucking either of them in this dark cell."

"That can be arranged."

"So what? I fuck one of them, and you don't kill any of my children? Then you throw us back in these cells?"

"Afterwards, I'll decide if you still love Langston or not. If you do, you'll go back in this cell to think about it for another year. If you don't, then we can start your transition to power and go after him together."

This is my chance. He'll take us upstairs. We will be out of these cells. We could find a way to kill him tonight. Or, at least, I could convince him I don't love Langston anymore and be free of this cell, giving me plenty of more time to kill him. Worst case, we end up back in these cells without succeeding.

We have to succeed. I won't survive another year.

"I'll arrange for you to be brought out of your cell in an hour. You can choose which of your cellmates you'd prefer to seduce then."

"What if I want to fuck them both?"

"If that's what you choose, then fine."

His eyes warn me, knowing why I asked. They're both on my side, and I want to improve our odds of defeating my father.

"You have one hour." He closes my door and looks from me to Corbin, then to Maxwell. "Plan well. You're only going to get this one chance to kill me. You don't want to know what's going to happen when you fail."

His words are a warning. If we make an attempt on his life and fail, he'll kill one of us.

He'll kill Corbin or Maxwell.

We can't fail.

♡

AFTER MY FATHER LEAVES, THE THREE OF US STARE AT EACH OTHER. None of us know what to do. We can't discuss a plan together—my father would listen in on the security cameras.

Instead, we sit quietly by ourselves, contemplating our plans. I try to go through all the possibilities. I try to come up with anything I can use as a weapon. All the tricks Langston taught me about how to get out of bindings, how to protect myself, I think of it all.

I don't know how fast or slow time moves. Since we've been locked up, time has been a strange element. We never know when it's day or night. It's hard to even keep track of the days when you have no sun to count, nor work or activity to mark the difference between days.

This hour passes in much the same—both slowly and all at once.

Corbin, Maxwell, and I exchange reassuring glances as we hear the approach of footsteps nearing the door that leads to our cells. We don't have to talk to know that we have a plan. We are going to succeed. We are going to kill my father. We might not all survive, but that isn't the goal. The goal is to put an end to this. Any sacrifice any of us make will be worth it.

We all stand and face the doors of our cells, ready to fight no matter what comes.

Suddenly, my world goes dark.

I OPEN MY EYES, AND THE ROOM IS BRIGHT—SO FUCKING BRIGHT that I immediately close them again, but not before I get a glimpse of Corbin standing over me.

"Where are we? The surface of the sun?" I ask.

He chuckles.

"No, we're in a room above deck with windows. That's the first ray of sunshine you've seen in a year."

I flutter my eyes, trying to open them, but honestly, I prefer the dark.

"Here," Maxwell says.

A second later, the blinds are blocking the light enough for me to open my eyes.

"Better?" Maxwell asks.

I nod and then sit up.

It makes me immediately queasy. Corbin notices the familiar motion and grabs a trash can for me just in time as the contents of my stomach come up.

"What happened?" I ask after my stomach stops heaving.

"He drugged you before he even entered your cell."

"Just me?"

Corbin nods. "Yea, he didn't have to drug us. He knew once he had you, we would do whatever he said. He brought us all into this room and then left. He hasn't spoken to us yet. Our best guess is you've been out for about an hour."

"Have you found any way out?" I ask, even though I know they can't answer me, at least not with words.

We did come up with signals for yes and no in situations like this to answer basic questions without my father or his men seeing what our real answers are.

"No," Corbin says.

He grabs my hand and helps me stand up off the couch I was lying on. He squeezes my hand twice before letting it go.

Our signal for yes was to make any motion twice, a single time for no.

Twice for yes.

They've found a way out of here.

The problem is they can't communicate it to me, so I just have to follow their lead of when or how to get out of here.

I look around the room. It's half living area, half bedroom. There is a couch I was lying on and two chairs. Then there is a large king-sized bed on the other side.

I gulp at the sight. I don't know if their plan of escape involves doing what my father wants before or after we use the bed.

I pace around the room as the two men's eyes are locked on me. I take in the two large windows that are now covered with blinds. I run my hand over the edge of the bed, the couch, the chairs, the door, the walls. I study the cameras I can see and guess where there could be more that I can't see.

I jump when I hear my father's voice.

"Prove to me that you don't love him anymore. Commit one of the worst sins."

And then his voice is gone.

I feel the two men behind me, and I know what I must do—fuck them like I want them.

There was a time when I would have been capable of this, even while loving Langston. But without seeing Langston for over a year, I'm not sure I'm strong enough. My heart longs for Langston so strongly that I'm not sure I can even go through the motions with someone else, let alone convince my father.

I don't turn around. I can't face Maxwell and Corbin. They've become friends, practically brothers in our year together.

"I can't," I whisper, letting them know I'm going to need all the help I can get.

I hear both men walk to me, stopping on either side of me.

They each take one of my hands and squeeze twice.

Yes.

I don't know what they are trying to say yes to; just that is the signal they are giving me.

"Close your eyes," Corbin says.

I do.

"Take a deep breath and let go of everything. Let your mind drift to what you want it to," Maxwell says.

And then I feel a blindfold placed over my eyes.

I gulp for air, like losing my sight also affected my ability to breathe.

They lead me over to the bed until the backs of my thighs graze the edge. A hand on my shoulder lowers me to the bed. I sit, but I don't fall back.

"Picture him, not us."

I can't tell if that was Maxwell or Corbin who said that.

I don't know how I'm supposed to show that I'm over Langston if they had to blindfold me for me to fuck them.

"It won't work."

"Trust us. It will."

Picture Langston.

Pretend it's Langston.

My memories of the last time we were together are so foggy that I can barely remember. *What did it feel like to have his lips pressed against mine? Were they soft and sweet? Hard and controlling? Would I lose my breath, or would my heart rate speed? Was I overcome with emotion, or so lost in him that I felt no emotion at all?*

I can't remember.

I've been living without him for so long that I've forgotten all of the little details. *What shade was his hair up close? Was his smile crooked or straight?*

Hands gently glide me down until I'm lying on my back.

I purse my lips and let out a slow, calming breath. Maxwell and Corbin aren't going to hurt me. They are just doing what is necessary for us to protect my kids and kill my father.

"Think of him," Corbin says. Then I feel warm, wet lips against mine.

The kiss takes my breath away. I wasn't expecting anything so intimate from either of them. Fucking yes, kissing no.

"Him."

The lips don't leave mine. I don't know if it's Corbin or Maxwell kissing me, but he's persistent in his drive to get my lips to part.

Think of Langston. Think of the man I've been so desperate to forget because thinking of him was too painful.

Finally, I open my lips.

His tongue takes full advantage, dipping into my mouth and controlling every part of it. It sweeps over my tongue, pulling a low moan out of me.

My body comes alive again. I never thought I'd be here, writhing under Langston again, but I am.

His hardness is hovering over my body but isn't pressed against me like I want. I tug on his bottom lip with my teeth, encouraging him to come closer.

I hear moaning, but it's not his.

It's Corbin or Maxwell, but somehow it feels distant, not close.

It's because I'm imagining Langston, not them. My mind is playing tricks on me, pushing their voices out, but I can't quite invent Langston's voice out of thin air, not when I haven't heard his deep timbre in so long.

I don't need to imagine his voice. Whoever is kissing me is doing plenty to stir my memories of Langston. I remember how his kisses would start off by taunting me, making me feel like I'm in control before demanding everything from me. I'd feel his kisses to the deepest parts of my core and all the way to the tip of my toes—it's how I feel now.

I grab for his shirt and yank him to me.

His body fits perfectly over mine.

How can a man who isn't Langston fit so well with my body? Is it Maxwell or Corbin?

No.

This is Langston.

Langston!

I let my fantasy of the man touching me being Langston fill my head. I won't think of Maxwell or Corbin again.

He pushes my shirt up my body as he kisses my stomach then up to the curve of my breasts. He pulls the shirt off my body, so he can stare at my body unobstructed. He pauses, not touching me, kissing me, or whispering dirty thoughts. He must be doing nothing but looking at me.

I bite my lip as I feel a blush come over me. *Does he not find me attractive anymore?* I know I've been through hell. My body is weak, bruised, scarred. I don't have the curves I used to.

It's been so long since we've fucked that I'm sure he no longer finds me attractive.

"Maybe you should wear a blindfold too and imagine someone else," I whisper.

He catches my wrist as I try to push him away and kisses the tender spot of my palm.

I can't help but moan at the softness of his lips. Then his lips are at my ear.

I shiver from the hotness of his breath building pleasure through my body.

"I can't take my eyes off you," he says.

My breath catches. His voice sounds like what I remember Langston's to be. My mind is fully committed to the fantasy.

He starts kissing down my body again, not missing a single inch of skin. I get lost in the pleasure. With my blindfold on and not feeling anything like this in a year, my body is tingling everywhere his lips press. So much so that I don't notice that he's removed my pants until I feel him kiss between my legs.

I gasp loudly—so loudly that he stops to check that I'm okay. He continues when he realizes it's just because the intensity of his touch is overwhelming me, not hurting me.

My body is torn between indulging in the feel of his hot lips between my legs and knowing how wrong this is. A tingle of fear simmers under the surface. *What if my body no longer knows how to do this? What if it hurts?*

My thighs squeeze against the sides of his head as his tongue slides up my slit. It's exactly the same way Langston used to lick me.

Waves of pleasure ripple through my body. His hands push at my thighs until they fall open for him, giving him complete access to my body.

I'm going to hell for enjoying this.

His tongue swirls around my clit, and I completely let go.

"Fuck!" I moan as I feel my orgasm climbing in record time. I've never come so fast.

The sensations and feelings overwhelm me. I lose all thoughts. I lose all sense of what I'm supposed to be doing. I can't help myself.

I moan loudly. "Yes, just like that! I'm coming. Lang—"

A hand covers my mouth, muffling my screams.

CHAPTER 25

LANGSTON

I want nothing more than to hear Liesel screaming my name as I fuck her. I don't know Corbin and Maxwell's exact plan, but I do know that her screaming my name right now is the opposite of helpful. I muffle her screams with my hand and then eventually my mouth.

I don't think she realizes that it is actually me who is kissing her, touching her, making her come. The reason her body is so responsive is because I'm the one fucking her.

Liesel is wearing a blindfold. She's not privy to Corbin and Maxwell's plan, although I'm not much either. I think they are afraid if she sees me, her reaction will give away my presence.

I snuck onto the yacht and into this room, realizing it was where Mr. Dunn was bringing them. I'm outnumbered by myself on this boat. If I were smart, I would've brought Enzo, Beckett, or Zeke, but I need to do this on my own. I need my own hands wrapped around Liesel's father's neck.

I've been hiding under the bed so the security cameras wouldn't spot me. It was almost impossible to stay hidden when Liesel's limp body was first brought into the room, but then I watched Corbin and Maxwell take care of her. They studied the room and tried to come up with a plan wordlessly. I knew they had a plan even though they didn't speak it out loud.

My heart raced when I heard her father's words, when I knew what she had to do.

I almost gave away my hiding spot when they blindfolded her and led her to the bed. I thought they were going to go through with it with me hiding under the bed.

I was just about to reveal myself when the lights flickered, and the electricity went out.

Maxwell crouched under the bed with a finger to his lips, telling me to be quiet, while motioning for me to come out.

So I did.

We all stared at Liesel sitting on the bed, scared out of her mind. Both men nodded at me to approach her.

It took every ounce of control in me not to lift her up in my arms and carry her away, but I put my trust in the two brothers who have kept her safe for over a year.

It didn't take me long to realize they had somehow fucked with the visual aspect of the security cameras, but not the audio.

They started moaning and making grunting sounds that were hilarious to watch and listen to. I realized my task was to make Liesel make sounds to match theirs.

If this is how I save Liesel, how I save us all, by making her orgasm, by fucking her—I can't think of a more enjoyable way to save us.

"My turn," Maxwell shouts.

They're standing near the door with their backs to us. They're trying to stall until they figure a way out of here. I don't know if we are going to live or die, but either way, I need Liesel more than I need air right now.

I don't move from Liesel. I don't want to think she's being shared. I want to tell her it's me, but I'm not sure what her reaction will be. And I'm having a hard enough time keeping her moaning and not shouting my name as it is. If she knows it's me for sure, it's going to be that much harder.

Plus, I enjoy watching her body respond to me even though she thinks it's not me. It's like we are fucking again for the first time. I have to convince her all over again that she wants me, remind her that she craves me.

As much as I want to feel her skin against my skin, I decide it's best to keep as many of my clothes on as possible in case I have to make a quick escape.

I notice Maxwell and Corbin are doing jumping jacks and push-ups and have removed half their clothes to make it seem like they were the ones who fucked her, not me.

Now, to actually fuck her, so her father has proof that she doesn't love me.

Liesel is still breathing hard as I lower my lips to hers. I kiss her as slowly as I can manage, but after missing her for a year, unsure if she was alive or dead, it's near impossible. It's especially difficult with the sounds she's making when I kiss her—soft, delectable moans.

I have to remember to let her moans escape my lips so they can be heard on the cameras. But damn, do I want to capture them all for myself.

She writhes beneath me as I press my body against hers.

"Why do I want you so much?" she asks.

Because you love me.

I tease her nipple with my fingers, squeezing it and making her arch her back into me.

"I'm sorry, Langston. I'm sorry, but I want you, whoever you are," she says.

I let her words out because they'll help convince Liesel's father that she's falling for whichever man is supposed to be fucking her.

But she has nothing to be sorry for. I know that if Corbin or Maxwell were really the ones trying to fuck her, she would be different. She doesn't want them like she wants me.

I consider telling her, but we need to keep the charade up longer. She can be a good actress when she wants to be, but I suspect seeing me again will end in a fountain of tears. It will take too long for her to compose herself to make the sounds she needs to make. So I make her endure for a little longer.

At least I can make her body feel good in the process.

I move back to her ear. "Trust me," I whisper, knowing that her mind isn't processing my words correctly. She doesn't recognize it's me.

I rub her clit to ensure she's as wet as possible. She's ready for me, but despite that, I don't want this to hurt for a second. I don't want her afraid.

I pull my cock out and ease it against her entrance.

She stiffens. Her thighs clamp shut while wetness oozes onto my cock. She's conflicted. Her body wants this, but her brain is telling her to stop.

Corbin and Maxwell notice her hesitation.

They walk over with their backs to us.

"Do you want me?" Corbin asks.

Liesel holds her breath like she doesn't want to answer.

"What about when I do this?" he asks.

I circle her clit then squeeze it.

She moans so loudly I'm sure the entire ship can hear her.

I stop.

"No, don't stop," she moans.

I slide my cock back to her slit as I continue to rub her clit, not letting up the pace this time as I ease her into the idea of letting me fuck her. But even with how riled up her body is, I can still sense her hesitation.

Corbin starts to speak again, and I take it as my opportunity to speak without being heard.

"I love you, huntress," I whisper.

She gasps, finally recognizing my voice. Her legs part immediately, and her body welcomes my cock in.

I bite my own lip to stifle my moan as Corbin groans loudly, pretending it's him instead of me. It's going to be impossible for me to keep my moans to myself when being inside her feels like heaven. She's wrapped around me so tightly that if I move, I'll come, so I don't dare move.

But Liesel is desperate for more of me. She rocks her hips, and I groan louder.

Corbin covers my groans with his, but I can't chance them hearing another voice on the recording.

I plant my lips on hers. "Don't stop kissing me."

She doesn't.

Now that she knows it's me, she devours me. Her kisses are frantic, hungry weapons she uses to put me at her mercy for making her think she was fucking another man. Her hands tangle in my hair as I sink deeper into her body.

Everything disappears except her and me.

We float away on a cloud, all the pain of the last year, of our lifetime, disappears. This time, there is nothing that will rip us apart. This time, we are going to last forever.

That's what I try to tell her with every thrust. It's what she agrees to with every rock of her hips.

I feel us both so close to orgasm. My body trembles over her, trying to drag this out as long as I can. Her lips suction to mine, trying to keep me silent as she moans around them.

I hope to hell Corbin and Maxwell have a plan because I know as soon as I finish, her father will burst through the door to look for proof of what he heard but couldn't see.

I look at Corbin out of the corner of my eye. He nods, letting me know he's ready.

Then I spend my last seconds enjoying Liesel before the battle begins. But this time, we are going to battle together, and we're going to win.

I drive hard into Liesel, and she comes a second before I do. My lips stay pressed to hers, and I do everything I can to suppress my own groans while letting hers out.

Then before I know what's happening, Corbin rips me from her body and pushes me back under the bed.

CHAPTER 26

LIESEL

I rip the blindfold off, so sure I'll find Langston on top of me. Instead, I find Corbin and Maxwell butt naked on either side of the bed next to me.

I frown.

Did I imagine Langston? I know I was trying to pretend, but there was no way my mind could so convincingly persuade me that I was fucking Langston if I wasn't.

Could it?

I stare at Corbin, then Maxwell, looking for clues of what happened. From the obvious evidence, it looks like they fucked me, and I imagined Langston. Both are covered in sweat and the smell of sex. Both are naked. Both are here while Langston isn't.

They must have fucked me, not Langston.

But his words...*I love you, huntress.*

Did I dream up those words?

Did I so badly want Langston to be here that I convinced myself he was?

The door bursts open, and my father steps inside.

Both Corbin and Maxwell move protectively in front of me, blocking my naked body from my father's peering eyes.

He studies the scene and then must come to the same conclusion that I did. "You did well."

He walks over to a door at the back of the room and unlocks it. "There's a shower and a change of clothes inside. You boys can clean up in there."

He tosses a robe in our direction. "Liesel and I need to have a chat about what we are going to do about Langston."

Maxwell hands me the robe, and I slip it on. I'm hesitant to leave alone with my father, but this is our chance. We all feel the shift in the air. I'll go with him. If the opportunity presents itself, I'll kill him.

In the meantime, they will break out of this room and come for my father if I don't succeed. This room isn't as secure as the cells were.

I stand in the fluffy robe, and I smile at both men, hoping they can read my thoughts. They tense protectively as I stand off the bed and walk toward my waiting father.

I should be thinking about how I'm going to kill him. Instead, all I can think about is that I fucked Corbin and Maxwell, and I enjoyed it. I'm going to hell. I hate that I betrayed Langston.

My father exits the room, and when I turn to follow him, something catches my eye, making me turn back—the slightest movement under the bed.

Was it a mouse?

Golden eyes are staring back at me with a smirk. He lifts a finger to his lips, reminding me to be quiet.

I didn't imagine him. *Langston is here.* I have no doubt he was the one who fucked me. I didn't betray him, not again. It was him this whole time.

My heart soars, but I'm also terrified that he's here. His being here makes my father's task of killing him easier, and it makes my task of eventually saying goodbye to Langston harder.

I force myself to stop staring at the only man I've ever loved and turn to follow my father.

None of them will have trouble breaking out of this room, but as I shut the door, I leave it cracked just the slightest, ensuring they can escape. Finally, I follow my father. I know what I have to do.

I just hope that Corbin keeps his promise.

CHAPTER 27
LANGSTON

The door shuts, and I scramble out from under the bed.

"Thank god you showed up when you did," Maxwell says, pulling me in for a hug even though he's still naked.

"I'm sure Corbin would have found a way to do what had to be done. He's done it before," I growl.

Corbin winces. "I deserve that, but things have changed. She's like a sister to me now. We've spent a year sharing a cell next to each other. It would have been hard to hurt her like that."

"Is that what's happened this last year? You were all locked up in a cell?" I ask, afraid of their answers.

"Yes, we've been locked up in a cell on this yacht for a year. We haven't been let out or seen the sun for a year. That's how long he gave Liesel to change her mind about you. If she didn't, he'd kill one of her children."

"I'm going to kill him," I growl.

"That's the plan," Maxwell chuckles.

Corbin walks into the bathroom and finds the change of clothes. They start getting dressed without showering. We don't have time to waste.

"You did a good job with your grunting and moaning. You convinced him at least," I say.

"Well, we had to grunt so loudly because someone couldn't stop groaning," Maxwell teases.

"It's been a year; what did you expect?"

He chuckles.

"What's the plan?" I ask.

"Do you have a gun?" Corbin asks.

I pull out my gun and two knives, which I toss in their direction. They each catch a knife, ready to fight.

"We need to figure a way out of here. I'm not sure about the door. It looks like it's been reinforced. We might have to try one of the windows," Corbin says.

I nod.

"Then we take any weapons we can from the guards, find Liesel and her father, and kill him. If we can't find him, we'll pretend we've captured you and are bringing you to him."

I nod, acknowledging the backup plan of pretending to be their prisoner.

Corbin and Maxwell go to the windows while I see if I can break out through the door. There's a crack of light shining between the door and the frame. I push, and the door pops open.

"Guys, this way!"

Corbin and Maxwell run toward me.

"How'd you get it open?" Maxwell asks.

"Liesel left it open," I say.

"She's going to kill him long before we get there," Corbin says.

I grin. "I know, but she's going to get our help whether she needs it or not."

CHAPTER 28

LIESEL

"Where are we going?" I ask.

"Somewhere where we can be alone."

I squeeze the robe tighter around my body as I follow my father to the furthest end of the yacht. I don't know how long it will take the men to follow us. I hope they are already behind us, watching where we're going.

We reach the back of the yacht, and then my father motions for me to climb down a ladder leading to a smaller boat.

This is a trap.

Perhaps the only reason I'm wearing a robe is so he knows I'm not hiding a gun. Thankfully, I don't need a weapon to kill him.

I want to ask again where we're going, but it doesn't matter. Everyone I love is safe. This is between my father and me.

I climb down onto the small boat. My father climbs down after me. He unties the boat and starts the motor. Then we're zipping across the water. I stare out at the unknown ocean instead of the yacht and men we just left behind. They can't save me now. I'm on my own.

My father knows, I realize.

He knows Langston is on the yacht.

He knows Corbin and Maxwell are planning to take him down.

He knows I didn't really betray Langston; I still love him.

Suddenly, my father shuts the engine off, and we're floating in the middle of open water. The yacht is no longer in sight behind us, and the island isn't visible either.

"You brought me here to kill me," I say, not looking at my father.

I try to figure out what my options are, but I prefer it this way—just him and me.

He doesn't answer, but then I guess I didn't really ask him a question.

I turn and face him. He doesn't move. He doesn't speak. He just stares at me with a blank expression.

I feel a cool breeze on my face and notice dark clouds stirring behind my father. We're going to get caught in a storm. I want to be the one to kill my father, but if I don't succeed, then I'd be happy for the storm to take my father's life.

"You can't kill me," I say.

"No, but I can make your life hell, so you'll wish you were dead."

"You're dying. I can see the gauntness in your eyes, the paleness of your skin, your lost weight—you're dying. And you need a successor, or everything you've spent your whole life working for will be for nothing."

"You think I'm a cruel man, don't you, Liesel? I'm a monster who left you and your mother when you were a child. I shirked my responsibilities to become a mob boss for money and power. You think I kill for the thrill of it."

"Don't you?"

"No, I was just taught an important lesson early in life—love always fails. It's the cruelest monster alive."

"I agree; falling in love is incredibly cruel. But it's too late to stop me from suffering the hardships of love."

"I know. I failed. I should have stepped in sooner."

"Why do you want me to take over for you when you're gone? Why does it have to be a family member? Couldn't your second in command take over for you? Then you could leave my family and me alone."

"I've tried that. I took some time off when I was first diagnosed with cancer and let my second lead." He stares off into the ocean. "I lost twenty men. More than I've lost in a decade, he lost in less than a month. He didn't understand his responsibility to the organization, not just himself and power. You understand that, though. It's why you agreed to come out here with me by yourself, instead of risking your friends or lover's life. You'd rather risk your own life than those you love.

"I think I've been going about this the wrong way. The way to get you to take over for me when I'm gone is not to get you to stop loving, but to get you to love my men, my world, as much as I do."

"I'll never love ruining people's lives for profit. I will never love stealing from them, selling them addictive drugs that will eventually kill them, or selling people like property. I will never love being a monster like you."

"Then it seems we are at an impasse."

"It seems we are," I agree.

"You think you're dying from your own illness; or you think I'm going to be the death of you. I can see you're prepared to die, but you don't realize love is going to be what kills you. Love makes you weak, dependent, selfish. You'll do things you wouldn't otherwise do because you fell in love. Let me help you, teach you, and you can learn to be the greatest—"

The roar of an engine interrupts him.

He squints his eyes in the sound's direction. I don't have to turn around to know who is coming toward us. I'm running out of time to kill my father before I'm risking Langston, Corbin, and Maxwell's lives too.

I see my father reach for something, assuming it's a gun.

It's not.

It's worse.

I jump, but I'm not sure I'm going to be able to save them. I'm not sure I'm going to be able to save any of us.

CHAPTER 29

LANGSTON

I hold my hands behind my back, pretending they are tied together, while Corbin and Maxwell pretend to be my captors.

We make our way quickly down the hallway until one of the guards walks toward us.

"We found him trying to break into Liesel's room. Where is Mr. Dunn?" Corbin asks the man.

The man frowns, looking at us suspiciously. He can't make sense of the situation, and I doubt he'll give us any answers, so I shoot him. Luckily I came prepared to be stealthy with my gun's silencer.

"Well, that was effective," Corbin says, reaching down to grab the man's gun.

"We need to hurry; I don't trust Dunn with Liesel for a second longer than necessary," I say.

I move to the front now that two of us have guns. Corbin follows with Maxwell, holding only a knife, trailing him.

I practically run down the hallway and up to the top deck, looking for Liesel. I see two more guards and shoot them both before they even notice us. Maxwell collects one of their guns, and then we split up, all searching for Liesel and her father.

Five minutes later, we are all huffing as we meet back on the top deck.

"I found nothing," I say.

Both Corbin and Maxwell shake their heads.

"Where could they have gone?" Maxwell asks.

I run to the railing of the yacht and look down. "One of the lifeboats is gone. Let's go."

I run down the stairs with Corbin and Maxwell following me. Thankfully there are two lifeboats on either side of the yacht. We can still find them; although, we have no idea which direction they went. They also could have hopped on a bigger, faster ship. They could have gone to land and be driving on the island. They could have gotten on a helicopter. They could already be long gone.

I try not to think about that.

We'll find her.

We have to.

We all jump on the small boat.

"Which way?" Corbin asks at the back. He'll be the one driving the boat.

I look in each direction. There is no obvious way to go, but my heart is pulling me west.

"This way," I point in the direction of the setting sun.

We take off. Each of us holds our gun at our side, ready to fight for a girl who has won our hearts. Before, I might not have believed they were on my side, but after everything that has happened, they are at least on Liesel's side.

"There they are!" Maxwell shouts from the front of the boat.

We all turn, and in the far off distance is their boat, floating in the middle of the sea.

"Hurry!" I shout back to Corbin.

"We're going as fast as this thing goes!" he shouts back.

Jesus, it's going to take forever to reach them.

There is nothing else to do but hope we get to them before he threatens her life. We are so close, and yet we can't protect her from here. We have to get closer.

I squint my eyes, trying to get a good view of what's happening, but I can barely make out their bodies sitting on the boat.

Liesel jumps.

Not off the boat like I want her to, but she tackles her father.

None of us speak as we speed as fast and as close as we can.

We all raise our guns, ready to take aim the second we can.

We watch in horror as Liesel battles her father.

She punches him hard in the face, knocking him out.

I breathe a sigh of relief.

Then, she does the craziest thing. She starts up the boat, but instead of driving it toward us, she drives it away.

"What is she doing?" Maxwell asks.

"No clue; follow her," I tell Corbin.

Our boat must be faster than hers, or she isn't driving at full speed because we are catching up to her.

"I'm going to jump," Maxwell says as the tip of our boat comes along the side of the back of hers.

He jumps onto her boat successfully. I move up to jump onto her boat as well when Liesel's eyes catch mine. She turns her boat sharply, and we speed past her.

"Liesel!" I yell, confused by her actions.

"Max will help her steer in the right direction," Corbin says.

I don't think she's having problems steering. I think she's doing it on purpose, but I don't tell Corbin that.

"Just get us back to her boat," I yell.

Corbin sharply course corrects our boat.

Maxwell furiously grabs Liesel.

"What the hell is he doing?" I ask, terrified that he's hurting her as she kicks and screams in his arms.

Corbin doesn't answer me. It's clear he isn't sure either. We are definitely missing something, but I don't know what.

He drops her into the sea as she screams something back at him.

Then he grabs the engine's controls, and the boat speeds off away from us.

"Liesel," I yell as we approach her, floating in the ocean.

I dive into the water and swim toward her just as her head comes up out of the water.

I wrap my arms around her, never feeling safer than I am now. I'm never letting her go again—never.

"You have to stop Maxwell. My father started a bomb. I couldn't diffuse it. It's got less than a minute before it explodes," she cries into my arms.

"Shit."

Corbin pulls up next to us, and I quickly help her onto the boat before I pull myself up.

"Maxwell! Jump!" I yell, hoping he'll hear me and jump. It's his only chance.

We won't make it to him in time. We can't get any closer without risking the bomb killing us all, either.

Maxwell turns and looks at Corbin before jumping into the ocean. He hits the water just as the bomb goes off.

Liesel shrieks.

Corbin freezes.

I close my eyes, unable to handle the most likely outcome.

I turn to Liesel, who looks the more stable out of the two of them. "Stay here until I tell you it's safe to come closer."

She nods, and then I kiss her on her lips. One passionate kiss to hold us over, but it won't be the last. I dive into the water to swim closer, hoping to find Maxwell alive and her father dead.

The boat has been blown into a million pieces. I have no doubt that her father was planning on tossing the bomb onto our boat at the last second. Instead, his own need to control his daughter's life led to his death.

I see blood and pieces of his body floating in the water, and relief of his death washes over me.

"Maxwell!" I shout when I see his head bobbing up and down.

I swim as hard and as fast as I can in his direction. His head sinks below the water's surface.

"Dammit, Maxwell, why did you have to be a savior?" I mutter to myself as I dive down and push him up out of the water.

I know before I pull his head up that he's gone.

I feel my tears fall instantly.

For him.

For Liesel.

For Corbin.

He saved us all.

"Thank you, Maxwell. You saved her. You told me you would do anything for her. Thank you for keeping your promise," I say.

I squeeze my eyes shut as I hold his limp body. Corbin and Liesel are going to lose it when they realize he's dead. They must have all grown close being locked up in a cell together for a year—relying on each other, protecting each other.

All I want to do is heal. To become a family again. To put this horrible past behind us. But there is no easy way to heal after losing what we've lost.

Corbin eases the boat close enough for me to hear him, but not so close that they can get a clear view of Maxwell. It's probably for the best.

"Is he...?" Liesel asks.

"They're both gone," I answer.

She collapses down on the boat. I want nothing more than to wrap her in my arms and take away her pain, but I need to figure out what to do with Maxwell's body.

I look to Corbin for guidance. *Does he want his brother buried at sea? Or does he want to bring his body back to be buried somewhere?*

Corbin gives me a stern look I don't understand. He aims his gun at Liesel.

"No!" I shout.

Instead of shooting her, Corbin speeds off away from me.

"Liesel!" I shout, letting go of Maxwell and starting to swim after them.

Grief makes people do crazy things, but I have no idea what the hell Corbin is doing. And I definitely didn't fight so hard to get Liesel back just to lose her all over again.

CHAPTER 30

LIESEL

As soon as we are out of sight of Langston, Corbin lowers his gun.

"Are you sure?" Corbin asks.

I stare back at the sea where we both left people we love floating in the ocean. Maxwell didn't survive. Langston will, but he'll have to learn how to live without me once again.

"I'm sorry. It was supposed to be me who died, not Maxwell," I say through my tears.

Corbin stops the boat for a second and wraps his arms around me as we both sob. "No, don't be sorry. Maxwell loved you. He wanted to protect you at all costs. He protected us all. We can miss him but don't be sorry that he died instead of you. You saved him a year ago. Without you convincing your father to help him, he would have died then."

I nod. He's right, but it's still hard.

Corbin grabs my cheeks and forces me to look at him again. "Are. You. Sure?"

I squeeze my eyes shut, closing off my tears.

"Kidnap me, make Langston think you killed me. Put an end to his

533

suffering. I don't want him to keep loving me, to keep hurting, because of me."

Corbin kisses my forehead, and then he begins to drive the boat again, fulfilling his promise to me.

I can't save Langston from heartbreak and pain, but I can end his suffering. I can save him from months of agony. It's time for him to start healing, no matter how hard it is. Maybe then I'll be able to rest in peace.

CHAPTER 31

LANGSTON

One Week Later

I don't know the truth from the lies, but I do know that Liesel isn't dead. Corbin tried to make me believe it. It was convincing. The pictures. The video. Payback for losing his brother is what he said.

A lie.

But why? I have no clue.

I've tracked him to Portugal. His cousin has some land here that he's staying at. He hasn't been using a credit card, nor his own passport—nothing that would allow me to track him electronically.

It didn't stop me, though.

I found him.

I searched every relation, friend, and person he's ever met until I found him. It was almost like he wanted to be found. He was doing just the bare minimum to hide, not enough to keep me away for more than a week.

I expect to be walking into some sort of a trap.

Yet, I didn't bring Zeke, or Enzo, or Kai, or Beckett, or Siren. I don't need backup to get Liesel back. I just need answers.

The mansion they are living in is gorgeous—three stories of beautiful curved arches with winding greenery and roses. A terrace over-looks a small vineyard for enjoying the wine grown here.

That's where I find them sitting on the terrace, drinking wine.

Liesel isn't dead.

And if she's his captive, he's treating her well. Although, if he's made her his sex slave, I guess he could be trying to convince her to like him. *Maybe she fell for him in their year together?*

No, she loves me.

If she loved him, she would have fucked him on the yacht, not me.

There is only one way to find out the truth.

I step out from the shadows.

"Spare any wine for me?" I fold my arms and lean against the side of the house.

Both Liesel and Corbin jump.

Corbin grabs his gun and aims it at Liesel.

"Move, and I'll kill her."

I scrunch my nose. "I thought you already did. Isn't that what the photos were supposed to convince me of?"

Corbin frowns and keeps the gun aimed at Liesel. I'm not really concerned with his actions. I'm worried about hers.

She hasn't moved, but her breathing hasn't sped either. She's not afraid for her life. There is no sign that he's tortured her. In fact, she looks better than she did a week ago. There's more color in her cheeks like she's been spending lots of time in the sun.

"Test me, and I'll make it a reality," Corbin says. *He's a good actor, but I don't believe him.*

"No, you won't."

"I will."

"No, you won't. I removed the bullets from your gun. You literally can't kill her."

He studies the gun before realizing I'm right.

I pull my gun out and aim it at him.

He freezes and looks at Liesel.

"Run, Liesel. I got this."

Prove my theories wrong, Liesel.

Run.

She doesn't run. She stands slowly and walks in front of Corbin. "Don't shoot him."

"Why?" I growl.

She doesn't answer, but she does step between Corbin and me.

"Why? He kidnapped you, faked your death. Why shouldn't I kill him?"

Break my heart, huntress. Tell me you love him.

"I told him to kidnap me."

I lower my gun. I don't want to threaten her life.

She looks away for a second. For a moment, I think she's looking at Corbin like she needs his assurance to tell me.

"I'm sorry," she starts. She doesn't have tears in her eyes, but I can tell whatever she's about to say is going to hurt me, possibly worse than anything she's ever told me before.

"I'll give you a moment to talk," Corbin says, sneaking away.

I don't give a shit about him. I don't care what he does. I care about her.

With Corbin gone, I close the space between us, but I don't dare make a move. Not until she speaks. Not until she breaks my heart.

"What's going on, huntress?"

One tear streaks down her cheek so fast I think I imagined it.

"I don't want to hurt you. I don't want to watch you in agony every day I'm alive. I can't."

I frown, not understanding.

I take her hands in mine. I can't help myself. I need to hold her in some way, even if she is leaving me for another man.

"You love him?" I ask.

She frowns into my eyes. "No—I mean, I love him like you love Siren. He's a close friend, nothing more."

"Then nothing you could say would break my heart."

She shakes her head.

"I'm dying."

"What?"

I look her up and down like I can somehow figure out what she's saying.

"I have colon cancer, and it spread. I don't have much time."

I pull her closer, not accepting her words.

"Atlas had cancer. I have cancer. And I'm pretty sure my father was also dying of cancer before the explosion. I think we have a hereditary gene that makes us all more susceptible. I've had it for a long time. It was in remission for a while, but in the last couple of years, it's come back. I don't know how I've lasted this long."

I wrap my arms around her and hold her firmly against my chest. I feel my tears welling, but somehow hearing that she has cancer and not that she doesn't love me is better. I can reverse cancer. I can't make her love me if she's in love with another man.

"Because you're the strongest person I know, that's how."

"I had Corbin kidnap me because I thought dying swiftly would be easier for you than watching me die slowly and painfully. I can't watch your heart break again."

I grab her cheeks and peer into her eyes.

"Do you love me?"

"More than I should."

"Then my heart will never have to break."

"But—"

"No, I refuse to let you die. We've survived too much, you and I."

I kiss her, showing her how much I need her no matter what.

I know I can't control the world. I don't have any real power over whether she lives or dies, but I'm a stubborn bastard. And for however long I have left with her, I won't waste one second.

She moans into me.

I push her lips apart, dipping my tongue into her gasping mouth.

I grab her legs and wrap them around my waist as I carry her toward the house. I don't know if I can make it to a bed, but I don't want to fuck her on the deck.

She devours me with her mouth as I throw open the door and step inside. She's ripping my button-down shirt while my hand is frantically dipping beneath her sundress, feeling her moisture spread over her panties.

"Jesus, can you at least wait until I leave a room before you fuck her? I've seen you fuck more times than I need to," Corbin says as he starts to rush out of the room.

We chuckle into each other's mouths as we kiss.

"And Langston, you're welcome!" Corbin shouts as he jogs down the hall. "I'm sorry, Liesel!"

Liesel frowns. "The bastard. He was supposed to keep his word, so you didn't have to suffer."

I shake my head as I rub my cock between her legs as we fall onto the couch. "No, I'll never suffer as long as I'm with you. You're wrong to think that you dying would somehow make my life easier."

I unzip my pants and ease my cock into her as she arches her back. Her eyes are hungry with need. She kisses me hard, which will make it hard for me to get the words out that I need to.

"I never wanted to love you. I tried for so long to not love you because I thought it would save you. In the end, it only cost me time with you. There was no way I couldn't fall for you," I say.

A tear brushes her cheek again.

I kiss it away.

"I never wanted to break your heart, but I've always loved you since you became my killer."

"I've loved you since I watched you hunt a spider and needed my help to kill it. But break my heart, huntress. Break it a thousand times if you must. Loving you will always be worth the heartbreak. Just promise me this—you'll let me love you for as long as we both have left. Love me as long as we are both living."

"I promise to love you and let you love me for as long as I live."

"I'll love you even when you're gone. But I don't accept that you'll be the first to die. I don't accept that either of us will die anytime soon. We have a lot of lost time your father cost us to make up for. Our forever won't end anytime soon."

And then I show her how much I love her by making love to her. Over and over and over. So loudly that we drive Corbin out of the big house.

She thinks this is the end of our story, that the end is near. We won't get our happily ever after.

Maybe she's right.

But I'm a believer that love can conquer all.

Our love is the greatest love story that's ever been told—call me biased.

Our story doesn't end with her slipping away in my arms before she turns thirty.

Our story is endless, and I'll fight every day to ensure it. We've fought the world before and won. *Why should this be any different?*

I look into her eyes; she doesn't believe me. It doesn't matter. Liesel may be right most of the time, but this time she's wrong. I'm right.

"Do you want to make a bet?" I ask.

She frowns. "A bet?"

"We are going to live happily ever after, for a very long time."

She smiles sadly. "What do I get if I'm right?"

"The ability to haunt my ass and ensure I'm never with another woman again."

It makes her laugh.

"And if I win, I get whatever I want. Deal?"

"Deal," she agrees.

"Good. I plan on winning."

She kisses me rather than continue our conversation, but when we are eighty and sitting in our rocking chairs together after living a long and happy life together, I'm going to collect on our bet.

FIRST EPILOGUE
LIESEL

One Year Later

"Mom!" Declan yells.

All three of my kids are running toward where Langston and I are lying on the beach.

They jump on me, ignoring their father.

"Why are you all jumping on me?" I ask as I laugh.

"Because Dad will say no," Rose says.

I laugh. She's probably right, but I have to hear this.

"Stop tickling me and tell me what you all want," I say, sitting up.

Langton is still lying still on the towel next to me; his cap draped over his eyes.

"The answer is no," Langston says without moving.

The kids jump at his voice.

Rose pouts.

Atlas smiles. "I told you he'd say no."

Declan rolls his eyes.

I look to each of my kids, one by one, seeing what it is they want. As much as Langston pretends he can be a firm dad who tells his kids no, he can't. He'll cave. The kids know it; they just like to rile him up.

"Yes," I say.

"You don't even know what we are going to ask," Rose says.

"I'm your mother, so I already know what you're going to ask."

"We were going to ask to only ever eat ice cream for every meal for the rest of our lives," Atlas jokes.

I shake my head. "Nope."

"We were going to ask for millions and millions of dollars."

"Nope."

"You want to go visit Uncle Enzo, Aunt Kai, and the twins and go to Disney World with them," Langston groans.

"They did know," Rose says, her eyes bugging out that we would guess what our kids want.

I laugh.

"The answer is no," Langston says.

I bite back a smile. He knows I'm going to say yes, and he doesn't have a choice in the matter.

I know this.

The kids know this.

Langston knows this.

"How about you go get Dad a bowl of his favorite ice cream and see if it changes his mind?" I tell the kids.

All of their eyes light up. They run off, but not before I hear Rose say, "Mom's going to convince Dad to let us go. This is just a diversion, so we don't hear them argue. But just in case, we should bribe Dad with ice cream."

I lift Langston's hat off his face and am met with a scowl. Somehow I find him more attractive when he's angry than when he's smiling.

"Do we really have to take them to Disney World? That's the least safe place in the world."

I roll my eyes. "Yes, they're kids. They want to go to Disney World with their cousins."

"They live on a private island with their cousins; why do they need to go to Disney World?"

"We're going."

He frowns. "No, we're not. It's not safe."

I raise an eyebrow at him. "We aren't in danger. And even if we were, we aren't denying our kids the joys of the world."

"Disney World isn't a joy. It's a crowded, disease-infested, capitalistic hell."

"We're going."

"No—"

"I didn't survive a year longer than I should to not take our kids to Disney World with their cousins."

He frowns and grabs my hips, yanking me toward him so he can kiss me. "Fine, but you can't use the cancer card for another year."

I smile into his lips, knowing very well that I can and I will. Langston would do anything for our kids and me. We've built the perfect world here for them on this island, but that doesn't mean we are afraid to venture out into the real world.

Siren and Zeke finished their house here. Phoenix and Corbin live here as well. Rose and Atlas still call Phoenix 'Mom,' and it doesn't bother me in the slightest. I'm happy they can have two moms, a dad, and plenty of aunts and uncles who love them and would be willing to die to protect them.

Enzo and Kai live with their kids on their yacht and spend time between Miami and here, still leading their empire like the badasses they are.

Beckett stays with them a lot, but he's found a new girl in Seattle who he's been spending a lot of time with. We're pretty sure he's in love, but we don't tell him that. We don't want to jinx his relationship. After all, all of our love stories put us through hell before we got to the happily ever after part.

SECOND EPILOGUE
LIESEL

Ten Years Later

My heart freezes when we get letters in the mail addressed to each of the kids.

My father.

I recognize the handwriting—the same handwriting that was on the letter that Langston and I tore in half.

I show the letters to Langston.

He immediately tosses them all in the fireplace, burning them all.

My father's empire is dead.

We've ensured it.

The decent people who used to work for him now work for Kai and Enzo. The rest we either killed or they found their way to new crime organizations.

We're safe.

Our kids have grown up only knowing love and safety. Even Declan has forgotten about the horrors of his past. We've protected them well, and they are all ready to fly the nest. I can't wait to see what adventures the world holds for them.

I pour myself a cup of coffee, needing an afternoon pick me up.

"You know what today is?" Langston asks after he gets over his grumpiness at seeing the letters.

"What?"

"Ten years exactly since we made our bet. Do you admit that I was right yet?"

I've been cancer-free for eight of the ten. Langston took me to every doctor in the world until we found something that worked.

"Would I ever admit that you're right? I would never lose a bet so easily. You said forever. Ten years isn't forever," I tease.

He wraps his arms around me and kisses my neck. "I'm going to enjoy the next fifty years proving how right I am."

THIRD EPILOGUE
LIESEL

Fifty Years Later

Langston holds my hand as we sit on the sand, staring out at the sunset.

"I win our bet, right?" he asks.

I grin.

"Yes, you win. So what do I have to do to pay my debt?"

He kisses me. "You already have, by giving me our forever."

Thank you so much for reading Langston & Liesel's story! Beckett's story is next in MISTAKEN HERO.

She mistakes me for her hero. I'm no hero. And I'm definitely not hers. But that won't stop me from making her mine.

One-click MISTAKEN HERO now>

ALSO BY ELLA MILES

LIES SERIES:

Lies We Share: A Prologue

Vicious Lies

Desperate Lies

Fated Lies

Cruel Lies

Dangerous Lies

Endless Lies

SINFUL TRUTHS:

Sinful Truth #1

Twisted Vow #2

Reckless Fall #3

Tangled Promise #4

Fallen Love #5

Broken Anchor #6

TRUTH OR LIES:

Taken by Lies #1

Betrayed by Truths #2

Trapped by Lies #3

Stolen by Truths #4

Possessed by Lies #5

Consumed by Truths #6

DIRTY SERIES:

Dirty Beginning

Dirty Obsession

Dirty Addiction

Dirty Revenge

Dirty: The Complete Series

ALIGNED SERIES:

Aligned: Volume 1 (Free Series Starter)

Aligned: Volume 2

Aligned: Volume 3

Aligned: Volume 4

Aligned: The Complete Series Boxset

UNFORGIVABLE SERIES:

Heart of a Thief

Heart of a Liar

Heart of a Prick

Unforgivable: The Complete Series Boxset

MAYBE, DEFINITELY SERIES:

Maybe Yes

Maybe Never

Maybe Always

Definitely Yes

Definitely No

Definitely Forever

STANDALONES:

Pretend I'm Yours

Finding Perfect

Savage Love

Too Much

Not Sorry

ABOUT THE AUTHOR

Ella Miles writes steamy romance, including everything from dark suspense romance that will leave you on the edge of your seat to contemporary romance that will leave you laughing out loud or crying. Most importantly, she wants you to feel everything her characters feel as you read.

Ella is currently living her own happily ever after near the Rocky Mountains with her high school sweetheart husband. Her heart is also taken by her goofy five year old black lab who is scared of everything, including her own shadow.

Ella is a USA Today Bestselling Author & Top 50 Bestselling Author.

Stalk Ella at:
www.ellamiles.com
ella@ellamiles.com